"I WANT YOU
SHE SAI[D]

Donall drew in a sharp br[eath] ... expected answer as he'd tho[ught] ... knowing he sounded like a simpleton, but unable to stay his tongue.

She nodded. "I wish to forge an irrefutable union with you in the hopes of ensuring lasting peace."

Donall's jaw still hung embarrassingly slack as he gaped at her. She stood firm, her lifted chin declaring her strength of purpose.

She wanted peace.

He wanted out of her clutches.

And he wanted her.

Donall let his gaze roam over her from head to toe. His hands ached to do the same. Something fine, warm, and bright began to pulse deep inside him.

The beginnings of a smile touched his lips. Mayhap giving the lass what she's after would allow him to have her, and his freedom. What better way to win her confidence than by bedding her?

Bedding her well.

APPLAUSE FOR SUE-ELLEN WELFONDER'S
DEVIL IN A KILT

"A lovely gem of a book. Wonderful characters and a true sense of place make this a keeper. If you love Scottish tales, you'll treasure this one."

—Patricia Potter, bestselling author of
The Heart Queen

Please turn this page for more quotes . . .

"*Devil in a Kilt* will catapult Sue-Ellen Welfonder onto 'must-read' lists. This dynamic debut has plenty of steamy sensuality, a dusting of mystery, and a touch of the paranormal. You'll be glued to the pages not only by her fresh, vibrant voice and strong emotional intensity, but by her ability to make you believe you are there."

 —Kathe Robin, *Romantic Times* (a top pick)

"An engaging read. Very fast paced with fascinating characters and several interesting plot twists . . . *Devil in a Kilt* is a keeper."

 —Writers Club Romance Group on AOL

"As captivating as a spider's web and the reader can't get free until the last word. It is easy to get involved in this tense, fast-moving adventure."

 —Rendezvous

Knight
in my Bed

ALSO BY SUE-ELLEN WELFONDER

Devil in a Kilt

Knight in my Bed

SUE-ELLEN WELFONDER

WARNER BOOKS

An AOL Time Warner Company

WARNER BOOKS EDITION

Copyright © 2002 by Sue-Ellen Welfonder

Cover design by Diane Luger
Cover illustration by John Ennis
Handlettering by David Gatti

Warner Books, Inc.
1271 Avenue of the Americas
New York, NY 10020

Visit our Web site at www.twbookmark.com

An AOL Time Warner Company

Printed in the United States of America

First Printing: April 2002

10 9 8 7 6 5 4 3 2 1

This book is dedicated with deepest appreciation to my own favorite author, Becky Lee Weyrich, who told me I should stop writing seventeen-page letters and start writing romance.

A fan letter to her turned into one of my most valued friendships and gave me the mentor without whose encouragement I would probably still be penning nothing more exciting than too-long letters and countless travel journals.

Becky, this one is for you. Thank you with all my heart.

Acknowledgments

The following dearly-loved individuals stood by me through this book's difficult deadline. Their generosity of spirit kept me grounded in a time I often felt as if my world was fast tilting out of control. I feel so blessed to call them my friends:

My writing sisters, Elizabeth Sinclair, Lauren Bach, Lauren Royal, Susan Grace, Brenda Novak, Pat Laye, and Rosalie Whiteman. Bless you for always being on the other side of the keyboard when I needed you.

Gaye and Jim Walton, for always caring and for the special stones. Kristine Hughes, for the good old days and assuring that my heroes never suffocated in those closet boxes. And Gwen McDaniel, for telling me about her brother, Drake Allen McLean, a true MacLean hero.

My intrepid travel companions, Karen D. Stevens and Pat Cody, a thousand hugs for keeping up talk about our next jaunt over the Big Pond. The anticipation kept me going!

Karen Kosztolnyik and Beth de Guzman for their

reassuring smiles when I was feeling most lost. Courtney Boissonnault, whose shining enthusiasm never fails to cheer me, for her incredible support. Larissa Rivera for being so sweet. And Michele Bidelspach, for not forgetting me.

My much-appreciated agent, friend, and rock, Pattie Steele-Perkins, for not letting me look down.

As always, for my knight in shining armor, my handsome husband, Manfred, who held the keep with a masterful hand and slew many dragons as I wrote this book.

And last but by no means least, for the real Bodo, my own four-legged champion, Em, for filling my heart with love and joy.

The Legacy of the Lady Rock

❦

*I*N THE MIST-SHROUDED waters off the western coast of Scotland, not far from the remote but beautiful Isle of Doon, lies a tidal rock known as the "Lady Rock." Visible only at low tide, the treacherous islet provided displeasured lairds with a means to rid themselves of unwanted wives: a barren or disobedient bride stranded upon the rock would drown with the incoming tide, leaving the laird free to wed another.

One such laird was a MacLean, and though his nefarious act took place in the distant past, the deed ignited a bitter feud between two clans who had once been allies if not friends.

At odds for centuries, the MacLean and the MacInnes clans have grudgingly shared the windswept Isle of Doon, neither clan willing to share an inch more of "their" island than absolutely necessary.

Now, in the troubled year following the death of Robert the Bruce, King of Scots, they've shared an uneasy truce as well.

A truce soon to be shattered.

Another MacInnes bride has been found dead upon the Lady Rock, murdered in the same manner as her ill-fated ancestor, and this time, when the ancient enmity flares anew, the Clan MacInnes wants blood.

Aye, they will seek revenge.

A most fitting revenge . . .

Chapter One

DUNMUIR CASTLE
THE ISLE OF DOON, 1330

✤

NIP HIS FLESH with white-hot pinchers, expose him to showers of offal and ceaseless floggings. Pour molten lead down his throat and force him to fetch pebbles from a cauldron of boiling oil.

Make him weary of drawing breath.

Hasten his mortal exit.

The hum of angry voices pierced the blessed refuge of Donall MacLean's deep slumber with all the subtleness of a heavy-handed peasant battling moonbeams with a rusted scythe.

Careful not to reveal he'd awakened, Donall the Bold, proud laird of the great Clan MacLean, opened his eyes to mere slits and squinted into what could only be called the antechamber to hell.

Trouble was, Donall the Bold, belted knight and warrior of untold renown, was not yet ready to pass into legend.

Pull him asunder by four stout oxen.

Get him to his knees until he pleads the mercy of God's holy blood.

"Pull me asunder? Make me plead God's mercy?" The words burst past Donall's parched lips, riding hard on a floodtide of fury he could no longer suppress.

Now fully awake, and uncaring if his malefactors knew it, he strained against the heavy bands of iron secured around his wrists and ankles. Outraged, he stared in disbelief at the unsmiling graybeards outlined in the open doorway to his dungeon cell.

An unlikely assemblage to be spouting brazen words, but the hatred simmering in their aged eyes brandmarked them as the crazed dominions who'd rained such vile threats upon him.

Behind them, a wall torch sputtered and smoked, its reluctant flames edging their gaunt figures with an eerie reddish glow—an odd effect that underscored the impression he'd awakened in the talons of the horned one and his cloven-footed minions.

Relying on a fast-waning reserve of strength deep inside his battered body, Donall raked them with a defiant glare. "A MacLean gets on his knees before no man." Incredulity warred with his fury over the very idea. "'Tis mad the lot of you are if you think to accomplish such a feat. The only getting I'll be doing is out of here."

"Aye, and leave us you shall," one of the men agreed, "as a corpse to be tossed from the cliffs, your cold flesh good for naught but carrion for the gulls."

Donall narrowed his eyes at his captors. He'd howl with laughter at their effrontery but regrettably, he lacked the vigor to do much more than glower.

Cold and shivering, he'd been left unclothed to wallow on a pallet of fouled straw, his every muscle screamed in agony and his temples throbbed so fiercely he'd almost swear some heavy-armed churl had cleaved his head in twain.

Giving heed to the urge to laugh would only increase his misery. Even scowling cost him.

With a low groan, he leaned his head against the damp wall and drew in a few shallow breaths. He instantly regretted doing so, for a bitingly rank smell assailed his senses with each ragged gasp.

A stench almost as sharp as the white-hot shards of agony shooting through his head.

Where, by the Holy Rood, *was* he?

And who were his stern-faced tormentors?

Donall peered hard at the one who'd spoken. Hawk-eyed and boasting an unkempt shock of hair the color of rusted iron, the graybeard returned his stare.

They *all* stared.

And waves of anger emanated from their ancient bones. Several of them seemed hauntingly familiar, but the throbbing in his temples kept him from thinking clearly.

And who was the lady Isolde?

The woman whose name the jeering old weathercocks had bantered about before they'd let loose their barrage of ludicrous threats.

Or had he imagined the name?

His mind's attempt to wrest his thoughts from his ravaged and aching state of being?

Or was *Isolde* the name of a long-forgotten paramour? A faceless victim of a one-time dalliance, come back to haunt him in his darkest hour?

Either way, the name wove a fine dance along the outer edges of his mind. Elusive as a nimble *sidhe* maid cavorting in the gloaming, the name taunted him with its familiarity but never came close enough for him to comprehend who she might be.

Snatches of angry words and a half-remembered scuffle joined the chaos of confusion in his mind but the red haze of pain banished each snippet of thought before he could make sense of aught.

"Not so mighty now, are you, Donall the *Bold*?" another of the graybeards commented, his aged voice laden with sarcasm. "Still, we purpose to grant you the preservation of your dignity by allowing you to repent your sins before our fair chieftain."

A female chieftain.

The lady Isolde.

Fragments of conversations he'd had with his brother's now dead wife, Lileas, joined the swirling morass in his head, adding to his bewilderment.

Hadn't Lileas called her sister Isolde? And hadn't there been some talk about Archibald MacInnes's eldest daughter assuming the role of chieftain upon Archibald's death two years past?

The answers teased him, hovering close but not near enough to grasp.

Not with his blood pounding louder than a smithy's hammer in his ears.

He opened his mouth to let loose a stream of choice epithets but the dark oaths died on his tongue when a tiny, four-footed *something* skittered across his bare feet. He jerked his legs in reaction, but the cold iron binding his ankles hindered any further movement and drove home the grim reality of his plight.

At once, the haze clouding his mind lifted, leaving only pain, anger, and indignation in its place.

With dawning clarity, the wretched details of his surrounds and the sorry state of his own bruised body became as clear as if illuminated by the flames of a thousand well-burning torchlights.

Not as clear but equally disturbing came the faint memory of a grizzle-headed female bending over him, a hell-hag who peered at him from clouded eyes. To his horror, he also recalled the crone lifting the tattered cloth someone had tossed across his vitals and, brazen as day, peeking at what lay beneath.

Saints preserve him if she proved to be the "fair chieftain" his captors thought to force him to do penance to. The very thought was enough to curdle his flesh.

"You appear vexed," said a third graybeard. This one had stark white hair and leaned heavily on a walking crook. With slow, shuffling steps, he came near to where Donall sat braced against a cold, slime-coated stone wall. "Dare we hope you are regaining your senses at last? Perchance remembering the ease with which we took you?"

The man leaned down, so close his stale breath fanned Donall's cheek. "Pray, how does it feel to have been bested by an insignificant clan such as ours? I doubt you e'er thought to awaken wearing naught but MacInnes irons?"

The MacInnesses!

At last, the remaining dredges of fog cleared from his mind and he remembered.

Everything.

But he hadn't been bested, they'd tricked him.

When his brother Iain's grief upon his wife's death had proved too great for him to perform the sorry task himself, Donall and his foster brother, Gavin MacFie, had set off alone to bear Lileas's body home to her clan's stronghold, Dunmuir Castle.

Upon arriving, they'd been welcomed, thanked, and even offered victuals and ale to sustain them before they continued on their journey to the mainland to purchase cattle and supplies for the MacLean holding, Baldoon Castle on the opposite side of Doon, the bonnie isle both clans had shared since time beginning.

A voyage Donall had expected to make together with a party of MacInnesses.

An excursion he'd meant to use to locate the true murderer of Iain's beloved MacInnes bride.

An endeavor of great and dire import, a matter he'd hoped to see resolved before his short-tempered brother awakened from the haze of his sorrow and set off on his own to avenge his wife's death. Iain's rashness would only make a bad situation worse.

Deep inside, in a hidden place Donall did not care to let his thoughts linger, he hoped Iain's hot temper and tendency to quick bouts of irritability had nary a finger in *causing* the tragedy.

And now his attempts to avert further turmoil were rendered impossible by the MacInnesses' addlepated plans to wreak vengeance on him!

He strained against his fetters, frustration hot and bitter in his throat. Cold iron emphasized the futility of his efforts to break free, while the closed expressions on his captors' faces bespoke the folly of trying to persuade them to form an alliance to seek the true perpetrators of their kinswoman's murder.

But futile or folly, he must try.

Donall forced himself to swallow his anger. If only Archibald were still alive, he might have half a chance. But the old laird was gone, and the graybeards holding him captive showed none of Archibald's desire to maintain at least a semblance of peace.

Though they had been bitter enemies for centuries, the old laird's efforts had enabled the two clans to enjoy an uneasy truce in recent years. Neither Donall nor Gavin had suspected the lass they'd come upon not long after their departure from Dunmuir of pretending to have twisted her ankle. Her supposed injury allowed the scheming MacInnes whoresons to fall upon them from behind when they'd stopped to help her.

"What ails you, laddie?" The white-haired ancient nudged Donall's bare thigh. "Are you so vexed o'er being bested that you've lost your tongue?"

Donall ignored the taunt and swept the cell with his gaze, peering deep into the shadowy corners to see if his pain-addled state had prevented him from spotting Gavin. But he was indeed alone, his foster brother nowhere to be seen.

"What have you done with Gavin?" He struggled to sit up straighter. "If aught has befallen him, it is your clan who will be bested," he swore, directing his words to the hawk-eyed man he at last recognized as the late MacInnes laird's brother, Struan.

"Proud words for a man in your position." Struan's gaze flicked over Donall's iron-bound limbs. "Your man rests in his own cell and more comfortably than you, never fear. We bear no grudges against the MacFies. Our fight is with you."

"Striking a man from behind has naught to do with fighting." Ire swelled in Donall's gut. "Such trickery was a sorry deed, one I doubt your brother would have allowed."

"Archibald is dead." The youngest-looking of the gray-beards stepped forward. He cast a sidelong glance at Struan. "Our *ceann cath* now advises us in war matters, and we possess the wisdom of our combined years. It is enough."

Without further discourse, he went to stand before the chink in the far wall that served as the cell's only window. Though painfully narrow, the opening had allowed a semblance of light and an occasional stirring of brisk sea air to enter the chamber. By blocking the air slit, he stole the scant comfort Donall had gleaned from the few stray breezes that had found their way into the cell.

As if Donall's thoughts were emblazoned upon his forehead, a knowing smile spread across the man's grim-cast face. "You see, Donall the *Bold*, brawn is not always required to make one's enemies squirm. Clever planning can often wreak a far more fitting revenge than a well-wielded sword."

"And it is the taste of my well-wielded blade's steel you shall suffer if you do not release me at once." Donall's anger heated his blood to such a degree he no longer felt the cell's damp chill.

"Your blade is secured far outwith your reach," Struan countered. "Indeed, your days of swinging swords are past, MacLean. Even your supposed prowess with another sort of, shall we say, *thrusting weapon* will serve you no more."

Bracing his hands on his hips, he gave Donall a wholly unpleasant smile. "I daresay you shall regret being denied the use of *that* sword once you glimpse the fair countenance of our chieftain, the lady Isolde. But alas, sampling such a tender fruit as she is a pleasure beyond your reach."

"I would sooner plunge my staff into a she-goat," Donall seethed, his shackles cutting into his wrists and ankles as he sought to lunge at the graybeard. "May my shaft wither and fall off afore I—"

"Be assured I find the notion equally displeasing."

Donall froze. Smooth and rich as thick cream yet irresistibly spiced with the bite of pepper, the woman's voice poured over, around, and into him.

Under any other circumstances, the pleasing tones would have banished the sting of his anger with ease, mayhap even ignited fires of an entirely different sort of heat, but he was in no mood to be swayed by the sweet lilt of a few saucily spoken words.

Especially when the melodious voice most assuredly belonged to Isolde MacInnes.

A woman he had no intention of being attracted to.

"Distasteful as your presence is to me, you are under my

roof and I am determined to have done with you accordingly," she spoke again, her words confirming her identity.

Donall shifted on his pallet of straw and wished more covered his manhood than a thin piece of cloth. If the lady Isolde's appearance proved halfway as provocative as the honeyed timbre of her voice and the avowals of her uncle, he would have preferred a more substantial modicum of dignity.

Cell-bound and fettered or nay, red blood yet coursed through his veins.

Nor had the blackguards put out his eyes.

Pressing his lips together, he pushed aside all thought of fetching lasses. It'd been longer than he cared to admit since he'd last taken his ease with a wench, but he did not want to be bestirred by Isolde MacInnes.

Not even a wee bit.

What he wanted was a way out of this cell.

With luck, he'd find her so unappealing, any unwanted surges of admiration would fly away at first glance. Holding his breath lest it not be so, he turned his head toward the door whence her voice had come.

She stood just inside the open doorway, holding a rush light, her aged kinsmen clustered around her. And much to his ire, he recognized her worth immediately.

Her uncle hadn't lied: she was indeed a beauty.

A powerful jolt of frank appreciation shot through him, boldly declaring his hot-blooded nature's refusal to cooperate with his avowals to resist her charms.

"Lady Isolde." He curtly inclined his head. Blessedly, his voice remained free of any indication he found her alluring. "I refuse to be a part of such foolery as your men intend to perform on me and demand you release me at once."

She stepped farther into the cell, her rush light held aloft. Its flame illuminated the finely formed contours of her face, emphasizing the smooth perfection of her skin and casting a bright sheen upon her plaited hair.

Hair the color of a thousand setting suns, its deep bronze tones shot through with lighter strands that shone like molten gold. Unbound, it would surely swirl around her gently curved hips and bewitch the good sense out of any man fool enough to try to resist his attraction to her.

She came closer and Donall caught her scent. A light, clean fragrance, fresh and feminine, with a trace of wild-flowers and summer days, yet laced with a breath of some warm and tantalizing spice that promised darker pleasures beneath her aura of grace and innocence.

The sort of pleasures he'd love to awaken in her.

Were she any other woman.

"I told you she was a prize. What a pity you can no longer indulge in such sweet pursuits." Struan laid his arm around his niece's shoulders and drew her closer to where Donall sat pressed against the cell wall. With his foot, he lifted the rag covering Donall's male parts and kicked it aside. "You appear fit and hale . . . I imagine it pains you to know your few remaining days will be abstemious ones?"

The white-haired ancient hovering to Donall's left chortled, a thin-sounding, old man's laugh. Isolde MacInnes gasped and turned away, her cheeks blooming near as red as her hair.

"By God's teeth, you base-minded miscreants, have none of you any shame?" Donall met the graybeards' smirks with a fierce glare. "If your chieftain is a maid, what madness possesses—"

"I *am* a maid, sirrah, and it is you who bears the weight of shame. You, and every other MacLean male ever born." She stood with her back to him, her stance rigid and proud, her shoulders squared.

A goddess carved of stone.

She turned back, and the light from her torch shone full on her face. Her eyes, beautiful and exceptionally large, appeared dull. The sparkle that should have lit eyes of such a rich amber color was extinguished, snuffed out by a pall of sadness. Marred as thoroughly as her expression of accusation and disdain turned down the corners of her lips, thus spoiling the sweet allure of a mouth that fair begged to be kissed.

Not that he was the man to do the kissing.

Delectable lips or nay.

Donall turned on the pallet, a vain attempt to shield his male parts from her view, but even more, a fruitless endeavor to free himself from the witchery she'd cast over him. Straw jabbed the backs of his bare legs and a gust of briny air swept into the cell, bringing with it the sharp tang of the nearby sea and stirring up the stale smell of the cell itself.

Dank and sour, full of shadows, darkness, and unnamed scurrying creatures, the pathetic confines and the cold iron of his fetters flooded him with renewed vigor and scorn.

Scorn, not for the lady, but for her aged advisers and their misplaced plans to wreak revenge on him for a deed he had naught to do with.

A nefarious act he prayed had not been born of Iain's lightning-quick mood swings.

Digging his nails into his palms, he banished the troublesome nigglings of doubt that threatened to eat away his very soul.

Iain could not be the murderer.

He simply would not allow it to be so.

The MacLeans, including his brother, condemned the foul deed, were stricken by it, and burned to avenge the gentle-hearted Lileas's death.

They would, too, if the MacInnesses would but listen to reason and release him.

And mayhap he'd lost all reason, too, for he half believed that whilst the graybeards turned a deaf ear upon his avowals of innocence, the lady Isolde might prove more open-minded. A wild-brained notion, to be sure, but he had naught to lose and everything to gain.

Only by securing his freedom could he locate the true blackguards and circumvent further chaos should Iain be left too long to his own devices.

Turning back to the MacInnes chieftain, he cleared his throat. "My brother had naught to do with his wife's death," he said, fighting hard to ignore his undignified state and hoping his words held more assurance than he felt.

Just broaching the matter caused his chest to constrict with pain. He could see the mild-mannered Lileas still, her red-gold hair tangled with seaweed, her slim body cold and unbreathing.

"Iain loved his wife. Ne'er would he have laid a hand on her," he vowed, focusing on the many times he'd seen Iain rain affection on his quiet wife rather than the rare occasions he'd ranted at her when beset by one of his black moods. "I'd swear his innocence on the holiest relics of the land."

Unbidden, Iain's haunted eyes loomed vividly in Donall's mind. His gut twisted at the memory of how inept he'd been in his attempts to ease his brother's sorrow. "He mourns her truly," he said, this time with more conviction.

"You lie." The two words fell upon his naked skin, cold as two chips of ice.

Isolde shivered. As so often since learning of her younger sister's death, waves of cold washed over her even as her heart burned with the need to avenge Lileas's murder. "You lie," she repeated, her gaze fixed on the opposite wall rather than upon the naked man sprawled at her feet. "No one else could have done the deed."

Slipping out of the reassuring circle of her uncle's arm,

she thrust her rush light into his hands, then began pacing the bracken-strewn floor. She'd looked at the MacLean longer than she could bear. His unclothed state unsettled her, and knowing she'd soon be even closer to him, and to *that* part of him, made her heart pound with trepidation.

But get close to him she would.

For Lileas.

For her people.

And for herself, a tiny voice in the recesses of her mind reminded her. But those other reasons seemed sorely insignificant now.

Still, she'd be strong. *Brave.* She'd follow her secret plan, even if it meant relinquishing her virginity to a man she reviled. Her sister's murder must be avenged and she had to ensure the survival of her clan.

Her council wanted the MacLean laird to die. They boasted his death would prove the ultimate revenge against the MacLeans. But such a plan, justifiable though it was, would destroy the MacInnesses. Vengeance would come swift and without quarter. She might as well unbar the gates and let the MacLeans storm within. Only a fool would think himself capable of staving off an attack by a clan so powerful.

Yet almost all within her household seemed bent on being fools.

She had no choice but to implement her own secret plan. A strategy to assure the MacLeans posed no future threat. For such a gain, the loss of her maidenhead was a small price to pay.

Especially if her couplings with the MacLean left her blessed with a child as she hoped.

"So if you believe me a liar, Isolde of Dunmuir, are you as bloodthirsty as your kinsmen?" Donall MacLean challenged her. His deep voice held a tinge of amusement and cut straight through her musings. "Are you, too, determined to torture me?"

What I am wont to do to you, Donall the Bold, shall be a torture unto myself. The words echoed so loudly in her ears, she half feared she'd blurted them for all to hear.

"Not as vocal as your wild-eyed band of elders, fair lady?" he taunted. "Have you no desire to recite the myriad cruelties you mean to inflict upon my flesh?"

Wincing, for his accusations came closer to the truth than he could possibly know, Isolde joined Lorne, the youngest of her clan elders, in front of the cell's narrow window.

She did not trust herself to meet her prisoner's dark and furious eyes. Keeping her back to him, she clasped her hands before her and took a deep, cleansing breath of salt-laden air. The muffled whoosh of waves washing over the pebbled beach just beyond the dungeon wall made her heart wrench.

How often had she and Lileas skipped along the shore's narrow reaches in the carefree days of their childhood?

And how often had her dear da scolded them for venturing onto a beach he deemed dangerous because of the quick-changing currents of its harmless-looking waters?

Now both Lileas and her father were gone.

Isolde blinked hard.

A speck, *something,* must've gotten into her eye.

She unclasped her hands and smoothed her palms against the woolen folds of her belted *arisaid.* The plaid's soft and nubby texture comforted her with its familiarity and provided a tenuous but reassuring link to normality during a situation that seemed to have skittered completely out of her control.

Not yet ready to turn around, she stared out the window slit. Too narrow to reveal more than a slim swath of brilliant blue sky, the view was enough to make her hands clench at her sides.

How could the sun shine when such darkness had settled over her heart?

She blinked again, no longer able to blame the stinging heat at the backs of her eyes on a mere speck of dust. But rather than give heed to tears, she squared her shoulders and braced herself to face her enemy.

The man she held responsible for her sister's murder.

Vengeance must be had but neither was all lost. She had much to be grateful for, and she wasn't alone.

She had the support and devotion of her clan. Her people now, for upon her da's passing, and following his wishes, she'd accepted her place as chieftain. And as such, she had to do what was best for the good of them all.

Especially in times of trouble, and including the daunting task of saving them from their own stubborn and foolish selves.

"One of our own, a fine young woman we trusted your brother to treat with respect, has been killed upon the Lady Rock," Lorne's commanding voice sounded beside her, his austere words calling her back from her silent reverie. "Murdered by her MacLean husband in the same manner as her ancestress so many years past. You, Donall the Bold, as MacLean laird, will do penance by—"

"Lorne, please." Isolde swung around and touched the elder's arm, unable to bear hearing the gory details of her kinsmen's intent spoken aloud yet again. "The MacLean is aware of what he faces."

Returning to her uncle Struan's side, she hoped naught about her bearing or expression revealed the turmoil swirling inside her.

Her voice as level as she could manage, she said, "I am weary and shall retire early. I trust verily no one will disturb me before cockcrow."

Bracing herself to play a role she already doubted she

could master, she cast a disdainful glance at the MacLean. "Niels and Rory have insisted on guarding my door so long as *he* remains within our walls. Rather than injure their feelings, I agreed, so do not be alarmed if you see them there. They've sworn to let none save the Blessed Mother herself cross my threshold." With that, she kissed her uncle's cheek, gave the MacLean a curt nod, then sailed from the chamber as quickly as her pride would allow.

A safe distance from the cell, she paused before a dark alcove set deep in the passage's wall. "See that he is properly bathed and brought to my chamber this eve," she whispered to the man concealed by shadows. "Late . . . not before the hour of compline. And, pray God, let none catch you."

The man opened his mouth to reply, but Isolde hitched up her skirts and hurried down the dank corridor before the words could pass his lips.

If her well-meaning cousin Niels tried once more to sway her purpose, she might well abandon her ambitious plan for securing peace with the MacLeans.

Indeed, after seeing their laird in the flesh, *completely in the flesh,* she harbored serious concerns about the wisdom of pursuing her goal.

Donall stared after her long after she'd gone, a multitude of conflicting emotions eating him alive. Saints, but she took his breath away, riling him with her blunt refusal to listen to reason, yet even as fury made his blood boil, he had to admire her courage and spirit.

She had to know what her clan elders meant to do with him. Her willingness to allow such barbarous acts beneath her roof spoke of her sheer will to see her sister's death avenged.

Whether he shouldered responsibility or nay, and he most assuredly did not, such strength of character as she displayed was something any Highlander or Islesman had to admire.

"An uncommon beauty, is she not?" Lorne MacInnes drew Donall's attention with a swift kick to his ribs.

Biting back a groan, Donall shot a dark look at the smirking graybeard. The tattered cloth that had covered his male parts dangled from the bastard's fingers.

"A sweetmeat the likes of you will never sample again," Lorne drawled, twirling the rag before letting it drop onto Donall's groin. "If good fortune is with you, mayhap our fair chieftain will grace your dreams," he added, then strode from the cell, the other MacInnes ancients trailing after him.

"Surely you cannot deny her appeal?" yet another male voice came from the darkness, robbing him of the welcome quiet that had settled over his cell since the graybeards' collective departure. "I doubt there is a finer lass in all of the Isles."

Donall clenched his jaw and said naught. He wouldn't give the insolent lout the gratification of an answer. Especially when none was necessary.

Isolde MacInnes was a prize grand enough to bring a king to his knees.

Most men would be afire with need at the mere thought of bedding a maid so fine.

Not that such thoughts had entered his mind.

Nor was he most men.

Though regional unrest and his duties as laird left him little time or inclination for wenching in recent years, none could claim he lived a monk's life.

But ne'er had he sampled the favors of a female as alluring as the MacInnes chieftain, and a merry pox on the whoreson who'd brought such unwanted notions to his mind!

His brows drawn together in ire, he sought the source of his irritation, ready to unleash the full wrath of his fury on the cur, only to have the words lodge in his throat when he spied the wretch in the shadows of the still-open cell door.

A veritable giant of a man, the overgrown ox with his outrageously red hair had the audacity to look amused by Donall's surprise. "Not all MacInnes men are old and bent," the giant said, holding out his well-muscled arms and flexing his fingers. " 'Twould be wise of you to remember it."

"And who are you?" Donall shot back, wishing fervently he could rid himself of his shackles. "Are you come from the lady to begin my torture?"

The man peered hard at him. After a long moment, he said, " 'Tis Niels MacInnes I am, and, aye, the lady Isolde sent me, but her reasons for a-wanting you have naught to do with breaking your bones, though I will not deny I wouldn't mind getting my hands on you."

"So why *are* you here?"

"I asked if you find our chieftain appealing. You didn't answer." Niels MacInnes folded his arms and pinned Donall with a piercing stare. "Do you?"

Thinking the great buffoon a mite short of all his wits, Donall snapped, "And if I did?"

" 'Twould lend ease to the covenant my lady seeks to offer you."

"Covenant?" Now Donall knew the man was witless.

"I will come for you sometime between the hours of vespers and compline," the giant informed him, his voice so low Donall scarce heard him. "If you do not cooperate, your daylight hours will be made as miserable as the night ones could have been pleasurable."

"You spout nonsense," Donall protested, straining his full might in a vain attempt to break free. "I'll go nowhere with you and I want naught to do with your lady and her covenant."

"Aye, you will go, and you will be gentle with my lady. If you are not, I shall grind your bones to powder. The decision falls to you." With a last sharp stare, the giant stepped back through the open doorway. "Misery or paradise," he added, and disappeared from view.

Miserable, indeed, and more than confused, Donall stared at the rough planks of the door the lumbering oaf had closed and locked behind him.

What the devil had he meant about Donall *being gentle with* his lady? Surely not the obvious? Heat sprang to the base of his neck at the very thought, and of a sudden, his lungs seemed incapable of drawing air.

Nay, it could not be anything so preposterous.

Beautiful, of exceptional grace, and very likely yet to be deflowered, Isolde MacInnes would be the finest paradise.

If such was the meaning behind the giant's riddles, a possibility Donall highly doubted. Still, none could call him dense. His sharp wit and keen sense of perception had guided him through many a treacherous encounter.

And the more he mulled it over, the more he came to the wildest, most absurd conclusion.

With a sigh, he fell back against the wall and stared at his cell's water-stained ceiling. May the saints and their entire retinue of holy men preserve him, but a trace of the wench's scent lingered in the air.

A mere whisper of wildflowers, but enough to tempt his senses and mock his determination to remain unmoved by her charms.

Should his suspicions prove true.

Donall closed his eyes and groaned. A deep, full-bodied groan straight from the very bottom of his soul. Had the giant truly said he had a choice?

Indeed, he'd most assuredly been given a choice. The trouble was, if his instincts hadn't failed him, he doubted he possessed the strength to make the right one.

Chapter Two

❦

*I*SOLDE HURRIED THROUGH the gloaming, her *arisaid* clutched tight about her shoulders. A stiff wind whistled past her ears, its chill bite ripe with the thick tang of the sea and the damp, earthy scent of coming rain.

She followed a narrow track through a landscape of wind-stunted trees and shrubs, a well-trodden path that hugged the sheer crags forming this end of Doon before ending in a cliff-top glade the old ones called the edge of the world.

A notion enhanced in its eeriness by the silver birch and rowan trees surrounding the clearing, and the presence of Devorgilla, the ancient crone who dwelled there.

Isolde struggled against the increasing strength of the gales sweeping in off the sea, eager to reach the only living soul she'd trusted with all her reasons for having the MacLean secreted to her chamber.

Not even the ever-faithful Niels knew everything, and certainly not his shadow, Rory.

Only the *cailleach*, and Isolde's little dog, Bodo.

And neither one of them would betray her confidences.

Even now, Bodo displayed his devotion, his eagerness to keep her safe. He trotted along a short distance ahead of her, his tail held upright, his gait self-important. Though diminutive and still playful as a puppy, the little brown and white dog would defend her to the death if need be.

And if he possessed such courage, who was she to harbor niggling doubts about going through with a plan to ensure a secure future for her people? Didn't she owe them as much loyalty as wee Bodo showed her?

Wouldn't lasting peace be a more noble tribute to Lileas than another death?

Wasn't an alliance of necessity with Donall MacLean preferable to seeing her clan fade from existence?

Isolde sent a quick glance heavenward. Bands of fast-moving clouds, deep gray and heavy with rain, stretched across the sky, stealing the early evening's luminous light as easily as the mere thought of Donall MacLean had robbed her of her nerve.

Determined, she continued on, but an unshakable sense of ill ease accompanied her, while doubt threatened to cloud her intentions.

She'd spent hours, whole nights, searching for a solution. She'd mulled over every minute detail . . . even questioning Evelina, Doon's own joy woman, about the art of seduction!

Quickly, before her cheeks could flame, she pushed aside all thought of her clandestine meetings with Evelina, a woman most womenfolk of Doon, MacInnes and MacLean alike, pretended didn't exist.

To Isolde's amazement, she'd even found herself liking her. But she rather doubted Evelina's claim she no longer plied her lurid trade, having supposedly given her heart to a mysterious benefactor she refused to name.

"Owwwwwwww . . ." Isolde grabbed her ankle and glared at the offending root stretching across the path. "By the bridge of St. Ninian's nose," she vowed, hopping on one foot. "May his manhood wither and fall off, indeed."

She frowned at the throbbing in her big toe.

It was *his* fault.

Had she not been dwelling on him, and the art of seduction, she wouldn't have slammed her foot into the exposed root.

Bodo bounded back to her, jaws open, a quizzical look in his golden-brown eyes, his perplexed expression all the more endearing for the crooked set of his teeth.

The way he gazed up at her thawed a bit of the frost that had settled 'round her heart since hearing Donall the Bold's insults. Forgetting the dull ache in her foot, she scooped the little dog into her arms for a fierce hug.

"*You* wouldn't compare me to a she-goat, would you, Bodo?" she whispered into his smooth fur, deftly ignoring the tiny voice of reason that reminded her the MacLean had not exactly stated *she* was a she-goat.

His insulting sentiments slighted her all the same.

Another hot spring of irritation welled deep within her and she hugged Bodo tight, taking comfort in the feel of his cold little nose pressing against her neck, before she set him on the path.

He scampered ahead, and eager to reach her destination, Isolde cast another wary glance at the ever-darkening sky and made to follow him.

But not before she pulled a small leather flagon from within the folds of her skirts and hurriedly removed its stopper. With a grimace, she held her nose and swallowed the remaining drops of Devorgilla's anti-attraction potion.

A great shudder tore through her as the foul-tasting infusion burned its way down her throat, but heedless of the potion's questionable taste, she meant to ask for more.

Enemy or nay, she would have to have been cloudy-eyed like Devorgilla herself not to have noticed the MacLean's fine form and bonnie face.

And the man had been well grimed and reeking.

The impact of his good looks once bathed and properly groomed didn't bear thinking upon.

Worse, his resemblance to the shadowy figure she'd dreamed of after placing sprigs of yarrow beneath her pillow on the night of Beltaine presented an even more disturbing aspect.

She was not looking forward to facing him again.

Yet face him and more, she must.

Much more.

Setting her lips in a grim line of determination, she picked up her skirts and hurried on. She caught up to Bodo at the edge of the circular glade Devorgilla called home.

Feeling half the fool for the chill skipping up and down her spine, Isolde crossed herself before she stepped into the clearing. Doing so was like surrendering oneself into a parallel yet unseen world.

The mysterious realm of the wee folk, the *sidhe*.

A world where the Old Religion still held sway, and the crone, Devorgilla, reigned supreme, heeding not whoe'er bore the title of MacInnes chieftain, but the ancient ones who served the Goddess.

Bodo's ears lifted, his hackles rising. He peered into the clearing . . . a strange place lit by an eerie silvery light despite the encroaching darkness.

A place where no wind blew, though the approaching storm raged all around them. Even the wispy column of smoke rising from Devorgilla's thatched cottage rose in a straight, bluish-gray line.

Low rumbles sounded in Bodo's chest, and Isolde reached down to touch him. "Do not fret, precious," she said. "The *cailleach* would ne'er harm either one of us."

Bodo ceased growling, but glanced up at her, his eyes white-rimmed and doubtful. Nevertheless, he trotted along beside her, his short, sturdy legs moving quickly over the grass as he sought to keep pace with her longer strides.

As always, a heavy silence cloaked the glade. Devorgilla's thick-walled cottage perched very close to the edge of the cliff. Fishnet weighted down by stones held the rough thatch roofing in place, and as in the glade itself, a luminous silvery light seemed to shimmer up, down, and around the humble dwelling's whitewashed walls.

Even the warm glow of lit candles, visible through two unshuttered windows, cast more of an otherworldly air than a welcoming one.

But Isolde knew she was welcome.

As the crone was always welcome at Dunmuir, her skills and wisdom appreciated, her person and property e'er assured of what protection the current MacInnes chieftain could offer her. And Isolde secretly suspected the *cailleach* had outlived more MacInnes lairds than just her da and his before him.

"You've naught to fear," Isolde reassured Bodo before she lifted her hand to rap upon the door. Never would she admit her own nerves were strung as taut as her little dog's appeared to be, nor that her so calm-sounding voice was meant to lend comfort to herself as well.

But unlike Bodo, Devorgilla and her enchanted glen were not the cause of her agitation.

Nay, the cause of *her* tension lay naked and bound in Dunmuir's dungeon.

Or, and a much more disturbing image, perchance even now, sitting in a washtub, having the grime scrubbed from his flesh in preparation for being hauled abovestairs to her chamber and the service she hoped to induce him to perform there.

The very thought sent a flood of heat spilling through her, and made her heart spurt into a faster beat.

Straightening her back against the madness she'd taken upon herself, she raised her hand to knock, but the door swung open before she could.

The *cailleach*'s tricolored cat, Mab, slipped through the opening, rubbing herself against Isolde's legs before sauntering off into the shadows without so much as a sideways glance at Bodo, who snarled his displeasure at the feline's familiarity toward his mistress.

"Welcome, lassie, have yourself in," the crone greeted her, a wealth of wisdom and compassion in her cloudy eyes.

Isolde swept past her into the low-ceilinged interior, Bodo hard on her heels. The cottage's tidy homeyness quickly unraveled what tenuous hold she'd kept on her nerves.

"You must give me more of the potion." The words came out in a rush and the desperation in her voice only unsettled her more. "I would know what you think of him. Is he the one? Pray tell me he is not."

Rather than answer her, the *cailleach* carefully closed the door and turned around with excruciating slowness.

A deliberate slowness Isolde suspected had naught to do with the natural limitations of the diminutive Devorgilla's age-bent bones.

"I must know. He—" she began, but the crone silenced her with one sage look.

"So many wants, my child," Devorgilla said, her voice annoyingly calm. "And such irritation thrumming through you. By the grace of the Mother, I vow I can hear the racing of your heart."

"You do not understand . . ." Isolde let her objection trail off when the *cailleach* lifted one straggly brow.

Ignoring Isolde's agitation, Devorgilla turned her attention to a dark-haired lad of about nine years who sat on a bench against the far wall, stuffing moss and ferns into a worn bed pallet. "Lugh, fetch a cup of heather ale for the lady Isolde, and a fresh bone for her dog. Then be gone with you for a while. The lady and I have matters to discuss not fit for your young ears."

The lad set aside his work and stood, a red stain coloring his cheeks. He gave Isolde a shy glance and a nod, then pushed aside a hanging partition of woven straw not far from where he'd been sitting, and disappeared into the darkness beyond.

Isolde listened to him moving about in the small larder that opened off the cottage's main room, and tried to ignore the hunger-stirring aroma of smoked ham and dried beef wafting out from behind the straw mat.

She had more serious issues to deal with than the rumblings of her empty stomach.

The partition moved again, and Lugh returned with a filled-to-the-brim cup of heather-scented ale for Isolde, and a good-sized bone for Bodo. His mistress momentarily forgotten, the little dog dashed forward and snatched the bone from the lad's fingers.

A stew bone with a nice portion of meat still clinging to it. Isolde's mouth watered at the sight, and she swallowed back the near overpowering urge to ask the crone's great-great-grandson to fetch her a spot of victuals as well.

As if reading Isolde's mind, Devorgilla laid a gnarled hand on Isolde's arm. "Would you like a bowl of rabbit stew?" Her hazy-eyed gaze went to the bubbling cauldron suspended over the central hearth fire. "I've some fresh bread almost finished," she added, glancing toward the circular bake-oven protruding from the thickness of the opposite wall.

A delicious smell drifted past the seams of the oven's closed iron-plate door, but Isolde ignored that temptation, too. "The ale will do," she said simply, accepting the cup Lugh offered her. "I thank you," she added with a forced smile for the lad. "And for giving Bodo a bone as well."

Lugh's cheeks flamed a deeper red and the corners of his mouth lifted in a hesitant smile before he turned away to head back to the bench and his unfinished task.

"Ho, laddie." Devorgilla shuffled after him, moving her hands in a flapping motion that underscored her resemblance to an oversized, black-garbed bird. "Out with you now." She urged him toward the door. "I'm a-thinking you ought gather a bit more moss and ferns for your sleeping pallet."

Without further protest, he took the basket Devorgilla handed him, and let himself out of the cottage. Isolde's heart twisted for the lad. He'd scarce uttered a word since his mother died of fever some years past, but as much affection as she bore him, she had other, heavier problems weighing on her mind.

She waited until Devorgilla hobbled away from the door, but the moment the crone paused at the central hearth and reached for a long-handled ladle to stir the simmering stew, Isolde's patience snapped.

"He compared me to a *she-goat*," she railed. "Claimed he'd rather see his manroot wither and fall off before he'd deign to bed me."

Devorgilla shot a sharp glance her way. "He already knows what you would have of him?"

"Nay, he knows naught . . . as yet." Warmth crept into Isolde's cheeks. "He simply meant to hurl nastiness at me."

Seemingly unperturbed by Isolde's outburst, the crone

dipped the ladle into the cauldron and began to stir the aromatic stew. A cloud of fragrant steam rose to encircle her grizzled head, and to Isolde's ire, she imagined she heard the old woman snicker.

"There is naught amusing in such insults," Isolde said, hoping her voice disguised the sound of her stomach growling in reaction to the delicious-smelling stew.

"'Tis not amused I am, but intrigued." Devorgilla glanced at her, a cagey expression on her wizened face. "Why do you wish more of the potion if he vexes you so? Riled as you are, I would think you'd have no need of my anti-attraction infusion?"

Isolde ignored the crone's questions and asked a few of her own. The same ones she'd posed upon arriving. "I know you went to see him. Is he the one? The man you glimpsed in the cauldron's steam?"

Devorgilla cast Isolde another of her impish looks, then waved her hand through the steam drifting up from her stew. "Would that he appear now so you could see him yourself. Then you'd ken the answer without asking me."

"But I *am* asking you."

"Such things cannot be rushed." The crone returned the ladle to the tabletop. "Ofttimes the answers we seek are already deep within our own hearts, if we'll but look."

"I have looked. *At him.* And I did not like what I saw." Isolde blew out a frustrated breath. "Nor did I care for what he said."

A tiny chuckle, nay, more a cackle, escaped the crone's lips, and her hunched shoulders trembled with what Isolde highly suspected to be mirth.

"I told you, there is nary a thread of humor in his slurs," Isolde said, relieved her great respect for Devorgilla kept her tone from revealing the depth of her indignation.

The cackling ceased and Devorgilla peered hard at

Isolde. As ever, she seemed to hear Isolde's unspoken words as clearly as the spoken ones.

"How many men do you suppose would keep a civil tongue under such circumstances?"

Isolde glanced up at the smoke-blackened ceiling rafters rather than give the crone a scathing look.

Devorgilla was right.

Donall the Bold's slights were born of his outrage at awakening bound and chained to a dungeon wall, and not truly directed at her.

But after seeing him, she preferred anger to acknowledging the way her heart had skipped a beat upon noticing his resemblance to the man she'd dreamed of on the night of Beltaine.

Would that she hadn't placed the yarrow sprigs under her pillow!

But she'd wanted to see if the herb's magic would conjure her true soul mate.

A man she'd hoped to recognize as anyone but Balloch MacArthur, the man the clan elders meant to name as her betrothed.

Now, may the Holy Apostles stay her by, she was sorely afeared the man in her dream, her *soul mate,* might be her worst enemy, Donall MacLean.

Isolde returned her gaze to the crone. "I must know," she said. "Is the MacLean the man you saw in the cauldron's steam the night of Beltaine?"

The *cailleach* pursed her lips and reached again for the ladle. Isolde gently pushed aside the old woman's arm. *"Is he?"*

"The man in my vision was the one, your soul mate," Devorgilla hedged, dusting an invisible speck of lint off her sleeve. "And he was not that bumbling ox, Balloch," she added, confirming Isolde's suspicions about the crone being able to read minds.

Relief washed over Isolde upon Devorgilla's last pronouncement, but not enough. The niggling fear that Donall the Bold might be the one was too bothersome a notion for her agitation to lessen.

"Your true soul mate is a braw man, a fine warrior," Devorgilla continued at Isolde's silence. Shuffling across the room to a rough wooden shelf that ran the length of one wall, she began rummaging through a jumbled assortment of clay pots, earthen bowls, and jugs.

"Images seen on the night of Beltaine do not lie, the power of the old gods should not be doubted," the crone said, lifting a small leather flagon off the cluttered shelf.

She hobbled back to Isolde. "The man I saw was dark of hair and eyes, his muscles spoke of hard training, and he was . . . good."

"Then he cannot be the MacLean, dark and well muscled or nay." Isolde felt better already.

Somewhat better.

But the crone merely shrugged. "The vision did not show me the man's face."

"Is this the anti-attraction potion?" Isolde held up the little flagon Devorgilla had given her.

"'Tis what you came here for, aye," the *cailleach* said, moving toward the door, then opening it wide. "Now you have it, mayhap you should be on your way. My bones tell me a storm will break soon."

Isolde swallowed the urge to tell the crone a storm already *had* broken, and its fury threatened to engulf her very soul.

Instead, she called Bodo to her side, thanked the crone for the shielding infusion, and stepped into the night.

To her great dismay, she caught another of Devorgilla's

cagey little cackles as the old woman closed the door after her.

About an hour later, on the opposite side of Doon, pounding sheets of rain drenched the massive walls of Baldoon castle and jagged streaks of lightning ripped across the night sky.

A sky gone as dark as the many ells of black mourning cloth draped across the chancel and high altar of Baldoon's private oratory.

A lone man knelt in prayer before the altar, his broad shoulders and lowered head silhouetted against the flickering light of countless lit candles.

High above him, the curved line of tall, round-topped clerestory windows sent rainbow beams of color streaming into the chapel with each new flash of lightning, but the man did not notice.

To his left and right, clustered groupings of slender, round pillars supported the vaulted ceiling and formed shadowy arcades where young boys stood, their heads lowered as they rang hand bells to ward off the demons that might attempt to torment the departed soul of the man's late wife, Lileas MacInnes.

Deafening booms and claps of thunder repeatedly rattled the precious panes of jewel-toned glass high above the altar, and even seemed to shake the oratory's cold stone floor, yet the grieving man prayed on, fully undisturbed by the fury outwith the sanctuary of the semicircular chapel.

A dark cloud of sorrow, thick and cloying as the incense-laden air, clung to the man who appeared to hear neither the mournful ringing of bells, the unbridled wrath of the storm, nor the repetitive clatter and scrape of scores of men sharpening their swords in the great hall just beyond the oratory's half-opened door.

Neither did he hear the soft footfalls of the slender, raven-haired young woman who approached him from behind. "Psalm chanting and prayer will not bring her back, Iain," the woman said, placing a hand on his shoulder.

Only then did he stir, lifting his dark head as if awakening from a dream, then pushing to his feet to stare at her with eyes gone dull with sorrow. Deep vertical lines next to his lips marred his otherwise handsome face, while purplish smudges under his eyes bespoke long nights without sleep.

"Mayhap not," he answered the woman, his deep voice weary, "but if the good Lord has any mercy, he will lend Godspeed to the men repairing our storm-damaged galley and gift us with fair weather and a safe passage to MacKinnons' Isle."

"And if He is wise, He will send more storms such as this so you have no choice but to await Donall's and Gavin's return before you set forth on such a foolhardy mission." The woman braced her hands on her hips and lifted her chin in a clear gesture of defiance.

"Foolhardy mission?" The man's face darkened. "Now is not the time to rile me, Amicia. Sister or nay."

Undaunted, she stared back at him, her own face coloring. "Setting sail now, with Donall gone, and upon a hastily repaired vessel, *is* foolish."

"Avenging my wife's murder is foolish?" The man grabbed the woman's arm and pulled her from the chapel. Keeping a firm hold on her, he drew her through the throng of men until they stood in the very middle of Baldoon Castle's vast great hall.

With a broad sweep of his arm, he indicated the chaos of activity all around them. "Every man and lad o'er the age of ten-and-four who calls himself a MacLean is ready to bear arms against the foul perpetrators of my lady wife's death. You alone object."

The woman yanked her arm from his grasp and drew a deep breath. "I, too, would see Lileas avenged. But I will not stand silent when your grief and anger drives you to set sail in a ship that could sink and cost me not only you, my brother, but all these kinsmen you mean to take with you!"

Iain MacLean pressed his lips together, the slight jerking of a muscle in his jaw saying more than any heated words could have.

"Donall would tell you so, too," Amicia pressed. "Why do you think he and Gavin meant to join the MacInnesses on their journey to the mainland rather than wait until our own galley has been made seaworthy again?"

When Iain remained silent, Amicia stepped forward to stand directly before him. "We have no proof the MacKinnons are responsible for Lileas's death. Mayhap the storm that damaged our ship did damage to theirs as well?"

She tilted her head to the side, her eyes pleading. "Can you not wait until Donall's return to seek your revenge?"

"It will be months before our brother has finished his business in Glasgow," he spoke at last. With a tired smile, an exceedingly grim one, he rested his hands on Amicia's shoulders. "As for the MacKinnons, who but they could have done the deed? Our clans have e'er been at odds, and they've no fondness for the MacInnesses either."

"But the ship—"

"The voyage to MacKinnons' Isle is not hazardous or long," her brother cut in. "I promise you we shall not set forth until the galley's hull has been fully and soundly repaired."

The woman drew back her shoulders and made to protest, but Iain silenced her by placing two fingers over her lips. "'Tis well I know that retaliation will not bring Lileas back to me, but I cannot rest until I know her murderer is cold in his grave."

Amicia gave a little sigh, and her shoulders sagged. "There is naught I can say to stay you?"

Iain shook his head.

"Then may God watch o'er you," she said, blinking to hide the sudden brightness in her eyes. "'Tis said He takes special care of fools," she added under her breath, but the softly spoken words were lost in a crash of thunder and the din of men making ready for war.

Chapter Three

✦

THEY'D CHAINED HIM to her bed.

Her cheeks flaming, Isolde quickly pulled shut the door she'd just opened. Too stunned for words, she stood staring at the two kinsmen guarding her bedchamber.

A keening wind whistled 'round the curving tower wall, and thunder rumbled in the distance, an unceasing series of deep, resounding booms. Somewhere, a loose window shutter slammed repeatedly against the stone masonry of one of Dunmuir's towers, and that noise, too, she heard.

Even the muffled rise and fall of the wind-whipped sea came to her ears, familiar and clear despite the thick walling and the loud fury of the storm.

But none of the night's clamor could match the wild roar of her own blood pulsing madly in her ears. Nor could aught erase the image of Donall the Bold's splendor.

Even though the closed door separated them, she still saw him standing there, fury sparking in his dark eyes. His black hair gleamed, damp from his bath. The broad expanse of his bare chest, hard-planed, imposing, and tensed in agitation. His shoulders broad and powerful-looking.

He was taller than she'd realized, his face more noble and handsomely formed than the dim light in his dungeon cell had revealed. Bathed and well groomed, he bore an even more striking resemblance to the dream man she'd glimpsed on the night of Beltaine.

Her senses reeling, Isolde stared at the door's solid wooden planking, but saw instead the two images. The man conjured by the yarrow's magic and Donall the Bold, both emblazoned across her consciousness and merged into one.

She also saw the heavy chain hanging between her bed and a single iron band around one of his ankles.

Niels and Rory had chained Donall MacLean to one of her bedposts and sheer black anger emanated from every glorious inch of him.

Praise be, he'd wrapped those inches in a bedsheet, thus sparing her an even greater shock.

Not that she hadn't already seen *that* part of him, brief though the glimpse had been.

If all went in accordance with her plan, she'd soon have to become far more intimate with him than merely peering at the majesty of his form.

His naked form.

At the moment, though, she found herself not yet ready to face him in *any* form. And the memory of her sister's form, still and lifeless, damned her for the unexpected thrill of excitement that had thundered through her upon glimpsing the MacLean's magnificence.

Isolde struggled to calm herself. Daunting or nay, she would not allow his manly graces to unnerve her. Circumstances compelled her to deal with him, and the sooner she got on with what must be done, the sooner she could rid herself of him.

She turned to the taller of the two men guarding her door. "Why is he bound to my bed?" Faith, but her heart still drummed against her ribs. "And why isn't he clothed?"

Niels, her cousin, had the good grace to look embarrassed. "He's less likely to attempt an escape if he's chained."

"But why is he unclothed?" Isolde persisted. "Did you purpose to vex him by leaving him thus?"

A flicker of guilt in Niels's light green eyes answered her. "And if he takes out his vexation on me?" She looked between her cousin and Rory. As with Niels, a look of discomfiture passed over Rory's face and he avoided her eyes, gazing instead at the floor.

Isolde pressed a hand to her breast, still struggling to regain her composure. "His fury came at me in waves when I opened the door. I am half afeared to do so again."

Niels straightened to his full height and patted the broadsword hanging at his side. "You've naught to fear, he will not lay a hand . . ." he started, then broke off, his face coloring. "I mean," he began again, his fair complexion flushing a brighter red with every word, "he is not armed. He will not dare harm you knowing we stand guard outside your chamber."

"Think you he would harm me were you not here?" Isolde fought to keep the blush from her own cheeks.

Niels slid a sideways glance at Rory, but the other man only made a noncommittal grunt and shrugged his burly shoulders. An uncomfortable silence welled up between them until Isolde's cousin finally said, "I warned the whoreson I'd grind his bones to powder if he isn't gentle with you."

"Lower your voice, will you?" Isolde admonished him, mortification stinging her cheeks, her battle against blushing instantly lost. Every inch of her blazed with the heat of ten fast-burning fires.

Fires fueled as much by her own agitation at being in such a position as by the meaning behind her cousin's words.

"Answer me, Niels. Do you believe he would hurt me?" She lifted her chin and set her face into her best imitation of what she thought of as her da's *laird's look.*

The stern expression her late father had oft used to intimidate those who sought to defy him. As Niels meant to flout her now, if the stubborn set of his jaw was any indication.

She peered deep into his eyes and tried not to blink. "Well?"

Her da's old trick must've worked, for she'd only stared at him a few moments before he blew out a breath and rolled his eyes. "Nay, I doubt he would from what I've heard and seen of him."

"I am glad to hear it," Isolde said, the firmness of her voice amazing her. "For I doubt I could go through with what I must do, knowing someone lingered outside the door."

Niels gaped at her. "You cannot think to dally with him without us close at hand?"

"Did you not just say you do not believe he would do me ill?"

Looking more uncomfortable than ever, Niels rubbed the back of his neck. Isolde seized her advantage. "I am not asking you to leave, merely to stand out of hearing range. I cannot be expected to—"

"'Tis dangerous in other ways," Rory broke in. "What if someone comes looking for you? If we are not here—"

"But you will be," she cut him off, "at least close enough to take up your positions should anyone approach." Pausing, she glanced over her shoulder, then lowered her voice. "This is difficult enough without having the two of you within hearing range."

Niels reached to touch her arm, but lowered his hand when she backed way. "'Tis for your own good," he said. "We don't *think* any harm will befall you, but we cannot risk the chance."

Yet you'd see me betrothed to a man I revile?

Balloch MacArthur's coarse face rose up in her mind, an image even more unappealing than the thought of facing an unclothed Donall the Bold in her bedchamber.

Turning aside, she stared down the shadow-filled passageway. As gloomy as the ill-lit corridor and the yawning stairwell beyond, so bleak would her life be as Balloch MacArthur's bride.

Isolde shuddered.

If she meant to rid herself of Balloch, she had no choice but to lie with the MacLean. Balloch, a brutish man, dull of wit but exceedingly proud, would surely extricate himself from a betrothal if she told him she carried another man's child.

And she'd have to conceive and give birth to that child if she hoped to forge an irrefutable bond between her dwindling and weakened clan and the powerful MacLeans.

A bond she saw as her clan's sole chance of survival.

Her resolve strengthened, she turned back to face her cousin and Rory. "Rory, you are about the same size as the MacLean. I bid you to fetch him something to wear. I've ordered a meal brought to my chamber, and I will not sup with a naked man sitting across from me."

Rory blinked. "We were told he is to have naught but table scraps, and he was divested of his garb a-purpose. The council gave ord—"

"And so have I," Isolde overrode his objections. She

paused to gather her courage. Ne'er had she been so assertive. "Would you seek to make me more uncomfortable with this *situation* than I already am?"

"Nay, my lady, 'tis only—" Rory began, but she silenced him with a pointed look.

"You may stand guard at the top of the stairwell. I will not have you lurking outside my door." Her tone dared them to deny her wishes. "And if the MacLean proves he can abstain from insults and is not rough with me, I want him unchained from my bed. That, too, I find unsettling."

Both men stared, twin looks of incredulity on their faces. So much so, Isolde felt a wee twinge of guilt. Even after two years, she was not yet comfortable exerting her authority as chieftain, but the gravity of her present predicament gave her no choice but to do so.

Without further objections, both men nodded and moved away. Isolde winced at the injured looks they'd given her. Niels and Rory were among the few able-armed men left beneath her roof. But an audience of listeners during her . . . *encounters* . . . with Donall the Bold would only heighten her ill ease.

The silence returned, a deafening quiet so loud she could hear the rainwater coursing down the castle stonework. Silence loomed on the far side of her closed bedchamber door, too.

A strange silence, for she suddenly realized that in her haste to exit the room, she'd unwittingly shut in poor Bodo.

Her little dog was inside the room with the MacLean.

And Bodo wasn't barking.

Bodo!

All else forgotten, she pushed open the door and rushed inside. Her breath caught in her throat at the sight before her. The MacLean knelt beside her bed, his handsome face relaxed and smiling as he rubbed Bodo's belly.

The wee dog lay sprawled on his back, completely at ease, whilst *he* trailed the backs of his fingers down Bodo's white-furred tummy.

And the little traitor appeared to enjoy the man's touch.

As if only now becoming aware she'd just burst into the room, fully prepared to rescue him from the MacLean's clutches, Bodo turned his head to stare at her. Jaws open, and tongue lolling out one side of his mouth, he appeared to be laughing at her.

But attuned to her emotions as he always seemed to be, his comical expression quickly changed to one of contrition. He leaped up at once, shook himself, then scrambled across the rush-strewn floor to his bed by the hearth. Looking duly chastised, he circled a few times, then curled up in a ball, his back to the room's two occupants.

Isolde returned her gaze to the MacLean, only to find he, too, stared at the dog, a shadow of a smile still playing across his too-sensuous lips.

As if he knew the instant she glanced his way, he pushed to his feet and turned toward her, the look on his handsome face so compelling she couldn't have moved if her life depended on it.

His gaze flickered briefly to Bodo. "I could see you well content, too, my lady," he drawled.

His smile turned wicked and something akin to amusement gleamed in the depths of his deep brown eyes. But then all traces of merriment faded and his expression grew cold, hard, and angry. "Aye, I could pleasure you," he said. *"If I was wont to . . . which I am not."*

Isolde swallowed hard. Embarrassment dampened her palms, and mortification rode hard on her shoulders, while her heart threatened to gallop out of all restraint and bounds.

"Your being here has naught to do with pleasure," she snapped, amazed the words hadn't stuck to her tongue.

Donall the Bold merely arched a brow.

Heat crept up Isolde's neck. "I would have words with you."

"Words that make you blush?" His lips curved in another cold smile.

A knowing smile.

He knew what she wanted of him.

He knew and was making sport of her.

"Private words of great import." She met his mocking gaze with another interpretation of her da's *laird's look.*

"I can scarce wait to hear them." One corner of Donall the Bold's lips quirked with what she hoped wasn't amusement.

"I've ordered a repast brought up," she blurted, hoping to steer the conversation in a different direction.

Anywhere but into the realm of what must happen between them.

What *had* to happen, and would, if ever she could embolden herself to seduce him.

Not yet ready to be so daring, she wet her lips and hoped the layers of her chemise and skirt concealed her trembling knees. "I've also arranged to have raiment fetched for you."

"You are full kind," he said.

Isolde knew he did not mean a word.

Hoping the meager light from the hearth's low-burning fire and the chamber's two hanging cresset lamps was too poor to reveal her discomfiture, she smoothed the folds of her gown. "Further, if you prove less . . . less slanderous of my person than you were earlier, and if I see no cause to be fearful in your presence, I shall see you unchained."

"So you are brave as well as kind." A half smile played at the corners of his mouth, but it was clearly another of his mocking smiles.

Definitely not a sincere one.

"I've no need to be overly courageous. Two of my best warriors guard the door." She declined to mention they now stood a goodly distance away, well out of decent hearing range.

"My guardsmen are well armed," she declared, fighting the unsettling impression he found her words . . . amusing. "Harm me and they will be upon you in a heartbeat. Let loose more of your slurs—"

"My *slurs?*"

Irritated more by his arching brow than his sarcastic tone, Isolde crossed the room to a row of tall, arch-topped windows. Cut into the thickness of the wall, the windows were the room's best feature and, in fine weather, provided sweeping views of the neighboring isles.

But they were shuttered now, not that it mattered. The storm raging beyond them suited her mood. And it was far more prudent to stare at the neutrality of closed shutters than to turn around and face *him*.

Him, and the heavily curtained bed looming so close behind him.

"To what slurs do you refer, lady?" Again, his tone held a trace of amusement.

Plague take the man!

Isolde whirled around, her patience flown straight through the shutter slats. "'May your manhood wither and fall off,'" she quoted, not caring if she sounded like a fishwife. "'You'd sooner—'"

"'Sooner plunge my staff into a she-goat,'" he finished for her, a slow smile spreading across his handsome face.

A smile so cold it chilled her to the marrow of her bones.

His glance lighted briefly on the iron band around his ankle and the length of chain binding him to her bed. "Pray tell me, fair one, what man with blood in his veins would not protest at such confinement?"

His words sliced away the last threads of her fast-dwindling composure and the knocking of her knees increased to such a degree the clatter could surely be heard by all within ten leagues of her humble castle's walls.

Worse, she found herself unable to answer him, for someone else's words crowded out her own.

As if Devorgilla stood beside her and whispered in her ear, the *cailleach*'s thin, reedy voice echoed in Isolde's mind . . . *How many men do you suppose would keep a civil tongue under such circumstances?*

Something light and cool brushed along the exposed nape of her neck, lifting the fine hairs there, and sending a delicate little ripple down her spine.

Isolde glanced behind her, half expecting the crone to be hiding in the shadows of one of the deep window embrasures, but naught was there.

Nothing stirred save the storm-driven wind racing through the night beyond Dunmuir's snug walls.

Of such a gentle, caressing breeze as had drifted past her there was no trace.

This time when she turned back to the MacLean, his dark countenance had turned to stone. "Know this, Isolde of Dunmuir, ne'er have I done harm to a woman, and ne'er shall I," he said, barely restrained anger tainting the rich timbre of his deep voice. "There is naught under God's heaven that could drive me to do so."

He crossed his arms. "Nor can you tempt me to touch you in *other* ways." He stared at her so penetratingly, she feared he could see clear into her soul. "Should you foster such ignoble intentions."

A particularly strong gust of wind rattled the closed shutters, a howling gale followed by a sharp clap of thunder, as if the very heavens meant to underscore his disdain.

He took two steps toward her, as far as the chain would

allow. A strange glint sparked in his brown eyes. "As for the slurs you find so distressing, were I to voice what I truly think of you, you would abandon your ill-chosen plans for misplaced revenge and run for the safety of your mother's skirts."

Isolde flinched. Would that she *could* seek the comfort of her mother's understanding. But the light had gone out of her mother's eyes long ago, and with it, her senses.

It was on the tip of her tongue to tell the insolent lout what she thought of him, his stance arrogant, his legs spread beneath one of her bedsheets, hands braced on his lean hips, and his too-bonnie face darkened with displeasure. But she said naught, for her mouth had gone too dry for her to speak.

The blackguard appeared as much a mind reader as old Devorgilla. And he made her feel as exposed as if she already stood before him wearing naught but her indignation.

Turning away, she rested her hands on the back of a chair. Exhaustion weighed heavily on her, and she was weary from the chaos and turmoil that had swept into her world since Lileas's death.

Damn the MacLean for reminding her she'd lost her mother as well. Isolde blinked back the hot sting of tears. Though, even now, the lady Edina sat belowstairs in Dunmuir's great hall, comforted by warm blankets and the elders' respectful attentions, Isolde's vacant-eyed mother might as well be long in her grave for what little notice she took of the world around her.

A hesitant cough sounded behind her, but she wasn't about to turn around. Some wild-brained notion entered her mind that he sensed he'd pushed her too far, that his next words might be different entirely from the insults he'd spewed at her thus far.

But she did not want his comfort.

Saints forbid.

She had ample solace from the *cailleach,* and from Bodo, when she needed it. She also had the rough-hewn devotion Niels and Rory afforded her. And she had the crone's anti-attraction potion.

Should she need it.

Not that she'd seen a fig of the MacLean's legendary charm. Still, his looks alone would've stolen her heart were he any other man.

And the fluttery sensations that whirled and eddied through her each time he turned his dark gaze on her were surely caused by irritation and naught else.

Isolde slipped her hand into the folds of her skirt and fingered the leather-wrapped flagon of anti-attraction infusion. The potion would purge her of any possible flarings of interest his alarming resemblance to her dream man might awaken in her.

Before she could think better of downing the bitter-tasting tincture, she unstopped the flagon, and lifted it to her lips. Three rapid gulps were all she could manage before a convulsive shudder swept over her.

"Mother of God, woman, what are you about there?" came the MacLean's outraged voice behind her.

"Naught that concerns you." She wheeled to face him, a leather-wrapped flask clutched tight in her hand. Her creamy skin had gone a shade paler, and her beautiful eyes were wide and overbright.

"So long as I am chained to your bed, lady, what you do does concern me," Donall said dryly. "I would know what foul brew you've swallowed and why?"

She pressed her lips together and simply stared at him. Proud, indignant, and obviously struggling to ignore the shudders still wracking her elegant, and temptingly supple body.

A body whose tremors he wouldn't mind stilling by

drawing her tight against him in a crushing embrace, saints preserve him.

As if she sensed her victory over his flagging will to resist his attraction to her, she lifted her chin and gave him a tiny, grudging smile.

A smile that sank into him like the sun's warmth on a fine midsummer's day.

Donall closed his eyes and concentrated on the cold iron pressing against his ankle until its chill vanquished the stirrings unleashed by a single, fleeting smile.

When he looked at her again, she was replacing the little flagon's stopper. She'd moved to the hearth, and the fire's glow highlighted her curves and gilded her thick braids with pure gold. His pulse quickened in reaction, and he frowned against the ease with which she seemed able to stir his blood.

And this time the damnable shackle did little to still his untoward urges. But to his immense relief, the thought of Gavin being held somewhere within her castle walls *did* quell his ill-placed lust.

"Where are you holding Sir Gavin and how fares he?" he demanded, his tone gruffer than he'd intended.

She met his guaranteed-to-intimidate stare full on, her eyes blazing with a fine boldness of her own. "No ill has befallen your man. He is comfortable enough in a cell far more habitable than yours and will be sailed to his clan's isle of Colonsay as soon as—"

"As soon as what?" Donall mimicked. "As soon as you and your graybearded minions have seen me draw my last?"

At once, the annoyance vanished from her eyes and she paled visibly, flinching as if he'd struck her. "I understand why you are wroth with me," she said, a hint of guilt lacing her words and flickering across her beautiful face. "But you err in thinking I—"

"*I* err?" His brows shot upward. "'Tis you and your buffoons whose heads are stuffed with falsehoods and nonsense."

She began pacing the chamber, the hem of her black mourning gown swirling around her shapely ankles, her light, wildflower scent floating out to bedevil him anew each time she passed.

"Aye, sir, I do believe you speak the truth," she said suddenly, peering sharply at him. "The notions that fill my head and haunt my dreams do appear foolhardy at the moment. Unfortunately, I am loath to relinquish them."

Too flummoxed by her speech to do aught but gape at her, Donall waited.

She came to stand before him.

Dangerously close before him.

So close, another scent rose up from her, but this one offended his senses as foully as the pleasant wildflower fragrance roused him.

The remnants of the sharp-smelling potion she'd gulped, still clinging to her tongue.

A pungency so strong Donall forgot all else.

With lightning speed, he reached out and seized hold of her wrist. "I would know what manner of brew you imbibed."

She tried to jerk away but he clamped his fingers in an iron grip. Apparently unaware of the offensive smell clinging to her, she glared at him. "What I swallowed, sirrah, was a potion to . . . to rid my complexion of freckles," she declared in a rush, her whole demeanor challenging him to doubt her.

"Truth tell?" Donall captured her chin in his free hand and turned her face toward the glow of the nearest cresset lamp. "I vow the mixture is potent indeed for I see nary a freckle to mar your fair skin."

"Then mayhap your eyesight is as lacking as your chivalry."

Donall tamped down a near irresistible urge to throw back his head and laugh. At her audacity as well as the lame pretext she'd so glibly tossed at him.

The woman was an inveterate liar.

The fair-skinned womenfolk in his household had tried every freckle-purging remedy known to man and not one had e'er smelled so abominably.

"Ah, I do believe I see one." Donall smoothed the side of his thumb over the curve of her cheek. "Aye, 'tis a great need you have of such an elixir."

"My needs are greater than you can know," she said, and a foul-reeking whiff of her breath caught him full in the face, even as the fleeting trace of vulnerability he'd glimpsed in her eyes caught him off guard and tugged at something deep inside him.

A disconcerting something he didn't care to identify or scrutinize.

A most unsettling something.

The laughter he'd been trying to suppress ever since she made her ludicrous pronouncements about freckle-banishing potions froze in his throat and he released her as if she'd scorched him.

With effort, he concentrated on the ramifications of his present predicament rather than how soft her cheek had felt beneath his thumb or how the smooth warmth of her wrist had seeped into his fingers, distracting him so thoroughly he near forgot who she was and why he stood, half-naked and fettered, in her bedchamber.

He could not allow himself to fall prey to her comeliness.

Nor dare he let himself be influenced by the disturbing aura of susceptibility that enveloped her at times, despite her obvious grace and courage.

She peered intently at him and he couldn't help but notice the faint purple smudges beneath her eyes. To his great annoyance, the barely there shadows only underscored the air of vulnerability he was fighting so hard not to be affected by.

"You spoke of needs," he said, holding her gaze but willing himself not to truly *see* her. "I, too, have needs most urgent. Detaining me ill suits my purposes and your own as well."

Donall struggled to contain his wrath over the chaos that could soon erupt at Baldoon. Iain would keep a cool head only so long. "Having me put to death before a jeering circle of feeble-witted graybeards will spell endless grief for your clan. 'Tis a consequence you should well consider."

Her far too appealing look of injured innocence evaporated at once and a flare of pure indignation blazed in her gold-flecked eyes. "Think you I am unaware of the folly of executing a MacLean?" She appeared to thrum with agitation. "Most especially the laird."

Donall shrugged. "So you mean to intercede on my behalf at the execution?"

"There will be no execution," she said, her obvious discomfiture announcing how much she resented making such a revelation. "I have other plans for you."

The giant's cryptic words rang again in Donall's ears but he strove to ignore them. The notion was too preposterous to bear even a seed of possibility.

More absurd than the wildest tales the most highly skilled *fili* could spin in a hundred endless winter nights.

Stifling an inexplicable urge to laugh at the outrageous images parading through his mind, Donall forced himself to look disinterested.

Mayhap even a bit bored.

"Other plans?" he spoke at last, casually lifting a brow to emphasize his indifference.

She nodded. "A covenant."

"A *covenant*?" An odd sinking feeling coupled with a distinctly perverse sense of hilarity soundly conquered his pretense of nonchalance.

He could almost see her redheaded dolt of a henchman looming up behind her, admonishing him to "be gentle with her" lest he wished his bones ground to powder.

"What manner of covenant?" Not that he cared to know.

Isolde MacInnes drew a deep breath. "A pact of peace. A plan to ensure the long-lasting harmony my father sought and my sister died trying to achieve."

Somewhere in the distance, thunder boomed. The low rumbles jarred the shutters and echoed off the walls, allowing Donall the brief respite he needed to gather his wits.

She could not possibly mean what he suspected.

No maid as exquisite as Isolde of Dunmuir would barter herself.

Not even for peace.

". . . the sooner certain conditions have been met," she was saying, seemingly unaware of the odious tang still tainting her breath, "the sooner you and Gavin MacFie may leave."

"I shall leave, your ladyship, the instant the first opportunity affords itself," he vowed. "And I vouchsafe Sir Gavin would tell you the same. Regardless of whatever conditions you think to suffer upon us."

Two spots of bright red appeared on her cheeks. "Only you must fulfill my conditions. I want naught from Gavin MacFie," she said in a huff, and Donall inhaled another whiff of whate'er wretched brew she'd swallowed.

The pestiferous scent, her own words, and those of her

oversized oaf of a guardsman combined to paint lewd and outlandish images in Donall's mind.

The laughter he'd been repressing all evening escaped him at last.

Isolde MacInnes's lovely eyes widened at his mirth, and the two spots of color on her cheeks suffused into a dull red flush that slowly spread clear across her pretty face.

"Lady, if you seek to bring about peace by the method I am sorely beginning to suspect you have in mind, namely by offering your bonnie self to me as my bride, then I must beg you not to imbibe any more of your foul-reeking brew," he said, regretting the words even as they hastened past his lips.

"Marriage to you, sirrah, was never a consideration." She bristled visibly. "What I had in mind was an alliance of . . . of convenience. One I was foolhardy enough to believe might benefit us both."

She glared at him for a long moment, then stormed away, fleeing to the row of tall, shuttered windows on the far side of the room. There she stood, her back rigid, her shoulders squared, and hell and botheration, but he wished he could tear out his tongue.

May the devil snatch his soul for mocking her. Ne'er had he spoken thusly to a woman, but she possessed the ability to rile him beyond the outermost bounds of his patience.

Yet, even now, he felt compelled to go to her, was beset by an overwhelming desire to caress away her anger and banish his insults with kisses, sharp-smelling potion on her lips be damned.

He would, too, were she any other woman.

Were he not manacled to her bed.

Tearing his gaze from her, Donall stared into the crackling flames lapping at the hearth log. Anger roiled and simmered deep inside him. Annoyance at himself for upsetting her, exasperation over the deep-seated longing eating a hole in his gut.

A longing he couldn't seem to extinguish despite his most ardent efforts.

Donall swore softly under his breath.

His brows drew together in a frown.

Heedless of what nonsensical and provocative proposals she might make once her agitation cooled, he would not bow to the temptation presented by his fetching keeper.

At the moment, though, if he was completely honest, doing just that was his most dread fear.

A fear he wasn't wont to share with her.

Gazing heavenward, Donall prayed for the cunning he'd need to persuade her to release him before she discovered how very much he desired her.

The lady would no doubt take sore advantage if she knew.

Chapter Four

✦

ℛELEASE ME AND a fine mantle lined with miniver shall be yours," Donall the Bold tossed out another bribe. The hundredth he'd dangled before her ever since Niels had deposited their evening meal upon the chamber's only table.

A sturdy oaken table he'd dragged across the room, placing it near the bed so she could share her repast with the MacLean without necessitating the removal of the iron shackle secured around his right ankle.

And already, Isolde regretted the simple gesture meant to hinder needless embarrassment between them during their first shared meal.

A fool notion he'd quickly seized to his advantage.

An ill-considered impulse that sentenced her to suffer his repeated and increasingly ludicrous attempts to talk his way out of confinement.

"Not interested in furs?" He rubbed his chin and feigned a look of astonishment. "May I tempt you with twenty ells each of exquisite samite and sendal silk?"

Ignoring him, Isolde tore off a piece of brown bread and popped it in her mouth.

"A circlet for your hair set with agates and sapphires?"

Isolde swallowed the bread. "Such frippery does not interest me."

With an exaggerated sigh, he leaned forward on one elbow and peered intently at her. "A coffer of gold?"

Isolde peered right back at him. "Your wealth cannot buy my favor, Sir Donall. What I want from you cannot be bought with coin."

He straightened at that, not answering her in words, but loudly declaring his frustration by the cold set of his jaw and the fury snapping in his eyes.

"My conditions, what I desire from you, will not lessen your riches." Isolde struggled to remain composed beneath his sharp perusal.

A scrutiny meant to needle her.

A game he enjoyed playing.

That she knew, for a decidedly false smile began tugging at the corners of his mouth and a telltale glint danced in his dark brown eyes. Truth be told, she couldn't quite shake the notion he found himself highly amused by her refusal to accept his absurd bids to ransom himself.

Not that she could fathom what about her rebuttals he seemed to find so entertaining.

Nor why he continued to stare holes in her rather than fill his belly or quench his thirst.

Isolde gestured to the victuals spread upon the table. "You have touched naught," she said. "This is finer fare than you have recei—"

"The finest fare I've e'er seen, lass," he interrupted, a strange huskiness edging his deep voice. Not taking his gaze off her, he leaned back against the bedpost and crossed his arms. "Still, I have good reason to abstain from such delicacies as you would offer me."

Unable to withstand his assessing stare or the shameless intimations lurking behind his guileless-sounding comments another moment, Isolde turned aside to glance at Bodo. The little dog still dozed upon his bed by the hearth.

"Ah . . . a soft bed and a crackling fire." The smoothly spoken words grated sorely on Isolde's nerves. The man seemed capable of making the most innocent observation sound mocking.

Scornful.

"Since you place little value on the treasures I've offered you," he droned on even though she'd turned her back to him, "I vow you hold such simple comforts in higher esteem?"

"Aye, sirrah, I do."

He made a noise that could have been a snort of derision . . . or a chuckle. "I cannot persuade you with baubles and rich attire?"

"Nay, you cannot." She twisted back around to face him. "I am content with little and neither needful nor desirous of finery or jewels."

"If that is the truth, Isolde of Dunmuir," he said, quirking a dark brow at her, "then I am most interested to hear what it is you *do* wish of me?"

Isolde felt her face flush. He noticed, too, for a near wolfish grin stole across his handsome features.

A knowing grin.

The grin of a victor.

Or a predator about to pounce upon its cornered prey.

Plucking idly at the folds of the well-worn *lenicroich* Rory had grudgingly relinquished to him, he glanced down at the borrowed plaid, his dark gaze rife with undisguised contempt. "Since there can be no question you and yours have dire need of the riches you scorn, I am indeed at a loss to imagine what conditions you mean to demand of me."

Too riled to think of an adequate retort, Isolde met his arrogant appraisal of her means or, more appropriately, her lack thereof with a wrathful glare of her own. Far from the legendary charmer the tongue-waggers claimed him to be, she found Donall MacLean naught but boorish.

A master of churlishness.

And much too bonnie for his own good.

Even the poor quality of the homespun *lenicroich* he'd draped around himself did little to detract from his annoying air of superiority.

Or his stunning good looks.

If anything, the faded saffron of the garment's soft folds emphasized the glow of his sun-burnished skin, even as the simple bone bodkin at his shoulder underscored her clan's inferior status.

Isolde flinched at that telltale representation of her clan's lesser standing. When he'd been taken, his own plaid had been fastened with a most noble brooch, one studded with glittering gemstones. His brooch now rested in the bottom of her locked strongbox, in safekeeping, until he'd met her conditions.

If ever he would.

Excruciatingly aware of the way he perched on the edge of her bed, *studying* her, Isolde helped herself to a too-large piece of green cheese. Half because she wasn't willing to let him see she'd erred, and half to appease the hunger gnawing inside her, she stuffed the entire chunk into her mouth and began to chew.

"If it is not my wealth," he boomed, his voice loud in the close confines of her bedchamber. His mirth, an insult. "Then it must be me you desire."

Isolde almost choked on the cheese. Her eyes tearing,

she reached for the single tankard of ale and helped herself to a healthy swallow.

"I desire naught but what is best for my people and this isle." She plunked down the tankard and dabbed at her lips with a napkin. *"Peace."*

The MacLean leaned forward again. "A piece of what, milady?" he probed, the mildness of his tone in stark contrast to the devilish glitter in his eyes.

Blessedly, a familiar whimper spared her having to respond to his double-edged rudeness. Bodo stood on his hind legs, his forepaws resting on the edge of her chair. He peered up at her, an expectant look in his bright eyes.

"One so eager should not be made to wait." With deft fingers, Donall selected a choice morsel of roasted seabird and offered the scrap to the little dog.

"Do you not agree?" He cast her a wholly innocent-looking glance as Bodo scampered to his side and took the proffered tidbit from his fingers.

Isolde compressed her lips and drew herself up straighter in the hard-backed chair. She would not be maneuvered into a corner by his knack for turning a clever phrase. The unchivalrous knave would need more than a tasty tidbit to win her favor.

She would not follow Bodo's example and lavish adulation on him simply because he waved some flavorsome delicacy in front of her nose. Be it a tantalizing piece of perfectly roasted meat, a selection of sumptuous raiment, or a chest brimming with sparkling jewels.

Yet she would have to lavish some kind of attention on him if her plan was to succeed.

"Have you lost your tongue, milady?"

"What I have lost, sirrah, is my sister," she snapped, driven to shrewishness by the sight of Bodo leaning contentedly into the blackguard's bare leg.

His dark gaze never straying from her face, Donall the Bold reached down and rubbed the dog's shoulders. "I share your loss." For once, his voice held not a trace of sarcasm, but considering who and what he was, Isolde found the sincere-sounding words a greater affront than his usual mockery.

"All in my household mourn the lady Lileas," he went on, smoothing the backs of his fingers down the length of Bodo's spine. "Most especially my brother."

"I find that difficult to believe." She hadn't missed the odd glimmer that flickered in his eyes when he'd mentioned his brother.

Iain MacLean.

Her sister's murderer.

"Had your brother not stranded Lileas upon the Lady Rock, binding her there by her own tresses, dooming her to drown with the incoming tide, there would be no need for you or those beneath your roof to share my grief." The sharp-toned litany rolled off her tongue with surprising rapidity, spurred on by her anger over Lileas's death, and her resentment over what she'd taken upon herself to do to ensure a permanent end to such senseless tragedy.

But do it she would.

And with aplomb.

As if he'd read her thoughts and meant to enlighten her as to the sheer folly of her intentions, an icy mask seemed to drop over his face. "My brother did not kill his wife," he said, his expression inscrutable, his words hollow-sounding.

Forced.

Not quite convincing.

"How do you know?" Isolde prodded, ire whirling inside her.

"I simply do," he said, his dark countenance still unfathomable, his tone as cold as a black north wind. "My word will have to suffice."

Isolde curled her fingers around the pewter tankard and brought it to her lips. "I am afraid it doesn't," she said over its rim before she took a fortifying sip.

"Then release me so I can search for the true murderer and quell your doubts." With lightning speed, he reached across the table, seized the tankard from her hand, and slammed it onto the table. "Keeping me here is madness!"

Isolde shrank back against her chair, her daring flown. Even Bodo took flight, dashing for the refuge of his padded bed by the fireside as swiftly as his short legs would carry him. Isolde stared after him, wishing she could flee the MacLean's wrath as easily.

Instead, she clung to the comfort Bodo's wee presence afforded her, even from across the room. Doubts, the man had said. Isolde fought back the bitterness rising in her throat. She had more doubts plaguing her than he could banish in a lifetime.

And the matter of his brother's guilt wasn't one of them.

Nay, it was her own ability to seduce him that she held in question.

That, and the wisdom of attempting such a feat.

"Why am I here, Isolde of Dunmuir?" he demanded, his words ringing hard in her ears. "To what purpose am I chained to your bed?"

Isolde expelled a deep sigh and met his furious gaze. "You are chained so you cannot escape."

For a very brief moment, something surprisingly akin to admiration flashed in his eyes, but a tiny muscle jerking in his neck betold the true depth of his anger. "Answer my question: why am I bound to your bed?" He leaned toward her. "Perchance to sleep there?"

Heat surged up Isolde's neck.

"With you?" His two words screamed outraged incredulity.

Isolde squirmed, embarrassment swelling her tongue to ten times its normal size. Not that he needed verbal confirmation of his suspicions. The hot flush stinging her cheeks surely told him what he wanted to know.

As if to prove her logic, he laughed.

Gritting her teeth, she struggled not to display any further reaction to his rudeness. But then he let his gaze roam boldly over her breasts.

Her breasts, and any other part of her not hidden from view by the table.

Her cheeks fired anew.

"Gracious lady," he said, blessedly ending his brazen appraisal, "had you presented me with such an honor at any other time, rest assured a chain would not have been needed to keep me at your side."

With all the dignity she could gather, Isolde lifted her chin and hoped he could not hear the wild thundering of her heart. Nor would she humiliate herself further by admitting he'd indeed guessed her intentions.

The seduction was supposed to follow a natural course.

Instead, she found herself held hostage by his drawled comments and probing stares, ill prepared to counter the verbal barbs he kept shooting at her. With amazing ease, he'd rendered her unable to do aught but sit calmly by and wait for the next brilliantly scathing observation to leap from his tongue.

A wicked gleam lighting his eyes, he ran his fingers along the edge of the table. "Much as I regret disappointing you, I must decline your tempting offer. Matters of greater import demand my immediate attention."

His arrogance chased the fetters from her tongue. "My offer to you, sirrah, is one of peace. 'Tis well I know you may not have personally stranded my sister on the Lady Rock, but by association, you are guilty of condoning the deed. You bear the stain of an innocent's blood on your hands."

His face darkened, the roguish glimmer in his eyes extinguished. She'd expected a sharp retort, his denial. But rather than proclaim himself blameless, he clamped his lips into a tight line and leveled a cold, silent stare at her.

"No protestations?" Isolde bristled. "You do not deny it?"

"Deny blood on my hands? What warrior could make such a claim?" He paused, obviously striving to contain his fury. "I am a belted knight, lady. Much blood has sullied my hands, but ne'er without a fair fight and nary a drop of a woman's."

"I said by association."

His eyes narrowed to slits. "May God the Father strike me dead if I lied to you."

"You are a master of words, e'er sidestepping the truth—" Isolde faltered, the accusations she meant to hurl at him sticking in her throat, trapped there by the utter futility of arguing with him. Each harsh word spat in anger lessened her chances of inducing him to crave her favor.

Not that she cared to begin testing her wiles this night.

The morrow would serve as well.

No doubt sensing her capitulation, the insufferable wretch arched a patronizing brow. "At the moment I am master of naught *but* my word," he said, his gaze lighting briefly on the heavy-linked chain binding him to her bed.

Isolde drew a deep breath. With but a few tersely spoken words and a single glance, he'd wrested control from her, imperiled her seduction plan by goading her into shrewish behavior, and unwittingly drawing her attention to the invisible chain binding *her* to the bed.

Her chain, one woven of all her sore troubles, condemned and confined her as soundly as his bound him.

Not that he'd spend her a smidgen of sympathy if he knew.

Impervious and proud, he sat upon the edge of her bed, peering at her, his steepled fingers slowly tapping his chin, his cold expression signaling he knew exactly what disturbing thoughts troubled her heart and creased her brow.

Mother Mary, but he unnerved her.

His piercing gaze made her feel as if he'd pinned her to the tapestried wall behind her, affixed her there with the brute strength of his supercilious stare.

Of a sudden, the lacings of her gown seemed overtight and an uncomfortable heat welled inside her. Quickly, lest he see how thoroughly he unsettled her, she glanced pointedly toward the shuttered windows.

Anywhere but at him.

The moment she looked away, he must've moved, for his chain made a loud clinking sound. An aberration in the thick silence hanging so heavily in the chamber, the noise sent a twinge of guilt straight to her core.

A trace of guilt shot through with a good dose of frustration.

Guilt at keeping her plan a secret from the elders.

Frustration, that their own stubbornness made such a deceit necessary.

Both emotions curled 'round her heart with startling tenacity, squeezing so fiercely she almost gasped. She would have, too, was she not keenly aware of the MacLean's penetrating stare. His all-seeing gaze had waxed bolder and she needn't look at him to know it.

She kept her own attention firmly trained on the closed shutters. Driving rain still beat down with a vengeance, and the dank, wet smell of water-sogged wood and cold, damp stone pervaded the chamber, but the worst of the storm had moved on. The loud cracks of thunder came with less frequency and each resounding rumble sounded more distant.

If only the tempest brewing inside her would pass as swiftly.

But the MacLean's sheer proximity rivaled the might of any storm. His compelling presence proved greater, more daunting, than the wildest gale ever to pound this windswept side of Doon.

Bound or nay, he exuded raw male power.

A shiver swept over her. One that had scarce little to do with the damp chill seeping in past the rain-drenched shutter slats. Steeling herself against his annoying ability to rile her, she stiffened her back and reached for her tankard of mead.

And another oversized chunk of green cheese.

She wouldn't let him spoil her appetite, nor allow his overbearing self to wreak havoc upon her emotions. She need only give him her body. Isolde ate the cheese and reached for more. Her heart would remain pure . . . untouched.

Unsullied.

Hers.

Feeling somewhat better, she washed down the cheese with a hearty gulp of the sweet-tasting mead.

"You fair astound me, milady," came her captive's deep voice, honeyed and smooth, yet still laced with unmistakable mockery . . . and totally spoiling the taste of the thick mead flowing innocently down her throat.

Isolde set down the tankard at once. "How so, *milord*?" she challenged him, placing the same irreverent emphasis on "milord" as he'd used when addressing her as "his lady."

His mouth curved in a slow smile that would've been devastating in its sheer potency had its warmth reached his eyes. Instead, his dark gaze flicked coolly over the generous helping of roasted seabird she'd piled high on the thick-slabbed trencher of brown bread set before her.

Embarrassment flooded her. She hadn't realized she'd taken such a large portion.

"For a maid, you are possessed of a most hearty appetite," Donall the Bold commented. "I am wondering if all your appetites are so . . . healthy?"

Her breath caught at the hidden meaning behind his dry observation. She might yet be virtuous, but she was by no means ignorant. And what she hadn't known about the *things* men and women do together, the joy woman, Evelina, had told her.

In great and shocking detail.

Determined to ignore her rising agitation, and especially the way his false smiles made her blood quicken, she lifted her spoon, intent on finishing her soup.

"I haven't eaten since yestermorn," she said, and her stomach growled as if to prove her hunger. "You'll surely agree I need all my strength, and my wits, to properly deal with t-this situation that's been thrust upon me."

"Thrust upon you?" For once both of his brows shot upward.

"Aye." She gave him a sharp look, daring him to claim otherwise.

But despite her best efforts to occupy herself with finishing her meal, ill ease pursued her with unflagging persistence. A pulsing heat inched its way up her throat, and became more bothersome with each moment she was forced to endure his disturbing perusal.

"Must you stare?" She set down her spoon, her raging hunger insignificant next to the turmoil his brazen scrutiny unleashed inside her.

"You are disturbed by my looking at you?" His brow furrowed but a hint of pure devilry gleamed in his dark brown eyes. "Do correct me if I misunderstood, but that which you would have me do for you, namely take you to wife, if I was wont to oblige you, would involve much more than merely gazing across a table at you."

Isolde's patience thinned. "I told you, I seek an alliance, not marriage."

"A pact that must be negotiated behind a barred bed-chamber door? With me attached to your bedpost?"

"Are you not hungry?" she quipped.

Another of his lazy smiles slid across his face. "Ne'er have I been more ravenous."

"Then eat your fill, there is naught stopping you."

For a moment, he looked close to laughter again, but then the smile that had been playing across his sensuous lips faded, and a dark, somber look settled over his features. "You err, Isolde of Dunmuir," he said, the rich timbre of his deep voice oddly stirring. "There is much that prevents me from staving the hunger consuming me this moment."

Undaunted, she shoved the platter of roasted seabird toward him. "The gannet is plump and tender . . . delicious."

"Plump?" He eyed the platter skeptically, his gaze skimming first over the gannet's crisp-roasted, golden breast, then boldly lighting upon her own. "I would not say plump." He narrowed his eyes then, and she could almost feel the heat of his gaze upon her flesh.

With deliberate slowness, he lifted the tankard in sardonic toast. "But of a certainty, well formed, tender, and *succulent.*"

Pretending not to have understood the ribald undertones in his silkily spoken words, nor to have noticed his brazen stare, Isolde lowered her own gaze to the spread of victuals Cook had undoubtedly taken great care to prepare.

Rather than scoff at her voracious appetite, Donall the Bold ought be grateful. If those in Dunmuir's kitchen weren't aware of her appreciation of fine and plentiful viands, there would be less food to share with him.

In addition to the roasted gannet, Cook had sent up a steaming mazer of leek soup and a goodly portion of soft green cheese delicately flavored with herbs. Precious little remained of the cheese, but she hadn't yet touched the small spiced cakes and the large ewer of honey-sweetened mead was more than ample for two.

Certainly not a noble feast, but the repast, though humble, had been carefully prepared and was the best Dunmuir's kitchen could presently conjure.

Those who supped belowstairs had contented themselves with the leek soup, of necessity much watered-down, coarse black bread, and simple ale.

Indeed, she'd rather down bitter ale and suffer through watery soup along with everyone else, but Cook enjoyed providing Dunmuir's chieftain with the best victuals he could. His pride would be sorely dented if she bade him to serve her the meager fare doled out in the great hall.

Swallowing her resentment at the deprivations her people had to bear *and* at having to endure the MacLean's taunts and stares, Isolde dipped her spoon into her soup. A delicious aroma rose from the mazer, and much to her dismay, her too-long neglected stomach gave forth another low grumbling noise the instant the fragrant steam reached her nose.

"Do keep eating. I enjoy watching you." The MacLean's voice, rife with undercurrents, sliced through the silence. "Indeed, if I were of a humor to—"

"Wedding you ne'er entered my mind," Isolde declared before he could finish whatever slur he'd meant to bestow upon her.

Far from appearing chagrined, the trace of amusement in his eyes blossomed into a merry twinkle. "As I was about to say, were I of a humor to *have* you, which I am not, such a robust appetite as you display would undoubtedly make our time together most interesting."

Isolde's spoon froze halfway to her mouth. She fixed him with a look she hoped would wither the tartness from his too-loose tongue. "I am not a bawd, Sir Donall."

"Yet you would play a bawd's game. A game that sends trepidation into the very fiber of your maidenly heart." He peered sharply at her hand, his all-knowing gaze taking in the way her fingers clenched her spoon. "Aye, for all your daring, sweeting, you are afraid."

"I fear naught. Least of all you."

"Then mayhap you should." A wholly different light came into his eyes and Isolde's heart turned over at the transformation. "I am not a man to have his passions trifled with, Lady Isolde."

To her growing mortification, he reached across the table, pried her fingers from around the spoon, then up-turned her hand. His dark gaze not leaving her face, he trailed one finger down the sensitive flesh of her palm.

She jerked in reaction, a startled gasp escaping her lips. His touch, brief though it'd been, had sent heated tingles racing up the length of her arm. And now, afterward, a strange warmth lingered where his hand still cradled hers.

A stealthy heat that seeped straight through her resistance and slowly spread through her entire body.

Even the tops of her ears burned!

"Or did you not have me hauled up here, to your bedchamber, so you could . . . *trifle with my passions*?"

"Of all the cheek!" She tried to yank free of his grasp, but his fingers encircled her hand like bands of steel.

"Be wary, my lady, of what you purpose to achieve." He gave her hand a brief squeeze. "Your folly could get you burned."

His taunt let loose, he released her hand, leaned back against the bedpost, and crossed his arms.

Her bedpost.

Her bed.

And yet he sat there, a self-satisfied look on his bonnie face, appearing completely relaxed . . . at home.

As if *he* were laird and master of Dunmuir Castle and not she.

"If not to offer yourself to me in marriage nor, as you deny, to have me initiate you into the joys of carnal pleasures," he goaded her, "then why all the secrecy? What mysterious revelation do you care to make, or expect to hear from me, that cannot be broached in a dungeon cell?"

"My reasons are my own and shall remain thus for a while at least." She clung to the image of his hands stained with her sister's blood rather than acknowledge how indecently attractive he looked lounging so casually upon her bed, one massive shoulder resting against her bedpost.

He emanated power, carefully restrained anger, and something she couldn't define. An elusive something she recognized as having to do with the natural urgings Evelina had claimed flared hot between men and women.

Certain men and women.

The joy woman had called such stirrings a rare and precious gift.

A special occurrence Evelina professed to have experienced only once: with the unnamed benefactor for whose love she'd abandoned her lucrative trade.

Isolde helped herself to another bite of cheese. If she concentrated on eating, maybe she could rid herself of the lurid images Evelina's instructions sent parading through her head.

But the wild and base acts pranced on, marching with shameless abandon all over her maidenly sensitivities. Most alarming of all, the brazen images now bore faces. Hers and the face of the man who'd visited her dreams the night of Beltaine.

Her soul mate according to Devorgilla.

A man who bore a disconcerting resemblance to Donall MacLean.

Isolde shuddered and snatched another piece of cheese.

"How much of a while do I have, then?" The MacLean's deep voice shattered the spell he'd cast over her with his damnable touch and his striking . . . *maleness.*

"A sennight, a fortnight?" he demanded. *"A day?"*

Isolde peered at him, her mind still befuddled, her senses even now reeling with torrid images. "Hmmm?"

Impatience glittering in his eyes, Donall the Bold shot to his feet. He braced his hands on his hips and scattered every last wispy illusion tumbling through her mind with the sheer weight of his stare.

"Lady, I have listened to the rants of your graybearded worthies. The oversized buffoon and his cohort standing guard outwith your door are overeager to visit all manner of unpleasantness upon me." His contempt leaped between them, palpable and menacing. "Should they make good their threats, I shall be offering my felicitations to my Maker in one month's time."

He slammed his fist on the table. *"One month,"* he thundered. "And you order me bathed and affixed to your bed yet refuse to tell me why or how long you would see me suffer through this perverse form of torture?"

"It is not my will to torture you."

"Nay? You torment me by your very presence and 'tis well I think you know it." He towered over her, his face dark with rage. "What *is* your will?"

Trembling, Isolde pushed to her feet, intending to shove her chair between herself and his wrath, but his arm shot out and he seized hold of her, his fingers digging into the tender flesh of her upper arm.

Before she could voice a protest, Bodo burst between them, his hackles raised, his barks piercing. The MacLean released her at once. Her pulse racing, she snatched up the snarling dog, pulling him close against her chest, as much to soothe him as to ease her own agitation.

"I do not have the frivolous leisure of time, your most fair ladyship," Donall seethed, his voice restrained though fury still blazed in his eyes. *"Why am I here?"*

"So I can save you," Isolde breathed, unable to stop the hastily whispered words from slipping past her lips.

"Save me?"

She nodded. "Aye."

Incredulity rendered Donall speechless. Stunned, he gaped at her, a plethora of possibilities whirling through his head. And not a one of them made a whit of sense. The wench had a warped view of the world if she thought to fatten him up nightly, keeping him alive for the sole purpose of driving him to madness with her bountiful charms, only to surrender him to the whims of her crazed menfolk come the morn.

Her henchmen had taken much pleasure in assuring him his visits to her bedchamber were to be of short duration, naught but a brief reprieve from the onerous agonies they meant to inflict upon him by the light of day.

Donall swore under his breath and raked a hand through his still-damp hair. "By all that's holy, woman, I want neither your food, the lunacy of being shackled to your bed, nor your deliverance from whatever ills you mean to save me from."

He paused, turning away from her to pinch the bridge of his nose. Saints, but the world had careened out of control of late! His household hovered on the verge of disaster, he'd walked blindly into a trap he should have seen coming at him full-tilt, and the lady would claim she wants to save him.

"What I want, Isolde of Dunmuir, is out of here." He wheeled around to face her. *"Now."*

She shook her head. "That, sir, is an impossibility."

"Yet you vow to save me?" he roared, balling his hands to tight fists to counter the tension thrumming through him.

She clutched her dog tight and peered at him from amber-colored eyes gone overbright. The entire length of her trembled, yet she lifted her chin and met his glower without flinching. And curse him to the gates of hell and back, but he couldn't help but marvel at her braw courage in the face of his blustering.

Did you kill her, Iain?

Swear by the Rood your quick temper had naught to do with this foul deed.

Donall's own words came back to haunt him, a repetitive drone in the darkest corner of his heart, cutting him to the bone and chiding him for the swiftness with which he'd let his own temper get the better of him.

The wench began inching backward, a slow and cautious retreat, leaving naught but her vacated chair and a lingering trace of her wildflower scent, within an arm's length of where he stood.

That she feared him, felt the need to flee from him, despite her valiant show of bravery, dealt him a more severe blow than the combined lot of her misguided minions could dare hope to achieve.

Including the giant.

Awash with shame at having frightened her, Donall took a step forward but the cold iron clasped around his ankle halted his progress, stopping him as irrevocably as recalling his own words to Iain had capped his rage.

Careful to keep his voice calm and his mien unthreatening, he repeated his question, "Why, and how do you purport to save me?"

To his relief, she stopped her backward retreat, but the way her fingers dug into her little dog's fur bespoke her continued nervousness. "Exactly how, I am not yet sure," she said, not quite meeting his eyes. "As for why, 'tis self-preservation. My own and that of every man, woman, and child residing under my roof or within the realm of my responsibility."

Donall folded his arms. "You fear the wrath of the MacLeans should I be put to death?"

"Aye," she affirmed, her face still pale. Nigh colorless save the lone freckle gracing the curve of her left cheek.

And, damn his fool hide, but his fingers itched to reach out and touch it.

His brows snapped together in a fierce scowl.

No doubt thinking he meant to lash out at her again, she spun around and hastened to the hearth, her black skirts pooling out behind her, her long braids swaying, their lush tips just brushing her sweetly rounded hips.

The devil take him, but his fingers itched to take hold of those braids, too. Undo them and revel in the silken mass he knew her unbound tresses would be.

What he'd do with her hips didn't bear thinking about.

It was a blessing she kept her back to him, for his frown raged even more fierce now. His blood ran thick and hot even as his fury coursed cold and uncompromising through every inch of him.

He stared long and hard at her rigid back, her squared shoulders, and the proud tilt of her head. The woman had already proven herself a consummate liar when she'd declared her foul-smelling tonic to be a freckle-banishing remedy.

And she'd lied to him just now, too.

Exactly how she meant to save him, she wasn't sure, she'd claimed.

Ha!

The lass knew what she was about and then some.

He knew, too.

Without a doubt.

Her intent was glaringly apparent . . . it loomed behind him in all its four-postered glory.

Loomed and waited.

As he, too, would wait.

For the first opportunity to free himself and Gavin and put Dunmuir's half-crumbling walls behind him.

Pompous graybeards, comely mistress, looming bed, and all.

Chapter Five

❖

$\mathcal{T}$HE WENCH TOYED with him.

With the well-practiced skill of a princeling's pampered harlot, she circled him, her lithe form swaying to some silent music only she heard. 'Round and 'round him she twirled, boldly enticing him with the smooth warmth of her supple curves one moment, only to pull away the next.

Always circling.

Ever teasing.

Rousing.

And wearing naught but her own creamy skin, the glorious mass of her unbound hair, and the rosy glow of the dying hearth fire.

She held a length of shimmering silk in her hands and used it in ways that would send him to his knees anon if she didn't soon grant him surcease from her lascivious display.

Her hips gently rocking, her eyes alight with all manner of licentious promise, she twirled the silk into a rope and slipped its taut length between her legs. For one agonizingly long moment, she held it there, pulled tight against the lush tangle of red-gold curls shielding her womanhood.

Slowly, torturously slow, she began drawing the rope back and forth in an intimate caress. Her eyes drifted shut, a soft sigh escaped her, and a look of pure, exquisite ecstasy slipped over her face.

Lust, raw and untamed, surged through Donall. More aroused than a beardless squire about to spill his seed in the throes of first rut, he watched her salacious performance, his gaze riveted on her hands, the length of silk, and the lush vee winking at him from betwixt her shapely thighs.

As if she knew he hovered on the very edge of his need and meant to bedevil him, she ceased her saucy antics and slid the makeshift rope from between her legs. Meeting his eyes, she laughed, a light, tinkling sound, and unfurled the silk.

She held its length before her, letting it hang between them like a banner, its rippling transparency clinging to the pert tips of her breasts and accentuating the dark, triangular shadow of her femininity.

Longing, fierce and uninhibited, swept through Donall. A swift and furious maelstrom, forceful as the racing white waters of a Highland burn after a cloudburst, his desire swelled and crested, out of control and unrestrained.

Wild.

Then she laughed again. A deeper, throatier laugh. Discordant and troublesome . . . almost a growl.

Donall stiffened, his senses alert with a nameless foreboding. A peculiar *something* skipping down his spine, strangely at odds with the other, more primal urges she'd awakened in him.

Using a wanton's coy tricks, she cast his fickle pricklings of doubt to the four winds by wetting her sweet lips and dipping the edge of the banner to afford him one lightning-quick glimpse of her hardened nipples.

Captivated, Donall reached for her, but she danced backward, maneuvering herself just outwith his grasp. Another mischievous tinkle of laughter escaped her and she snapped the silk, whipping it once more into a taut rope. Still chuckling, she whirled away to slip behind him, the rapid fluidity of her movement leaving a trace of her wildflower scent hanging in the air.

Fully besotted, intoxicated with need, and driven to savor even the faintest whisper of her sweet perfume, Donall drank in the smell of her.

Smell?

Again, a flurry of ill ease stirred inside him, but before the sensation could leap to life, she began sliding her hands up and down his arms, deftly massaging his aching muscles and caressing his hands, *milking* his fingers with a proficiency he'd ne'er before enjoyed.

Not even from the most talented stewhouse harlots.

Would that she'd milk his tarse thus.

Giving free rein to the bliss of her touch, Donall drew in another deep breath of the heady scents surrounding him.

Bewitching him.

Her light wildflower fragrance, the tangy musk of her own arousal, and the reek of that noxious potion she'd poured down her throat.

Only, of a sudden, the odious tonic smelled more stale than sharp. Seemed somehow . . . different. As did her hands. No longer soft, smooth, and gentle, the hands holding his in place behind his back were calloused, rough, and large.

Too large to be a woman's. And the coarse rope some heavy-handed varlet wound ever tighter around his wrists was anything but silken. A vicious kick in his shin ripped away the shroud of deep slumber.

"Blood of Christ!" Donall roared, now fully awake, the last vestiges of his dream spinning away in a red cloud of throbbing pain.

"I bid you a good morn." The giant stood before him and Donall knew at once the source of the stale smell he'd noted while yet asleep.

'Twas the dullard's breath.

Donall glared at him, a new kind of desire pulsing thick and hot through his veins. The irresistible urge to give the smirking whoreson a fine taste of his blade's steel. Saints, but his fingers itched to curl 'round the hilt of his broadsword!

Instead, he swore.

A volley of dark oaths menacing enough to send the devil's most debased miscreations scuttling for cover.

"Speak thusly in our lady's presence and I'll cut out your tongue for offending her gentle ears." The oversized oaf matched Donall's glare.

"Speak thus to *me* again, and 'tis I who shall do the carving," Donall shot back, aching to test the skill of his sword arm against the ham-fisted ox.

So long as he was kept against his will, he'd speak however the mood seized him. If Isolde MacInnes took umbrage at his vocabulary, she could release him and spare herself having to suffer through his rantings.

Ready to spout another stream of nastiness simply to prove his point, he sent a pointed glance toward her bed, fully expecting to see her cowering there, her beautiful face pale, her amber eyes wide with shock. But the timber-framed monstrosity loomed empty, its heavy curtaining flung wide to reveal a jumbled whirl of furs, sheets, and pillows.

The massive four-poster looked as if it'd hosted a wilder night of passion than he'd e'er had the good fortune to indulge in.

Following his gaze, the giant eyed the snarl of bedcoverings with undisguised disapproval. "If you used her roughly, start saying your prayers."

Donall bristled. "I didn't use her at all."

His aching limbs and screaming back muscles bore testament of his denial. Irrevocable proof he'd spent the night asleep on his feet. Propped against the unyielding hardness of a bedpost rather than plying the fair lady's softness with a rigidity of a most different nature than the cold wood of her bed frame.

Not that he hadn't been tempted.

A temptation he'd ignore even if the strain turned his vitals blue.

"I want naught of your chieftain save my release." As if to mock his lie, frustration, twisting and writhing like a trapped serpent, spewed its venom deep in Donall's innards. "I would sooner present myself to the nearest holy order and spend the remainder of my days living under the cross than take my ease with your lady."

"'Tis the salvation of your mangy hide, she claimed as much when we passed her on her way to the chapel just now," a second male voice said from behind him.

"On her way to pray for her dead sister's soul, she was," the same man added and gave the rope around Donall's wrists a sharp tug. "Her *murdered* sister."

Donall twisted around to glower at him, but having tied Donall's hands, the miscreant now kneeled on one knee and appeared to be fumbling with the end of the chain binding Donall to the wench's bed.

"A poor lass drowned by her own husband's hand," the man mumbled as he inserted a large iron key into a rusted lock, then began easing the heavy-linked chain from around the bedpost.

Fury welling inside him, Donall cast a quick glance at Niels. The giant still glowered at the mussed bedsheets. Seizing his advantage, Donall smiled maliciously and drew back his unbound left foot. The kneeling gaoler grumbled on, "We're hopeful our lady will come to see the folly of—"

"Folly indeed!" Donall roared, and sent him flying.

"Oopphhh!" The man landed facedown in the rushes, arms and legs sprawled wide.

Donall lunged at him, but the giant was upon him in a heartbeat. "Try that again," Niels hissed, pricking Donall's throat with the tip of his dirk, "and I'll pare you to bits an inch at a time."

Spitting out sprigs of dried meadowsweet, the second man scrambled to his feet, his mien murderous. "You just earned yourself new quarters, MacLean," he ground out, anger blazing in his eyes.

"Let's hie him to the sea tower," he suggested to the giant, then snatched up the end of the chain. Straightening, he leveled an icy stare at Donall. "The sea tower's dungeon is Dunmuir's oldest and well suited for your noble taste. 'Tis near the jakes, boasts a plentiful supply of water, and has all the comforts of hell."

The guard Donall now recognized as Rory gave the chain a jerk and headed for the opened bedchamber door. In perfect sync with his still-fuming cohort, the giant took his knife from beneath Donall's chin and gave him a rough shove forward.

At the door, Donall planted his feet far apart and spread his elbows wide, hoping to use sheer might against his two gaolers. "Have done with this nonsense and give me my blade," he challenged them. "Let us cross swords like warriors. One on one or two against one, I care not, but a fair fight."

"Fair like your brother treated his lady wife?" Niels snarled behind him. "I think not." Without warning, he slammed the flat of his foot into the back of one of Donall's knees. Before Donall's leg could even buckle, the whoreson jabbed a rock-hard elbow into Donall's lower back.

Sagging against the doorjamb, Donall pressed his lips together, stifling a moan rather than give voice to his pain. The giant shoved him into the dimly lit passage. "No more stall tactics, MacLean," he warned. "'Tis past lauds and we've orders to fetch you back to your quarters before the castle-folk stir."

Rory glanced over his shoulder with a leer of spiteful satisfaction. *"Your new quarters."*

Careful to first scan the shadows for movement, Isolde slipped quietly from the fusty-aired oppression of Dunmuir's chapel. But, as so oft of late, the vaulted passage outside the small oratory loomed dark and empty.

At this silent hour, not long past lauds, and later on, well after cockcrow and even deep into the day, scarce few save herself and the priest ventured to this gloomy corner of the castle.

With less than a full month since her sister's burial, it was common knowledge Lileas's soul still lingered close to her dead body. Or mayhap whiled inside the chapel, hovering near where her corpse had last lain, cold and black-shrouded, two lit tapers flickering near her head.

A light rustling, perhaps a stealthy footfall—or the gliding passage of a ghost—sounded in the darkness ahead of her, and Isolde flattened herself against the wall. Heart in her throat, she waited.

Her pulse racing, she held her breath. The noise came

again, closer this time, and then a rat shot past her. The creature disappeared around a curve in the corridor, leaving silence in its wake. Shuddering, Isolde drew her woolen *arisaid* tighter about her shoulders and crossed herself.

A simple rat.

No bleary-eyed kinsman, unable to sleep, and so wandering Dunmuir's twisting passageways in lieu of a night spent tossing upon his pallet. Nor the restless shade of her sister, come to bemoan the pitifully low number of masses being said for her soul.

Isolde sighed. She understood why the elders avoided the chapel. With the demise of one so young and innocent as Lileas still permeating the oratory's very walls, she suspected the old men shunned the reminder of their mortality, their own nearing deaths.

She could not claim such a sound excuse for exiting the chapel so soon after entering its cloying confines. Her intentions pure, she'd hastened there, her heart set upon praying for Lileas's swift passage through purgatory.

But *he'd* followed her.

Even though she'd left him in her bedchamber, propped against her bedpost and snoring, he'd accompanied her every step of the way. Though many stone walls stood betwixt them as she'd knelt upon the chapel's cold stone floor, his accusing eyes damned her while his slow smiles, false or nay, quickened her pulse and warmed her flesh in ways it shamed her to admit.

Especially when she'd meant to be reciting paternosters for her sister's soul.

Disgracefully, she'd been unable to purge herself of his presence. He haunted her in a worse way than Lileas's ghost could hope to do, and she hated that . . . as she hated him.

Her cares pressing on her, she fled down the corridor, pursued by guilt. Guilt and something else. A terrifying condition fearsome enough to steal her wits and crush every shred of good sense she possessed.

A sob tore from her throat and she pressed the back of her hand against her mouth to stave off the escape of yet another such unwanted admission of her plight. Running now, she reached the end of the passage and burst into the stair tower.

She took the curving stairs two at a time, making for an iron-studded door set deep in the gloom of the third landing. As if a pack of snarling hellhounds and not wee Bodo chased at her heels, she threw open the door and fled into the chill night air of the battlements.

Cold, damp air she'd hoped would be cleansing but proved anything but. The gusty drizzle underscored the bleak path she'd sworn to follow, while the salty taste of the brine-laden wind reminded her of the tears she didn't want to shed.

For several long minutes, she stood unmoving in the darkness. Her ears heard the familiar roar of breakers against the rocks far below and, closer, the soft pattering of rain on stone.

Her heart heard something else.

Something she wanted to blot out, but couldn't.

May the merciless hand of God smite her, but she heard *his* voice. Not his words, his mocking taunts, but the melodious tones of his richly timbred voice. Deeply masculine, yet smooth as the rarest silk, his voice fascinated her. And made her wonder what magic he could weave if e'er he chose to speak words as bonnie as his face.

She shuddered at the thought.

Scooping Bodo into her arms, she clutched him tight and began pacing the deserted wall-walk. Even the stars, winking high above and so distant, seemed to chide her.

Chastise her.

As she deserved to be chastised.

"Oh, Bodo, what am I to do?" she whispered, shifting his weight in her arms, desperately seeking the solace his soft warmth usually afforded her.

But even Bodo, so precious and loved, could not save her now, for she'd committed the most grievous of sins.

She was attracted to Donall MacLean.

Down, down, down, they pushed and pulled him.

A spiraling descent ever deeper into the dark, dank bowels of Dunmuir's ruinous sea tower. Repeatedly, Donall slipped on the slick stone steps, coated as they were with foul-smelling slime and so ancient they bore curves, rounded indentations worn smooth by countless pairs of trudging feet.

Each time he stumbled, his tormentors laughed. Especially at the base of the stairs when he nearly landed on his back in the thick muck covering the floor. Praise the saints he hadn't, for the oozing sludge glistened a most unappetizing shade of blackish-green and reeked of raw sewage.

Manhandling him roughly along the low-ceilinged passage, Niels and Rory gave him nary a moment to ponder the source of the smell. Not that contemplation was necessary to know where he was.

One whiff told the tale.

He'd been escorted to the equivalent of a cesspit.

Donall's skin crawled with revulsion. The dank passage through which they trudged served as receptacle for Dunmuir Castle's latrine chutes.

"I told you your new quarters were hard by the jakes." Rory guffawed behind him. "And, as you'll soon see, there'll be water a-plenty to freshen your fine self for your nightly visits to our chieftain."

A chill sea wind swept around a curve in the tunnel, but

before Donall could draw in a deep breath of the tangy salt air, the giant halted him with an iron-fingered grip around his arm.

Tilting his head to the side, Niels appeared to be listening to the hollow-sounding drip-drip of water echoing from an opening in the tunnel wall to their left. Rory drew up beside the giant and cocked his head toward the crevice as well.

Little more than a vertical-running crack and scarce wide enough for a man to slip through, the gap cut deep and dark into the rock's slime-coated surface.

An ominously silent entrance to some hellhole.

Silent save for the ceaseless plop-plopping noise of dripping water and the light crunch of someone's hesitant footsteps over loose stones.

"Mother Mary preserve us," Rory muttered, and began backing away from the opening.

Donall suspected he feared being accosted by the vengeance-seeking ghost of some poor wretch whose bones had long since been picked clean. The giant showed no such qualms and, turning sideways, wiggled his bulk through the crevice, quickly disappearing into the darkness beyond.

"By the Rood, lad," came his bellow a moment later, his deep voice reverberating from within the hellhole to bounce eerily off the tunnel walls.

To Donall's amazement, Niels squeezed his way back out of the gap almost immediately. He dragged a thin, wide-eyed boy behind him. His meaty hand wrapped soundly around the lad's spindly arm, the giant fixed the boy with a stern glare. "How many times must I warn you to stay out of this pile o' rubble?" he scolded, his voice full of reproach.

"That devil's den contains an oubliette." He jerked his

head toward the dark crevice they'd just exited. "Do you ken what that is, Lugh?"

The dark-haired lad nodded, his gaze downcast, his hands clutching a grimed sack of . . . something.

Small, writhing somethings with wings, from the look of it.

Niels snatched the pouch and peered inside. Donall caught a quick glimpse of the sack's contents.

Bats.

The child had been gathering bats and his bag was stuffed full of the winged creatures. Displaying none of Donall's surprise, the giant closed the pouch and returned it to the boy with nary a raised brow. "Does old Devorgilla ken where you are?"

Lugh shrugged.

"'Tis a hellish place, an oubliette," Niels elaborated when the child began shuffling his feet instead of answering. "A jug-shaped hollow deep in the bowels of the earth. Evildoers are dropped through a long, narrow shaft into a place so small they can neither sit nor stand."

His nerves now recovered, Rory tousled Lugh's dark head. "You don't want to be a-poking around in there," he said with a sideways glance at Donall.

Lugh glanced at him, too. The boy's expression held curiosity. Rory's betold how fervently he'd enjoy plunging Donall into the dread chamber of little ease. A muscle in Donall's jaw twitched at the thought while outrage curled icy claws around his innards and squeezed.

Squeezed hard.

Hunched in such cramped confines, waiting for the release of a priestless and unabsolved death, was not how he cared to end his days.

The giant patted the boy's shoulder. "Off with you now, ere you land in more mischief."

Lugh took his lower lip between his teeth and cast one last wide-eyed glance at Donall, then bolted away.

"Ho, lad!" Rory called after him when he tore off in the opposite direction from the stairs. "Where do you thi—"

"Leave him be," Niels said, watching the boy disappear around the bend in the tunnel. "He'll be after a frog from the sacred well to go along with his bag o' bats. He'll hie hisself out of here once he gets what he's after."

Rory shook his head. Mumbling to himself about stagnant wells, and frogs being more useful in one's belly than in a witch-wife's cauldron, he tightened his hold on Donall's chain and began slogging forward through the muck, Donall and the giant following hard in his wake.

The moment they rounded the curve, Donall's breath caught in his throat, for the vaulted tunnel vanished as if it'd never been and they stood upon a narrow skirt of rock jutting precariously above a choppy sea, its tossing surface gilt silver by a near full moon.

A wild wet wind blew, bracing and untamed, its ceaseless howl giving stiff competition to the thundering crash of the waves breaking against a mass of black, barnacle-encrusted boulders and a jumble of fallen masonry that could only be the tumbled walls of Dunmuir's ancient sea tower.

Stinging salt spray bit into Donall's wrists and ankles, cruelly searing skin rubbed raw from days of wearing manacles, but he scarce noticed.

Nor did he puzzle overlong about where young Lugh had taken himself off to. Though he'd come this way, the lad was nowhere to be seen.

Another matter plagued Donall far more.

An issue fraught with ramifications for his entire clan and weighing much heavier on his heart than the odd disappearance of one strange boy.

A chilling notion ghastlier than the bother of abraded flesh.

The bastards meant to drown him.

The laird's solar at the MacLean stronghold, Baldoon Castle, gave itself as dark and gloomy as the drizzle-plagued night pressing hard against the chamber's arch-topped windows. Other than the muted glimmer cast by the last feeble flickers of a near extinguished hearth fire, nary a ray of light graced what had oft been called one of Baldoon's most opulent rooms.

Not a one of the resinous wall torches burned. And though several elaborately wrought candle stands stood about the chamber, the beeswax tapers they held remained unlit. As did the candles adorning two multibranched candelabra of finest silver.

For days now, the sumptuous solar, the pride of every MacLean laird since time immemorial, had been purposely plunged into darkness and desolation.

By order of Iain MacLean.

To suit his glum mood.

"Drowned," he muttered under his breath, and whirled to stomp across the solar's rush-strewn floor for what had to be the hundredth time. "Drowned, drowned, drowned," he chanted the word like a litany-singing monk gone mad and kicked the sturdy leg of an oaken trestle table.

A slight shuffling noise sounded somewhere behind him and he swung around to catch Gerbert, Baldoon's e'er meddlesome seneschal, attempting to light a brace of candles just inside the door.

His dark eyes widening in disbelief, Iain stared at the white-haired steward a long moment before he marched across the room and blew out the old man's handiwork with one furious huff of air.

Straightening, he glared at the graybeard. "Think yourself above heeding orders, Gerbert?"

"Nay, sir, begging your pardon, milord." Gerbert excused his blatant disregard for Iain's orders with a falsified tone of obeisance.

Almost as perturbing, he possessed the impertinence to return Iain's glare with an unblinking stare of his own.

Scowling, Iain waved his hand through the dissipating smoke of the extinguished tapers. "Is this affront because you doubt the bounds of my authority in my brother's absence?"

Gerbert's face remained a careful mask of mildness. "Of a certainty, nay, my good lord."

The bland expression grated sorely on Iain's nerves. *"Of a certainty, nay, my good lord,"* he mimicked.

Unruffled, Gerbert fixed his watery blue eyes on his laird's brother.

And said not a word.

"Explain yourself!" Iain bellowed, his face turning scarlet. "By whose leave did you begin lighting tapers?"

"By no one's, sir."

"Then why?"

"Because none are lit and 'tis dark in here."

"By the bloody lance of St. Peter!" Iain kicked over the candle stand. "None are lit because I *want* it dark in here, you fool!"

"Candles should be burning in your lady wife's honor." A film of perspiration on the seneschal's forehead bespoke the heavy toll it cost him to remain calm in the face of Iain MacLean's outburst. "Her soul—"

Turning his back on Gerbert, Iain strode to the table and swiped up an ewer of wine. He filled his chalice and downed the contents in one swallow.

"There are enough candles ablaze in the chapel to light

her way to heaven and beyond," he vowed and slammed down the empty wineglass. "And nary a one of them does a whit of good." Whirling around, he stared hard at the other man. "Do you not see?"

As if he saw indeed and dreaded what was to come, the aging seneschal's shoulders sagged and he lowered his gaze. For the first time since entering the solar, he evaded Iain MacLean's glass-eyed glare. Instead of meeting the younger man's wrath, he stared at the floor and began shaking his white-tufted head.

"My wife does not need blazing candles a-lighting her way to the blessed beyond," Iain snapped. "She doesn't belong with saints and martyrs. She belongs with me!"

"She is dead, Iain." A dark-haired woman stepped into the room, a bulging sack clutched in her hands. "You cannot bri—"

"Nay, I cannot bring her back." Iain turned on his sister, Amicia. "On our sainted mother's soul, I vow I would kiss the devil's buttocks if I could!"

"Iain!" Amicia gasped.

"Iain!" he echoed, throwing his hands in the air. "If it pleases you more, I can fall to my knees and shout a hundred thousand holy hosannas." He peered sharply at her, a fiery challenge sparking in his dark eyes. "Think you it would do me aught good?"

"Iain, please." His sister came forward, her free hand extended. "You are making yourself miserable."

"The MacKinnons have made me miserable!" Iain roared and snatched the wine ewer off the table. With a loud, unintelligible cry, he hurled it into the hearth. "Scourges of the earth, they are, God rot their pestiferous souls!"

Gerbert cleared his throat. "Come, my lady," he said, placing a gnarled hand on her arm. "Let us speak to him by the light of day. We can do naught when such misery is upon him."

As if his two unwelcome visitors had already quit his presence, Iain resumed his pacing, his scowl more thunderous than before, his handsome face a closed mask.

"But the dog hair . . ." Her pretty forehead creasing with doubt, Amicia cast a troubled glance at the overstuffed linen pouch she carried.

"Dog hair?" Iain lifted a scornful brow as he stomped past her on his unceasing round of the chamber.

"Aye." His sister plunked the sack on a chair. Sidling closer to the old seneschal, she hooked her arm through his and lifted her chin. "Gerbert informed me you have been pushing the men to use great haste while working on the galley a-and . . ."

She let her words trail off when Iain stopped in his tracks and planted his hands against his hips. "What would you intimate, sister?"

"Simply that, in your rush to finish, you've been using an inferior hotchpotch of moss and pitch to caulk the strakes," she blurted. "Donall always ordered animal hair added to the caulk mixture when he oversaw repairs to hull planking, so my ladies and I have gathered dog hair for—"

"By Lucifer's tarse!" Iain exploded. "Think you I have time to comb dogs when my wife's murderers are free to loll about and make merry in their hall?"

"Donall will be—"

"—well on his way to Glasgow. As the two of you shall be on your way out of here." He raked his sister and old Gerbert with a look intimidating enough to curdle vinegar. *"Now!"*

Anger blazed in Amicia's eyes as well, but she gathered up her skirts and sailed through the opened doorway, Bal-

doon's long-nosed goat of a seneschal tagging along behind
her.

"Your temper will see you to your grave," her voice
drifted back to him from the gloom of the corridor.

"And if going there would reunite me with my Lileas,
'tis a fate I'd embrace!" Iain countered and slammed the
heavy, oaken door.

Still grumbling, he dropped the bar in place, thus assuring his undisturbed solitude.

Peace again at last.

A grim smile stole across his features.

With Baldoon's two most persistent needlers out of his
hair, Iain MacLean leaned his back against the locked door
and cast a self-satisfied gaze about the darkened solar.

Not a candle flickered.

Even the smoldering hearth fire had spent its last dubious tendrils of warmth.

Nary a spark dared defy him with a single cheery pop.

The jug of wine he'd flung onto the firelog had suffi-
ciently squelched that particular danger.

Heaving a great sigh, he pushed away from the door and
resumed his circuitous march around the room. "'Tis right
you are, Amicia," he carped to himself as he stomped past
the chair with her fool bag of dog hair.

"Temper might well hasten my journey into infinitude,
but I am not going there or anywhere until I've sent on a
multitude of MacKinnons before me!"

Chapter Six

❖

I AM ATTRACTED to him.

Like a persistent gnat or, worse, a swarming cloud of midges buzzing 'round her head, the same five words rang ever louder in Isolde's ears, dogging her hurried progress along the gray-shingled beach.

Bedeviling her with relentless tenacity.

I am attracted to him.

Simple words. Yet possessed of such power. Her face flamed despite the soft mizzle dampening her cheeks and seeping into the very fabric of her clothes.

Without breaking stride, she glanced over her shoulder and drew a deep sigh of relief. No one followed. Not a living soul pursued her along the stony cove's crescent-shaped shoreline.

Thanks be to all her patron saints. Unthinkable, should the scandalous purpose of her trek to one of Doon's most isolated corners become known. *Her* knowing was degradation enough.

And while the breaking morn brought a welcome cessation to the night's howling winds and the sea's wild tossings, the quiet calm of the new day only sufficed to remind her of the turmoil spinning inside her.

Sheer panic, a goodly dose of desperation, and a smidgen of courage had borne her from the lofty refuge of Dunmuir's deserted battlements, right back to the emptiness of her bed-chamber. But once there, the tangled bedcoverings had taunted her, recalling with shameful clarity the nightmarish images that had beset her all through the awkwardness of a sleepless night spent with the MacLean slumbering against her bedpost.

A blessedly short night fraught with seemingly endless bouts of tossing and turning.

Unable to return to sleep, she'd left Bodo slumbering peacefully on his bed, and fled to the great hall where she'd summoned the most dignified bearing she could muster, then whisked past those clansmen just beginning to stir upon their pallets.

She'd bestowed a quick nod in passing on the few elders already gathered near the hearth fire, cups of ale cradled in their hands, before pure nerves alone had lent her the strength to wrest open the hall's cumbersome iron-shod door without a single wince.

I am attracted to him.

The humbling admission had propelled her out the door and through the arched tunnel of Dunmuir's outer gate with nary a backward glance.

Damning her to the core, the five words hastened her flight across a scrubby stretch of moorland until she reached the dark belt of trees everyone knew hid the secluded cove where Evelina, Doon's joy woman, lived in a stone cottage set near to the sea's edge.

Knew, but cared not to acknowledge.

Sheltered by towering cliffs and the deep shadows they

cast, the little cottage with its sturdy whitewashed walls and gray-slated roof blended almost seamlessly into the folds of the rugged bluff rising up behind it.

The perfect hideaway for hermits and holy men. An ideal sanctuary for those wishing to live in utter solitude. Or shield their doings from disapproving eyes.

Isolde stopped in her tracks. Evelina's cottage stood not far ahead, wispy gray smoke curling lazily from its squat, rounded chimney-stack. Within minutes, she'd be there.

Naught but a few more paces.

Her pulse began to race and her mouth grew dry. Thanks to her own badgering, she now knew exactly what kind of goings-on took place behind the thick walls of Evelina's cozy little home. Or rather what *had* taken place if she was wont to believe the joy woman's claims about no longer peddling her . . . wares.

Either way, Isolde could scarce condemn her. Unless the saints saw fit to grant divine favor to the isle of Doon, miraculously restoring peace to its troubled shores, she fully purposed to perform at least some of the sordid practices Evelina had revealed to her.

Lewd acts she meant to carry out with *him*.

At the thought, another fearsome blush stole up her neck and the wee smidgen of courage that had carried her this far evaporated with the speed of two nimble fingers pinching a burning candlewick.

Regrettably, her panic and desperation remained.

Isolde glanced at the pewter-colored sea. The water's surface, sullen and still, stretched clear to the distant shores of MacKinnons' Isle with hardly a ripple to mar its glassy calm. She hurried on, a slight frown knitting her brow. The day's calmness robbed her of her last opportunity to make a stealthy return to the comfort of Dunmuir's protective walls.

On less tranquil days, a thin white mist often drifted in

from the sea to enfold everything in its path in concealing sheets of slow-drifting fog.

Had this been such a day, a discreet withdrawal would have been possible. But it wasn't. Not this morn. Despite the new day's gray persistent drizzle, nary a thin tendril of mist was to be seen.

But *she* had been.

At her approach, the cottage's door swung open and Evelina stepped outside, a wooden bowl in her hands, her glossy black tresses unbound and flowing free to her hips. Her full lips curved in a serene smile. "My lady," she greeted Isolde. "I bid you a good morn."

Isolde swallowed nervously. "And to you, lady."

"Evelina will do," the joy woman said in her soft, throaty voice, then set the bowl of milk on the hard-packed earth before her doorstep. Straightening, she wiped her palms on the skirt of her near transparent camise and gave Isolde another of her gentle, oddly *knowing* smiles. "What brings you here so early in the day?"

Isolde opened her mouth to reply, but her tongue seemed affixed to the roof of her mouth. And it seemed to swell larger the longer she stood gaping at Evelina's near naked state. Though simply robed, the older woman, with her silk gauze attire and easy charm of manner, oozed sensuality.

Blatant, uninhibited carnality.

Yet she appeared somehow . . . *dignified,* as well.

She would have Donall the Bold eating comfits from her hand with one worldly-wise glance from her dark, sultry eyes.

Isolde swallowed again, but the response she meant to tender the other woman still lodged firmly in her throat. Much to her discomfiture, for she knew she was gawking, she couldn't tear her gaze away. The neckline of Evelina's camise dipped so low it scarce covered the dusky tips of her full bosom, while a long slit up the front of its skirt revealed her shapely legs almost to . . .

Embarrassment tore through Isolde.

Merciful saints, if she wasn't mistaken, the gown's sheerness revealed a thin gold chain slung low around Evelina's hips.

A chain with a large, sparking bauble dangling from it.

A precious gemstone of a brilliant green, nestled against the abundant-looking triangle of dark curls at the apex of the joy woman's thighs!

Lifting her chin, Isolde met Evelina's unruffled gaze. Keenly aware that her cheeks glowed, she blurted, "Were you expecting a . . . er . . . a *friend?*"

"Aye, indeed I am," Evelina affirmed. "But my lord is a well-occupied man. He will not come for some hours yet." She peered down at the wooden bowl of milk. "Other than him, I await none save Mab."

"Mab?" Isolde asked before she realized the other woman could only mean the crone's multicolored feline.

"Old Devorgilla's cat," Evelina confirmed Isolde's guess. "Mab often visits me. She welcomes a bowl of fresh, sweet milk and cares not from whose hand it is poured."

Isolde winced at the flicker of regret in the older woman's eyes. "I did not mean—"

"I know you did not, my lady. 'Tis most high in esteem I hold you for your trust in me." Evelina made a dismissive motion with her hand when Isolde tried to interrupt her. "You did not come here to exchange niceties. Will you not come inside and tell me what troubles you?"

She stepped aside so Isolde could duck beneath the door's low-set lintel. Though yet early, a small stone hearth glowed with a freshly laid and kindled turf fire. Its scent, smoky sweet and earthy, lent the spotlessly clean cottage a welcoming air of warmth, peace, and contentment.

Isolde followed her across the stone-flagged floor to a smallish wooden table and two exceptionally fine high-backed chairs. Gratefully, for her legs suddenly felt quite wobbly, she took a seat on the chair Evelina pulled out for her.

Her back a mite too straight and her hands clasped tightly in her lap, she watched the joy woman slide a tall screen of woven willow branches in front of a low, open archway cut into the opposite wall.

Evelina's bedchamber.

Despite her fervent desire not to offend the older woman by showing any form of judgmental behavior, Isolde couldn't hinder the dampness beading her forehead and palms, nor relax the wooden manner with which she perched on the edge of her chair.

And her nerves didn't fail her because the tiny bedchamber held a bed and naught else, but because she'd had the audacity to peer into it on her last visit. Quite boldly, she glanced behind the screen when Evelina had busied herself fetching them both a cup of her self-brewed redcurrant wine.

This time, too, she caught a quick glimpse of the bed before Evelina could shove the screen into place. A simple oaken four-poster, uncurtained, but graced with exquisitely embroidered coverings and pillows.

For a long, uncomfortable moment Isolde kept her gaze on the well-swept floor rather than watch the joy woman hovering so near the place where surely countless passions had been indulged and spent.

Where, within a few short hours, Evelina would no doubt tryst with her secret amour.

Isolde squirmed on the chair.

Her palms grew clammier.

And the unobtrusive popping sounds of the peat fire crackling in the hearth swelled to a great roar in her ears until she recognized the noise as the loud thudding of her own heart.

She cleared her throat. "Your champion sounds brave and valiant, a man any maid would rejoice to have. Do you not wish to wed him?"

No sooner had the words spilled from her tongue, than she realized the hurt they could inflict. "Pray forgive me, lady. I—"

"We cannot marry," Evelina began, taking a richly bordered mantle of heavy silk off a peg on the wall and draping it discreetly over her see-through camise. "Because, as you know, I am not a lady."

"But—"

Evelina stopped Isolde's protestation with a raised hand. "But I have quit my wicked trade?" Fastening the mantle's girdle around her still-slender waist, she gave Isolde a half-amused smile.

Isolde's heart wrenched at the sadness hiding behind it.

Coming forward, Evelina took one of Isolde's hands between her own. "Think you it matters I've . . . *reformed*?"

"I vow it should."

"But it does not." Evelina released her hand. "Some stains ne'er wash out, my lady. The people of these isles have long memories."

Taking two earthen cups off a shelf, she poured them each a portion of her famed redcurrant wine. "I have a reputation for evil living." She placed a cup in front of Isolde. "Many are they who would chase after me with sticks, their faces a-glow with zeal whilst they wish all the terrors of hellfire upon me."

Her voice was firm, her expression placid, but the telltale glitter of moisture swimming in her dark eyes made Isolde forget her own woes.

And the reason she'd come.

"Tell me on whom you've hung your heart, and I shall intervene." Isolde clutched at Evelina's arm when she made to move away, but her fingers grasped at air as the joy woman slipped past her to stand at the opened door, her back to the room.

"Is he a MacInnes?" Isolde probed. "A MacLean?"

Evelina turned around. "As I will not betray your trust, nor can I violate my lord's. Not even to you."

"He can be naught but one or the other," Isolde reasoned, undaunted by Evelina's refusal to reveal the man's name. "If he is of my blood, I shall speak to the elders on your behalf. If he is a MacLean," she hesitated, then rushed on, "mayhap there, too, I can soon wield some small influence."

With a quiet sigh, Evelina gestured to the row of wooden pegs lining the far wall. For the first time, Isolde noticed a faded *arisaid* hanging there.

MacInnes colors.

Her heart began to thump, but then she recognized a MacLean plaid dangling from the next peg.

And there were others.

The implication blossomed on Isolde's cheeks.

"I see you understand." Evelina took the seat across from Isolde and lifted her cup. "He could fare from any of these isles, my lady. Be glad I will not allow to befall you the havoc that would erupt should you attempt to champion someone like me."

"But—"

"You are too kind, Isolde of Dunmuir." Evelina took a sip of her redcurrant wine. "Would that all were as pure-hearted as you. But they are not, so it must suffice you to know your generosity is much appreciated."

Isolde curled her hands around her own cup and stared at the tabletop. "Of late I feel anything but generous, and certainly not pure-hearted."

"Your intentions are noble."

Isolde looked up. "And the means?"

"The means?" Evelina smiled. A wide smile that lit her face and made her appear years younger. "Did you know, once when I yet lived in Glasgow and was the . . . er, *guest* of a great and noble lord, I heard the bards sing Donall the Bold's praises?"

A mischievous light danced in her eyes. "Aye, 'tis true. There wasn't a storyteller worth his salt who couldn't recite a rousing tale about Donall MacLean's valorous deeds."

Isolde took a healthy swallow of her wine.

Evelina leaned forward. " 'Twas also claimed he is fired with enough romantic ardor to please ten women at once."

The wine cup near slipped from Isolde's fingers. "I find him boorish and rude."

Sitting back, Evelina lifted an elegant brow and peered across the table at her. "Can you blame him?"

Isolde glanced away.

The joy woman's raised brow and penetrating scrutiny reminded her too much of the looks *he* gave her. And her words sounded disconcertingly similar to those of the *cailleach.*

Agitation began to bubble in Isolde's belly. She studied the other woman's face but couldn't discern what she wanted to know. "Who holds your loyalty?" she finally blurted.

"Why, you both do, of course," Evelina said as if her answer made perfect sense.

"Impossible." Puzzlement joined the irritation churning inside her. "It was you who feigned a twisted ankle to trap him!"

"A weak moment, my lady." For a fleeting instant, a wistful look crossed Evelina's face again. "And I pray God the head-veil I wore hid my face. One such as myself should e'er traverse the path between and ne'er take sides."

A sharp jolt of something inexplicable shot through Isolde, zeroing in on only half of what the joy woman had said. *I pray God the head-veil I wore hid my face.* "Donall the Bold would have recognized you?" she asked, ashamed for the question but unable to stay her tongue.

To her astonishment, rather than appearing offended, Evelina reached across the table and squeezed Isolde's hand, another beaming smile lighting her face. "Nay, he never darkened my door, though I will not deny there was a time I would have welcomed his attentions."

"Then why would you worry about him glimpsing your face?"

Still smiling, Evelina shook her head. "I meant Gavin MacFie."

"Oh." A floodtide of relief replaced the tight, burning sensation that had plagued Isolde a moment before.

A wash of shame quickly followed.

She'd forgotten all about Gavin MacFie.

"I see," she said to cover her embarrassment.

"No, I do not think you do," Evelina told her. "'Tis Sir Gavin's widowed father with whom I was once quite, shall we say, *friendly*? Now, years later, I vow we are indeed true friends. The elder MacFie has grown too ill to plow the sea routes as he once did, but his son is most faithful in keeping me supplied with whate'er provisions I might need."

"Oh," Isolde said again, wishing she could sink into the floor.

"Gavin is a man of good repute."

Isolde set her jaw and tightened her grip on the wine cup.

"A man well born and not given to frivolous leisure or vile deeds." Her gaze locked on Isolde's.

"I cannot release him."

"You can speak with him," Evelina said, unblinking. "Sometimes simply talking with someone can reveal much more than the words that are spoken."

"Such as?" The devil made Isolde ask.

The merry sparkle returned to the other woman's eyes. "Such as how our talk has revealed the reason of your visit."

"I came to seek advice because I find it difficult to proceed with the ... ah ... *instructions* you gave me," Isolde lied and pushed her chair back. "No other reason."

Evelina brought her steepled fingers to her chin. "Indeed?"

"Aye," Isolde fibbed again and stood. "And now I must return to Dunmuir before I am missed."

The joy woman stood, too. "Then I will not ask you to linger," she said, and accompanied Isolde to the door. "Perhaps the next time you visit, we can discuss what is truly troubling you?"

Halfway out the door, Isolde froze. "What is truly troubling me?" she echoed before she recognized the trap.

"Aye, my lady," Evelina said with an air of angelic innocence. "Your attraction to Donall MacLean."

Donall the Bold's ill humor had simmered for hours.

The echoing tread of many pairs of feet tromping down a distant stairwell made it boil over. Especially when a small dog's high-pitched yaps joined the muted thump, thump, thump of the trudging feet.

So she deigned to pay him another visit.

Here, in the devil's own kitchen where her two favorite minions had dumped him.

A great murky chamber, enclosed on three sides by rough-hewn stone walls, but fully open to the sea on the side they'd entered through. And save the jumbled mound of fallen masonry rubble at the extreme rear of the cavernous dungeon, wholly vulnerable to the whims of the running tides.

The dank walls bore the floodmarks to prove it.

A telltale dark stain high enough to freeze a lesser man's blood.

As were the grisly tools of torment scattered about and hung from the walls.

A shudder rippled down Donall's spine as he glanced around what he'd first believed to be a sea cave, his gaze taking in ever more implements of horror.

Not a cave at all, his new quarters appeared to be the remains of the bottommost chamber of an ancient broch tower. The saints knew enough of them dotted Doon's landscape. Remnants of a perilous past, the round stone towers provided Doon's earliest dwellers with their last refuge against hostile raiders.

A safe bolt-hole no longer, this broch, or what remained of it, would be underwater if the tide ran fast and furious enough.

Death by drowning or through the nefarious deeds of a dullwit giant. Or, may the old gods preserve him, at the hands of a doddering headsman too frail to properly wield his ax.

Donall clenched his jaw at the grim absurdity of being held captive in a place where his distant ancestors had run for shelter.

The view out across the open sea fueled his vexation even more. A menacing line of jagged black rocks broke the surface some distance offshore, soundly emphasizing the futility of an escape by sea, should he manage to free himself of his shackles. Nor could his own men rescue him should they get word of his capture, for the reef's sharp teeth would shred any boat's hull within minutes.

But what galled him most lay at a greater distance than the hazardous rocks.

His blood running hot with fury at the sight, Donall stared out the open end of the chamber to the dark outline of MacKinnons' Isle riding low on the horizon.

Had he not been taken, and were the MacInneses not such stubborn fools, he might now be dropping anchor on that distant shore.

Dropping anchor and delving into the truth behind his brother's wife's murder.

The dog barked again, louder this time.

Nearer.

Much nearer.

Donall's nerves snapped to attention, the MacKinnons and their distant isle forgotten. He recognized the dog's bark without question now. It belonged indeed to Isolde MacInnes's wee champion. There could be no doubt her fine ladyship accompanied her gaggle of graybearded poltroons.

His brow drew together in a heavy scowl as he strained to hear above the loud slapping of waves and the hollow whistle of the ceaseless salt wind.

The sound of his tormentors' approach came from a different direction than the harrowing sea ledge the would-be strumpet's two henchmen had jostled him along shortly before dawn.

Not that he cared a whit whence his visitors came. All that mattered was their prompt arrival. And soon, before he lost the strength to hurl blasphemies at them. Regrettably, he could do little else, fastened as he was to a rusted chain hanging from the ceiling.

"God's wounds!" he shouted when his feet near flew out from under him as another wave, icy cold and white with foam, swept over the seaweed-draped rock he stood upon.

Had been stranded upon.

Left to endure chills and roiling water swirling 'round his legs with the incoming tide; the rank smell of shallow, brackish pools, scum-caked and oozing mud, when at last it receded.

Far from the drowning death he'd expected, the scourgers had inflicted on him a punishment more fitting to his crime.

Or so they'd expounded.

Amazingly, with his arms stretched taut above his head and his fettered wrists stinging as if Lucifer himself stood spewing fire on them, he must've slept away most of the day.

Slept or passed out.

Deep blue shadows now crept along the damp and glistening walls. Unless the fierce tingling in his numb fingers and aching arms impeded his judgment, the gloaming would soon be upon them.

Another wave crashed into his legs and he struggled to recover his balance, his hobbled feet slip-sliding over the rock's slippery surface.

Sheer force of will helped him gain a foothold. He would not allow *her* to witness him floundering in the surf like an inept nithing unable to stand or swim. What he would do was badger her and her phalanx of ancients with mockery until they grew so weary of him they desired naught but to see his retreating back.

Or at least withdrew themselves from his presence long enough for him to discover a means of escape.

For the thousandth time, a fat drop of water plopped onto his forehead and rolled into one of his eyes, then down his cheek. With a curse, Donall shook his head to rid himself of the bothersome bead of bedevilment.

And as before, he'd no sooner shaken off one droplet before the next plunked down to vex him anew.

"Fine new quarters, eh, MacLean?" a man's voice jeered from somewhere above and behind him.

Rory.

Donall jerked his head around. Fully intending to smite the pock-faced churl with a barrage of fierce invectives, the profanities drowned in his sharp intake of breath at the sight before him. At the *possibilities* revealed by the glare of Rory's blazing rushlight. And at his own tardiness in realizing the full potential of his new quarters.

Choking back the urge to shout his small victory, Donall met the dolt's leer with a narrow-eyed stare.

Oblivious to having unwittingly exposed aught of interest, Rory gave Donall a mocking bow. "Noble enough for your exalted tastes?" he jibed with a malicious grin.

The muscles in Donall's jaw worked and a nerve beneath his left eye began to jerk, so great did it tax him to keep his expression bland. "The accommodations suit me well," he said, his tone wholly without a querulous note.

The perplexed look that crossed Rory's broad features afforded Donall ample recompense for his hard-won restraint. The lout hovered outside the narrow opening of what appeared to be a low-ceilinged tunnel set about halfway up the dungeon's rear wall.

An intra-mural gallery, or corridor, that would run between the broch's double walls.

All such ancient brochs and duns were possessed of them.

Though Donall kept a carefully impervious stare on the other man, his mind whirled. Concealed by dark shadows before, the flaming torch in Rory's hand illuminated not only the tunnel's entrance but also the jutting rock projection on which he stood, a broad ledge that would have once supported timber floors and rafters.

Also revealed were crudely carved stone steps leading from the ledge to the mound of rubble piled against the chamber's back wall.

A possible escape route.

If e'er he won the chance to test it.

And if the broch tower's partial collapse hadn't rendered the centuries-old intra-mural gallery useless.

Hope swelled in Donall's chest and his pulse quickened

with excitement. Rory's very appearance, and that of the aged buffoons traipsing out of the narrow opening to join him on the ledge, lent the tunnel promise. If they'd traversed the corridor without peril, he could pass through with ease.

Slowly, and much to his irritation, another kind of excitement built inside him. The sensation thrummed his nerve endings like a harp string as the graybearded worthies assembled themselves in a line along the ledge.

Without exception, they glowered at him, their faces grim-set, pure hatred oozing out their aged pores. But their number appeared less plenteous than before. The eldest, the bent-shouldered wretch with the thick mane of white hair who used a walking crook, was missing, as was the youngest. The angular-faced one with the booming voice who'd stood before the air slit in Donall's old cell. Isolde had called him Lorne.

Of the giant was no trace either.

And the comely chieftain kept her distance, too, although the sharp yaps of her dog revealed her proximity.

Donall's blood pumped faster.

He'd know she lingered near even without her pet's noisy behavior. *Why* he'd know was something he would not admit even if the heaven's entire host of winged angels fell to their knees and cajoled, begged, stormed, and pleaded.

Soundly routing the wench from his mind, he centered his attention on Struan, the MacInnes's *ceann cath.*

The lady's uncle.

With his stony visage and cold glare, the barrel-chested war leader vanquished any threat of Donall growing soft the moment Lady Isolde stepped into view. A derisive laugh rose in his throat. The fair maid inspired many stirrings in him, but growing soft was not one of them.

"Good sirs," he called up to the graybeards, suddenly overcome with a fearsome urge to goad them.

To goad anyone.

"Do you wish to bathe your limbs in the restorative sea waters?" he mocked, reveling in the perturbed looks his taunts put on their lined faces. "Do join me, for the temperature is fine!"

Struan's lips curled. "Heed your tongue, MacLean, lest I order it bored through."

Nods of approval and rumbles of agreement rippled through the ranks of the ancients. One of them produced a short iron stake the width of a woman's small finger, and held it high. "Aye," he shouted, waving the rod over his grizzled head. "A tongue piercing will teach him the virtues of humility."

A feral gleam in his eyes, Struan snatched the iron stake from the other elder's hand. Running his thumb over its end, he said, "'Tis blunt enough to well purge his arrogance."

Donall spat into the surf.

"The cur!" Struan hissed and started toward the crude stone steps. "Of all the insolen—"

"Hold, Struan!" Clemency in the form of Rory surprised Donall and earned the blackguard a furious glare from the *ceann cath.*

Rory thrust his torch into a wall bracket, then laid a staying hand on Struan's shoulder. "As fond of water as he professes to be, do you not think it would be more fitting to deprive him of what he purports to savor?"

"A parched throat is punishment for petty misdemeanants," Struan argued, his face dark with fury. "Donall MacLean's crimes must be expiated by harsher means."

"Aye, and it is not such a trivial penance I had in mind," Rory rejoined, casting a pointed glance at the rusted chain holding Donall's arms pulled taut above his head.

Slung over a heavy crossbeam that stretched the breadth of the chamber, the chain's weighted end rested beneath the white-foamed waves swirling around Donall's legs. Further weights were stacked beneath the ledge, not far from the base of the steps.

Taking his hand off the war leader's shoulder, Rory folded his brawny arms. "What say you we hoist him up until his feet dangle above the water?"

The babble among the ancients reached a fevered pitch, but rather than join the heated clamor, Struan clamped his lips together in a tight scowl. Still holding the iron rod in his clenched fist, he glowered at Donall.

By the time he hurled the stake into the surf in a great huff of anger, Rory was already halfway down the stone steps. Cold dread dug its talons deep into Donall's gut when the bastard hefted two good-sized weights under his arms and started toward the water's edge. He hadn't gone three feet before pandemonium broke lose.

She finally made an appearance.

Her face ashen, she hurried to her uncle's side, her squirming dog tucked beneath one arm. Before she could reach Struan, Bodo wiggled out of her grasp, sprang to the ground, and streaked down the steps. A whirlwind blur of brown and white fur and furious, snapping jaws.

"Seize the pesky little rotter!" Struan yelled, his eyes near bugging out of their sockets.

He chased after the dog, his balled fist raised in the air. Frantically calling Bodo's name, Isolde pushed past him, almost plunging down the crude steps in her haste to reach her pet first.

Heedless of those in pursuit of him, the little dog shot across the rubble, barking fiercely.

And not at Donall, but at Rory.

He launched himself into the surf, thrashing forward through the swirling water, sparing himself by a mere hairbreadth from Bodo sinking his fangs into his meaty calves.

The bugger's gone mad!
What ails the wee beastie?
. . . ne'er seen the like . . .

Agitated twaddle flew back and forth between the knot of old men as they teetered precariously close to the lip of the rock projection to observe the spectacle unfolding below.

Donall gaped, too.

The lady Isolde and her uncle, his face mottled with rage, both chased after Bodo. And neither appeared nimble or fleet-footed enough to catch him. Bodo raced to and fro along the edge of the water, his hackles raised, floppy ears flying, his sharp barks piercing. The wench tried repeatedly to snatch up the little dog while her uncle ranted and kicked at him.

"In the name of St. Ninian, are you daft up there?" Struan thundered, pausing to rake his fellow elders with a furious glare when one of them tittered.

The rest quickly followed suit with a chorus of chortles and wheezes.

"Decrepit lot!" Struan bellowed and took up the chase again.

Then Rory slogged up to Donall, the weights still pinned beneath his arms. Dropping one, he grabbed Donall's chain and began affixing the first weight to its length. His broad back to the chaos behind him, he mumbled, "You won't hang long. Niels will fetch you down as soon as the rest of us clear out."

Donall paid him scarce heed, for the tumult beneath the ledge had come to an end. Isolde MacInnes clutched the still-growling dog to her breast. Her uncle leaned heavily against the base of the ledge, his barrel chest heaving, his mien furious.

"No need to thank me, 'tis my lady's orders," Rory

sneered, bending to retrieve the other weight from beneath the foam-capped water.

The second weight attached, he began to back away. His own weight straining against his burden, he slowly hoisted Donall higher.

Only a foot or so above the water's surface, but high enough that Donall's arms would soon be disjointed. A groan of agony, full-bodied and hot, swelled in his throat, pushing hard to break free, but he drew on every last shred of his strength to quell it.

He would not abase himself by acknowledging the pain.

". . . dinna ken what's gotten into her fool head of late," Rory groused.

Or so Donall thought, for the wench and her wee dog still claimed his interest. Despite the fire shards shooting through his shoulders.

. . . to me, I'd fasten weights onto your feet as well and have done with you . . . Rory's carping faded as he sloshed away through the surf. The moment the surly scoundrel reached the shore, Donall expelled his groan.

In teensy increments.

And without much regard.

For some strange reason even the wisest of men would have difficulty deciphering, the flames eating into his shoulders didn't grieve him half as much as the disturbing scene on the stairs that led up to the ledge.

The lady Isolde carefully traversed the steps, Bodo cradled safely in her arms. Her uncle followed close behind her, a still-palavering Rory fast on his heels.

But it wasn't Rory's fulminations that plagued Donall.

'Twas the murderous look Struan trained on his niece's back as she ascended the steps before him.

Chapter Seven

❖

"WHAT IS YOUR intent, lady?" Donall asked a short time later, the frustration in his tone lost on the fair Lady Isolde.

He stared across the bedchamber at her, stung because she continued to ignore him.

Curled on the floor near the hearth, she cradled her wee dog in her lap. Gently stroking him, she made soft cooing noises as if Donall still dangled from a rusted chain in her dungeon and wasn't once again affixed to her bedpost.

Newly bathed, though this time he'd used the icy water gushing from an underground spring rather than the warm tub he'd enjoyed the night before, he stood beside her bed, garbed in borrowed raiment, manacled and seething. Every much an ornament as the precious baubles she claimed to scorn.

Ire brewed inside him, its mounting heat rivaling the searing ache in his shoulders.

"I would know your purpose." He tried a different tone.

Undaunted, she dipped her head and pressed the side of her face against the little dog's furry shoulder. And continued to mumble unintelligible nothings to her pet rather than address his concerns.

His most urgent concerns.

"Hell and botheration," he muttered between clenched teeth.

No lass had e'er provoked him more. Mayhap he had not provoked *her* enough.

"By all the Prophets and Apostles!" he thundered. The bellow caused a near imperceptible jerk in her shoulders . . . and an odd, wholly unexpected stitch in the region of his heart.

A most unwelcome reaction.

Donall squared his own aching shoulders against the sensation. "I would have an answer," he said, his tone no longer gruff, but undeniably commanding. "Your intent, Isolde of Dunmuir."

She finally deigned to glance at him. "I have told you. My sole purpose is to gain lasting peace."

Donall bit back another fierce epithet at her evasive answer. "Dare I hope to be enlightened as to how you think to achieve this wonder?"

A haunted look entered her beautiful eyes and its appearance sent scores of red-hot needles jabbing into a vulnerable area near his heart. An accursed weak spot he hadn't been aware of until a moment ago.

"How?" he persisted.

"I know not," she said, and he recognized the lie.

Blessedly, her glaring untruth promptly sealed the newly exposed tear in his resistance to her.

"I shall think on it after I've soothed my dog." Dismissing him, she turned her attention back to her four-legged champion and resumed her cooings.

Donall's vexation surged anew. Weary of the game she played, he sank onto the edge of her bed and dragged a hand through his damp hair. "My patience has flown, wench. I am not a chess piece to be pushed about, used or ignored at will."

She gave an exasperated little sigh—Donall heard it—then scooted around on the floor rushes so she faced the hearth head-on, her rigid back to the bed.

To him.

Thus depriving him of the satisfaction of unsettling her with penetrating stares, carefully chosen words of mockery, and a wicked smile or two to fluster her maidenly heart.

Worse, with her attention fully focused on coddling her pet rather than countering his barbs, or shooting off her own at him, she unconsciously freed him to observe her without the constraints of having to disguise his strong attraction to her.

Donall studied her, relieved she couldn't see how deeply her beauty and grace affected him. Firelight cast a coppery sheen on her thick braids. She'd wound them into coils over her ears, and the flickering light made her already-lustrous hair gleam like spun gold and bathed her supple form with a shimmering halo of soft, rosy hues.

Yet while the front of her glowed with angel fire, her back appeared kissed by starlight, gilded a fine silvery-blue by the wide swath of moonbeams streaming through the row of opened windows to her left.

Half fiery goddess, aglow with radiance. Half ice maiden, cool and aloof.

A potent combination.

Heady enough to stir any man's passion and befuddle his every last vestige of good sense.

As if she had a second pair of eyes appended to the back of her head and could see him shifting on the edge of her bed, could see *why* he squirmed about, she peered over her shoulder and gave him a cool little smile.

"You find it displeasing to be used as a pawn, Donall the Bold?" The feigned astonishment on her beautiful face offered a superb imitation of the mocking looks he'd so oft bestowed on her. "I rather doubt my sister cared for the role either."

Donall's stirrings ceased immediately.

She peered hard at him. "Shall we see how *you* fare as a game piece, my lord?"

"So your boasts of saving me from execution were naught but a poor jest?" Donall said, unable to think of a better retort. "Or mayhap you overestimated your influence?"

A glimmer of doubt crossed her face, but his triumph at putting it there proved mightily short-lived when she set her dog on his cushioned bed and pushed to her feet with more easy grace than he would have credited her for, considering the game she played.

"Perchance I have overestimated myself," she said, and lifted her hands to the bodice of her gown. She began unfastening its ties. "Regardless, I mean to test my skill."

The need to squirm assailed Donall with renewed vigor.

"Skill at . . . *what?*" Not that he needed to ask. The clumsiness of her fingers and the crimson stain on her cheeks shouted the answer.

Silently cursing himself for the need to do so, Donall snatched up the leather-wrapped drinking jack she'd offered him earlier and took a healthy swig of ale.

And another.

Saints, but his throat had gone arid as a young lad's about to catch his first peek beneath the well-aired skirt of a willing and fetching lass. Blood surged into his loins at the very thought. The image of Isolde MacInnes lifting *her* skirts, and for *him*, made his manhood swell beneath the worn folds of his borrowed *lenicroich*.

Fury at his body's reaction rose as well.

With great effort, he struggled to tear his gaze from the expanse of creamy skin she'd bared . . . and failed.

She'd only revealed the base of her throat and the delicate line of her collarbone, but what an alluring feast even such a wee glimpse presented. And her fingers still worked. Already, he could see the top of her camise.

The empty drinking jack slipped from his fingers and landed on the rushes with a dull *thunk*.

A most welcome distraction.

As was the sharp rap upon the door.

The enthrallment shattered, the heated quickening in his blood slowed and cooled. Banished by the persistent knocking at the door, someone's attempt to cough discreetly, and his own well-developed instincts of self-preservation.

She seemed to have realized the folly of her actions, too, for her face no longer glowed scarlet. She'd gone quite pale, and the lone freckle on her left cheek stood out in stark contrast to her sudden pallor.

More telling still, her attempts to refasten the lacings of her gown proved even more inept than her bumbling endeavors to undo them.

Donall lifted a lazy brow. "Do you require assistance, my lady?"

"I am in need of a great deal!" she snapped.

High amusement, sublime and rare, spread its unaccustomed warmth through Donall. Unable to curb himself, his lips curved into a slow smile.

"And I, sweeting, have a great deal to give." He winked. "Mayhap more than you can take."

She stared at him, incomprehension clouding her amber-flecked eyes, but then the double meaning of his words must've sunk in, for her brows shot heavenward and her pretty lips formed a shocked-looking little "o."

Donall laughed.

A deep, mirth-filled rumble the likes of which he hadn't indulged in in years. But whoever stood outside the door did not share his humor. The raps and discreet coughs ceased immediately, and the door's heavy oaken panels shook beneath a veritable hail of fist poundings and loud callings of the wench's name.

Rory.

Donall leaped off the bed, his hands curling to fists, his brief merriment flown. He glowered, waiting. The wench had scarce unbolted the door before it burst open, cracking loudly against the wall.

Her two dullard guardsmen loomed on the threshold, their hulking frames edged by the leaping flames of a well-burning wall torch opposite the door.

His countenance thunderous, Niels's gaze went straight to Isolde's half-gaping bodice. "What manner of havoc goes on here?"

"Your lady's virtue has in nowise been disturbed. I am not a despoiler of women." Affecting a disinterested mien, Donall leaned against the bedpost and crossed his arms. He fixed the giant with a haughty stare. "Nor shall I allow her to despoil me . . . despite her most valiant efforts."

Isolde drew a sharp intake of breath, but it was lost in the outraged sputterings of her two henchmen. Rory's face contorted with rage, while the giant's suffused a deep purple.

"I'll see you howling in hell before you utter such slurs again." Niels reached for his sword. The large platter he'd been holding with both hands tilted sideways, the viands atop it near sliding onto the floor. "Damnation!" he roared, struggling to rebalance the tray.

"Hush, please!" Isolde leaned around the two guardsmen and peered into the passageway. "Naught but ill will befall us should you be heard."

Her pained embarrassment sent an unexpected twinge of contrition to Donall's newly discovered soft spot. Thankfully, the sensation ebbed quickly. Riling her was his purpose, not seeking solace for a weakness he would not acknowledge.

"Please leave us," she pleaded of her men. "Make haste about your business, then be gone. *Please.*"

Looking duly chastised, Rory pressed his lips into a thin, hard line and stepped forward. A streak of brown and white halted him. His short coat bristling, Bodo planted himself in front of Rory's booted feet. Barring his crooked teeth, the little dog growled his displeasure.

"Hail Maria!" Rory exploded. He slid a livid glare at Isolde. "Call him off."

"Bodo, go to bed," Isolde ordered, her voice firm. *"Now."*

Reluctant to oblige, the little dog glanced at his mistress before he toddled off, disgruntlement rumbling in his throat. He paused once or twice to cast a look of high reproach over his shoulder.

"Crazed mutt!" Rory swore, then stalked across the room to haul the table before the bed as he'd done the previous night. His task accomplished, he retrieved the platter of victuals from the giant.

Stone-faced, he plunked the generously apportioned meal on the table. Niels stayed where he was, blocking the doorway with his bulk, his hand hovering near the hilt of his sword.

"Succubus swine," Rory mumbled as he passed Donall on his way to the door.

"And you are a clumsy fool!" With lightning speed, Donall thrust his unmanacled foot in Rory's path. The oaf stumbled, pitching forward. Seizing him from behind, Donall yanked him up by the back of his tunic.

Holding fast to the lout's bunched neckline, Donall twisted the material until the other man gasped for air. "Can't walk without falling over your own feet, can you?"

The giant whipped out his sword and lunged at Donall. "Cease!" Isolde flung herself at her cousin and grabbed hold of his arm. "I beg you."

Niels gave her a sharp look, but sheathed his blade. "He's turned your head."

"'Tis this fool's head I'd like to give a few spins," Donall swore, releasing his hold on Rory. He gave the lout a hefty shove. "We shall tangle again, my friend. Do not doubt it. And when next we do, your lady will not be around to save you."

Bent at the waist and coughing, Rory staggered toward the door. Niels caught him by the elbow, roughly yanking him out of harm's way when he almost plowed into a hanging cresset lamp.

His large hand steadying Rory, Niels narrowed his eyes at Isolde. "I have sore concerns about your ... ambitions, cousin," he said, then withdrew into the corridor, pulling Rory along with him.

But Rory balked. Shaking himself free of Niels's grasp, he sagged against the doorjamb. "T-the *cailleach* was in the kitchens," he wheezed, his pockmarked face still flushed. "The flagon on your tray is for that w-wretched d-dog ... a tincture against f-fleas."

"*A flea tincture?*" Isolde stared at him, her face blank. "Bodo has ne'er ... *oh, yes,*" she corrected, comprehension dawning. "They've been plaguing him of late."

Rory drew a breath. "She said w-whene'er you have ne—"

Isolde closed and bolted the door in his face. Quickly, before his loose tongue could reveal more than he already had. Even now, she could feel the MacLean's knowing smirk boring into her back. She turned to face him and knew her instincts hadn't deceived her.

Leaning arrogantly against her bedpost, he'd crossed his ankles and another of his supercilious smiles tugged at the corners of his mouth.

"So this eve it is to be called a *flea tincture*," he drawled, his amusement leaving no doubt his observation was a statement and not a question. "A most creative ruse."

His gaze lighted on the flagon. "My curiosity is piqued. Who shall imbibe the reeking brew tonight? You, or your dog?"

Isolde stiffened, but she kept her dignity. She refused to acknowledge his barbs. Nor would she permit him to see he'd guessed the truth about the flask's contents. Admiration for Devorgilla's swift thinking almost brought a slight smile to her lips, but she vanquished the impulse and took her seat at the table with quiet grace.

At least what she hoped passed for quiet grace.

She met Donall the Bold's unwavering scrutiny with a penetrating look of her own. Holding his gaze, she placed her hand upon the little flask and slid it to the extreme edge of the table.

"My curiosity is aroused, too, my lord."

"Only your curiosity?" Pure devilry crackled in his tone. "Such a pity."

Ignoring his deliberate ribaldry, she tilted her head to the side. "How long will you continue to agitate my cousin and Rory?" She took a sip of ale. "You cannot fight your way out of here."

To her surprise, his lips twitched as if he struggled to suppress a smile . . . or a gloat. But he kept his silence and simply peered across the table at her.

"It is quite pointless, I assure you." She smoothed her

napkin over her lap. "May the good Lord grant you the wisdom to recognize that."

A strange glint sparked in his brown eyes, its appearance sending a trace of ill ease to join the hunger stirring in her belly. He was hiding something from her. It was writ all over his bonnie face.

"I have recognized more than you would care to know," he said.

Isolde wet her lips. "Aught I can persuade you to share?"

She meant whate'er vital secret he was keeping from her. The way his eyes darkened, *he* harbored notions of a much bolder nature. Proving her suspicions, he reached across the table and closed his hand over hers.

The memory of the last time he'd done so flared in her mind and she tried to jerk away, but he'd encircled her hand firmly within his own, his long fingers, dry, warm, and surprisingly . . . *soothing*.

Save the unsettling tingles rippling up her arm.

Just like the other time.

"There is much I could share with you," he said, and began making slow circles over the top of her hand with the pad of his thumb.

Isolde drew a quick breath.

This was worse than the last time.

"Aye, a wealth of . . . *sharing*." He slipped his roving thumb beneath her hand and used it to massage the hollow of her palm. "And I vow you would be most receptive."

Her heart thundered out of control. A veritable floodtide of sensation spilled down the length of her, cascading from the tops of her ears clear to the tips of her toes.

He must've felt it, too, for his eyelids lowered and the look he leveled at her warmed her from the inside out and in ways she scarce comprehended.

She recognized the look, though. The man she'd

dreamed of on the night of Beltaine had worn the same expression. A great shudder shook her at the implication.

The MacLean's cold smile returned. "I see you tremble in anticipation. A pity, for I cannot be amenable to your persuasions." He released her hand. "Tempted though I am."

His arrogance doused the fires he'd stoked in her more thoroughly than if he'd upturned a barrel of frigid seawater over her head.

"Have a care with your bold words and daring, Sir Donall." Anger overlaid her voice with a shrewish tone. "I am yet desirous of sparing your life, but I have not forgotten who you are, nor why you are here."

He opened his mouth as if to protest, but closed it as quickly and simply arched a brow.

His air of lordliness pushed her past restraint. "If you remain so obstinate, sirrah, I may see no course but to heed my elders' council. Already they are discussing the merits of walling you alive in the broch's intra-mural gall—"

"Fairest maid," his deep voice intruded, "your aging council is neither cunning nor sagacious if they believe to confine me within those crumbling walls."

Grasping the edge of the table with both hands, he leaned forward. "Think they I am unaware of the numerous passages running between the double walls of every such broch to grace these fair isles?"

He sat back, a smug look on his handsome face. "I would be gone before your ancient worthies had time to mason me in."

Isolde gave him a gloating look of her own. "You do my elders an injustice. Not even a knight of your exalted skill could bare-handedly dig through the thick walls of our broch's gallery."

When her words put nary a dent in his annoying air of superiority, Isolde ran the tip of her middle finger slowly around the lip of her tankard. "I said intra-mural *gallery,* not galleries. Dunmuir's broch only has but a single passage. A short, thick-walled one that ends at a heavily guarded door to our great hall. All other galleries caved in on themselves centuries ago and are no longer passable."

Lifting the pewter tankard, she helped herself to a fortifying swallow of ale. "Escape that way is impossible."

At last his insolent demeanor took a hard blow. Something indefinable flared in his eyes. Anger, shock, or fury, it leaped at her with such force she almost felt the impact.

But whatever emotion her pronouncement had evoked, he squelched it with amazing ease. His lips curved in a wry smile. "I shall not bandy words with you," he said, his voice as bland as if he sat in his own hall discussing the weather.

He swept her chamber with another of his coldly assessing glances, then fixed his dark gaze on her. "You shun adornments and coin. A locked chest in my bedchamber at Baldoon contains a treasure I suspect will hold more appeal for your pious soul."

Isolde folded her arms and waited.

He hesitated but for a moment. *"Lint scraped from the robe of St. Columba."*

More amused than anything, and certainly not impressed, Isolde gaped at him. An awkward silence descended. One he obviously misunderstood, for his cynical smile widened. He leaned forward again, a hawk spreading its powerful wings to swoop in for the kill.

Lowering his voice to a near whisper, he said, "The knob on the hilt of my father's sword contains the dried blood of Christ himself."

Isolde laughed.

She couldn't help herself. It started deep in the pit of her belly and bubbled upward until she could do naught to contain it, and had no course but to set it free.

Donall the Bold flushed a deep red.

Heedless of his ire, Isolde let her merriment follow its natural course. The saints knew she'd had little reason to laugh of late and doing so felt good.

Even in *his* fuming company.

"My good Sir Donall, I told you once your freedom cannot be bought. Splendor and riches do not impress me, and neither do boasts of holy relics." She paused to dab at the corners of her eyes with her napkin. "Not even if I believed them to be real, which I do not."

Rather than answer her, he continued to frown.

Her laughter finally subdued, she met his glower full-on. "I shall visit the chapel this night and kneel for a dozen extra Ave Marias if my next words offend the saints and angels, but I vow, sir, were you truly in possession of such marvels, the late Edward Longshanks of England would have sent his armies decades ago to seize them."

To her astonishment, his anger appeared to ebb away. Even the hard glint in his eyes began to soften. His expression took on a wholly different quality. "Might I convince you a horde of roaming monks once sought to purloin Baldoon's collection of prized reliquaries?"

"Nay, you cannot," Isolde countered, stiffening her back against the transformation wrought by his rare attempt at sincere-sounding humor. "I will not be prevailed upon to believe thieving holy men ply these waters nor will I fall for any other such tall tales you might attempt to regale me with."

Mother Mary, but he held a mighty weapon against her!

The trace of true amusement in his deep-timbered voice and the way his brown eyes had darkened with an inner, glowing warmth imperiled her greatly, for should he continue to assail her with such disarming *honest* charm, she'd soon be adrift in a chaotic sea of conflicting desires.

"And if they are engaging tales?" he asked softly.

Isolde drew a breath and strove to ignore the oddly soothing quality his voice took on when he spoke in such low, gentle tones.

"You can recite the entirety of your amassed wealth and concoct enough spurious sagas to claim yourself a master of the bardic arts, and you shall still not sway me in your favor," she said, sounding far more peevish than she'd intended.

Just please stop looking at me as you are now and cease speaking in such a lulling manner or I shall soon break faith with all I hold dear.

"Indeed?" he drawled, his mouth curving in a knee-melting smile.

Isolde's eyes flew wide and for one frightful moment, she thought she'd spoken her last thoughts aloud.

"Indeed, aye," she mimicked, hoping her raised voice disguised the thumping of her heart. "And unless you become more cooperative, I shall face even greater difficulties when trying to keep my council from visiting untold torments upon you."

"Naught they can inflict on me can be a greater torment than being bound to your bed each night." His gaze lowered to her half-undone bodice. "Most especially if you are finally intent on being forthright about your reasons for having me brought to you."

Embarrassment and something else, something much more disturbing, ripped through Isolde. Acutely aware of his lingering perusal, she tore off a piece of crusty brown bread, stuffed it into her mouth, and began to chew.

Furiously.

Until the bread's unusual pungency reached her taste-buds. Fighting the urge to gag, she snatched up her tankard and washed down the bread with a generous gulp of ale.

"Not so fond of this eve's victuals?" He eyed her with mock astonishment.

"The viands are fine." She helped herself to a nicely crisped frog leg, but the closer she brought the fare to her lips, the more difficult it became not to wrinkle her nose.

One bite confirmed her suspicions.

Old Devorgilla had not only slipped a flagon of the anti-attraction potion onto the dinner tray, she'd also used her foray into Dunmuir's kitchens to liberally douse the food with the sharp-smelling brew.

Now she knew why Bodo slept so peacefully. Blessed with a more sensitive nose than she, he'd undoubtedly been aware of the despoiled food the moment Rory plunked down the platter.

Her face a careful mask of innocence, she placed the offending delicacy on the thick-slabbed trencher without a further bite.

A devilish gleam danced in Donall the Bold's dark brown eyes. "You ate most heartily yestereve. Has your lusty appetite abandoned you?"

"Cook seems to have used a heavy hand with the spices," she improvised, glancing away.

Anywhere but at him.

Sincere or forged, she'd had enough of his glinting eyes and slow smiles.

"With my appetite is naught amiss." She smoothed her palms over the napkin on her lap. "Pray indulge your own."

"Mayhap I shall."

The way he'd said the words made her glance sharply at him. He'd schooled his features to appear as guileless as she hoped her own did, but a nearly imperceptible twitch at one corner of his mouth revealed his pleasure in shooting his double-edged innuendos at her.

"It has been overlong since I have . . . *indulged*." He

began piling frog legs onto his side of the trencher. "Utter satiety might prove most restorative."

She gave him a fuming look, but then recalled the anti-attraction potion. All her carefully drawn plans would be at grave hazard should he imbibe the tincture-steeped comestibles.

"Hold." She grabbed his wrist just before he bit into one of the frog legs. "Those are fouled. I would not see you ill."

Saints, but the wench could lie!

"Fouled?" Donall shook himself free of her grasp. Holding the frog leg between two fingers, he pretended to examine it. Though oddly seasoned with a strong-smelling spice he recognized but couldn't quite place, the tidbit appeared well larded and nicely crisped.

"Most gracious lady," he said, "I do not believe you."

"'Tis true, the frogs hail from an old well and the water is oft tainted."

"Truth tell?"

"Oh, aye." She nodded.

Nodded a mite too vigorously.

He had her now. "Your cook knows this?"

"All know." She fell for his trap. "The sacred well has been stagnant for years."

Donall held back a victorious smile. "Then pray explain why the good man who oversees your kitchens would send his lady chieftain a blighted supper?"

She opened her mouth, but snapped it shut again as quickly.

The tops of her ears turned scarlet.

She'd lied.

Again.

Donall's empty stomach growled. "Lady, I have not eaten in days." He eyed the morsel in his hand. Its heavily spiced aroma promised anything but a palate-pleasing taste, but it was plump and roasted to a fine golden brown.

His mouth watered. He needed sustenance if he was to escape. Looking pointedly at his comely captor, he bit into the frog leg. "Most fair eating," he commented the moment he'd forced the spice-laden piece of meat down his throat.

The wench gasped and tried to snatch the food from his fingers. "You cannot eat that."

"Ah, but I already have, sweeting," he said, holding the foul-tasting tidbit above his head when she made another swipe for his wrist.

"I am not your 'sweeting.'" Irritation snapped in her amber-colored eyes.

"Nay, you are not," Donall agreed. He drew his brows together in feigned confusion. "But if the notion so distresses you, why should you care what I ingest?"

A huff of exasperation answered him.

Burying his own pique—for the moment—he scanned the array of victuals, using the distraction to steel himself against the thousandfold more magnificent bounty *she* presented.

"'Tis I who has reason to be grieved," he said. "Sore reason."

"That, sirrah, is a matter of opinion," she said at last, then pressed her lips together in a way that made them appear lush and soft-looking.

Kissable.

Donall focused on the lone freckle on her cheek rather than the temptation of her mouth. "Would you but listen to reason, I vouchsafe you would share my views."

"I will not be wheedled into releasing you." She returned his stare. "Not by your ludicrous ransom offers, silly tales, nor by your boorish airs."

Donall placed his free hand against his chest. "Fair lady, you pain me greatly."

"You will suffer worse sorrow if you persist in eating that frog leg," she said, the tumult thrumming inside her visible in the pulse throbbing wildly at the base of her throat.

To rile her, he took another bite. "I am famished," he said the moment he'd gulped down the odious scrap. He let his gaze drop briefly to her breasts. "Starving for nourishment, for—"

"I shall have other victuals brought up," she quipped, agitation staining her cheeks.

"Too late," he taunted, emboldened by the way she squirmed upon her chair. "I regret naught else will satisfy after what you have so generously offered me."

She clutched at her gaping bodice in a vain attempt to shield her exposed flesh and her trembling fingers confirmed what he already knew: she meant to seduce him yet did not possess the daring to try.

And she understood each and every bawdy intimation he shot at her. Did she not, were she wholly innocent, she would not appear so panic-stricken each time he indulged himself by egging her thus.

Without question a maid, she also seemed well versed in the subtleties of carnal passion.

A potent combination.

The innocent and the siren rolled into one wondrous package. Something deep inside Donall broke loose. An odd tugging and swelling that caught him unaware with its intensity.

"You have yet to take what I've offered," the temptress in her said, proving his assessment as soundly as the white-knuckled fingers still holding tight to the top of her gown.

Donall tightened, too.

His gut, his throat, and another part of him that was growing increasingly difficult to control.

He watched her closely, his every nerve taut. Her fingers dug deeper into the black linen of her bodice. The tip of her tongue darted out to moisten her lips and Donall's loins contracted in immediate response.

Merciful martyrs, she'd likely disrobe and do his bidding at the slightest indication he'd have her, yet her very willingness to do so seemed to terrify her.

Alarm of his own furrowed Donall's brow. Until this moment he had been able to deny his attraction to her. "Exactly what *are* you offering?" he challenged, daring her with words and the fierceness of his stare to admit what he already knew.

She lowered her hand from her bodice. "I believe you know."

The lilting cadence of her voice flowed over and into him, *soothing* him, even as its sweetness fired his blood.

He looked deep into her eyes. "And if I do?"

She held his gaze, her eyes pure molten gold. "Then I would ask you to oblige me."

"Oblige you *how*?" He wanted her to say the words.

Her cheeks bloomed scarlet, but she pushed to her feet. Though she held her back straight and her chin high, the glowing blush staining her creamy complexion revealed the cost of her boldness.

"Tell me what you want of me, Isolde of Dunmuir."

She lowered her gaze, but the haunted look he'd glimpsed in her beautiful eyes just before she had, sank into him like the sun's caress on a warm summer day, wrapping itself soundly around his heart.

Squeezed hard and unrelenting, yet with a gentle grace that shamed him for pushing her.

Cursing himself for the way his fool heart reacted to her,

thumping hard and steady in his breast, he stared at her bowed head, a cascade of emotions tumbling through him.

Unwelcome emotions, every last one of them.

Saints, but she was beautiful.

Light from the cresset lamp bathed her with a luminous glow, glossing her coiled braids to a fine, richly burnished bronze. Her bodice once more gaped free, baring the elegant column of her throat, the soft shadows formed by the hollows beneath her collarbone, and other enticements as well: the lush swell of her breasts rising sweetly above the edge of her camise.

Breasts yet to know the pleasure of man's touch.

A camise wrought of transparent, filmy fabric such as he'd ne'er seen.

Donall shoved a hand through his hair. He could scarce breathe. And, by God's bleeding wounds, when had the chamber grown so warm? A film of moisture dampened his forehead and the back of his neck burned hotter than if a fork-tongued firedrake crouched behind him spewing him with flames!

He swallowed hard and rubbed his nape.

To no avail.

The dryness in his throat and the heat searing him inside and out remained. She looked up at him then, her eyes wide, shining, and so filled with trepidation he felt like ten kinds of a rotting varlet for what he was about to do.

As if the devil himself had absconded with his last shred of chivalry, he cast down the half-eaten frog leg and stood.

"Tell me, Isolde," he said, his tone a command. "What is your will?"

"I want you to take me," she said softly.

Donall drew in a sharp breath, not as prepared for the expected answer as he'd thought. *"Take you?"* he mimicked, knowing he sounded like a simpleton, but unable to stay his tongue.

She nodded. "I wish to forge an irrefutable union with you in the hopes of ensuring lasting peace."

His jaw hung embarrassingly slack as he stared at her, but she stood firm, her lifted chin declaring her strength of purpose.

She wanted peace.

He wanted out of her clutches.

And he wanted her.

Donall swore and snatched up her tankard. A few dregs of ale remained, so he tilted back his head and let them slide down his throat. "Lady, you are full mad," he said, slamming down the empty drinking vessel.

"I wish you hadn't eaten those," she said, staring at the platter of frog legs, the cryptic words proving her addled state of mind.

Totally flummoxed, and sorely agitated at the way his heart still pounded, Donall glared down at the foul-tasting mound of roasted frog meat.

Would that he found the wench as unpalatable.

Would that he could have her *and* his freedom.

Unbidden, the image of her redheaded cousin rose in his mind. The frog legs loomed into sharp focus, too, while the giant's words, spoken to the strange lad called Lugh, rang loud in his ears.

He wants naught but a few frogs from the sacred well.

He'll hie hisself out of here once he gets what he's after.

For the first time since he'd been taken, true hope surged within him.

As did rampant desire.

Donall let his gaze roam over Isolde from head to toe. His hands ached to do the same. Something fine, warm, and bright began to pulse deep inside him. Aye, giving her what she wanted might hasten his escape.

The beginnings of a smile touched his lips. Mayhap he *could* have her and his freedom. What better way to win her confidence than by bedding her?

Bedding her well.

His body tightened at the thought. And once he'd conquered her affection, she'd slacken her guard and he'd make good his escape. Something akin to guilt pinched his conscience, but he brushed aside the damning notions before they could form, concentrating instead on the supple curves of her body and the gleam of firelight on her hair.

As if she sensed his capitulation, or by the grace of God, his victory, she raised her head and met his gaze full-on. "You have decided," she said, the words a statement, her tone dull and flat.

Resigned.

For the space of a heartbeat, Donall considered relenting. But too much depended on his swift return to Baldoon. He had to assure the well-being of those dependent on him by any means he could, fair or foul.

His mind made up, he cleared his throat. Feeling master of his destiny once more, he reached across the table and cupped her shoulder.

"Isolde of Dunmuir, you have convinced me," he declared, and the tiny smile that had been playing across his lips turned wicked. "I have decided to oblige you."

Chapter Eight

❖

THE WARMTH FROM Isolde's shoulder seeped into Donall's hand and spread through him with all the melting languor of the most rare and precious Tuscan wine. Exquisite, proud, and yet utterly vulnerable, she roused him to the very core of his being, her allure slipping past his barriers to curl and pool in the most unexpected of places.

His conscience.

Donall's brow furrowed.

He attempted to withdraw his hand, but couldn't. His fingers remained pressed firmly against her shoulder as if they'd magically acquired the ability to ignore his will.

A black oath crept up his throat but he thwarted its escape by coughing. Her shoulder began to tremble. Or mayhap it was his hand that shook? He coughed again simply for good measure.

"Are you ill?" came her soft voice, cutting through his improvised hacking with the surety of steel slicing butter.

"*Ill?*" Donall cocked his head, momentarily confused.

She nodded. "You were coughing."

"I swallowed wrong," he said, fuming inside at the ease with which the lie had passed his lips.

Isolde MacInnes was a bad influence.

Her constant fibbing had *him* spouting untruths.

And the courage and grace she displayed when she wasn't spinning fabrications inspired yearnings that could only lead to turmoil and disorder.

"I have taken my ease with many women." The unexpected revelation leaped from his tongue before he could squelch it with another cough. "If you persist in following this . . . *path,* I must make known to you that although having you would indeed be a pleasure, it would not be a rare one, would not enable you to bend me to your will."

Her eyes widened but she held his gaze. "You are a renowned warrior," she said, a slight tremor underlying the calmly spoken words. "A man well traveled and . . . a-and pleasing to the eye. I would not expect you to have abstained from such inclinations."

Pleasing to the eye?

His newly discovered soft spot warmed at the compliment, while his heart turned over, then began to thump with a slow, deep rhythm.

"An untold number of women, my lady," he said, cursing himself for letting her praise affect him. "All sweet interludes I recall with fondness, but do not ask their names for I have forgotten all but a scant few."

She stiffened and his hand came free from her shoulder at last. "Only holy men live a life of abstinence and fasting," she demurred, her voice smooth despite the tension he knew rippled through her.

He steeled himself against the slight crease his illuminations had put between her brows. "There are some whose faces have also slipped my memory."

She glanced away. "It is the way of men to partake of

such t-*things* so oft and whene'er the urge befalls them. I doubt there are many who can remember every place they've lain."

Donall rubbed the back of his neck. Frustration rode him hotter and heavier than a band of long-tailed and horned demons fresh from the gates of hell.

"Yet you profess to believe our carnal union will bless this isle with everlasting peace?" He paused, his lips curving into a skeptical smile. "Why should you not slip from my mind as easily as those before you?"

Her posture rigid with pride, she said, "I shall suffer the risk."

Donall smothered a dark oath. Saints, did she not realize he was giving her one last chance to abandon the foolish course she seemed determined to follow? Could she not guess he sought to shock her maidenly sensibilities into withdrawal before she crossed the threshold she might soon regret?

Before *he* turned his back on what ragged shreds of chivalry he yet possessed and, meritorious no more, slaked his thirst for her only to abscond with his freedom?

He cleared his throat and braced himself for one final attempt before he cast caution, hers *and* his, to the four winds. "Do you understand what I am telling you, Isolde of Dunmuir?"

She turned luminous eyes on him. "Aye, Donall of Baldoon, I do. You are wondering why I would esteem myself capable of holding your interest long enough to ensure the peace I desire for this isle."

"No lass has e'er held my attention longer than the time it took to enjoy a few mutually pleasing tumbles." He deliberately withheld the revelation that would seal his fate and end her virginal state faster than she could produce another of her funny little flasks of multidubbed potions.

The simple truth that, for *her*, he'd gladly abstain from any and all other amorous pursuits . . . and if he lived to a riper dotage than the lot of her graybeards combined!

Risking a resurgence of self-determining appendages, Donall stepped around the table and placed his hands lightly on her shoulders. "You still wish to pursue this . . . *endeavor*?" he asked, his heart already thumping roughly o'er the answer he knew she'd give.

"Aye, I do," she said on the wings of a little sigh, then lowered her gaze.

Something wild and fine, hot and untamed, surged through him. He stared at her bowed head, his mouth too dry to speak. Her lashes, thick and lustrous, fluttered against her pale, creamy skin, their tips looking as if they'd been dipped in liquid gold.

His hands on her shoulders tensed . . . wanting more. Donall swallowed hard, losing himself and his resolve.

Gold-tipped lashes.

Eyes kissed with amber.

What other enticements would he discover when he embarked on the sensual journey she'd invited him on? Closing his eyes, he drew a deep, ragged breath. A sore error in judgment, for with the cool night air came her fresh, feminine scent.

The light wildflower fragrance swirled around him, wrapping him in her spell as surely as if she'd wound a length of sturdy netting 'round him and 'round him, then bound the whole with rope.

He opened his eyes to find her watching him, her face calm, her whole demeanor . . . acquiescent. *Ready.* Something inside him smoldered and melted.

But even the fierce longing he couldn't deny did naught to dispel the queersome premonition seizing him in a relentless, cloying grasp.

A damning sense of being conquered rather than conquering.

Pushing the disturbing sensation aside, he took his hands from her shoulders and placed them on his hips. He narrowed his eyes at her and tried hard to see behind her mask of serene determination. "You are certain?" he asked one more time. "You truly understand what shall transpire if I avail your wishes?"

"Aye," she reconfirmed without the slightest hesitation.

"Then so be it," Donall said, his voice thick . . . husky.

Holding her gaze, he smoothed the backs of his knuckles down the petal-soft curve of her cheek. She blinked and a visible shiver rippled through her, but her wee quiver was tame compared to the raw need coursing unchecked through him. Too long were the months since he'd last seen to his manly needs.

And ne'er had he done so with a lass as fine as Isolde of Dunmuir.

Glancing away from her, he focused on the pattern of silvered light and dark shadows stretching across the floor where wide bands of moonbeams slanted through the unshuttered windows.

Saints, but he was a man split in twain.

"Lady, you are a most desirable maid, untouched, yet you would give yourself to me," he said more to himself than to her.

She must've heard him, for she gave a soft sigh. "The loss of my maidenhead is a small sacrifice for the good I hope to reap by surrendering my innocence to you."

Still staring at the dancing shafts of moonlight, Donall momentarily saw her as he had in his lascivious dream: not surrendering or innocent at all, but twirling in an erotic dance, garbed in naught but a length of silk, ethereal and shimmering as the moonbeams spilling into her bedchamber.

His body tightened in reaction. His spirit reeled in confusion. And he didn't know whether he should feel exultant or ignoble. One part of him, though, was most assuredly not plagued by such qualms.

Keeping his back to the source of his quandary, he pinched the bridge of his nose until the sharp need pulsing in his groin ebbed and ceased.

The moment it did, he turned to face her. "What do you know of coupling?" he asked far too gruffly. "What knowledge do you have of men? Are you aware of what will happen if . . . *when* I mount you?"

She drew a shaky breath at his bluntness and took her lower lip between her teeth, clearly allowing the pink stain tinting her cheeks to answer him.

Isolde of Dunmuir knew little if aught of men.

The vulnerable area near his heart surged with undeniable triumph.

And . . . awe.

Ne'er had he bedded a virtuous woman.

"I may be of gentle blood, sir, but I am not ignorant," she said at last, and like her blush, the tremor in her mellifluous voice revealed more than her words.

Donall struggled to keep his mouth from curving into a silly grin. Allowing himself to savor the taking of such a prize would only vex him later. Maiden pure or accomplished siren, his dallying with her could serve no purpose other than his escape.

"Ignorant?" He concentrated on the cold iron weighing down his right ankle and schooled his features into an impermeable mask. "Ne'er would I call you thus," he vowed. "Sheltered mayhap, but of a certainty not unenlightened."

"I *am* enlightened." Her tone held a note of challenge.

"The men of Dunmuir are not monks. I have observed more than one disappear into the shadows with a serving lass, and I have seen what they've done there."

Donall arched a brow. "So you know *how* a man takes a woman?"

She nodded.

Taking an earthen jug from the table, he poured ale into a tankard. He glanced at her. "And catching glimpses of clansmen having their way with willing kitchen wenches is the summation of your knowledge?"

Her color deepened and something odd flickered in her eyes. She moistened her lips. "I have observed animals."

"Animals?" A harsh laugh formed in Donall's throat but he choked it back and relieved his astonishment by shoving a rough hand through his hair. "Old men diddling serving wenches in dark corners," he muttered. "Rutting dogs. Think you I would handle you thus . . . even under these most unusual circumstances?"

Her expression hardened. *"How* you treat me is of little import, only that you do. It is the result that matters, not the means."

Donall swore under his breath and took a long, slow sip of ale. He watched her over the tankard's rim. An unusual play of emotions flickered across her beautiful face, and plague take him, but he couldn't decipher a one of them.

Yet he knew she was lying.

Or hiding something.

He could taste the fibs and deceit hanging in the air between them. A needling sense of foreboding skittered up and down his spine, and his warrior's instincts tensed with the certainty she wanted more than mere peace.

When the heat of his stare sent her hand to pluck at the wispy strands of hair escaping her coiled braids, he knew his intuition hadn't failed him.

"I am not one of your feeble-brained graybeards, easily cozened, my lady," he said. "Something deeper than your sought-after alliance troubles you."

And being cast in the same kettle with doddering fools and ruttish dogs troubles me! his deepest masculine pride railed at her.

Her hands clasped demurely before her, she met his ire with a look more innocent than ten self-sacrificing virgins singing psalms. "Cozening you is the last thing on my mind, Donall the Bold. Nor did I lie about being enlightened."

The corners of Donall's lips twitched in response.

"I am," she insisted, squaring her shoulders against his ill-veiled doubt. "Enlightened, I mean."

"Sweeting, you are as enlightened about the ways of fleshly pleasures as the cold, thick wood of yon door," he said, warming to the urge to show her exactly how erroneous her views were.

A flare of anger crossed her face. "You are not only tainted with the stain of murder, Laird MacLean," she said, her eyes alight with agitation, "but you are a poor judge of women. I truly am well apprised of all aspects of carnal passion and learned in the art of seduction."

"Your sister's death soils neither my hands nor my brother's," he said, flinching, unreasonably annoyed by her persistence in laying the blame on him. Her *other* statements bordered on the absurd and roused his mirth.

Learned in the art of seduction!

He let his gaze traverse the length of her. "Well apprised of fleshly delights, are you?"

She had the daring to nod. "I have trained in the ways of pleasuring men," she said, bold as day.

Driven by most unknightly urges, Donall narrowed his eyes and took a slow step forward. A predator about to pounce on a lamb. "Has no one e'er warned you to be careful of what you allow to pass your lips?"

She swallowed and took a backward step.

His own lips quirking with amusement, he closed the short distance between them. "Schooled in seduction, hmmm?" Towering over her, he held her in place by the sheer might of his stare. "Prove it," he said, and folded his arms.

Her head tilted at a defiant angle, she matched his stare with one of her own. "As you wish," she said, lifting both hands to her bodice.

She began undoing the remaining stays, and to Donall's surprise, rather than watching her with sharp anticipation of the moment her lovely breasts spilled free, the near imperceptible trembling of her lower lip and the more obvious shaking of her slender fingers cooled his ardor.

She unintentionally initiated an onslaught of emotions in him of a much more perilous nature . . . ones he did not care to identify beyond crediting them to the lingering influence of the scattered shards of his chivalry.

Wincing at her inept attempt to seduce him, Donall seized her hands and lowered them to her sides. "Fair lady," he drawled, releasing her, "I commend your willingness to disprove my assessment of your professed . . . er, *talents,* but upon earnest consideration, I believe I prefer to do the proving myself."

The creamy swell of her breasts rose with her indignation. "Pray do not trouble yourself, good sir."

"Ah, but I must." Stroking his chin, Donall eyed the fine display she presented, wittingly or unwittingly. "I have warned you I am not a man whose passions should be trifled with, and you, most revered lady, have offered too much for me to now refrain from partaking of such a delectable bounty."

She stood still as stone, her gaze fixed on his, fierce pride shining in her magnificent eyes, defiance in the tight set of her jaw. "Then what is stopping you?"

Your innocence, his conscience shouted.

"Naught but my desire to prolong the pleasure we shall have with one another." His deep voice, low and deliberately lazy, cloaked his true concerns.

She crossed her arms. "Why should you care about extending the pleasure, or tedium, of our . . . ah, joinings, when you profess to forget the names and faces of your amours the moment you've had your way with them?"

Because you are not them, and neither will I deflower a maiden, any maiden, with all the finesse of a stag in season!

"Do not tell me you would seek to spare me a rough taking?" Tilting her head to the side, she peered at him, the look on her face, and her words, making him wonder if she possessed the uncanny ability to read minds. "'Tis not consideration I seek from you."

Donall shoved a hand through his hair. "I know full well what you want. And I have vowed to fulfill your . . . *needs*, and shall." He paused to draw a breath. "Most adequately, too."

He stepped closer.

So close he caught another tantalizing whiff of her wild-flower scent. "Aye, sweeting, I ken what you want. 'Tis the *why* behind the wanting that puzzles me."

The panicked caught-fibbing-again look flashed across her face. "I want naught but pea—"

"Your alliance, I know," he said, silencing her by placing two fingers against the lush fullness of her soft lips.

Only the certainty she hid some dark and disturbing secret motive saved him from succumbing to the powerful urge to replace his fingers with his lips. "Lady, I have seen nigh onto as many battles as you have seen days. I would not be here to stand before you, had I not learned at a very young age to heed my instincts," he allowed.

"And at this moment, they are telling me you have more than one reason for desiring peace." He paused to purposely let a wicked gleam enter his eyes. *"For desiring me."*

"I do not desire you."

"Nay?" He slipped his fingers beneath her chin and eased her face upward. "Then why do you tremble?"

"Because I am cold."

"What you are, lady, is a liar," he said, softening his words by gently tracing the line of her jaw with the side of his thumb.

A tiny gasp escaped her and Donall smiled. "Sweet Isolde," he murmured, "there is nary a cold bone in your body."

Emboldened because she did not pull back from his caress, he indulged himself by touching the tip of his middle finger to the freckle on her cheek.

A grave mistake.

Something fierce and elemental ripped through him at the contact, a fearsome rush of raw desire that near buckled his knees. A veritable torrent unleashed by placing a single fingertip to one fetching freckle!

But a freckle he'd burned to touch from the very first moment he'd noticed it perched so jauntily over her left cheekbone.

Donall the Bold, laird of the great Clan MacLean and master of Baldoon, champion knight of the Scottish realm, stalwart defender of the Isles . . . brought to his knees by a freckle.

His brows snapped together in consternation and he yanked his hand from her cheek. Saints, what stirrings would assail him when he first touched his arousal to her sweetness? His breath hitched at the thought, and the nigglings of ill ease that had been plaguing him intensified to a most alarming degree.

Clasping his hands safely behind his back, he looked at her but strove to see Baldoon and all those within its great curtained walls. Forced himself to dwell not on her, and the temptation she posed, but on the chaos facing his household if he could not soon charm his way out of her clutches.

Needing the sanity of distance from her, regardless of how scant, Donall returned to her bed and resumed his usual stance against her bedpost.

"Aye, 'tis a teller of tales you are," he said, and this time his words held not a trace of softness.

Nor did he smile.

And neither did she. "Weighted down by onerous burdens is what I am, sirrah. Naught else."

The bitterness edging her voice tugged at *his* onerous burden, the wretched soft spot she'd unknowingly bestowed on him, but he could not pursue and slay whate'er dragons bedeviled her.

He had too many pressing problems of his own.

But not pressing enough apparently, for almost of its own accord, his tongue paid humble obeisance to her. "A burden shared is a lesser one." The saintly sounding words spilled from his lips before he realized he'd even formed them.

Donall frowned. By all the Lord's disciples, he'd almost swear she'd cast an enchantment o'er him.

"I do not want to apportion my woes to others, least of all to you," she was saying, wholly unaffected by his growing vexation. "What I want is to rid myself of them."

"And peace." Donall reminded her, not even trying to keep the mocking note from his voice.

She nodded. "Aye, that above all else. God willing, if my plan bears fruition, I shall see all my goals achieved."

Donall lifted a brow. "Dare I hope you are about to reveal the nature of those other goals?"

A ghost of a smile flitted across her lips. "Nay."

"Nay, I dare not hope, or nay, you shall not divulge your plans?"

She glanced briefly toward the bank of narrow windows. "You are already privy to my most ardent wish. 'Tis why you are here."

Donall pushed away from the bedpost. The wistful tone in her voice sent prickly little shivers dancing over the back of his neck. "I am here to bed you," he said bluntly, stating the fact as the cold truth it was in the hope of jarring loose her secrets.

But instead of oiling her tongue, she merely nodded her agreement, a guarded little smile stealing over her lips and into her eyes.

The gooseflesh breaking out on Donall's nape spread down his arms. "You still wish to pursue this foolery after what I've told you?"

"Told me?" She cocked her head, a vision of innocence. Contrived innocence.

Donall planted his hands on his hips. "I would know if you still wish me to take you, knowing my interest will wane after I've done so?" Narrowing his eyes to slits, he peered hard at her. "It always does."

She gave a little sigh, a *resigned* little sigh, and came forward to stand right in front of him. She looked up at him and his heart plummeted.

Her expression boded ill.

He was about to receive a goodly portion of her "onerous burden."

"Think you I am desirous of keeping your interest, Laird MacLean?"

Bracing himself, Donall simply waited. Blessedly, he didn't have to for long.

"You flatter yourself overmuch, Donall the Bold. It is not your lasting attention I wish to hold, but your bairn," she said, determination glinting in her eyes. "I want you to get me with child."

In the deepest, most silent hour of the night, Iain MacLean lay still upon his bed and frowned at the elaborately carved canopy looming darkly above his head. His hands rested atop several layers of embroidered coverlets of the finest quality, his fingers growing more tense the longer he glared holes in the bed's timber-framed ceiling.

Heavy, drawn curtains sumptuous enough to please a king's exalted tastes enclosed him in a cocoon of darkness. A sequestered sea of smooth silks, noblest furs, and . . . emptiness.

With a cry of anguish heard by none save his bedchamber's well-built walls, he flung aside the coverings and sat bolt upright.

"Lileas!" The name burst from his throat, torn from the very depths of his soul.

Fierce pain clamped 'round his chest, icy cold bands of steel that squeezed the breath from him and crushed his soul. "My beloved." This time the words were scarce more than a whisper, softly murmured pearls of misery borne on an agonized sigh.

His hands clutched the heavy folds of the bed curtains, his fingers digging into the opulence of the richly embroidered silk as if letting go would plunge him into the most vile abyss of hell.

He hung his dark head. "Lileas, I miss you . . ."

His great shoulders, rounded and hunched, began to shake. When the sobs rumbling deep in his chest breached his lips, Iain released the bed curtains and buried his face in his hands. Only after he had no more tears to shed and his voice became too hoarse to voice his pain, only then did he part the curtains and push to his feet.

The oppressive stillness of the dim chamber was nigh as great as the damning silence that lurked within the massive four-poster bed when its enveloping curtains were drawn. Even the hearth gave itself quiet and cold, its fire long extinguished.

Dead.

Spent as completely as his lady wife's precious life.

His steps slow and heavy, he followed the path of the room's sole illumination, a wide swath of pale moonlight, until he reached its point of entry: a splendidly arched window embrasure cut deep into the thickness of Baldoon's stout walling.

Heaving a great sigh, he leaned his shoulder against the masoned recess and let the briny night air cool him. He rested the flat of his hand on the cold stone of the window tracery and stared out at the endless expanse of the sea.

A soft mist, washed silver by the moon, drifted slowly inland from the distant horizon, muting the rhythmic surge and withdrawal of the night-calmed sea, and cloaking its surface like a finely spun shroud.

Iain stepped farther into the window's dark recess and pressed his forehead against the transom, welcoming its chill, grainy texture just as he welcomed the eerie quiet filling the room.

With the turn of a single fast-moving tide, light and softness had become as distant and unattainable as the disk-shaped moon shining high overhead.

Straining his eyes, he peered deep into the night's silver-black darkness, probing the shadows until he found what he sought. The Lady Rock, half-hidden by wispy sheets of drifting fog, but there.

A harmless-looking hump broke the surface surprisingly close to Doon's rugged shoreline, mockingly set smack in the middle of the broad, whitish-silver path of light cast across the dark waters by the impervious moon.

A rocky islet of death, as much a taker of life as the bastard MacKinnon whoresons who'd stranded his lady wife there, dooming her to drown.

Dooming his heart to die with her.

His hands clenched to fists, and fury, raw and unbridled, swelled within him until the force of it threatened to burst him asunder. But his grief weighed heavier than this strange, quiet night, and his anger receded, leaving sheer nothingness in its wake.

Pushing away from the window, he dragged a hand over his face and sank wearily onto one of the two opposite-facing seats carved into the embrasure walls.

His-and-her seats hewn of stone, hard and uncomfortable, but once piled high with beckoning mounds of gaily colored silken cushions.

A favored trysting spot where he and Lileas had spent many long hours lost in the simple joy of each other's company.

Now the cushions were gone, and so was his wife . . . he sat alone on cold, naked stone and cried.

Or would have had he not already shed his every last tear.

Letting himself fall back against the wall, Iain turned his head toward the sea. The Lady Rock had slipped from view, swallowed either by the cloaking sea mist or engulfed by the fickle tide.

But he continued to stare, peering into the darkness and its mantle of silvery mist as if his will alone could summon forth the tidal rock once the waves had claimed it for the remainder of the night.

After a long while, he shoved to his feet and closed the shutters. "Soon you shall be avenged, my sweet," he said to the dark and silent chamber, his hand yet resting on the damp, wooden slats now blocking the sea and its menaces from view.

"A sennight, no more, and vengeance shall be mine." Turning his back on the window, he glowered instead at the vast emptiness of his magnificent bed.

His cold comfortless bed.

"Seven days, and I set sail, Lileas," he said, and started forward . . . toward the hulking mass of carved oak and heartache. "Seven days and the MacKinnons will wish they'd ne'er been born."

During the same small hours, but far and away across the boggy moorland of tumbled stones and stunted trees that stretched between MacLean and MacInnes lands, old Devorgilla hovered in front of her hearthstone, deftly jabbing at orange glowing clumps of peat with an iron poker. A shower of sparks and a smoky sweet curl of smoke rewarded her efforts and wreathed her lined face with a satisfied smile.

Stoop-shouldered, her free hand pressed to her hip, she prodded the smoldering peat until the sparks became lapping, dancing flames, and the fragrant smoke thickened and began drifting up toward the chimney hole cut in the low ceiling.

Her ancient bones warm again, she leaned the poker against the wall and returned her attention to the black cauldron suspended above the fire and its bubbling, foul-reeking contents. Leaning forward, she squinted at the steaming concoction, then sniffed.

And sniffed again.

"Harumph," she grumbled, and took a long-handled ladle off the nearby table.

Still muttering, she dipped the spoon into the gurgling brew and brought a small sample to her lips. One taste, and she fair cackled with glee.

A second sampling, and she was convinced.

Her excitement mounting, the crone used the ladle to fill a dented pewter cup to the brim. She drained it in one gurgling gulp.

"Incense and holy water are not as potent," she informed Mab, the tricolored feline curled fast asleep on the stone-slabbed floor.

The cat opened its eyes and stared at her. A supercilious look, a reprimand for daring to disrupt her sleep. But Mab's haughty glare only increased Devorgilla's glee.

'Twas the first time she'd noticed Mab's eyes were of two colors.

Chortling with mirth, her gait sprightlier than usual, the crone crossed the cottage's main room to the long wooden shelf that held her assortment of healing and spell-casting ingredients and preparations.

"Nigh good enough to make oxen fly," she complimented herself as she studied the jumbled collection of herbs, powders and oils, and other charmed objects.

Her lips pursed, she rubbed her chin and let her cloudy-eyed gaze dart from one earthen container or leather-wrapped flagon to the next. After a moment, she took a small wooden bowl and began filling it with a wee pinch of this and a more generous dash of that, mixed them together, then carried the bowl outside, where she lifted it up to catch the pale light of the moon.

"In the name of the old gods," she chanted, "by the moon and the stars, I conjure you . . ." A fine and rare wind, blue-white and shimmering, swept into the glade to snatch the blessing from her tongue and speed it heavenward.

Well content, Devorgilla lowered the bowl and gave the moon a humble nod of thanks. When she stepped back into the cottage, she went straight to the cauldron and tipped the bowl's contents into its bubbling brew and stirred.

Stirred and planned.

All manner of mischief.

All manner of good.

Even if some would not yet thank her.

Chapter Nine

❖

GET YOU WITH child?" Donall the Bold's jaw dropped in a most unflattering expression of incredulity.

Isolde flushed with acute self-consciousness at the look of total astonishment on his handsome face. "'Tis the natural course of t-things when a man and woman have . . . l-lain together," she stammered, hating the way his gaping made her stumble over her tongue.

He threw back his dark head and stared at the raftered ceiling. A sound that could have been a growl of bottomless outrage, or a snort of utter derision, came from deep in his throat.

When he finally looked at her again, his brown eyes had darkened to a dangerous degree. "And to think *I* am called bold."

Her cheeks burning, Isolde said, "Were I truly thus, I would surely not find this situation so distasteful."

"Distasteful?" His vexation almost scorched her. "If you, the accomplished seductress, find being bedded by me offensive, then release me and spare yourself the agony."

Mortification rose in Isolde's throat, hot, thick, and stealing her breath. "I cannot," she choked out, pushing the two words off her tongue.

I cannot because a child who shares our blood is the only salvation I see for this isle, for my dwindling clan, and to spare me a marriage to Balloch MacArthur, thus freeing me to wed my true soul mate.

A man I pray to God isn't you!

"Nay, lady, you cannot," came his cold reply, scattering her cares as swiftly as if a chill, black wind had swept through the chamber. "You cannot force me to wed you by swelling with my get. Think you—"

"It is the babe I want, not marriage. Ne'er di—"

"Think you," he overrode her protestations, "think you I would see my child, *my firstborn,* spring from *you*? A MacInnes? *The* MacInnes? An inveterate liar? A wench so cold-hearted she has me tortured by day yet would spread her bonnie legs for me come nightfall?"

Isolde flinched beneath his blazing wrath. "Nay, you are wrong. You misunder—"

"Nay, woman, 'tis *you* who are wrong," he seethed, his face dark with fury. "And sorely *un*enlightened." He tossed back his mane of thick, black hair. "Or were you truly not aware a man can pleasure a woman, even take his own ease, and leave nary a drop of his seed behind?"

Isolde opened her mouth, only to promptly close it. She'd almost blurted that, aye, she did know of such impediments to her plan.

Her pulse jumping, her discomfiture high, the tops of her ears burned at the memory of Evelina's warning, her calm assurances a skilled seductress could persuade a man to spill his lust whether he cared to or not.

"Shall I prove it to you?" the MacLean drawled, his deep voice low, smooth, and frightfully . . . *compelling.*

Another of his slow smiles began to spread across his bonnie face, tugging at the corners of his sinfully appealing mouth. Isolde's heart flip-flopped at the sight of it.

At the sight of *him*, saints preserve her.

Darkly handsome, so like her dream man, his bold glare and crackling anger made him seem larger than life, more brazenly masculine than e'er before. His daunting presence filled her bedchamber, claiming mastery of all within its tapestried walls with such ease she could do naught but stand and stare at him.

Wholly captivated.

Wholly his.

"Aye, I believe I shall," he said, pure wickedness glinting in his eyes.

"Shall what?" Isolde blurted, her voice little more than a squeak.

"Enlighten you," he said, and had the audacity to wink at her.

Then his expression went cold and heated at the same time and he advanced on her. His confident air of pure, unbridled *maleness* filled her with an odd rush of exhilaration even as whirling panic careened through her.

"You are a knight," she squeaked again, holding up his ennobled status as a shield. "A champion renowned for—"

"I am many things and renowned for much," he said, stopping at the table's edge, halted by his chain. Something dark and far too stirring flashed in his eyes, but then they warmed, turning a rich, liquid brown. As he looked at her, the hard line of his jaw relaxed, and his lips curved in a disarming smile.

The first of its kind he'd turned on her. A smile so devastating in its power, its impact surged through her. An unrestrained cascade of sensation spilling from the crown of her head clear to the soles of her feet, and warming every place between.

Half-afraid to breathe, she began inching her hand toward Devorgilla's little flask of anti-attraction elixir. The flagon still rested near the table's edge, and she needed it.

Badly.

"You are honorbound to be chivalrous," she argued, hoping to distract him as she curled her fingers around the flask. "A knight—"

With lightning speed, he lunged to the side and snatched the potion from her fingers with one hand, while seizing her wrist in an iron grip with the other.

"I am a *man*," he said, holding the flagon high above his head. "And I am about to show you how very unknightly a man can be."

She stared at him, her heart thundering. His raven-black hair, lustrous and wild, just skimmed the wide set of his shoulders. A pagan god, untamed, lusty, and more breathtakingly handsome than any mortal man should be.

As if the devil himself meant to tempt her, an overwhelming urge to run her fingers through his hair's glossed thickness beset her. A strange and disturbing quickening deep inside her. Faith and mercy, but she needed the crone's tincture.

Now.

And more than one wee flask.

She peered at the flagon he still held out of her reach. "Sir Donall, please. . . ."

"And I shall, sweeting," he said, his voice dark and husky. "Do not doubt it."

Isolde blinked. "I am not your sweeting."

She wouldn't have believed it, but his smile grew a shade warmer, a touch more . . . intimate.

"Not yet," came his drawled reply.

In a bold display of self-confidence, he released her wrist and stepped away from the table's edge. "Nay, Isolde of Dunmuir, you are not yet mine." A new look entered his magnificent dark eyes. A *knowing* one. "Nor are you running."

Isolde expelled a furious breath at his arrogance. Equally aggravating, she couldn't have fled if the table before her turned itself into a fire-spewing sea dragon.

Her fool feet seemed nailed to the floor!

So she stood where she was, gaping at him, her white-knuckled hands clutching the top of her chair, frozen in place as if the old gods had cast her to stone.

Her brow knitted at the MacLean's self-satisfied countenance. Not taking his dark gaze off her, he pulled out the flagon's stopper and sniffed.

His nose wrinkled in a clear display of distaste, and in truth, her own nostrils twitched in reaction to the potion's reek. He gave her an arch look that said more than any words could have, then upturned the flask and poured its contents onto the floor rushes.

"An astounding concoction," he said, dropping the empty flagon and its stopper onto the oaken table. "Vanquishes freckles and purges wee dogs of fleas."

Tensing, Isolde held her breath and waited, afraid of what he'd next say . . . or do.

He didn't leave her in suspense long. "What other miracles does your sharp-smelling wonder potion procure?" he asked, his tone a clear warning the worst was yet to come. "Mayhap save you from being kissed by stealing the sweetness of your breath?"

A gasp escaped her at how close he'd come to guessing the elixir's true purpose. The *implication* behind his guess made her pulse race and set her heart to hammering.

Surely he didn't mean to kiss her?

Not yet.

She wasn't ready for such intimacies. But the lazy beginnings of another of his languorous smiles, and the devilish gleam in his dark brown eyes, indicated *he* was.

As if fully aware she would not bolt, he took up his favored stance at the foot of her bed. With one shoulder resting against the intricately carved bedpost, he folded his arms across his well-muscled chest and simply watched her.

Nay, not simply.

Isolde wet her lips and her fingers clutched the chairback tighter. Far from simply, he watched her with a slow burning fire in his eyes. A smoldering gaze of such intensity it wrested a choked gasp from her. His thick-lashed eyelids lowered in frank appraisal, he slid his gaze possessively up and down the length of her.

His heated perusal warmed her inside and out, searing her flesh with tiny little flames wherever his gaze lighted, breathing to life a fire of her own somewhere deep inside the lowest, most intimate part of her belly.

"Come here," he said, his eyes darkening to a shade close to peat.

Isolde shook her head.

He raised one black brow. "Afraid, Isolde of Dunmuir?"

She stared at him, scarce hearing his silkily spoken words for the rush of her own pulse pumping loudly in her ears.

"Come here."

That, she heard. It was a command. Irrefutable, assertive, and so compelling her feet began to shift on the rush flooring as if they sought to carry her toward him, acting on their own volition, heedless of her will.

"Well?" he prompted when she didn't budge.

Isolde swallowed thickly. Her mouth had gone unbearably dry, her throat so tight she could scarce breathe, and her heart thudded painfully against her ribs.

Worse, her fingers had somehow relinquished their firm grip on the chairback, defiantly joining her feet in their brazen betrayal of her determination to stay rooted to the spot. Panicked by the strange witchery he lorded over her, she dug her heels into the rushes and hugged her midriff.

Donall the Bold tilted his dark head to the side, one corner of his mouth lifting in an amused half smile. "I would have but one kiss," he said, his amusement apparent. "A lesson in enlightenment, if you will."

"No," she finally found her voice. "Not now, not this night."

"Nay?" His gaze flicked briefly to her lips before he lifted a hand to carefully rub the side of his jaw. "Sweeting, am I so pursued by ill luck of late that I have not only lost my freedom but also my wits?"

"Sir?" The instant the word passed her lips, Isolde realized she'd once more taken his cleverly tendered bait. Her heart sinking, she watched the look of feigned confusion settle across his handsome face.

"Aye, my wits seem to have scattered," he said, idly scratching his chin. "Or did you, with your vast knowledge of men, think to have me sire a babe on you by sharing the air in this chamber with you?"

Heat burst onto her cheeks. "I am well aware how bairns are made."

He raised a brow. "Truth tell?"

"Aye." She fixed him with a peppered glare. "I've told you so."

"Then you surely know a mere kiss is innocent?" he drawled, extending a hand toward her. "Come, Isolde of Dunmuir, prove to yourself you are bold."

"You, sirrah, would incite a piece of wood to be bold!" she said hotly, striding forward to slap her hand into his.

"Ah, but you please me," he fair purred, the firm press of his strong, warm fingers closing around hers heating more than just her hand. "And now, my sweet, I shall please you."

Something indefinable in the low, huskily spoken words sank into her, exciting her, while the oddly soothing feel of his large, well-formed hand encircling hers cooled her ire and sent pure languid heat spooling through her.

A wondrous warmth that threatened to melt every shred of resistance she held against him.

"I am not desirous of being . . . pleased," she managed, struggling to ignore the fluttery feeling his nearness touched off inside her.

Keenly aware of the way he looked at her, truly *looked* at her, deep, deep into her soul it seemed, Isolde let her own gaze flit from the sensual curve of his triumphant smile to the discarded little flask lying on the table. Saints, but she needed a swallow.

"Be that so, why do you tremble when I touch you?" he whispered above her ear, and smoothed his knuckles along the curve of her cheek.

Isolde leaned away from the contact, even though, true to his word, a flurry of pleasant shivers had cascaded down her back the instant he'd touched her.

"'Tis shaking from vexation I am, not quivering with pleasure." She purposely kept her head angled away from him.

"Indeed?" He captured her chin with one hand and turned her face back to his. The look in his remarkable dark eyes made her heart skitter a beat. "Most beautiful lady," he said, "I do not believe you."

She looked right back at him, straight into his all-seeing brown eyes. "You vex me mightily, that is all."

Releasing her, Donall lifted his hands, holding them

palm outward. "Then retreat to your safe corner behind the chair . . . if you so desire."

She didn't move. "What I desire—"

"I ken what you desire." He circled his hands around her upper arms, holding her gently but firmly in place by letting his hands glide smoothly from her elbows up to and over her shoulders, then back down again. "There is a very fine line betwixt passion and ire," he said. "Sometimes it blurs."

"And you think to show me the difference?"

"Not think to, I *will*," he murmured, his fingers lightly kneading her upper arms. "With a kiss."

Unsmiling now, but with a heat smoldering in his eyes that she instinctively recognized as pure, untamed passion, he slid his arms around her back and pulled her flush against him. "A thorough and leisurely kiss," he said, looking deep into her eyes.

The warmth Isolde saw there chased her rising whimpers of protest right back down her throat, and stilled the hands she'd been about to press frantically against the hard wall of his chest.

"Must you?" she gasped, already losing the battle to conquer the heart-stealing sensations spinning through her at being held thus.

Held thus by *him*.

"Must I what, lass? Kiss you?" He lowered his head until their very breaths mingled. "Aye, I must," he said, and did.

He touched his mouth to hers with such sublime tenderness, the sheer power of his kiss rivaled the iron-hard strength of the arms he'd curved around her back.

A tiny sigh escaped her as he moved his lips over hers with exquisite gentleness. A soft, smooth warmth, headier than she'd e'er dreamed a kiss would be.

Her pulse quickened, her blood thickening, even as a

heavy languor settled over her, pooling deep in her lower belly. A mindless, swirling, pulsing ache.

An ache for more.

A deeper yearning her body understood better than she. Easing her hands from between them, she cupped her palms over his broad shoulders, reveling in the warm, solid feel of his warrior's strength beneath the soft linen of the *lenicroich*.

"Holy saints," Donall breathed against her lips when she tilted her head to the side, parting her lips in an instinctive invitation for him to deepen the kiss.

He obliged at once, slanting his mouth over hers, claiming her lips with a firmer, more commanding kiss, its heated fervor stealing her breath and unraveling her very senses.

Another little moan rose in her throat, and he caught it with his tongue, masterfully blending her gasp of pleasure with his own until both sighs were indistinguishable from the sweet sighing of their mingled breaths.

Somewhere deep inside her something broke free, setting loose a wash of torrid, liquid pleasure that spilled down the length of her to pool around her feet in a rushing, soul-stirring torrent.

A sea of sensation swirled 'round and 'round her, tantalizing and powerful enough to sweep her into a wild, frenzied abyss of pure bliss.

His arms tightened around her, his hands moving over her back, caressing her, molding her to him. He deepened the kiss, and cupped her lower bottom, splaying his fingers over her curves, drawing her so close she could not deny his arousal, the unbridled might of his need.

A delicious haze engulfed her, and she opened her mouth wider, accepting his passion with an increasing need of her own. Letting herself melt into him, she slipped her hands around his neck and twined her fingers in the silken thickness of his hair, losing herself in the wondrous maelstrom of yearning.

Losing herself so completely naught else mattered.

Not his name.

Not why he was there.

Nothing.

As if he sensed her capitulation, he gentled his embrace and eased the kiss to an end by degrees until, as he'd begun, he simply grazed the soft warmth of his own mouth tenderly over hers, then finally pulled away.

He looked at her, his head angled so near his breath caressed her cheek. "Lady," he said, and naught else. But the softly spoken word held enough awe to kindle anew the raging fire he'd ignited in her blood.

With great gentleness, he brushed the pad of his thumb over her lower lip. "Ne'er compare me to lecherous graybeards and mating dogs again," he said, and a spark of his rare yet oh-so-fine humor flashed across his handsome face.

Though fleeting, the wee glimpse of genuine amusement warmed her, melting her heart with the same mastery his kiss and embrace had melted her resistance.

Feeling much the enchantress she'd professed to be, she gave in to the irresistible urge to touch her fingers to his mouth. Firm, yet smooth and warm, the feel of his lips fascinated her. Her breath caught on a captivated sigh as he curved his mouth into one of his slow, disarming smiles right beneath her fingertips.

"Now you know how a *knight* kisses," he said, the low, silky words causing a shower of light, fluttery shivers to ripple down her spine.

Holding her captive with the heat of his gaze, he captured her wrist, upturned her hand, and planted a searingly soft kiss on her palm. "One to dream on," he murmured, folding her fingers over the kiss.

Isolde blinked, too shaken to speak.

He offered her his palm. "Will you grace me with one, too?"

"One, too?" she echoed, full aware of what he wanted her to do.

"A simple hand kiss," he said, ardor still simmering in his warm brown eyes. "To see me through the long, lonely hours in your dungeon."

His last few words doused the fire in her blood in one fell swoop, at once reminding her of the constraints of her plight and smashing his expertly spun illusion of gallantry and dashing knights with all the finesse of a mailed fist crashing down on a goose egg.

"You said one kiss," came her rebuff, edgier than she would've liked, but at least her fool lips had ceased quivering. "It's now been two."

He closed his hand over her shoulder. "I would have more," he said, an indefinable undercurrent in his deep-timbered voice. "And you, most desirable maid, *should* have more . . . if you seek to further enlighten yourself."

"You are a shameless imposter, Donall MacLean," she accused, trying to wrest herself free of his iron clamp hold on her shoulder. "An arrogant boorish blackguard with nary a knightly bone in your body."

"Think you?" He arched a brow.

"Aye, I do!" she cried, anger scorching her cheeks. An acute and shameful awareness of the wild abandon she'd so easily succumbed to filled her with enough fury to ignite ten roaring fires.

Afraid traces of that abandon might still be blazing in her eyes, she whipped her head around, turning her face away from him. Unthinkable, should he be able to tell her lips yet tingled, aching to be kissed again.

Kissed as knights kiss.

"Ohhhhhh . . ." Fury bubbled and churned in her at the ease with which he'd so deftly played on her most secret desires.

"Ohhhh, you enjoyed my kiss, or ohhhh, you are wroth with me?" he whispered above her ear, then planted a quick kiss on the crown of her head. "That makes three."

She shot him an angry look. "You are mad."

"So some have claimed." He shrugged. "This night, though, I am simply mad for you, my lady," he added, and his mouth began to curve into another of his disarming smiles.

Isolde glanced away before it could fully form. "And come the morrow, another maid would catch your favor."

"Mayhap," he said, the speed with which the unflattering retort had sprung from his lips irritating her even more. "I have warned you my affections are fickle."

With an agitated huff, she wriggled from his grip. Free at last, she quickly darted behind her chair. Gripping its top, she drew a fortifying breath. "And I have told you I do not want your . . . affections."

He folded his arms across his chest, his entire mien exuding pure male superiority. *Triumph.* "Aye, you have told me." Tilting his head a bit, he peered at her with another of his feigned looks of consternation. "Tell me then, why your body says something else?"

Isolde pressed her lips together in a tight line.

His lips twitched in high amusement. "Ah, wench, you are fulsome beautiful when riled."

Her cheeks burning, Isolde promptly stared at the table. Anywhere but at him.

Devorgilla's little flask was still where he'd tossed it earlier. Empty, innocuous-looking, and as yet wholly ineffective.

She frowned. Thus far, the *cailleach*'s anti-attraction potion hadn't done her a whit of good in resisting Donall

MacLean's charms. Blessedly, though, neither had it stilled *his* apparent ardor.

He cleared his throat. "I find I am quite smitten with you, Isolde of Dunmuir," he drawled, as if uncannily privy to her thoughts.

And we with you, your lordship magnificence, the meddlesome butterflies still fluttering madly in her most private reaches chimed in answer.

She stiffened her back, refusing to deign him a response. Instead, she kept her gaze firmly focused on the flagon, vowing to have the crone brew a more potent batch.

"Knights admire wenches with steel in their veins."

The beguiling note underlying his observation, and the observation itself, almost brought a tiny smile to her lips.

Almost.

But she caught the wee tuggings at the corners of her mouth before they betrayed her. Squaring her shoulders, she made certain her posture displayed enough steel to set the handsome devil's head spinning.

Her effort was rewarded by a deep, rich chuckle.

Refusing to acknowledge his mirth, she walked to the opened windows with as much dignified grace as she could muster. Folding her hands in front of her, she let the brisk salt air cool her flushed cheeks and stared out into the rosy-gray luminescence of approaching dawn.

Niels and Rory would come for him soon.

A sharp pang of guilt jabbed into her at that, and she risked a quick, slanted glance over her shoulder. He'd resumed his favored position: lounged against her bedpost, ankles crossed, arms folded, one mocking brow arching heavenward the instant he saw he had her attention.

Resplendent in his dark, masculine beauty.

Proud.

"A farewell kiss before your henchmen fetch me?" His deep voice shattered the spell she'd almost sunk back into.

I would like a thousand kisses, her lips called to him.

She let silence speak for her.

Wincing at her weakness, and sorely in need of escaping his presence, Isolde gathered her skirts in preparation for a swift departure from her chamber.

From him.

The man was insufferable, but possessed of enough exalted prowess and high looks to win any maid's heart.

He kissed like a knight.

And his name was Donall MacLean.

That alone helped lift her chin to a haughty degree as she sailed past him, not stopping until she reached the door. With shaking fingers, she freed the stout drawbar and opened the door. "Sir Donall," she called, stunned by the audacity of what she meant to say even before the brazen words could leap off her tongue.

"Aye, sweeting?" he called from behind her, the two words rich with telling eloquence.

She steeled herself, and a teensy spark of warmth sprang to life somewhere inside her.

Donall the Bold liked steel.

"It would please me to resume our discussion about enlightenment on the morrow," she blurted, then scooted out of the chamber.

"You are bold, indeed, Isolde of Dunmuir," he called out as she shut the door. "A fine bold lass."

His words chased her through the dimly lit passageway, even pursuing her into the stair tower and down its winding stone steps.

She would have dashed right into the darkened hall the moment she reached the bottom, for her intent had been to seek the bailey and the quietude she'd find there at this early hour, but grumbling voices, some raised in anger, halted her as soundly as if she'd run full tilt into a wall.

Pausing, she searched the murky darkness. Most of the pitch-pine torches had burned out, but a low-burning hearth fire and a few braces of tallow candles on a nearby trestle table managed to cast some illumination.

And it was around the trestle table that the elders huddled, their collective grousing and cross-tempered snorts echoing in the vastness of the otherwise empty hall.

Slipping into the shadows outside the stair tower's arched entrance, Isolde tilted her head to the side and listened. The youngest council member Lorne's commanding voice rose above the others' grumbles. "I say a resounding nay. Balloch MacArthur is a braggart. He will not keep silent about such a coup."

A chorus of gnarled fists pounding on the long, oaken tabletop signaled the council's agreement.

All save one.

The war leader, Isolde's uncle, Struan, glowered at the others, anger flashing in his hawklike eyes. "And what would the lot of you have us do with them? Put good horse-flesh to the cliff along with the MacFie?"

Isolde clasped a hand over her mouth, and shrank deeper into the shadows, her heart thudding.

"'Tis madness to harm the MacFie," Lorne argued. "We have no quarrel with his people."

"I'm with Lorne," came white-haired Ailbert's quavering voice. "Every clan in the Isles will ill-wish us for such a misdeed."

"Aye, doing so would be placing a spark to tinder," yet another agreed, slamming his tankard on the table for emphasis. "We cannot kill Gavin MacFie, nor can we give Balloch MacArthur the horses. The pompous arse has a loose tongue."

With a furious oath, her uncle shot to his feet. "Blithering idiots! MacArthur also has a stout sword arm and a fat purse," he thundered, raking the others with a furious glare. "What shall we give him for our lady's dowry if not the MacLean's two fine steeds?" he demanded, his barrel chest heaving. "A chest of old stones?"

Ailbert, clan oldest, tittered. His perfidy in doing so earned him a sharp glance from the *ceann cath.*

"Think before you cackle, you feeble-headed nitwit," Struan upbraided him. "Old stone is all we have, and it isn't a precious commodity since every last one of these isles and all the land beyond is riddled with them."

"Archibald says we must honor the old," came a singsong female voice, and only then did Isolde spot her vacant-eyed mother. The lady Edina sat in a dark corner near the council members, a thick woolen plaid draped like a winding sheet around her slight form. "Archibald says—"

"Archibald is dead." Struan cast an irritated glance at her, but when her once-beautiful face clouded with confusion, his countenance softened. "You should be abed," he said gruffly and started toward her. "Come, I will help you abovestairs."

Lady Edina grabbed the arms of her chair. "Nay. Not until Archibald returns."

Struan muttered something under his breath and turned back to the table, his countenance dark. Taking his seat again, he took a long swig from his ale cup. "We've no choice but to dispatch the MacFie after the MacLean's execution. If we release him, and the two horses with him, as you simpletons would have us do, he'll ride straight for Baldoon. Within hours we'd have the full gale of the MacLeans' wrath blowing down our necks."

"I do not like it." This from the end of the table.

The others joined in.

A fool plan fraught with peril.

Too dangerous.

Lorne pushed to his feet. "Donall MacLean has thus far proved himself manly and resolute under his sufferings," he said, candleglow casting a play of light and shadow across his angular face. "We have no reason to inflict a penance on MacFie. Mayh—"

"What would you say?" another elder cut in, his voice laced with ill humor.

Still well concealed by the hall's deep gloom, Isolde held her breath, and kept her gaze trained on Lorne, her favorite among the elders.

"What I am saying," Lorne answered, "is that mayhap we should release both men *and* their horseflesh afore a worse fate is visited upon us than we could possibly wreak upon the MacLeans."

Isolde's heart swelled with gladness, but her elation proved short-lived. Outraged huffs and rants filled the hall as each graybeard present voiced his disapproval.

. . . we'd vowed to have no pity . . .

. . . make him pay until he shrieks with agony . . .

Lorne compressed his lips. Isolde expected him to attempt a second assault of wisdom upon the council, but he sank back onto his chair with naught but his troubled expression declaring his displeasure.

Struan, though, fair glowed with victory. "Donall the Bold and his friend will be executed within the month. Balloch MacArthur's men should arrive shortly thereafter to arrange the betrothal of his lord and our chieftain, the lady Isolde," he announced. "When he leaves, he shall take the MacLean's two horses as our gift to his liege."

He aimed a needling glance at Lorne. "Should any come

nosing about, we will claim we lost the MacLean, Sir Gavin, and their steeds, on the voyage to Glasgow. No one will be able to prove otherwise."

Isolde stared at her uncle, straining to hear more. She could see his lips moving, but his words were lost in the babble and mayhem that had erupted among the gray-beards.

With the exception of Lorne, their agreement with her uncle's views could not be denied. Only Lorne seemed to have found the same path she followed, but even he would balk if he knew exactly *how* she hoped to attain peace.

Then, with a look of utter disgust on his face, Lorne pushed to his feet again and strode from the hall. She would have to leave, too. But at the moment, her feet felt too much like lead for her to go anywhere.

One month.

She'd known the MacLean's execution had e'er been loosely planned for on or around the Summer Solstice, but somehow the date had seemed to loom in the far future. Struan's words had driven home the harsh truth. Midsummer would soon be upon them, a scant month and a few days away.

A shudder snaked down her spine at the date's bitter irony.

Just as the days following the Summer Solstice would shorten in length, their light gradually swallowed by longer and longer hours of darkness, so would blackness engulf all she held dear if she could not dissuade the elders from going through with their plans.

And she had but a few short weeks to do it.

Her heart heavy, she slipped back into the stair tower, all desire to seek the quietude of the bailey forgotten. Without a backward glance, she mounted the circular stairs, her progress much slower than her hasty descent a short while before.

And this time, the demons following her had naught to do with a handsome devil's roguish words and everything to do with the cold dread laying bold claim to her heart.

Chapter Ten

❦

IT TOOK ISOLDE several hours of plunging through bramble patches, trudging across the eerie grandeur of Doon's cairn-strewn moorland and worse, before she spotted the *cailleach* picking her way along the edge of the bogs.

Her stooped shoulders bent, a large willow basket on her arm, the crone searched the ground as she shuffled along the peaty bank of the nearest bog pool.

"Devorgilla!" Isolde hurried forward, Bodo on her heels.

The old woman plucked a dark purple flower from a small cluster of green by the water's edge and dropped it into her basket before she greeted Isolde. "A good morrow to you, lass."

Isolde almost told her a more foul morn had ne'er dawned. Instead, she peered into the willow basket. It held all manner of greenery. Roots still clumped with earth, tiny purple bog violets, and something that smelled most familiar.

Something she wished worked as powerfully as it smelled.

"Are you gathering ingredients for the potion?" Isolde's nose twitched at the pungent reek clinging to the basket.

"My bones told me you'd be needful of more," Devorgilla said, her voice oddly guarded, the look on her wizened face unusually bland, somehow . . . closed.

Secretive.

As if she'd been taking lessons in feigning indifference from a certain insufferable knight.

"Your bones are accurate as always." Isolde pushed a damp tendril of hair off her face. "I do need more . . . *much more*, and of a stronger potency."

Devorgilla's hazy eyes widened. "How so?"

"The potion isn't very effective," Isolde said, her cheeks coloring at the admission. "And do not taint my viands again. He noticed."

Devorgilla clapped a knotty hand to her face. "By the moon and stars, but I forgot he's dining with you," she said, and Isolde knew she was lying through the gaps in her teeth.

"Just double or triple its strength, I pray you," Isolde said. "And see it's delivered only into my own two hands."

"As you will." The crone bobbed her grizzled head in a ludicrously poor attempt at humble acquiescence. "Did the MacLean eat the victuals I treated with the potion?" she wanted to know, the barely suppressed excitement in her voice a sure sign she'd hoped he'd done exactly that.

Isolde ignored her question. "I've been searching for you since cockcrow. I vow I still would be had Lugh not told me where to look."

"He spoke?" A spark of interest shone in Devorgilla's cloudy eyes.

"Only a few words as he is sometimes wont to do." Isolde glanced out across the still, black-surfaced pool. "He worried I'd lose myself out here if he didn't tell me the direction you'd taken," she said, trying to ease her way into asking what she must. "I told him I must speak with you on a matter of great urgency."

The crone bent to pick another teensy bog violet. "More urgent than being needful of the potion?" She parted the cluster of leaves until her bony fingers found the wee purple bud.

"Aye, something most grave." Isolde glanced at the clear blue sky and wished her life could be as cloudless. "A favor I would ask of you," she said, looking back at the crone. "Nay, a request. Something you must do for me."

Straightening, the crone held up the tiny flower and peered intently at it. "A favor borne of a grave matter, that is a request I must do?"

Isolde nodded.

The *cailleach* clucked her tongue. "Be it Laird MacLean's bonnie smile or his braw embrace that's tied your tongue in knots?"

What would you know about his bonnie smiles and knightly kisses? Isolde almost blurted. "You speak as if you know him," she said instead.

"I know *of* him," Devorgilla quipped, her foggy-eyed gaze remarkably bright. "And I have seen him."

"In the cauldron's steam?" Isolde tried to outsmart her, hoping she'd reveal if he was indeed the man shown to her by the yarrow sprig on Beltaine.

The true soul mate Devorgilla claimed to have seen that night as well—in the vapor rising from her great iron kettle.

"In your dungeon, lass." Devorgilla gave her a sly little smile. "'Twas enough."

"Enough for what?" Isolde blurted, her voice agitated and loud enough to make Bodo jump up at her, his forepaws slamming against her skirts, his quizzical expression and crooked teeth making her smile despite her woes.

"Simply enough," Devorgilla evaded. "You should ken I

dare not reveal all I see. Doing so would vex those who confer such gifts."

Shuffling forward, she touched the violet lightly to Isolde's cheek. "Ah, child, do you not yet ken there are some things we must see for ourselves?"

Uncomfortable, Isolde glanced at the little flower in Devorgilla's age-spotted hand. "Then tell me how did you see *that*?" True puzzlement drew her brows together. "Even I wouldn't have noticed it, hidden as it was beneath so many leaves."

A sage smile curved Devorgilla's lips. "'Tis the most precious of treasures we find when we look in unlikely places," she said, and dropped the violet into her basket.

Knights admire wenches with steel in their veins.

The MacLean's words swept past her ears, riding the tail of a soft, sun-warmed breeze.

So soft and warm, chill bumps broke out on her arms.

Isolde frowned.

Then she squared her shoulders. "I want you to get a message to Balloch MacArthur," she blurted before her rush of steely courage could desert her.

Devorgilla blinked. "Even the worst winter storm will spend its force, lass," she said, worry replacing her usual spry caginess. "Those who are wise do not disturb sleeping dogs."

Isolde turned away. Seeing the crone's distress only stoked the flames of her own. "It is too late," she said, swallowing the cold lump of dread rising in her throat, gulping it right back down to join the larger ball of icy apprehension spinning in her stomach.

As if he knew she needed comfort, Bodo pressed himself hard against her legs, and she reached down and scratched him behind his soft, floppy ears. "Can you get a message to

MacArthur?" she asked when she straightened. "Is it in your power to do so?"

Devorgilla pressed her lips together and stared at her black-booted feet.

"Devorgilla," Isolde prodded when the old woman began poking at a clump of grass with the scuffed toe of her boot. *"Can you?"*

"I would know why."

Steely wenches.

"Because I am asking you," Isolde said, feeling quite bold.

The crone glanced heavenward. "It will rain soon," she claimed. "A fierce storm."

Nary a cloud marred the brilliant blue sky.

"Lives depend on my getting a message to Balloch." Isolde tried another tactic. "And not just Donall MacLean's."

That caught the *cailleach*'s attention. "Whose lives?"

"Gavin MacFie's for one," Isolde said, hoping to impress the crone with the urgency of her task. "And two fine horses."

Without batting her cloudy eyes, Devorgilla set down her basket. She planted her fists on her hips. "You'd best tell me what is amiss."

And Isolde did, repeating everything she'd heard in the hall that morn. When she finished, Devorgilla shook her head, then stared out across the moorland toward Dunmuir.

"I do not like this," she said, unwittingly repeating what one of the elders had also stated. "'Tis perilous ground you'll be venturing on if you do this."

A fine bold lass.

"I must." The two words sprang from her lips. "Can you reach Balloch?

The crone picked up her basket. "Aye, I can," she affirmed after a long, uncomfortable moment. "What would you have him know?"

"That I am with child," the steely wench in her said. "I want him told I am to bear another man's child."

Many hours later, Isolde stood in the vaulted passage outside Dunmuir's chapel and listened to the resounding boom and clash of thunder. The deep rumbles, mighty enough to shake the stone floor beneath her feet, also rattled her nerves.

Devorgilla had predicted a violent storm, and Isolde hadn't believed her.

Not until much later when, sometime after the hour of none, the clouds had set in, swiftly darkening the afternoon sky. Roiling thunderheads, deep gray and menacing, driven by chill, fast-moving gales racing in from the open sea.

Just as the crone had said would happen.

Isolde shivered and drew her woolen *arisaid* closer about her shoulders. May the Blessed Virgin help her if Devorgilla's other predications came to pass. An outraged Balloch MacArthur raising a clamor would cost more fortitude than she could presently spare. Dunmuir shouldered enough grief of late without a false move of hers unleashing yet more turmoil and disaster.

Her stomach knotting, she reached for the chapel door's iron latch. She'd placed votive offerings at the sacred well earlier, and now she'd say her daily chants for her sister's soul, plus a few for her own.

For everyone's.

Thus determined, she let herself into the quiet dimness of the small oratory, and closed the door soundly behind her. Terror seized her at once. All the steel she'd been convincing herself she possessed fled faster than *he* could shoot his brows heavenward.

She wasn't alone.

Someone was inside the chapel with her.

Someone she could feel but not see.

Lileas?

Her hand pressed against her heart, she took a few backward steps until she bumped into the closed door. There she remained, and would, until she could summon enough courage to flee. Fear a cold metallic taste on her tongue, she peered into the gloom, her eyes slowly adjusting to the darkness.

One of the elders must've visited the chapel, for a blaze of candles lit the side altar, the glow thrown by their flickering light not enough to dispel the murkiness, but enough to soothe her a wee bit.

Puzzlement drew her brows together.

She'd not known anyone else lit candles for Lileas.

Hoping to steady her nerves, she drew in a deep breath of the stale, incense-laden air. Another scent, faint and oddly familiar, came along with the fustiness.

A feminine yet dark note not quite blended into the chapel's mustiness and the damp chill of wet stone. Again, the sense that she wasn't alone sent icy shivers tumbling down her spine and lifted the fine hairs on the nape of her neck.

Taking her lower lip between her teeth, she scanned the shadows. Something stirred, an air current or perhaps her very own nerves, but a distinct swishing noise quickly followed. Jerking her head toward the sound, Isolde screamed.

Her dead sister, shroud-wrapped and cowled, was rising from the cold stone floor in front of the side altar!

"Do not be afraid, 'tis only me," Lileas said, her beloved voice smoother, huskier than in life. Death had made her more voluptuous than Isolde remembered, too.

The wraith glided toward her with fluid grace, her black

shroud swirling 'round her, a dark, feminine scent wafting ahead of her to drift around Isolde like an exotic cloud.

A rich, musky fragrance the unassuming Lileas would ne'er have favored.

"Do not look at me as if you've seen a ghost, my lady," the specter said, shoving the cowl back off her face. "'Tis me, Evelina."

Relief washed over Isolde in great waves. "On my life, but you frightened me, lady."

Evelina smoothed her raven tresses, then carefully adjusted the cowl's folds around her shoulders. "I've told you, I am not a lady, but it warms my heart when you address me thus." She gave Isolde a gentle smile. "'Tis good of you."

"W-whatever are you doing here?" Isolde gasped, her blood still pumping furiously. "You're the last person I'd expected to see."

"In your chapel or at Dunmuir?"

"Both," Isolde said honestly.

Evelina gave a little shrug. "Naught is impossible if one is discreet." She gestured to the enveloping black mantle and hood she wore. "No one's sensitivities were injured."

"I didn't mean . . ." Isolde folded her arms against the hot shame swelling in her breast. "You are welcome here. I have told you that."

Evelina's smile turned rueful. "I know you have, and I honor you for it."

Her pulse finally back to normal, Isolde glanced at the row of candles burning on the side altar. "You lit them?"

The older woman nodded. "Someone was kind enough to tell me you come here to pray for your sister. So I said a few prayers for her while I waited."

Isolde sighed. "Thank you."

Evelina touched her hand lightly to Isolde's sleeve. "Many were the good things I have heard of Lileas," she said, a wistful note creeping into her voice. "I wish I could have known her."

"But you did not come here to speak of my sister."

"Nay, I did not. I came because I must speak with you," Evelina said, her voice rife with concern. She grasped Isolde's hands. "Pray forgive me for speaking out of turn, but I would beg you not to send your message to Balloch MacArthur."

Isolde gasped in surprise. "But . . ." She let her voice trail off, too embarrassed to voice the probing questions tickling her tongue.

The joy woman had no such compunction. "But how did I gain such privy knowledge?"

"You know what the message is?" Discomfiture inched up Isolde's throat.

"Why else would I be so concerned?" Evelina released Isolde's hands. "I came straightaway after I heard. MacArthur is a violent man." She glanced away, but Isolde caught the way her jawline had tightened upon mentioning Balloch's name.

"You . . . ah . . . you know him?"

"I *knew* him, yes." Evelina looked back at her, and her beautiful dark eyes appeared dulled. "But only once. That was more than enough."

"I am sorry." Isolde touched her hand to the other woman's sleeve, much as Evelina had sought to comfort her a moment before.

"It happened long ago and is best forgotten." Evelina's eyes gleamed with a hint of moisture. "But I thank you for caring."

"You didn't say how you learned of my message?"

Evelina's gentle smile returned. "How do you think old Devorgilla thought to speed your tidings clear to MacArthur's distant isle?"

"You?" Isolde stared at her, then recalled Evelina telling her Gavin MacFie kept her supplied with provisions. "But Sir Gavin—"

"Aye, Sir Gavin is hindered." Evelina waved a dismissive hand when Isolde made to protest. "There are other, shall we say, former friends who look after my needs. Any one of them would be gladful to help me deliver a missive."

She fixed Isolde with a piercing look. "'Tis I who would rather not be entrusted with the task." Moving away, she took to pacing in front of the side altar, the hem of her cloak rustling about her ankles like a shifting black cloud.

A storm cloud.

She lifted a hand in supplication, then let it fall. "Sending such tidings to a man like Balloch will have naught but the gravest consequences for you."

Isolde clasped her hands before her. She could not let the other woman sway her. "Nor do I like voicing falsehoods, but if I do not, he will send his man to arrange our betrothal within the month. I cannot allow that to happen."

"And you purport to avoid this man's coming by sending word to Balloch you carry another man's child?" Evelina's beautiful face mirrored her concern. "Lady, he shall be livid. Naught would bring him here faster. Balloch MacArthur is a proud man."

Isolde glanced at the place where her sister's body had lain, her heart aching at the memory of Lileas waxen and silent. The image forever etched in her mind. Poor, sweet-tempered Lileas had looked as if she merely slept and would awaken any moment.

But she hadn't, and would no more.

And her death had set Isolde's own life on a course she'd fast lost control of. Sighing, she pressed the tips of her fingers to her temples and closed her eyes. Heavy silence filled the chapel, its weight pushing hard on her shoulders.

A tangible burden, thick, cloying, and interspersed only with the deep rumbling of thunder and the pounding of her own heart.

At last, she opened her eyes and met Evelina's troubled gaze. "His pride is my sole hope," she conceded. "The elders plan to execute Donall MacLean on or around the Summer Solstice." Isolde's blood ran cold at the thought. "He and I have not yet . . . there is not enough time for me to . . . t-to truly become . . ."

She let her words die and began pacing just as Evelina had done moments before, her footsteps tapping loudly on the stone-flagged floor.

"It is my hope, if Balloch is told I swell with another man's seed, his pride will stay his tongue." She paused before the altar, absently smoothing wrinkles in the black cloth still draped there in Lileas's honor. "I am certain he will forfeit the betrothal once such word reaches him."

"I see." Evelina's tone was anything but encouraging.

"But you do not share my conviction his pride will keep him away?" Isolde kept her gaze trained on the altar cloth and the flickering candles.

"No, I do not," Evelina said, confirming what Isolde had expected her to say.

Isolde turned back to her. "Will you still see the message delivered?"

Evelina paused a long moment before she nodded. "If you so wish, aye."

"I do," Isolde said, wishing she hadn't seen the shadow that had crossed the other woman's face as she'd uttered the two words.

"Then so be it," Evelina said, and came to stand before her. Though her dark eyes were sorely troubled, she managed one of her gentle smiles.

The sight of it tugged at Isolde's heart. Hot moisture

jabbed into the backs of her eyes. Blinking, she reached for Evelina's hand. "I thank you," she said. "Someday I shall repay your kindness."

Evelina's own eyes gleamed then, and she glanced away as if embarrassed by showing emotion. "You already have," she murmured. "A thousandfold."

But her quiet dignity soon returned, and she pulled her hand from Isolde's grasp to retrieve a small leather pouch from the folds of her cloak. She handed it to Isolde. "This is the blush of rose I mentioned to you. Use it as I advised, and you should be able to hasten your progress with the MacLean."

Blush of rose.

Isolde's fingers closed around the little pouch. She could feel the small jar it contained. *Vermilion.* Red-tinted goose fat scented with rose.

A whore's paint to be dabbed on one's nipples.

A sure way of striking powerful lust into any man's loins, Evelina had promised when they'd discussed the myriad methods Isolde could employ to seduce Donall the Bold.

Blush of rose.

Just the feel of the tiny container in her hand made her blush scarlet.

"You must use it," Evelina encouraged. "Especially now."

Isolde swallowed thickly, but nodded.

Evelina placed the back of her hand against Isolde's hot cheek. "The sooner he succumbs, the better your chances, my lady."

And if I succumb?

The words echoed boldly in Isolde's heart, loud and frightful as the cracking thunder renting the night. As if she'd heard them, too, Evelina arched an elegant black brow. "If you well please him, you might find he pleases you as well."

Embarrassed, Isolde shifted her feet. Her face, her entire being, grew warmer by the minute. Soon, she'd be glowing brighter than a well-dipped resin torch.

Evelina drew a deep breath.

"I must go," she said, taking her hand from Isolde's cheek. She made to move away, but Isolde caught her arm.

"You cannot leave in this storm. Stay the night here, I will order a meal and—"

"Thank you, but I have already been offered a fine pallet for the night, and even a hearty repast," Evelina said, an odd catch in her voice. "I wish you well with the MacLean," she added, then made for the door.

Her hand on the latch, she paused and looked back. "Never forget, the road to the greatest happiness is sometimes fraught with peril and ofttimes the longest we must traverse." Her words sailed straight at Isolde's heart, as she'd no doubt intended.

As if she knew they'd found their target, she gave Isolde one last little smile. "Know, too, my lady, the rewards we reap at journey's end are worth more than a king's ransom."

That said, she stepped out the door and closed it soundly behind her.

Donall grunted as the largest wave yet slammed into his ribs. "Christ's wounds!" he swore, blinking hard against the stinging wetness in his eyes. "Saints, Maria, and Joseph!" he cursed again as an even greater roller crashed over him.

Sputtering, he tossed his head in a vain effort to clear his vision. Not that he cared to see how much higher the tide had risen since the storm's full fury had broke about an hour before.

Lashing rain slanted sideways through the ruined broch's

sea entrance. Cold and hard as steel pellets, the blinding sheets of rain sliced into him with a force to rival the waves sweeping into the dungeon with ever greater ferocity.

Squinting, he glanced out at the open sea and saw ... naught. Only blackness. Roiling, surging water, and jagged bolts of lightning slashing across the angry night sky.

Summoning all his might, he clung to the cold, wet chain stretched taut above his head. Using his shoulder and arm muscles, he heaved himself above the tossing waves. Screwing his eyes shut against the bite of the salt water, he prayed to all his patron saints.

And a few others as well.

If the lightning didn't soon claim him, the furious surf would. Either way, if the wench's two buffoons didn't soon haul him out of this hellhole, he'd not have to send prayers heavenward much longer. He'd be able to make his felicitations in person.

Fetch him down.

The three words boomed in the darkness. Strong, commanding, and sweet in Donall's ears.

Too sweet.

For they were promptly swallowed by the roar of the sea and the fierce howl of the wind. A figment of his imagination or mayhap the taunt of a sea sprite, eager to claim yet another mortal man's fast-approaching demise.

"Make haste!" the voice came again, oddly familiar, though not belonging to the two dolt-headed guardsmen.

But, of a certainty, a *human* voice.

Not a sea siren lusting to pull him into her watery clutches.

"See to it. Now!" the voice commanded, and Donall muttered a prayer of thanks.

He'd make his felicitations to the revered saints at a later date ... one more suitable to his inclinations.

Hoping his relief didn't show, he craned his neck toward the voice and opened his burning eyes to narrow slits. Three male figures moved about on the sea ledge. The two buffoons, and another man. He couldn't make out the third clearly enough to discern his identity.

They'd thrust torches into the wall brackets, and the sputtering flames leaped and danced in the wind, casting an orange-red glow on the dungeon's rough, wet walls, and o'er themselves as well.

Three firedrakes risen from the depths of hell itself, but looking sweeter than heaven's holiest host of angels as two of them hurried down the steep flight of steps, then plunged into the surf, making straight for him.

And he'd be damned if he'd say thank you.

Not to *them*.

Fixing his features into a mask of indifference, Donall awaited their approach.

"Don't try to look grateful, you whoreson bastard," Rory groused the instant he reached his side. Glowering fiercely, the lout thrust his arms below the foam-capped waves, grumbling to himself as he fumbled to free Donall's chain from the weights that had held him aloft since daybreak.

The giant slogged up to them a moment later. He, too, glared at Donall. "It would seem you have more than one friend abovestairs," he said, and wrapped his great arms around Donall's waist, catching him just as the chain gave way, thus saving Donall from plunging beneath the waves.

"I'd rather push your ugly face under the water than haul you out of here," Niels swore, grabbing Donall's upper arm in a fierce hold the same instant Rory seized his other arm.

Together, they dragged him through the surf and up the slick stone steps to the ledge. Still holding fast to his arms, they drew him before the third man. *He* handed Donall a coarse drying cloth, then swirled a warm, woolen blanket around Donall's shoulders.

For the space of a heartbeat, Donall considered tossing both the drying cloth and the blanket into the sea, but his sheer will to persevere, and escape, vanquished any such foolhardy behavior.

Standing as straight as his numbed and aching body would allow, he ground the drying linen into his eyes until most of the stinging subsided. Then he opened them and recognized his unlikely savior.

He was none other than the stone-faced blackguard who'd so arrogantly placed himself in front of the air slit on Donall's first day of captivity. The youngest of the graybeards, the one Isolde called Lorne.

The man stood straight and proud, every bit as arrogant as before, but something else lurked in the backs of his eyes.

Something indefinable.

"You," Donall said, naught else.

The graybeard gave him a curt nod. "I am Lorne," he said, then glanced at Rory and Niels. "Fetch him water.

"*Fresh* water," he added as Rory stalked away.

While the pock-faced oaf dipped a cup into a wooden bucket set on the ground near the entrance to the mural passage, Lorne glanced at Donall's hands.

They shook.

Donall pressed his lips together and tried to still the shaking, but his hands were too numb from the chill, too weak from supporting his body weight for countless hours as he'd dangled from the ceiling.

"Help him." Lorne gave Rory a sharp look when he returned with the water cup.

Rory's face suffused with indignation, but he did as the elder bade him, and brought the cup to Donall's lips so he could drink.

The water, cool and sweet, flowed down Donall's throat, the most welcome libation he'd e'er imbibed. But the moment Rory took away the cup, he returned his attention to the graybeard. "To what honor do I owe your clemency?" he asked, cringing inwardly at the rasp in his voice.

Lorne's hard-set features didn't soften a whit. Nor did his stance. His broad shoulders thrown back, he held his hands clasped behind him and peered unblinking at Donall. The inscrutable glimmer still flickering in his eyes gave the only indication something had sparked his unusual show of consideration.

"Make no mistake, MacLean," he said, his deep voice imposing enough to be heard above the storm and the sea. "I yet hold you responsible for our lady Lileas's death, and you shall surely forfeit your life for the loss of hers, but I am a man of honor."

Donall lifted a brow. He wouldn't embarrass himself again by speaking with a voice that sounded more like a croaking frog than a man.

"And as such," Lorne continued, "I respect your valor. As a warrior, the warrior I once was." He drew a breath. "As a man, I revile you for your part in an innocent's murder, but my honor as an old knight myself will not allow me to see your strength of will and your astonishing endurance go unheeded."

Donall stared at him, too flummoxed to have commented even if his throat wasn't parched and hoarse.

After inclining his head in a nod one could almost deem respectful, Lorne turned to the two poltroons. "Take him to his friend's cell."

Rory's jaw dropped.

Niels pressed his lips into a tight seam and stared up at the dripping ceiling.

"But, sir," Rory protested. "The counc—"

"I will speak with the council," Lorne said. "See he receives a warm bath, his own garb, and decent victuals. Enough for himself and the MacFie."

"Holy alleluia," the giant swore, and raked a big hand through the wet tangle of his red hair.

Rory's face turned deep purple. "I would rather scratch the devil's backside."

Having already dismissed them, the graybeard had been heading toward the entrance to the intra-mural passage, but he broke stride, turning slowly to face Rory and Niels.

The torchlight shining on his stern-set face revealed a trace of the commanding presence he must've been on the field of battle. "Do as you've been told," he said, and Donall knew instinctively that neither Rory nor the giant would defy him.

As if he knew it, too, Lorne glanced once more at Donall. "Do not give me cause to regret my lenience," he said.

And then he was gone.

Swallowed up by the orange-glowing mouth of the ruined broch's intra-mural passage.

Leaving Donall alone with the fair maid's volatile guardsmen.

Alone with them and his utter astonishment.

Chapter Eleven

✦

BY THE ROOD, Donall!" Gavin MacFie scrambled to his feet and came as far forward as his ankle chain would allow. "Saints be praised!" he cried, pulling Donall into a rough, comradely embrace.

"I thought you were dead. They wouldn't give me word of you." He released Donall, a broad smile lighting his beard-stubbled face.

Donall returned his friend's smile with a grin of his own. "There are varlets a-plenty here who'd savor naught more than to see me swing from a gibbet," he said, casting a glance at the two scowling churls affixing his chain to a heavy iron ring on the wall of Gavin's cell.

"But," he vowed with as much purposeful joviality as his hoarse voice would allow, "I refuse to oblige them."

"Pompous bastard," Rory snarled under his breath and jerked on the chain, testing the iron ring's hold. Apparently satisfied, he strode to the door. "Were it not for our misguided ladyship, I'd smash my fist into your jeering mouth until you spit out every last one o' your teeth."

"Cool your temper," the giant admonished him, stepping aside to admit a stream of wide-eyed kitchen lads, each carrying a bundle of some sort in their scrawny arms. "Summer Solstice is fast upon us. Soon the crows will be picking his bones clean."

"Oh, aye?" Gavin balled his hands to fists. "Give me my blade and we'll see whose carcass ends as carrion fodder."

Donall leaned against the rough-masoned wall and feigned a look of detachment. Lifting his hand, he pretended to examine his knuckles. "You ken what they say, Gavin. A dog who barks overmuch does so because he cannot bite."

Gavin tossed back his shaggy reddish-brown hair and laughed. To Donall's amazement, even the giant's lips twitched a bit before he caught himself. Rory sputtered, his eyes blazing with such fury it wouldn't have surprised Donall to see steam shoot from his ears.

"Say your prayers, you whoreson knave," Rory seethed, whipping out his dirk. He took one menacing step forward before the aged knight, Donall's unlikely champion, entered the cell, his thick brows drawn together in a near solid line.

"Becalm yourself, lest I am tempted to have you muck out the cesspit," he said to Rory. Grim-faced, he took up a position by the door, hands propped against his hips, his still-muscular legs planted apart.

He slanted a pointed glance at the double-edged dirk in Rory's hand. "Sheathe it."

"Ram it down his gullet is what I'd like to do," Rory groused. With a last, outraged glower at Donall and Gavin, he jammed his blade into the leather holder at his belt, and stomped out the door.

"See he cools his blood," Lorne said to the giant, then inclined his leonine head toward the door in a clear gesture for Niels, too, to exit the cell.

Niels obliged him, ducking beneath the doorway's low

lintel to disappear into the dimness of the passage beyond. The kitchen lads scurried after him, clearly relieved to make a hasty retreat.

The moment their collective footfalls faded, Donall let himself sag a bit more heavily against the cold stone wall. If the stony-faced graybeard didn't soon hie himself away as well, he might not be able to maintain the pretense of invincibility much longer.

He glanced at the pallet the kitchen lads had hurriedly assembled for him. Though fashioned of naught finer than a coarse linen sack stuffed with straw and dried bracken, topped with a worn-looking blanket, its dubious comforts beckoned as his own noble four-poster at Baldoon had ne'er done.

Saints, but he was weary.

Scowling as darkly as he could—to hide his pain—he expelled a deep, hopefully not so glaringly ragged breath. By God's good grace, his hands no longer trembled, but as if some vicious demon of rascality sought to test his limits, the instant his hands had ceased shaking, his fool knees had gone weak on him.

Wobbly.

They knocked and shook with a fervor he feared would soon make more clatter than the storm raging outside the cell's wee excuse for a window.

Sure enough, Lorne's gaze flicked briefly to Donall's knees. His heavy-browed eyes widened imperceptibly, but naught else signaled he'd noticed aught amiss.

He simply gave Donall a curt nod. "Victuals should arrive anon, and later a bath." Gesturing to the cloth bundles lined against the far wall, he added, "Your clothes. Everything is there. Untouched, save your weapons. I can do naught else for you."

"You can let us—" Gavin halted in midsentence at Donall's warning glance.

Ignoring Gavin's puzzlement, Donall returned the graybeard's nod. "'Tis enough, and appreciated," he said, astounded by his own words. Amazed his lips had held back the snide rebuff dancing on the tip of his own tongue, and replaced them with pure frippery.

Grudgingly spoken, but were he wholly honest, not without respect. And in keeping with the odd rules of chivalry that existed among those who'd once knelt to take the coveted blow of honor. Enemies or nay.

"Then, sirs, I bid you a good night." He acknowledged their knightly bond with a stiff bow, then took his leave.

Gavin blew out his breath on a gusty sigh. "Who the devil was that?"

"A friend." The answer came from someplace so deep inside Donall even he couldn't fathom its reasoning. "Do not ask me why, but I believe he is a friend."

"But not one well disposed enough to free us?" Gavin sank back onto his pallet.

"I rather think not," Donall said honestly, and sought out his own resting place.

"And who is the 'misguided ladyship' the pock-faced cur referred to?" Gavin wanted to know. "The fetching MacInnes chieftain perchance?"

Donall slanted a sideways glance at his friend. As he'd suspected, an odd glimmer of amusement shone in Gavin's hazel eyes.

A look Donall knew well.

And dreaded.

Or would if the MacFie's glib tongue and sunny charm of manner had not oft taken the sting out of many an awkward situation.

The man was a veritable font of good cheer.

A loyal friend and skilled warrior, oddly blessed with more uncanny insight than the most far-seeing henwife.

At times.

And Donall sorely hoped this was not one of them.

In case it was, he busied himself . . . a method sometimes successful in staving off Gavin's launches into uninvited philosophical discourses. Pretending great care, Donall flicked out the woolen blanket Lorne had provided, and smoothed its scratchy warmth over his outstretched legs.

Gavin cleared his throat.

Loudly.

Grimacing, Donall steeled himself for the good-natured jab he knew was about to come his way.

"The incessant plucking of your fingers on that moth-eaten rag gives you away, my friend." Gavin began tapping his chin with steepled fingers. "So she *is* the lady Isolde."

"What do you know of her?" Donall shot back before he could cloak his words with a cool layer of aloofness.

Warming to his topic, Gavin stretched his arms and deftly cracked his knuckles. "Some claim a fairer maid ne'er graced these isles."

Donall leaned his head against the wall. "She is passable."

"You've *seen* her?" Gavin sat forward, keen interest sparking in his eyes. "Faith, but you are e'er a fortunate buffoon," he said, but cheerily, wholly without malice. "I've had naught to leer at but these miserable walls."

"I haven't been leering," Donall snapped, inexplicably annoyed by Gavin's word choice.

"Ahhhh . . ." The corners of Gavin's mouth tilted in a crooked smile. "So that is the way of it."

"The 'way' of it is far outwith the bounds of anything even one possessed of your rife imagination could dream up." Donall pinched the bridge of his nose. "You would not believe me if I told you."

"Compel me to try." Gavin rested his arms on his up-drawn knees.

"Pray desist, Gavin. 'Tis woefully exhausted I am, and would but sleep." Donall closed his eyes. "You'll soon learn the nature of my involvement with the lady."

"Sleep?" Gavin leaned sideways and poked his fingers into Donall's ribs. "Don't dare even think to do so after making such a statement. What manner of involvement are you enjoying with her?"

Donall's eyes snapped open. "By the devil's arse, Mac-Fie, do I *look* as if I've been enjoying myself?"

Gavin rubbed his bristly chin. "Wet and disgruntled-looking as you are, I'd say you *were* enjoying yourself. Mayhap trysting with her in the sea?" His voice hummed with merriment. "And now you are vexed because the storm broke, thus wresting you apart?"

"Would that I hadn't asked you to tender an opinion." Shutting his eyes again, Donall sought the sweet oblivion of sleep.

The saints knew he needed the rest.

But Gavin's lopsided grin and good cheer, despite the graveness of their plight, crept insidiously beneath his closed lashes, stealing Donall's sleep, and his ire.

Reminding him why he loved the MacFie as if they truly were brothers, and not merely fostered ones.

Cracking his eyes a slit, he slanted a sidelong glance at the grinning lout. "Saints, 'tis glad I am to see you," he said, and dragged a hand through his hair.

Gavin's smile flashed even brighter. Leaning across the space between their pallets, he gave Donall a friendly whack on the shoulder. "And I you."

"Owww . . ." Donall winced.

"God's teeth!" Gavin's face paled. "What have they done to you?"

"All manner of villainies," Donall sighed, struggling to keep his eyelids from drifting shut.

Villainies, and a bounty of such exquisite tortures I can think of scarce else.

Gavin fell back against the wall. He dragged a hand down his face and blew out a long breath. "My God, but I am sorry," he said. "Jesting about wenches and such frivolity. I but meant to cheer you."

"And you did . . . *do*." Donall gently rubbed his shoulder as he spoke. "Already, my heart is lighter."

"Do you wish to speak of it?"

"Mayhap later." Pushing those lush charms from his mind as best he could, Donall filled his lungs with the invigorating scent of rain and salt spray.

But even the brisk storm-washed air streaming through the cell's small, squarish window couldn't fully cleanse her from his thoughts.

"When later?"

"Perhaps after they've brought the supper and bath they've promised," Donall said, readjusting the woolen plaid over his legs. "But be warned, you will think I've taken up the bardic arts and am spouting the most outrageous tale when you hear what I've been about."

"Where have they been keeping you?" Gavin prodded, his all-seeing gaze, sharp and keen, flitted from Donall's plaid-covered legs to his still-dripping hair. "Do not tell me they've taken their twisted pursuit for revenge so far they've kept you bound on a rock in the sea?"

Donall cocked a brow at his friend. "'Twas nigh as debauched," he confirmed. Seeing no purpose in evasion, he expelled a long sigh, then described the old broch's sea dungeon and how he'd spent his days suspended by a chain from its dripping ceiling.

"By all the saints and prophets!" Gavin's light green eyes widened.

Donall gave a bark of mirthless humor. "I vow such venerable worthies deserted this end of Doon centuries ago, my friend."

Glancing around the tiny, stone-walled cell, he added, "'Tis glad I am they've rendered you a less odious form of hospitality. No slime-coated walls, nor slithering creatures breeding in fouled floor rushes."

"Upon my word, they've gone too far—"

"Aye, too far indeed," Donall agreed, his sufferings in the wretched confines of his first cell, and even in the sea dungeon, farther from his mind than the splendor of the late Bruce's court and all the fine and willing wenches he'd bedded there.

Setting his mouth into a grim line, he fell silent and fixed his gaze on the dancing flames of the resin torch Lorne had thrust into an iron bracket near the door.

The torchlight gave off a soft, buttery glow. A pool of comfort amidst the deep shadows. A warm contrast to the cold silver light bursting into the cell with each new crack of thunder.

A bright golden flame in a sea of darkness.

The same burnished gold as the wench's braids.

The same leaping fire he knew coursed through her veins.

Unbridled passion she didn't even know she possessed. *Until he showed her.*

Donall started, then shot a quick glance at Gavin. Saints, he must've drifted to sleep . . . he didn't know whether he'd muttered those words, or if they only circled through his consciousness, taunting and teasing him . . . just like the fair maid who'd inspired them.

"What did you say?" came Gavin's too-innocent-sounding voice. "I cannot hear you above the thunder if you persist in mumbling beneath your breath."

Donall grimaced. He needn't see the MacFie's all-knowing gloat to ken he'd indeed spoken aloud. And, regrettably, loud enough to be heard.

"I said, 'Wait until you hear where I've spent my nights,'" he said, trying to make the best of his slip.

"You spent them elsewhere?"

Now he truly had Gavin's full attention.

"Aye." Keeping his gaze lowered, deliberately away from his friend's prying eyes, Donall tucked the warm blanket more firmly around his legs. They *still* trembled. Or at least his knees did.

And ne'er had he been more cold.

Or exhausted.

A warm bath would be the finest bliss.

"Did they torture you nights?" Gavin coaxed, and Donall didn't dare look at him. He could hear his friend's wild imagination gearing up for a full assault.

Hard fingers poked into Donall's ribs again.

Donall raked a hand down his face in sheer frustration. When he'd banished enough of his vexation to meet Gavin's probing gaze, he sent the lout a fierce glower.

"Aye, I have been plagued evenings as well," he admitted. "And those trials proved a far worse torment than that which they inflicted on me by day."

Gavin tilted his shaggy head to the side. "Why do I think you are referring to the lady chieftain?"

Donall glared at him, his lips compressed into a tight line. Saints above, but Gavin could read a man's mind. He wouldn't be surprised if the knave could peer through the stoutest of Baldoon's walls.

Gavin's crooked grin emerged. "Aye, why can't I shake the feeling you are referring to her?"

Donall expelled the breath he'd been holding.

"Because," he said, acceding his friend's sound victory, "I *am* referring to her."

He wasn't coming.

Isolde bit down on her lower lip and tried not to think about the lateness of the hour. It was well past matins, deep into the small hours. Even the raging storm had passed, its bluster gone, blown away to haunt its terrors upon another unsuspecting corner of the night.

But while the wrath of Devorgilla's so accurately predicted gale had lessened, leaving only a damp chill and the soft patter of a lingering drizzle in its wake, the turmoil whirling through Isolde increased with each beat of her thumping heart.

Intensified with each long, agonizing moment of waiting for Rory and Niels to usher *him* into her chamber for the night.

For lessons in . . . *enlightenment.*

For more knightly kisses.

She stared at the fine silver candelabrum gracing her table. A treasure she'd secretly resurrected from her parents' old chamber, a room void of life since her da's passing. A dark place filled with cobwebs and memories.

And a few fine things like the candelabrum.

A frown creasing her brow, she smoothed her fingers over its gleaming silver base. She'd spent an hour polishing it to its former glory, even seeking out sweet heathery-scented beeswax tapers . . . all to impress the MacLean.

But he hadn't come.

And like the candles, no longer elegant and glowing, but ugly clumps of misshapen wax guttering deep in their sockets, her hopes for the night, too, had died a humbling death.

At least she'd dined well.

As had Bodo.

Naught but the thin rind of her trencher remained of the fine meal she'd assured they'd partake of this eve. She'd even ordered Cook himself to deliver the victuals, not trusting Rory should Devorgilla accost him along the way, outsmarting him with more of her meddlesome trickery.

Aye, she'd supped well.

But she hadn't been kissed like a knight kisses.

With a deep sigh, she pushed to her feet. For the hundredth time that night, she crossed the bedchamber, opened the door, and stole a glance down the long, shadow-filled hall.

The long, shadow-filled, *empty* hall.

Her hands clenching to fists, she vowed to have words with Niels and Rory first thing on the morrow. Neither of the good men had deigned to tell her why the MacLean hadn't been brought to her.

Furious at herself for caring, she shut the door again, and leaned her back against its solidness. A hard, unbending firmness that instantly reminded her of the hard, well-muscled plane of Donall the Bold's broad chest.

"Bats' wings and frogs' toenails!" She borrowed one of the *cailleach*'s pet curses, and leaped away from the door.

Foolish twaddle or nay, uttering the crone's oath made her feel good.

Faith and mercy, she'd even painted her nipples for the arrogant Lord Good-Kisser!

Heat flooding her cheeks—and other unnamed places as well—she snatched up the little pot of blush of rose and glared at it. Had she truly thought to stand before Donall the

Bold wearing the see-through camise Evelina had foisted upon her, her nipples red-tinted and thrusting at him through the gown's shimmering bodice?

Aye, she had.

And the admission sent her sailing around the chamber, following the circular track her constant pacing had worn in the freshly-strewn floor rushes. Bodo watched her from his bed, his head resting on his forepaws, his eyes puzzled.

Sympathetic.

Only she didn't crave sympathy.

Not even from her wee Bodo.

A dark scowl, worthy of the magnificent Donall the Bold himself, pulled her brows together and her lips downward.

Lips that ached to be kissed.

Her circuitous route took her past the bedpost.

His bedpost.

Unable to help herself, she paused long enough to trail her fingers down its intricately carved length.

Smooth, hard, and cool oaken wood . . . perfection.

Like him.

Her fingers curled tighter around the pot of vermilion. Its earthen coolness in her palm restored her wits. It was the man's coolness, too, upon which she must dwell. Not his bonnie smiles and the occasional warmth in his liquid brown eyes.

And most especially not the mastery of his touch.

His kiss.

'Twas *she* who meant to seduce.

And would.

She need only cling to his one imperfection . . . the cold stain of Lileas's blood. A great, wracking shudder . . . *shame* . . . washed over her. Even *that* damning thought couldn't quite dispel the desire she felt for him, the need he'd awakened in her.

Feeling utterly defeated, she released a long, deep sigh.
The little pot of blush of rose slipped from her fingers. She
almost bent to retrieve it, but a great weariness propelled her
toward her bed instead.

With shaking fingers, she grasped the heavy bed curtains
and eased them farther aside before she slowly divested herself of her black mourning gown and Evelina's scant slip of
an undertunic.

She'd scrub the paint from her nipples on the morrow.

One last time, she let her fingertips glide down the
carved swirls of her bedpost.

The bedpost.

His bedpost.

Then, before her feet carried her to the door for yet another fruitless peep into the silent corridor, she doused the
candle stumps, and climbed into the dark recess of her
empty bed.

Not that she expected to sleep.

Nay, she'd likely spend the remainder of the night doing
what she was already doing: lying on her back, fully unclothed save the vermilion staining the peaks of her breasts,
the many layers of coverlets pulled to her chin, staring at the
bed's canopy, and wishing her evening had been filled with
knightly kisses.

In a dark and quiet corner of Dunmuir, a *hidden* corner
where naught but the damp scent of rain and the earthy musk
of spent lust could intrude, Evelina breathed a soft sigh of
pleasure, and allowed herself to be pulled more snugly into
her old knight's arms.

Sated and content, she toyed idly with the smattering of
gray hair on his broad chest, and pressed sweet kisses into
the warm hollow where his neck joined his shoulders.

The age-worn warrior gave a well-satisfied moan of his

own, and smoothed his calloused hand down the curve of her hip. "Ne'er have I known more contentment than holding you," he vowed, skimming his fingers along her thigh before letting them brush lightly over her damp intimate curls, toying with them in the same lazy manner she moved her own fingers over his chest hair.

"And now that you've spent yourself once, you mean to be content with merely holding me?" Evelina purred, parting her thighs to invite a more thorough exploration.

Her lover obliged, dipping his hand deeper between her legs, no longer gently, but firm and demanding, palming her dampness with a rough, circular motion until she arched her hips, pressing herself against his hand, opening her thighs even wider in unrestrained need.

"Taste me," she urged him, the words a command, but cushioned on a breathy sigh no man could possibly deny.

Her once-time knight didn't even think to. With a ragged moan, and an agility that belied his age but paid fine tribute to long years of physical training, he eased her onto her back, and settled himself at the core of her sweetness, gladly partaking of all she offered him.

And he didn't lift his gray-shot, thick-maned head until he'd coaxed every sigh, every sweet shiver out of her. Sighs, shivers, and the most thunderous release he could give her.

With a deep, satiated sigh of his own, the old knight stretched out beside her on the simple pallet and drew her back into the circle of his arms. "You are my life, Evelina," he said, and she stiffened.

"You must not speak such foolery," she warned, a tremor rippling down her back.

A tremor she hoped he'd mistake for the last, lingering vestiges of her release.

"*Foolery?*" He lifted up on his elbow to peer down at her, and the fire in his eyes made her wince. Snatching the end of the worn plaid, he swirled it over her lush curves, protecting her from the chill damp of their trysting place. "You dare call my feelings for you thus?" he demanded, smoothing the blanket in place.

She sighed and gave him a wistful smile. "Not your feelings, dear heart," she said, smoothing a lock of coarse, brown-gray hair off his damp forehead. "Never your feelings."

"Then what, by God?" His voice came deep and harsh against the gentle patter of rain and the low, rhythmic snores of those sleeping on their pallets not far away, blessedly ignorant of the two lovers nestled in a dark, secluded niche tucked in a corner of the slumbering hall.

"Leave be," she pleaded, touching her fingers to his lips. "It will serve no purpose to rile yourself."

"Then dinna rile me!" The aged knight grasped her hand in his, bringing the soft underside of her wrist to his lips for a scorchingly possessive kiss. "If you would not see me vexed, then have done with *your* fool notions and wed me."

Evelina sighed. "Do not make me regret I stayed the night here, my love."

"I would harry you with regrets to the gates of purgatory and back if it would help my cause," her lover vowed, his agitation thrumming in his voice, crackling in the chill, damp air between them. "I love you, Evelina. I am a man of honor, and would see you where you belong . . . as my lady wife, at my side."

Evelina's heart twisted. "It is *because* you are a man of honor, I will not marry you," she breathed, pulling on her own long years of "training" to cloak the pain it cost her to refuse him. "I will not see you scorned."

"Think you I care a whit what the tongue-waggers might say?"

"I am full aware you do not care," Evelina said, closing

her eyes against the hurt she knew she was putting into his. "'Tis *I* who care. Now, pray, be silent before all and sundry hear you ranting and discover us."

"Mayhap they should!" the old knight swore, his frustration palpable.

"Please, my love, be still, and let us glory in what we do have." Evelina slipped her hand beneath the blanket and began making slow, gentle circles on his heaving chest.

Soothing circles . . . she hoped.

"Becalm yourself, and let us sleep." She pressed a gentle kiss on his shoulder. "We have had a full night together. Our first. Let that be enough."

"It will never be enough," her lover murmured, but already his breathing slowed, and soon his quiet snores joined those of his sleeping kinsmen.

Only Evelina didn't sleep.

She simply awaited the dawn as she did on countless other sleepless nights.

Staring into the darkness, listening to the gentle fall of the rain and the soft sigh of the wind.

And, every once in a while, wiping the dampness from her eyes.

Chapter Twelve

⚜

*E*ARLY THE NEXT morning, Isolde sat stiffly in her chair at
the high table, her straight back pressed firmly against the
elaborately carved seat of honor, the laird's chair that had
once been her father's. The defiant angle of her chin her
only concession to the emotions warring within her, she listened to her uncle Struan expound on Lorne's intervention
in the treatment of Donall MacLean.

Intervention he dubbed a gross erring in judgment.

An intervention that explained why she hadn't received
further tutelage in the fine and noble art of knightly kissing.

Bodo's cold nose nudged her ankle, and she reached
down to stroke him, gladful of the comfort his presence afforded her. Grateful, too, for any excuse to turn aside, thus
hiding the warmth blossoming on her cheeks.

A blush brought on by the mere thought of Donall the
Bold's irrefutable kissing skills.

"Lorne, you have overstepped your authority." Struan's
booming voice rose to the smoke-blackened rafters and
echoed off the great hall's weapon-hung walls.

"And I say you overstep yours," Lorne countered, his own voice every bit as commanding as the war leader's. "We've already broken the code of hospitality, let us not further shame ourselves by disregarding the rights of—"

"Rights?" Struan half rose from his chair. "Have you grown so high-minded you think to confer *rights* on the blackguard?"

"He *is* a knight." Ailbert's thin voice chimed in. "Laird of Baldoon."

"Laird of Baldoon," Struan mimicked the white-haired elder before he sank back onto his chair. "He is a murderer who forfeited all vested rights granted to his class the moment our Lileas drowned on the Lady Rock."

"We cannot be certain the MacLeans did the deed." Isolde's pronouncement rang strange in her own ears, the statement surprising her as much as it had her council.

To a man, they gaped at her, slack-mouthed.

All save Niels and Rory.

Standing a short distance away, near the hearth fire, Niels averted his gaze. Rory showed no such discretion. He narrowed his eyes at her, his face dark, his hand on the hilt of his sword as if Donall the Bold and his army of stout-armed MacLean warriors might charge into the hall any moment, blades drawn, and tempers high.

A thrill of excitement shot through her at the thought of seeing the MacLean exercise his sword arm. If his mastery with a blade was aught near his skill at kissing, it'd be a fine sight to behold.

Her heart began a slow, hard thumping. The stirring image almost lulled her into the soothing fog of a pleasant daydream, and *would* have, did her uncle not call her name.

Blinking, she tore her gaze from Rory's sword. "Aye?"

Her uncle was staring at her. "Who do you think did?"

"Did what?" She blinked again, trying to rid herself of

the image of a bare-chested MacLean swinging his sword, his glossy black hair swirling just above his powerful shoulders, his magnificent form sweat-sheened and glorious.

"Where are your thoughts, girl?" Struan stared at her, his gaze laden with reproach. "If not the MacLeans, I would know who you think is responsible? One of the selkie people?"

A bark of laughter rose from the far end of the table. "The selkies? We'll have to ask Gavin MacFie about that. 'Tis said his people hale from a selkie woman!"

Struan silenced the upstart with a stern glance. To Isolde, he said, "Well, lass, who do you think did the deed if not Iain MacLean?"

"I know not," she admitted, her voice wooden. "Certainly not the seal people."

Near as disturbed by her sudden desire to believe Donall the Bold had naught to do with Lileas's death, as o'er the tragedy itself, she added, "I only know it couldn't have been MacKinnons. We would have seen them pass through our waters."

"But we did not, did we?" Struan lowered his voice for the first time since he'd upbraided Lorne. "We have lookouts watching MacKinnons' Isle every hour of the day and night." His hawkish eyes glowed with an inner fire. "Yet nary a galley of theirs—not even a single hide-covered coracle—has plied the sea in months."

"The MacKinnons have been feuding with us *and* the MacLeans for years, so a motive is there. They could have used stealth to reach Doon." Lorne's argument drew angry looks from the others.

Struan gave a derisive snort. "Only the veriest of innocents would believe thus."

Lorne shot to his feet. "You bray like a mule," he vowed, earning a titter from Ailbert. "With the exception of Lady Isolde, there isn't an innocent at this table. We are all possessed of our own vices and follies, my own self perhaps more than most."

Ribald chuckles rippled through the ranks of the elders. One or two of them jabbed their elbows into their table partners' ribs, and wry sidelong looks flew the length and breadth of the table.

Lorne swept the lot of them with a withering glare, then sat back down. "That the MacLean must do penance is without question. Grounds to suspect the MacKinnons exist but are slight. So long as no one amongst the MacLeans admits the act, their laird is honorbound to shoulder the blame."

His words chilled Isolde.

She'd hoped his show of lenience had meant he'd discovered something new, that he might speak out in favor of releasing Donall the Bold and his friend.

Taking an ale mug off the table, Lorne drained it. "Heedless of the MacLean bearing the guilt, my conscience as a belted knight will smite me cold if I do not condemn the disregard we've shown his gentled status."

"Since you're the only knight amongst us, I vow the rest of us are safe from being thus afflicted?" someone called.

A chorus of hoots and guffaws followed.

Struan helped himself to a deep draught of ale. "You are alone with your views, Lorne. The council sees no need to grace the MacLean with chivalric concern." He slammed down the tankard. "They crave a long and odious death. As do I."

"I am not gainsaying his demise," Lorne argued. "I would but enjoin you to consider the valor he has shown despite the agonies we've suffered upon him. His bravery and noble rank should be respected."

"Respect?" someone cried. "Noble rank? I dinna care if the ghost o' the Good King Robert Bruce hisself vouchsafes

the scoundrel's character. I say hie him back to the sea tower."

"Aye!" others agreed.

Lorne slammed his fist on the tabletop. The grumblings ceased. When the silence held, he gave a satisfied nod. "Let us not besmirch our good name by denying him a dry pallet to sleep on between now and his execution. I would ask naught else."

"Spoken with the eloquence of a limp-wristed courtier," someone muttered.

A mere whisper, but enough to put the fire of self-righteousness back in Struan's eyes. "Besmirch *our* good name?" He threw up his hands. "I vow you speak more like a woman than a tarse licker."

Isolde's sharp intake of breath was swallowed by Lorne's outraged roar. He pushed to his feet so quickly, his chair toppled over. His right hand, balled to a white-knuckled fist, hovered menacingly near his dirk. "Slander me thus again, and I shall kill you," he seethed. "Kinsman or nay."

"Do so, and you'd sully yourself with a darker stain than taints the MacLean." Lounging in his chair, Struan leveled an impervious stare at Lorne. "What would such a grievous sin do to your fabled sense of honor?"

Lorne's only response was the jerking of a muscle in his jaw.

"You do not know?" Struan flicked his fingers. "Cast your honor to the four winds is what it'd do."

Dark waves of anger rolled off Lorne, but after a painfully long moment, he unclenched his hands. "I shall keep my honor until I breathe my last," he said. "*You* would be wise to acquire some."

Pandemonium broke loose. Struan laughed. "You wax proud if you think to advise me what I ought or ought not acquire." He waved a careless hand at the assemblage. "Nor are we a company of gentles, gathered to sing praises for the supposed valor of a roistering devil the likes of Donall MacLean."

Several of the council members thumped their fists on the tabletop, others stamped their aged feet. All heartily voiced their accord.

Fickle faithless fools.

Isolde forced a tight little smile, a contrivance, but necessary to conceal her true purpose.

"We are here," Struan declared, his chest swelling, "to wreak vengeance on a man Lorne would have us admire simply because, like Lorne, he wears the spurs and belt of knighthood."

Beside her, Isolde could sense Lorne's ire churning inside him. Quite boldly, she slipped her hand onto his knee and squeezed. Blessedly, his tensed muscles relaxed a bit beneath her fingers.

"Conferred knighthood does not make a man," Struan thundered on. "The MacLean's vestments are no longer white as befitting those claiming such ennobled privilege, but soiled red with the spilled blood of one of our own."

Nods and grunts of approval rippled around the table, but a few mumbles about "Archibald" could be heard as well.

Struan sent a dark look in the direction whence the references to his brother had come. "Were Archibald here, he would not want us cozening the perpetrator of his daughter's death."

Lileas's sweet face rose up in Isolde's mind. Her guileless blue eyes loomed troubled, her pale lips moved in wordless distress, but whatever message she hoped to convey was lost. The fleeting image was overpowered by Struan's diatribe.

Struan stood. "Archibald would want us to protect his remaining daughter and we shall! To the death, if the good Lord so wills it."

His watery blue eyes clouding with a trace of perplexity, Ailbert lifted a hand. "How shall we protect her if the MacLeans attack?"

"Not by the bite of *your* blade." Struan shook back his coarse mane of rust-colored hair. "The MacLeans will not seek to avenge a death they'll think befell the wretch at sea."

"What if they wax suspicious?" Ailbert's grizzled chin jutted forward. "*Your* sword arm cannot be of much better use than mine."

Muted laughter erupted around the table. Struan glowered. "Am I surrounded by fools? '*How shall we protect her?*'" he groused. "Why do you think we're wedding her to MacArthur?"

Isolde's breath caught at the mention of the dread name, but she maintained an air of indifference. Ailbert pursed his lips, belligerence oozing out of every line in his wizened face.

"Dinna tell me you doubt the stoutness of Balloch's sword arm?" Struan carped at him. "The man has never been defeated."

"His braw arm will have to stretch a fair distance to defend these walls." Ailbert spread his hands in emphasis.

Isolde glanced at Lorne. He'd leaned forward and watched the exchange with growing interest.

"What fool twaddle is that?" someone asked. "Balloch has sworn to bring a whole company of warriors to man Dunmuir's ramparts."

Isolde's hand clenched on Lorne's knee.

"And so he will," Struan declared, reclaiming his seat. He lifted his tankard to his lips but paused in mid-sip when Ailbert rapped his walking crook against the table edge.

"By the devil!" he railed, spewing ale foam onto the table. "What ails you now, *Ail*bert?"

"I would know how we are to defend our lady," Ailbert piped, his reedy voice glazed with self-importance.

"MacArthur will bring neither his own nor his men's might to defend us."

Struan slammed down his tankard. "What prattle-monger has been filling your head with such tripe?"

"More than one." Ailbert met Struan's glare. " 'Tis claimed he'd be wise to keep his strength at home. His father will want all his men to guard their own holdings."

"From whom?" Struan's brows lifted. "Their isle is so remote, there's hardly any would care to claim it."

Ailbert drew back his bony shoulders. "The Sassenachs would."

Something flashed in Struan's eyes, and whatever it was, it lifted the fine hairs on the back of Isolde's neck. Her uncle appeared riled, but not surprised by Ailbert's comments.

"The English?" Struan snorted. " 'Tis bleating like an old goat, you are—full of stuff and nonsense. Edward of England signed a treaty two years ago. He will not be harrying our waters."

Ailbert shook his head. "The Treaty o' Northampton was signed before Robert Bruce died. Times are perilous now."

"Perilous for *you* if you do not cease spouting such drivel," Struan snarled.

Ailbert raised his walking crook in the air. " 'Tis the God's truth. My sword skills may not be what they once were, but I've still got my wits." He lowered his stick. "All of 'em!"

"Could have fooled me," Struan muttered.

Lorne expelled a long breath. "Ailbert speaks the truth. Many claim Edward Balliol would seek English aid to wrest the Scottish throne from young David's tender hands."

"Aye, and Edward the Third is granting him that support, and much of it," someone else tossed out. "The young English king is said to have his grandfather's success at arms. He'll prove a greater threat than his loose-hipped sire should he turn his attentions northward."

Ailbert puffed out his chest. "The MacArthur will want his men atop his own walls. Each last one o' them, most especially his son."

Lorne placed his hand on Isolde's shoulder. "Balloch has vowed to live here and reinforce Dunmuir."

A speculative gleam entered Struan's heavy-browed eyes. "If such tidings be true, should we not accommodate our lady's future husband in these perilous times?"

Isolde could feel the blood draining from her face. Surely Struan would not suggest she live with Balloch on *his* isle?

Not that she intended to live with him at all.

Lorne's hand tightened on her shoulder. "What are you suggesting, Struan?"

"Only that, a *suggestion*," he said, stroking his chin. "Mayhap our lady should reside at Balloch's holding after they've wed? He can better defend his father's walls, she is removed from marauding MacLeans, and we gain prestige by impressing on the MacArthurs what congenial allies we are."

He paused to draw a breath. "Once the Sassenach threat has passed, the happy twain can return to Dunmuir."

Stunned surprise held Isolde's protest firmly in her throat. Blessedly, Lorne spoke for her. Fixing an accusatory stare on Struan, he said, "Ne'er have I heard a more unblessed pack of fool ideas. The lady Isolde belongs here."

As one, the council sided with Lorne.

Startlingly unperturbed, Struan shrugged. "As the council deems," he said, waving a dismissive hand. "It was only a consideration."

"And so I wish it to remain." Isolde found her voice at last. "I also wish Donall the Bold to remain in Gavin MacFie's cell. I care not what is done to him days," she lied, "but I want him granted the respect a worthy man of the sword deserves. Friend or foe, doomed to die or nay."

She pushed to her feet. "Such is the way of our Isles,

how my father would have ruled, and"—she lifted her chin—"how I rule."

Her authority asserted, her gaze flicked from Struan's tight-lipped countenance to each of the other council members. Some gaped, some grinned. Ailbert tittered. All save her uncle had a spark of admiration in their eyes.

Admiration she didn't deserve.

She was an imposter whose fibbing tongue boasted more forks than the devil's own.

Quickly, before they noticed, she excused herself and exited the hall, Bodo scampering after her.

Bodo, and her pack of lies.

She *did* care what happened to Donall the Bold.

And she did not want him kept in Sir Gavin's cell.

She wanted him with her.

"You've a visitor."

Something about Rory's tone gave Donall a niggling notion just who the visitor was.

Who he *hoped* the visitor might be.

His eyes snapped open, the sleep he'd been chasing forgotten. The pock-faced guardsman filled the threshold, his feet pressing against the doorjambs, his meaty arms folded. He wore a scowl darker than the crack of the devil's arse.

Donall frowned, too.

'Twas easy enough to do, giddy as he was just knowing he'd see *her* again any moment. Giddified elation at the mere sniff of a wench's swishing skirts was a frightful enough state to vex any man.

A powerful urge to see Rory vexed as well assailed him, so he folded his arms behind his head and fixed the oaf with an impertinent stare. "Pray, who can it be?" he pretended to puzzle. "A priest to fumigate the cell with smoke of myrrh

or a well-skilled henwife with her basket of charms and in-
cantations?"

Donall could feel Gavin's sidelong stare, but couldn't
have swiped the taunts from his tongue if the sainted Holy
Mother herself asked him to. Watching the whore-dog bastard Rory sputter and fidget provided too costly an enter-
tainment to easily relinquish.

"I regret to tell you, neither are welcome," Donall called
to him. "Myrrh makes Gavin sneeze, and I ceased believing
in the dubious talents of self-professed wise women at the
ripe age of four."

Rory's hand flew to his sword. "Ingrate MacLean whoreson," he hissed.

Donall crossed his ankles and flashed his most winning
smile.

"Step aside, Rory." *Her* voice, soft and smooth as sweet
cream, came from behind the lout. "I cannot enter if you
would block the door."

Donall's heart leaped, knocking against his fool ribs with
all the abandon of a callow youth mooning after the first
doe-eyed, long-limbed lass to cast a coy smile his way.

*By the warts on my grandmother's nose, I ne'er thought
I'd see the day* . . . Donall thought he heard Gavin mumble
beside him, but his friend's words had as much a chance of
stealing his attention as Donall did of slipping his foot out of
the cold band of iron cuffed 'round his ankle.

She was slipping past Rory, and everything else in Donall's field of vision, and consciousness, faded. He hadn't
seen her in a full four days, and though he'd half convinced
himself she couldn't possibly be as fair as his fantasies
painted her, he now saw he'd gravely erred.

Isolde MacInnes was even more fetching than his most
wild imaginings.

"Lady," he said in greeting and pushed to his feet.

Gavin stood as well. "Gavin MacFie, my lady," he said, bowing respectfully. "I'd humbly offer you my devoted services, but"—he shrugged good-naturedly—"I fear I am in no position to be of use to you."

"Sir Gavin," she acknowledged, inclining her head. "Your name carries many badges of honor, and I regret we meet under these . . . circumstances."

"Sir Donall." She scarce looked at him.

The slight bit hard and deep.

The fool lopsided grin spreading across Gavin's face bit deeper. Donall shot the wretch a dark look, but Gavin was oblivious, wholly captivated by Isolde of Dunmuir's beauty and grace.

Donall frowned. He wouldn't be surprised if his gaping friend's eyes didn't soon glaze over, so thunderstruck did he stare at the wench.

She appeared oblivious, too.

Of Donall's rising irritation at being ignored, and even of having won Gavin's devotion with a smattering of flattery and a single glance from her amber-flecked eyes.

Without a further word, she headed for the small window opening, her black skirts swirling, her wildflower scent light and precious in the musty confines of the cell.

She stood looking out the window, her shoulders straight, her back proud. Her quiet dignity stirred his heart almost more than her lithesome form roused his blood. She held her hands clasped behind her, and Donall's gaze clung to the sight of them.

The memory of those slender fingers pressed against his chest, kneading his shoulders, then sifting through his hair during their shared kiss, sent shards of white-hot desire spiraling through him. His loins tightened with burning need.

Gavin stared, too, and Donall couldn't decide if his fingers itched more to throttle his friend's gawking neck, or to undo the two long braids hanging down Isolde's back.

Thick, satiny-looking, and glossed to a deep golden sheen by the torchlight, she hadn't coiled them 'round her ears in the ramshorn style she seemed to favor, but had let them swing free, their tips just grazing her hips.

"Saints a-mercy," Gavin whispered beside him, and clapped a hand roughly over his heart.

Donall scowled at him.

Any moment, the smitten knave would be on his knee reciting a love sonnet if Donall didn't soon intercede.

And so he did.

Promptly.

By jabbing his fingers into Gavin's ribs.

Unfazed, Gavin sidestepped Donall's reach, and continued to gape. It was a merry wonder his tongue didn't loll from his grinning lips!

Donall cleared his throat. "To what honor may I credit your visit, fair lady?" He leaned against the wall and affected a most unimpressed, *casual* pose, should she turn to face him . . . as he sorely hoped she would.

"Mayhap to discuss the merits of . . . *enlightenment*?" he added when she paid no heed to his first, more courtly, attempt at catching her attention.

Gavin shot him a look of rabid astonishment—for he now knew exactly what sort of "enlightenment" Donall had shared with her—and was no doubt amazed he'd have the cheek to utter the word in his presence.

His cheek stunned Donall, too. But her sheer proximity did strange things to his senses, and her silence frustrated him beyond all bounds, soundly chasing his chivalry out the window. Leaving behind naught but a raw urge to rile a reaction out of her.

She turned around. "I came to see Sir Gavin, not you."

Donall's heart seemed to lurch to an abrupt, jerky halt, and the hot pumping in his loins instantly cooled. *"Sir Gavin?"*

She averted her gaze. "Truth be told, I did not think you'd be here. I thou—"

"You thought I'd be off undergoing some new and devious form of agony at the hands of your two henchmen?" he finished for her, a new kind of heat surging through him.

The heat of anger.

"Well . . . aye," she possessed the boldness to confirm. "I wanted to speak to Sir Gavin about . . . about your brother."

"My brother? You wish to speak to Gavin about my brother?"

She nodded, then turned back to the window.

She couldn't look at him.

She'd almost fled back abovestairs when she saw he was shirtless. The last time she'd seen his bare chest, it'd been grimed with dirt from his first cell's muck-covered floor. Smeared so darkly, she'd scarce been able to discern where he began and that cell's murky shadows ended.

The sight of his naked chest free of grime, its well-muscled expanse cast a-glow by the torch flames, his sheer *magnificence* of form almost too overpowering to bear, taxed her composure more sorely than she could control.

Control, and voice the questions she must ask.

So she kept her back to them both, thus shielding herself from his dark beauty, his darker temper, and the strange way he made her feel.

Instead, she stared at the *other* source of her ill ease. Its looming presence devoured convictions she'd ne'er doubted, and left crumbs of meddlesome doubt in their place. A dark mass rising low above the horizon to taunt her:

MacKinnons' Isle.

Chapter Thirteen

✦

MacKinnons' Isle.

Its rugged coast gentled by distance, its stern-faced cliffs softened by the luminous glow of a Hebridean gloaming, the MacKinnon holding appeared scarce more threatening than a dark, elongated lump on the far horizon.

But the onerous burden it betokened for Isolde lay so near she tasted its foulness with each indrawn breath.

A taste more bitter than the lingering vestiges of Devorgilla's anti-attraction potion yet clinging to her tongue. Praise the saints, the crone had upped its potency.

Sadly, it still did not seem to work.

Or mayhap Donall the Bold's bare chest was simply too bonnie?

Isolde expelled a sigh. She'd simply pay no heed to his braw form or the pleasant flutters pulsing low in her belly since seeing him thus displayed. She'd keep her attention riveted on the one thing incapable of stirring her senses.

Stirring *those* senses.

She wet her lips with the tip of her potion-flavored tongue. "Have either of you looked out this window?" she asked, a chill working through her, blowing its icy breath on each corner of warmth the MacLean and his hard-muscled chest had kindled inside her. "Do you ken what lies on yon horizon?"

One of the men, she suspected *him*, gave a snort of derision.

"Some things need not be seen to ken they are there," he spoke up. "The weight of their influence alerts us to their presence, or in some cases, their . . . smell alerts us."

Isolde blinked at the double meaning of his oh-so-smoothly spoken words.

He'd noticed the potion and wanted her to know.

"Gracious lady," Gavin MacFie intervened, "I vow we would have looked out the window were we not manacled to your wall." A trace of mirth took the sting out of words that could have been ill understood if not spoken with such courtly grace.

A tiny smile curved Isolde's lips. Gavin MacFie was a gallant, and she was beginning to understand why Evelina thought so highly of him.

"Our chains are too short to permit us to enjoy whatever view so engages you," he added, and Isolde could almost hear the smile in his words.

She turned around. "The view is not one I favor, milord," she said, purposely keeping her gaze on Sir Gavin. "Nor is it one I can avoid. It greets me every morn."

"I vow you speak of the same view visible from your sea dungeon?" *he* drawled. "MacKinnons' Isle?"

Isolde nodded, the bitterness in his tone making her risk a glance at him.

Light from the resin torch played over his glossy, black hair and highlighted the width of his shoulders. "Upon my word," he said, his dark eyes intense, "you could not broach a topic that vexes me more."

"You wished to speak about Iain?" Sir Gavin cut in, ob-

viously trying to ease the tension crackling between her and
the MacLean.

She glanced at Gavin, half amazed at his sunny, indefati-
gable charm of manner. Almost as tall and well built as *him*,
a cheery sparkle lit his hazel eyes, while a spray of freckles
and his easy, lopsided smile made him seem years younger
than Donall even though they had to be of similar ages.

Isolde found herself smiling at him.

And trusting him.

"What would you know of Iain?" he asked.

Isolde drew a breath to speak, but before she could, *he*
shifted noisily on his pallet. "She has already been told all
she needs to know about him," he said, a warning tone in his
deep voice. "Iain is innocent."

She risked another peek at him, and the sight of him, re-
posed so casually on the pallet, stole her breath. He'd folded
his arms behind his head, and stared at her from eyes dark
and smoldering. "Can you swear your brother's hands are
not stained with my sister's blood?" she challenged him.

As she had before.

And, as before, he pressed his lips together and simply
looked at her with those compelling, deep brown eyes.

Knowing eyes.

As if he knew she'd spent sleepless nights reliving his
kiss, craving more, and yearning for other things as well.

The sort of things she'd learned about from Evelina.

"Why ask me when you came to council with Sir
Gavin?" he returned, irritation humming in his voice.

Something in his tone sent a little thrill tripping through
Isolde's heart. He sounded miffed in a wholly different way
from the other times she'd questioned him about his brother.
Could he be perturbed by her desiring to speak to his friend?

Jealous mayhap?

For some inexplicable reason, the notion pleased her.

"Aye, I came to speak with Sir Gavin . . . not you." She studied him as she said the words. The tight set of his jaw grew a bit more stubborn, his artfully casual pose on the pallet, a mite too contrived.

He *was* jealous.

Before her smile could spread from her heart to her face, she turned to Gavin. "Good sir, can you tell me if the rumors I've heard are true? Is Iain MacLean possessed of an uncontrollable temper?"

A hint of ill ease passed over Gavin's boyish features. He opened his mouth to reply, but Isolde spoke first. "So it is true," she said, her heart sinking.

"Aye, 'tis true!" *He* shot to his feet, his eyes blazing. "All MacLean men have tempers, but they do not murder their wives."

Isolde flinched beneath his black fury. "And the MacLean who started our feud?" she pressed. "The one who drowned his MacInnes bride on the Lady Rock?"

"May the wrath of God sink that accursed islet beneath the sea!" Donall threw back his head and stared at the ceiling. When he looked back at her, a cold mask had settled over his handsome face. "That happened so many centuries ago there is scarce a MacLean *or* a MacInnes who recalls the names of that ill-fated pair."

"But we know the names of Iain and Lileas," a wee demon inside made her say.

Donall spun away from her. His great shoulders tensed with agitation, and when he dragged both hands through his hair, Isolde would've sworn his fingers shook. "My brother loved his wife," he swore, wheeling back to face her.

"MacLean men are strong-passioned," he vowed, his tone daring her to deny it. "When a MacLean loves a woman, he *loves* her. With every breath he takes, he gives her all of himself, protects her with his life. She *becomes* his life."

Isolde took a step backward, almost reeling from the sheer power of his outburst. From the corner of her eye, she saw Gavin start toward her. "You're frightening her, Donall, have don—" he began, but Donall the Bold shot his arm out and clamped his fingers around his friend's elbow, halting him in midstride.

And midsentence.

"I am *not* scaring her." He glowered at Gavin. "She is a bold-hearted lass with more steel in her back than her two fool guardsmen have combined. I am telling her what she wants to know: the truth!"

Isolde gulped, her heart galloping in her chest. She didn't want to admit, even to her own self, that, indeed, his braw show of ferocity—of passion—excited more than frightened her.

His calling her a "bold-hearted lass" sent warmth spooling through her while the look on his face as he'd said the words laid claim to her heart as soundly as his strong arms and knight's kisses had claimed her passion.

Keeping his gaze on her, he released Sir Gavin's elbow and folded his arms across his chest. "You did come to hear the truth, did you not?"

Isolde glanced at Gavin. Like her, he stared at Donall, his jollity replaced by a queer look she couldn't quite place. He appeared as spellbound by the MacLean's dark temper and bold words as she.

Donall arched a brow at her. "Well?"

"By the Rood, Donall, cease trying to intimidate her with your glowers," Sir Gavin said. "'Tis plain to see she came for honest answers."

Donall the Bold flashed one of his glares at his friend.

"She has heard the truth often enough, but refuses to listen," he said, stepping in front of her.

Isolde's heart stocked. The pulsing male power streaming from him kept her as firmly in place as his chain held him.

Cupping her chin, he lifted her face to his. "Do you seek the truth, Isolde of Dunmuir? Will you listen if I tell you?"

She could only stare at him.

He smoothed the side of his thumb along her jawline. "Will you?"

Her pulse pounding in her ears, she nodded.

His fierce countenance softened immediately, but the heated flare of male triumph in his eyes was near as unsettling as his glower.

Mayhap more so.

He lowered his head slightly and her heart slammed against her ribs . . . he was going to kiss her! But he merely inclined his head in a succinct acknowledgment of her surrender. To her disappointment, he took his hand from her chin and stepped back from her.

Returning to his pallet, he stood beside it, one massive shoulder resting against the wall. "For a MacLean to kill his lady would mean killing himself as well," he said, his voice low, smooth, and sure.

The smoldering in his dark brown eyes became a full-fledged burn. "*That*, Isolde of Dunmuir, is the truth. My brother did not murder your sister. He loved her."

To Isolde's utter amazement, she believed him.

Or *wanted* to.

But Lileas's sweet face loomed before her, pale lips moving, trying desperately to tell her something, but the image spiraled away, shattered by the hammering of Isolde's own heart.

She expelled a gusty sigh. She knew what Lileas

wanted—she sought to warn Isolde not to fall for the perfidy of a lying tongue.

Regardless of how bonnie.

One undeniable obstacle kept her from accepting what Donall the Bold would have her believe. And it rode the far horizon.

Cold and silent as Lileas's body in its grave.

Donall MacLean stared at her, his eyes demanding an answer. At her growing silence, his confidence began to visibly fade. The hurt lurking in the depths of his eyes stung her as mightily as the red-hot needles jabbing into the backs of her own.

"I *want* to believe you," she finally said. "I truly do."

"I would know what keeps you from seeing the truth?"

Isolde glanced at the small window. "That which I did not see, my lord."

"That which you did *not* see?" He lifted a brow higher than she'd have thought possible.

"Leave be, Donall," Gavin interceded. "She will believe Iain's innocence and the MacKinnons' guilt when she is ready, not before."

"She speaks in riddles." Donall's mask of indifference slipped enough to reveal his frustration. "She will not see because of what she did not see!" He dragged a hand down over his face. "'Tis utter nonsense."

Blinking back the moisture she refused to let become tears, Isolde returned to the window. The gloaming had almost fully claimed MacKinnons' Isle, but her gaze found it . . . as always.

"I do not speak riddles or nonsense." She clutched the rough edge of the window. "What I did not see were MacKinnon galleys passing through our waters. Were they guilty, as you'd have me believe, my lookouts would have seen them sail past on their way to your end of Doon."

She heaved a great sigh. "That simple fact, sirrah, is the reason I cannot believe your brother is innocent. No one else could have done the deed."

Both men inhaled sharply, and she could feel the MacLean's stare boring holes into her, but she kept her back to them, her stance rigid.

Facing them might mean capitulation.

So very much did she wish to believe him.

A rustling noise and the clank of a chain broke the silence, only to be quickly followed by a hefty oath.

Him.

He'd tried to come to her, and her heart turned over at the implication.

"I am loath to ask, but must," he said then, his voice gruff, rife with undertones she didn't want to understand. "What exactly are you intimating?"

"I am intimating naught." She pressed her fingers harder against the cold stone of the window ledge, clinging fast to its solidity, vainly trying to tap its strength.

The mere act of putting her suspicions into words had torn away a vital strand of her fortitude.

Left her weakened.

Shone glaring light on a fragility she did not want exposed.

"All I have done is but give you the truth *you* will not see," she said. "The MacKinnons have ne'er been our friends, but they did not drown my sister on the Lady Rock."

"Neither did my brother," came his fervent reply.

"Then who did?" she asked, hating the way her voice cracked. "Please tell me, for I sorely need to know."

Heavy, black silence answered her.

And she didn't like the sound of it at all.

*   *   *

Several mornings later, Iain MacLean and all the MacLean fighting men who'd been able to fit onboard the newly repaired galley stood upon the sandy beach of Mac-Kinnons' Isle and . . . *gaped.*

Of the massed might of the renowned MacKinnon warriors, nary a hair was to be seen, much less a well-muscled sword arm swinging a finely honed blade.

Of their formidable sea-going fleet was *much* to be seen.

And all of it in ruin.

The once-proud vessels, from the most impressive galley to the lowliest skin-covered coracle, lay in wrack. Broken and sea-blistered, their smooth lines now twisted, jagged, and draped with dried seaweed.

Some of the wreckage had already been half claimed by the shifting sands.

Sad flotsam, tragic remnants of a foundered fleet, made all the more pathetic by the day's brilliant sunshine and cloudless sky.

A day gripped in the talons of freezing winds and a dense, black fog would have better suited the grotesqueness littering the wide stretch of curved shoreline.

Better suited Iain's dark mood upon glimpsing the devastation.

"Begging your humble pardon, sir, but it appears something is amiss." Gerbert, Baldoon Castle's doughty seneschal, nudged a low mound of barnacle-encrusted oak clinker strakes. He scratched his bristly chin. "Aye, sorely amiss."

"God's wounds!" Iain whipped out his sword and thrust it into the sand. "Think you I am blind? *All* is amiss." His face dark with rage, he glowered at Gerbert, the only man along whose purpose wasn't the skill of his sword arm.

And at the moment, Iain didn't know *what* his purpose was.

Save to needle him.

As he'd known the meddlesome seneschal would do even before he'd wheedled his way onboard. But as the only MacLean to have e'er set foot on MacKinnons' Isle, Iain had been hard-pressed to deny the old goat.

Iain scooped up a handful of sand, then jabbed his clenched fist at the air over his head. "The MacKinnon scourges will not slip through our . . ."

He broke off, and lowered his hand. Opening his fingers, he frowned at the rusted nails lying on his palm. With a curse, he hurled them into the surf.

Then he sank to his knees and buried his dark head in his hands. His men, and even old Gerbert, kept a respectful distance, standing where they could amongst the wreckage. After a long while, he pushed to his feet. The shadows beneath his eyes appeared a shade darker; his eyes, to have lost their spark.

No one spoke.

Without exception, each man kept his gaze averted. Anywhere was safer to look than at Iain MacLean during one of his moods. He didn't look at them either, much to their relief.

He stared at his galley.

A fine vessel, sleek of line with high stem and stern posts, its mast straight and proud, a furled sail, and the row of oar ports staring blankly back at him.

Staring *accusingly* back at him.

And with reason.

The war-galley could ply the seaways with great speed at sail, and maneuvered well under the balled might of stout rowing arms if the wind died. She'd borne them to MacKinnons' Isle with a swiftness Iain had not dared hope for, and now . . .

Now, she rocked in the surf, moving in gentle time with

the incoming tide, and their whole journey, the arduous days spent repairing the storm-damaged hull, might prove to have been in vain.

A foolhardy mission, as Amicia had repeatedly harangued him.

Iain stared heavenward. The glare of the sun hurt his eyes, but he welcomed the discomfort. Gulls circled and screamed high above, and the sight sent another piercing shard of pain into his heart . . . had there ever been a time when he'd been so free of cares as the wheeling seabirds?

He started when one of his men sidled up beside him. "Good sir—" The man's voice was hesitant. "What are we to do now?"

Ignoring him, Iain yanked his sword from the sand and held it up to the light, catching the bright rays of the sun in the gleaming steel of its blade.

"We do what we came to do," Iain said, his voice as cold as the day was warm.

"But—"

"*But?*" The look on Iain's face was enough to silence the other man.

Iain swept the circle of men with a penetrating stare, his sword still held to sun. When no one challenged him, he sheathed his blade.

"One MacKinnon for each year of my lady wife's life, and all the rest of them for the grief they've wrought," he vowed, raising his voice above the rising wind. "We've tolerated their antics for years. This time they went too far. Now they shall pay."

But rather than drawing forth their weapons and roaring their support as they'd done in Baldoon's great hall, Iain's men turned into women. They shifted restlessly, shuffled their feet in the sand, and looked everywhere but at him.

They seemed to have lost their tongues as well.

Iain snarled. A deep, roiling rumble wrested from the blackest corner of his soul. And then he hollered for the one man whose knowledge he needed.

Gerbert.

Unlike his younger kinsmen, *he* wasn't afraid to meet Iain's eye. Iain peered hard at him, too, hoping what he saw in the old man's face was a mere trick of the light, and not what it appeared to be.

But it wasn't the light.

Gerbert's watery blue eyes swam with pity.

"Still think you can lead us to the MacKinnon stronghold?" Iain asked him, his voice gruff, his heart choosing to ignore the look on Gerbert's face.

"Well?" he prodded when the old man remained silent. "Can you?"

Gerbert hesitated but a moment. "Aye, but I'd rather not, now we're here."

"And why not?" Iain asked curtly, his balled, white-knuckled hands giving proof of his mounting anger.

His increasing dread.

For deep inside, he knew why Gerbert didn't want to seek out the MacKinnons after they'd journeyed so far.

"Why not?" Iain repeated, the words caught by the wind and whisked away as swiftly as God the Father had snatched Lileas's life from her sweet lips. *"Why not?"*

To his horror, the old man's eyes welled with sympathy. "It would not be wise to disturb them, I'm a-thinking," Gerbert said, his voice laden with compassion. "Now we're here, 'tis clear we've accused them falsely."

"No!" Iain lifted his hands before him as if doing so would ward off what he knew Gerbert was about to say.

What he didn't want to be true.

"No," he said again as the old seneschal stooped to fetch a piece of sun-bleached ship's planking off the sand. *"No."*

Gerbert shook his head and held out the wood for Iain's inspection.

Iain looked away.

He'd seen enough. He didn't need to hear Gerbert put the damning evidence to words to recognize the truth.

The storm that had damaged the MacLean galley had not been the one that had smashed the MacKinnons' entire fleet. The condition of the wreckage gave irrefutable proof that whatever storm gales had lashed at MacKinnons' Isle with such fury had done so long ago.

Too long ago for them to have used one of the ships to sail to Doon to murder Lileas.

The MacKinnons had not killed his lady wife.

"This eve," Isolde emphasized to Niels and Rory. "If he is not there by the hour of compline, I shall fetch him myself."

At her feet, Bodo stared up at the two guardsmen with an unblinking gaze as if admonishing them to heed her wishes. Rory glared at the dog, then jerked his head toward the iron-banded door behind them.

With its heavy drawbar in place, the door's solid strength kept all those behind it where they belonged: locked away within whate'er dark corner of Dunmuir's dungeons they'd been cast into.

"We told you," Rory began, "Lorne has joined us during the late watches every night since he had the bastard pulled from the sea dungeon."

He cast a wary glance at Bodo. "How're we supposed to hie the churl out of the MacFie's cell, past Lorne, and up to your bedchamber, without alerting all and sundry to your tawdry doings?"

Isolde lifted a brow in perfect imitation of *his* favored gesture of pique. "Tawdry?" She folded her arms. "Some would say my goals are bold and daring, their execution costly to none but me."

She declined to say she no longer viewed gaining Donall the Bold's favor as an ugsome task.

Rory pressed his lips together.

Niels scratched the side of his neck. "I don't know how we'll get him past Lorne."

Isolde began tapping her foot. *"Try."*

"A mite eager, aren't you?" Niels commented.

"The devil's done cast a witchy spell o'er her," Rory said. "O'er Lorne, too."

"Aye," Niels agreed, "the whole of Dunmuir's gone crazed of late."

Isolde glanced over her shoulder at the stairs to the great hall. Rustling noises, the clatter of cutlery, and the low hum of voices drifted down the curving stair tower, an indication preparations for the evening repast were well underway.

Bodo glanced at the stairs, too, no doubt looking forward to whate'er tidbits could soon be had.

Isolde turned back to the guardsmen. "Can you not suggest Lorne guard the dungeon entrance in the hall? The one that opens into the broch's wall passage?"

Niels and Rory exchanged uncomfortable glances.

"What is it?" Isolde looked from one to the other.

Rory averted his gaze and began mumbling under his breath.

Her cousin drew a big hand through his unruly red hair. "'Tis not guarding the MacLean and his friend, Lorne is, but a-watching o'er us," he said, a pink stain tingeing his broad face.

"Watching *you?*"

"We told you the world's gone mush-brained," Rory said. "Lorne is worried Struan and the others will have us hie the MacLean back to the sea dungeon when he isn't looking."

"And would you?" Isolde flipped a braid over her shoulder.

"Saints, but we'd like to," Niels admitted.

Isolde assumed her da's laird's look. "But you won't, will you?"

"Nay," Niels conceded in a disgruntled tone.

Rory spat on the floor, blessedly not anywhere near Bodo. "Nay, we will not," he agreed. "Much as the arrogant knave needs the pride washed out of him."

Satisfied, Isolde released the breath she'd been holding. "There is not much time. Not this night, not . . . at all. I can waste no more. You have not brought him to my chamber in a full sennight. I want him there this eve."

With that, she hitched up her skirts and walked away, her little dog bounding ahead of her. She hadn't taken three of the winding stone steps before Rory called after her. "We can't promise. Lorne—"

Without halting her upward climb, Isolde called over her shoulder, "Find a way. I want to see him."

I want to be kissed like a knight kisses.

Chapter Fourteen

❦

$\mathcal{S}$HE'D MISPLACED THE *blush of rose.*

Isolde made another circuitous sweep of her bedchamber, peering into every crevice and niche as she went. She looked into the aumbrey set deep into the thick walling, looked *everywhere*, but the little pot of vermilion nipple paint was nowhere to be found.

She even wrested the bed dressings off her great fourposter and aired each layer: linens, coverlets, furs, and all.

A peek under the bed proved equally fruitless.

The blush of rose was gone.

She'd need another method to draw Donall the Bold's attention to her breasts.

To her nipples.

To her . . . *everything*.

A languorous heat spread through her at the thought. An exquisite sensation that curled low in her belly, its pleasurable warmth teasing her with a slow, insistent pulsing at the very core of he femininity.

And whatever it was, she wanted more . . . and soon.

Wild and wanton images ran rampant through her mind, each one more tantalizing than the last.

And she couldn't find the wretched pot of nipple cream!

"By the moon and stars," she grumbled, snatching one of Devorgilla's pet epithets. She blew out a frustrated breath and would have continued her frenzied search, did she not catch the muffled trundle of approaching feet.

They were bringing him at last.

Quickly, before they could reach her door, she dashed to the row of windows and struck a casual, unconcerned pose. Bodo dashed to the door, tongue lolling and tail wagging, looking as eager as she . . . only *she* had no intention of displaying her feelings so openly.

But when the door swung open, her resolve sailed through the opened windows, flying away on wings of stunned surprise so great, she vowed its impact could carry her to the stars.

Donall MacLean wore his own raiment.

And looked so outrageously handsome in them the sight weakened her knees, lit a fire in her blood, and melted every bit of steel he claimed she possessed.

A light brown tunic hugged his smooth-muscled shoulders while a finely tooled leather belt slung low around his hips drew her attention to the well-defined bulge of his masculinity.

A most impressive display, braw and bold.

Daunting.

Her pulse racing, she lowered her gaze to his well-formed legs. He'd donned snug hose of a lighter brown than his tunic. The fine chainsil linen clung to his calves and thighs, the soft fabric caressing each muscular contour.

Only his feet were bare, a concession to the iron manacle around his ankle. Though Rory and Niels had surely removed it long enough for him to dress.

Heat sprang onto her cheeks at the thought of him standing naked, easing his legs into the fine linen hose. The image of him rolling the hose *down* his legs, stepping *out* rather than into them, turned the blush on her cheeks into a flaming burn.

A scarlet blush of epic brilliance, and one he took high note of, if his cocked brow and slow smile could be trusted as an indication. Lifting her chin, Isolde tried to pretend her cheeks weren't burning, and attempted to assume an air of dignified grace.

At least until Niels and Rory departed.

Then she intended to seduce him.

Bodo, though, had no intention of waiting for the two guardsmen to leave before he showed *his* affection. With a sharp bark of excitement, he launched himself at the MacLean with such force, he toppled backward. For a scant moment, he lay on his back, white belly exposed, his short legs plowing the air, before he bounded up to tear around the room, leaping playfully at Donall each time he streaked past.

The MacLean grinned, his handsome face losing all trace of lordly swagger. Even his perpetually arched brow descended to a normal level. The transformation did irreparable damage to Isolde's heart, his genuine amusement at Bodo's antics warming her soul.

The irony brought a smile to her own lips.

Bodo's display of canine affection easily won what she, with all Devorgilla's potions and Evelina's advice, had not yet managed to achieve.

The little dog had a firm hold on Donall MacLean's heart.

"I told you the whole of Dunmuir's gone mad," Rory carped, dropping to one knee to affix Donall's chain to the bedpost.

Bodo was on him in a heartbeat. "By the holy sepulcher!" Rory bellowed, leaping away before the dog could bite him. The moment Niels and Rory closed the door behind them, Isolde left her post by the windows. With a calm she didn't feel, she ordered Bodo to his bed.

"Your wee champion would defend you to the death, my lady," the MacLean said, something warm and indefinable in his voice.

Something that reached deep inside her to wrap itself around her heart, caressing her in a wondrously comforting way. Wholly different from the way his strong hands had felt upon her. Or even his masterful lips.

But no less powerful.

"Bodo meant to defend you," she said, still stunned by the dog's attachment to the MacLean.

Donall shrugged tunic-clad shoulders. "The little fellow loves you mightily," he added, one of his slow smiles beginning to spread across his bonnie face. "He could be a MacLean."

He could be a MacLean?

Bodo loves her mightily . . . he could be a MacLean?

Isolde's heart thudded slow and hard in her chest. Was Donall the Bold implying he *loved* her?

Impossible.

But if it were, why did she find the notion so thrilling? She certainly didn't love him. She merely found him attractive.

Somewhat attractive.

A means to expedite her goals.

Every fiber of her being laughed at the lie.

She swallowed thickly, and at last the words came, bursting forth with all the more force for having been snagged in her throat.

Snagged in her heart.

"What do you mean Bodo 'could be a MacLean'?"

"You cannot guess?"

Isolde shook her head.

"I meant the dog loves you as fiercely as a MacLean loves his lady," he said, his voice husky, his answer . . . disappointing.

"Oh." She glanced downward. "I see."

"Do you?" he asked with that odd tone again, the one that did funny things to her heart.

Such funny things, she sought the safety of the far side of the chamber. Standing before the unshuttered windows, she inhaled the briny night air, her hand going instinctively to the small linen pouch hanging from her girdle, her fingers moving idly over the small, solid object hidden within.

"Gavin sees," came Donall's voice, the odd tone unsettling her more by the moment. Then, to her surprise, he chuckled.

Or, at least, she thought he had.

"Aye, he sees all," he called out, his amusement unmistakable now. "The varlet sees by the warts on his grandmother's nose, or so he claims."

Isolde started, and not because of his nonsensical pronouncement, but because the words rang so loud in her ears, he might have been standing right behind her.

She whirled around . . . and gasped.

He *was* right behind her.

Or rather, in front of her, now that she'd turned around.

"Your minions neglected to chain me to your bed." His dark eyes twinkling, he held the loose chain with one hand.

Isolde gulped.

His smile widened. "I vow our four-legged champion frightened them off before they thought to do so," he said, casting a quick glance at the sleeping dog.

Isolde glanced at him, too, her mind racing almost as fast

as her pulse. Bodo would ne'er sleep so peaceably were she
in danger. Her decision made, she looked back at the
MacLean.

He watched her closely, a smile of such disarming appeal
on his face, she *knew* she ought to heed the perils it might
conceal, but she chose to heed her instincts instead.

Hers and Bodo's.

Before she could change her mind, she plunged her hand
into the folds of her skirts and withdrew the hard object from
the hidden pouch. She offered it to him on her outstretched
palm.

He stared at the iron key, his dark eyes widening in astonishment. The chain slipped from his fingers, dropping to
the floor with a rush-muffled thud.

Slowly, he lifted his gaze to hers. Soft light from a
nearby cresset lamp illuminated the inscrutable expression
he wore, but as she stared at him, his lips curved in a broad,
flashing smile. "I knew you were a fine bold lass," he said,
and accepted the key.

Isolde heart turned over upon hearing him call her "a fine
bold lass" again. "Do not make me regret it," she said,
watching him kneel to unlock the iron ankle cuff.

He glanced up at her as he slipped the key into the lock.
"Never."

And for some inexplicable reason, she believed him.

Faith, but she wanted him to kiss her again!

Her heart melting, her *senses* reeling with his nearness,
she moistened her lips. "The key will release the manacle
around Sir Gavin's ankle as well," she said. "I will see that
neither of you are chained again."

His brow lifted at that. "Ah . . ." he drawled, pushing to
his feet, "dare I hope you have finally accepted the truth?"

Isolde turned to the windows and stared out at the great

sweep of the night-darkened sea. MacKinnons' Isle rode low against the dark horizon.

"I know the truth," she said, a wistful note in her voice. "And I truly wish our truths were the same."

"And why do you wish that?" The words came from just above her ear.

He'd stepped closer. So near she could scarce draw a breath, so compelling was the sheer weight of his presence. He placed his hands on her shoulders and the warm contact sent a floodtide of pleasure streaming through her.

With great gentleness, he turned her to face him, but the last vestiges of her courage, all her bold seduction schemes, clung to the bank of windows, staunchly threatening to leap away into the night, traitorously joining her strength and resolve.

Both of which had taken the same escape route earlier.

Her steel wholly vanquished, she wriggled from his grasp and crossed the room to her strongbox. She fumbled with its lock, then threw open the curved, iron-banded lid. She thrust her hand inside. "Here!" she called, his jeweled brooch in her hand. "Your gold brooch."

Mayhap the return of the jewel-studded treasure would distract him, take some of the heat from his gaze, until she could summon back her nerve.

Her boldness.

The courage she needed to ask him to kiss her again.

The daring she needed to drop her gown and display her breasts.

Evelina had sworn naught stirred a man faster than a woman's bared bosom.

But when she held out the brooch, he shook his head. "Nay, *you* keep it," he said. "It is of great value and shall recompense you most liberally for . . . for the enjoyment of your company."

Isolde's eyes flew wide. She dropped the brooch as if it'd become a writhing snake. But as quickly, she snatched it up again. Holding the offending piece by the tips of her thumb and middle finger, she let the brooch fall onto the tabletop.

Bristling inside and out, she whirled to face the MacLean.

And immediately wished she hadn't.

His handsome face was unsmiling, but something unfathomable glowed deep in his eyes. A warmth that belied the cold words he'd tossed at her. "You do not want the brooch?" His voice held a peculiar thickness. "Truly not?"

Isolde shook her head, her ire swept away by the power of his stare. "I-I told you, I have no use for such frippery," she stammered.

Saints, but he could look at a woman.

The corners of his mouth twitched in the beginnings of a smile. "You mean that, don't you?" he asked, and Isolde heard his astonishment.

His incredulity.

"I do not lie."

One dark brow shot upward.

She blushed. "Not about such things."

The ghost of a smile that had been playing across his mouth burst to life in a full-bodied, flashing grin of such intensity, its brightness near blinded her.

What the smile did to *his* eyes stole her breath.

"You please me more than you ken, Isolde of Dunmuir," he said, the soft note in his voice going straight to her heart.

Her steel returning, she wanted naught but to be pulled against his hard body, to feel his arms around her once more, and sink into the magic of his kiss.

"Come here." His remarkable dark eyes smoldered with warmth.

A longing such as she had never known filled her. His

brooch forgotten, she simply looked at him, too moonstruck to move. Silvered light from the windows shimmered on his raven hair, while warmer light from the cresset lamp danced over the planes of his face and his broad shoulders.

Isolde took a deep breath, half-amazed she could, so deep were the stirrings he aroused in her. But she wasn't about to go to him. He was supposed to come to her. That had been her plan.

She'd meant to seduce him.

His smile changed, became a shade more intense.

More *compelling*.

Would that she'd found the blush of rose!

Scarlet-tinted nipples peeking at him would surely give her the advantage.

Expelling a gusty breath of pure frustration, she closed her eyes. Only briefly. Just long enough to shield herself from the wild attraction he presented.

He didn't appear similarly stricken. He stood bold and proud, legs apart, hands braced on his hips, his dark eyes flashing. And staring right at her, into her.

Into her very soul.

Her heart.

"Come here," he repeated. "There is something I would ask you."

When she didn't move, he lifted his hands, showing her his palms. "Fairest maid, did I have my gloves at hand, I would present one to you on bended knee. A knightly tribute to your grace and beauty." His courtly words came just smooth enough to impress her, and sincere enough to soften her heart.

"But alas, I find myself bare-handed," he went on, his words warm and mellifluous. "Thus I must employ other knightly devices to win your favor."

But you already have, her heart answered.

"A kiss?" the maid of steel wanted to know.

"Aye, a kiss." He extended his hand, beckoning her. "But first a simple question."

"A question?" Isolde hoped he couldn't see her disappointment.

He lowered his hand. "You desire more?" He feigned puzzlement. "More than a kiss and a few words?"

She did.

She desired . . . everything.

"Can I not answer from here?" she ventured, fingering the end of one of her braids in a feeble attempt to disguise the trembling in her hands.

And to attract his attention to her hair. Another infallible lure for unsuspecting seduction victims, Evelina had assured her.

"As you wish." He gave her a casual shrug, but the glitter in his eyes was anything but indifferent. Folding his arms, he regarded her with a penetrating look. "Why did you avoid looking at me when you came to speak with Gavin?"

Her eyes flew wide.

She could not tell him why.

"I await your answer, lady."

Isolde looked down. "I . . . I . . ." She threw up her hands. "'Twas your chest," snapped the steely wench, much to her dismay. "Your bonnie chest. I-It unnerved me."

His shout of laughter filled the room. She glanced at him, horrorstruck at her own tongue's brazenness.

"*Unnerved* you?" He peered at her, and for once, *both* of his brows shot heavenward. "You find my bare chest bonnie and that unnerves you?"

She nodded, unable to lie.

His wicked smile returned, more devastating than ever. "Then mayhap you should see it again?" Not taking his gaze off her, he divested himself of his fine leather belt and tossed it aside. He reached for the bottom of his tunic. "Aye, I believe you need to see my bonnie chest again," he said, and pulled the shirt over his head.

Isolde eyed his splendor, keenly aware of the wondrous urgings gazing upon him called forth in her.

Faith, but he was magnificent.

As he well knew.

The knowledge gleamed in his rich brown eyes. His strapping good looks and his sublime self-confidence sent eddies of feminine awe whirling through her and lit fires in all her dark and mysterious womanly places.

"And now, sweeting, I believe we shall have another lesson in *enlightenment*."

He came forward, his each step firing a new stab of pure heated desire straight to her core. His dark allure swirled around her like a warmed, silk-lined mantle, enveloping her in his mastery until she could do naught but stand and stare at him.

His eyes crinkled in amusement. "A bonnie chest, you say?" Tilting his head to the side, he took her hands in his. The feel of his fingers closing over hers, strong and warm, set her senses to reeling.

"So look upon me, Isolde of Dunmuir, until I unnerve you no more."

And she did.

The bold lass in her reveled in the wide set of his shoulders, the play of hearth fire over the hard-muscled expanse of his chest. A delicious tension spread through her, a sensation both disturbing and exhilarating.

He was gloriously handsome.

She yearned to trace her fingers along the smooth contours of his powerful arms. Her gaze dropped to his taut stomach, flat and well-honed. Iron strength and carefully restrained power emanated from every bold male inch of him.

His high looks and charm of manner proved more potent than all of Devorgilla's love concoctions combined.

Not that *her* potion had been blended to cull a man's favor.

Taking her leisure at studying his noble physique, she returned her attention to his face. First to the hard, firm line of his jaw, then to the full, sensual curve of his lips, the silken fall of his thick black hair, and finally his eyes.

A knight's eyes.

Heavy-lidded with desire, dark and full of ardor.

Ardor for *her*.

A soft sigh escaped her, and she glanced away, unconsciously seeking a reprieve from the sheer headiness of just gazing at him. She needed her wits about her if she hoped to seduce him.

Thus far, 'twas *he* who was doing the seducing.

She who would succumb.

Her brow knitted in perturbation.

"I vow you must look some more," he said, the levity in his deep voice striking the balance she needed to offset her burgeoning ill ease at having her plans so easily wrested from her control.

He brought her hands to his lips and kissed all ten fingertips. Each kiss sent showers of tingles washing over her. "You still appear . . . *unnerved*."

"I-I have seen enough," she said, hating the quiver in her voice.

Releasing her hands, he spread his arms wide and turned in a slow circle. "You've no reason to be afraid," he said, coming to a stop before her. "I told you, knights admire wenches with steel in their blood."

His gentle teasing made her heart skitter wildly. Then his jollity faded, and the look of the predator returned.

Dark, stirring, determined.

The look alone would have sent a less bold lass diving under her bed.

The look made Isolde want to dive into her bed.

With him.

Now.

"And what do knights like wenches to *do*?" she asked, striving for a low, sultry tone like Evelina.

She must've failed sorely, for rather than darken with desire, his eyes crinkled with renewed mirth.

He'd seen through her ploy and was laughing at her.

But then he scratched his chin, and she recognized his ploy as well. He meant to play along with her. One finger moving oh-so-slowly along his jawline, he gave her question a new twist. "What do knights like wenches to do *for* or *to* them?"

For or to them?

The possibilities, everything Evelina had taught her, landed in one great rush . . . *there*, close by the tops of her thighs where a pulsing ache had begun.

Do such things for or to him? Mercy, but she wanted *both* options.

In every variant.

"Well?" He stepped so close the heady musk of his dark male scent did powerful things to her senses.

And to her fool tongue, for it seemed to have swelled to ten times its size. She couldn't speak, could only stare at him, waiting for him to relieve the unquenched stirrings he roused in her.

Waiting for his knight's kisses.

"This knight would like you to do something *for* him," he said, and touched his fingers to the smooth curve of her cheek.

She leaned into his touch, a brazen maid, silently urging him not to take away his hand.

Not to withdraw its magic.

"Will you do something for me?" The low, huskily spoken words sank into her soul.

She nodded, not even considering denying him.

Not caring what it was he wanted.

A blush stole up her neck, for the truth was, she *hoped* whate'er it was, would be bold. Lascivious and daring enough to quench the fire raging in her blood.

May the saints preserve her wanton soul.

He slipped his hand around her neck, let his fingers caress her nape. "Will you do *two* things for me?"

She gulped, and nodded again. "If you wish," she agreed, the words an embarrassing squeak.

He looked sharply at her. "Have you imbibed more of that wretched potion?"

She started to shake her head in denial, but before she could, he'd lowered his mouth to hers. Her heart stopped, she was sure of it, so intense were the flames of desire flaring inside her, licking at her very core.

So *thrilling* to have him kiss her again.

But rather than the sweeping knight's kiss she'd hoped for, he merely flicked the tip of his tongue over her lips.

Tasted her.

A soft, gentle lick, naught more. Fleeting and light as a butterfly's wing, a simple taste to see if he could detect the anti-attraction potion on her lips.

Lightning quick though it'd been, the mere touch of his tongue on her lips had been powerful enough to send a surge of white-hot need shooting through her.

She slid her arms around his shoulders and thrust her fingers into the thick gloss of his hair. She pressed herself into him, not caring if she exposed herself to be as shameless as Evelina. Parting her lips, she used her urgency to beg for more, ached for him to kiss her deeply, thoroughly, as he'd done before.

"So eager, my love." He set her from him, his use of the endearment melting her heart as surely as his touch ignited her blood.

He rested his forehead on hers, his warm breath a sweet caress on her skin. "Your appetite pleases me immensely. Aye, lady, you rouse me to the limits of my restraint," he murmured. "And I shall give you all the knight's kisses you desire and more, much more, but before I do, you must fulfill your two promises."

He placed his hands on her shoulders. "Will you?"

"What is your will?" she breathed, nigh melting at the thought of giving herself to him so wholly she'd do whate'er it was he wanted of her.

Do *anything* for him.

He lifted one of her braids, rubbed his thumb over its thickly woven strands. "You are not blessed with much restraint, are you?"

She shook her head, beyond speaking, so eagerly did she crave his will.

His touch.

He let the braid fall. "There is much I would have you do for, and to me, sweeting. And I to you," he said, his eyes darkening, his voice low and . . . seductive. "But the keen edge of anticipation is almost as sharp as the final pleasuring and should not be missed."

He smoothed his hand over her shoulder, down her arm. "I want to initiate you into carnal pleasures one luscious step at the time," he vowed. "Such a tender fruit as yourself ought to be savored fully, but slowly. *Very, very slowly.*"

"And how do you wish to . . . t-to savor me?" her newly discovered wanton self wanted to know. "What two ways?"

He reached for her braids, taking them both this time.

Looking deep into her eyes, he said, "I want you to undo your hair for me, Isolde."

Disappointment and confusion welled inside her. The pulsing need she'd hoped to see quenched, cried out in pained rebellion. "Unbraid my hair? That is all?"

"That is the *beginning*." He lifted her braids. "To look at your hair," he told her, "to watch my fingers touching the strands, watch me *feel* them, caress them as they slide like ropes of golden-bronze silk over my palms."

The pulsing in her belly flared anew, and with a greater vengeance than before. Faith, but he could work a fine wizardry with simple words.

"Do you see, my sweet Isolde, how aroused you are merely by watching me fondle your braids?" he asked, and she knew he spoke the truth.

He *was* arousing her.

His lips curved in a slow, lazy smile. "How do you think it will make you feel, make *me* feel, to revel in your unbound tresses?"

A deep, throaty sigh rose in her throat, and she released it. The thoughts he put into her head, the shivery tremors his words sent tumbling through her, inspired a whole fleet of breathy sighs.

One more gusty than the other.

"I want to *bathe* in your hair," he told her, finally relinquishing her braids. "Drink in its fragrance, lose myself in its satiny warmth."

Isolde swallowed. She wanted that, too.

Badly.

But he'd had one more request.

One more desire.

Her pulse raced with anticipation. "And what is your second wish, milord?"

The slow burn in his eyes turned wicked.

Very wicked.

"I want to see your breasts," he said, and her heart slammed against her ribs.

She'd waited all evening to bare her breasts to him, fretting she'd not have the nerve after losing Evelina's nipple cream. A veritable fire wall of heat swept through her, and a wild tingling began in her breasts, its intensity mirroring the pulsing sensation in her belly.

"You want to *look* at them? Simply look?" the steely wench asked, inexorably pleased when he slowly shook his dark head.

"Nay, sweeting." He smoothed the backs of his hands very lightly down the outer swells of her breasts. "I want to do much more than look." He paused. "Dare I?"

She nodded. "But I would hear the words," she said, already finding this . . . this *speaking* of such acts highly stimulating.

Just as Evelina had promised.

"Aye, I would hear in the greatest detail what you mean to do to my breasts," she said, the heat pooling in her woman's core now pulsing with heavy urgency. "Tell me and I will undo my hair, then free my breasts to your will."

"You please me well, Isolde of Dunmuir, and so I shall oblige you," he said, tapping a finger against his chin. "First, I shall simply *look* at you, but from all angles. From afar, and up close. *Very close.*"

"I would hear more," she urged, enjoying the game, her cares and woes forgotten.

He smiled. "I shall touch you with my hands, and in many ways." He let his gaze roam over her breasts as he spoke. "I will smooth the backs of my fingers down, around, and under your breasts, move my fingertips over you in featherlight circles that will send shivers of delight the length of you until, finally, I turn my attention to the peaks of your breasts . . . your nipples."

He peered at her, waiting for a nod, a word, for him to continue. She purposely stalled, just a short moment, then inclined her head. "Your words stir me," she admitted, scarce believing her wantonness. "Pray continue. What else shall you do?"

"Ohhhh . . . I shall lift and weigh your breasts. I will fondle and *palm* them, mayhap a bit roughly, but only enough to heighten your pleasure."

"Is there more?" she asked, a pleasing warmth coursing through her, her woman's core weighted and pulsing.

"Aye, much more," he promised, the intense bliss his words instilled in her startling and amazing her. "I shall worship you with my lips and my tongue. I shall lick, lave, and—" He broke off, hopping on one bare foot.

"What the . . ." He reached down to retrieve something from the thick layer of floor rushes. He examined whatever it was, then held out his hand, a little earthen pot resting on his palm.

Isolde flushed scarlet.

'Twas the blush of rose.

Evelina's nipple cream.

"Is this yours, my lady?" He snatched his hand back when she reached for it. "I see it is by your flushed cheeks."

He opened the jar and peered inside. A look of astonishment, then recognition flashed over his handsome face.

He knew what it was.

He looked at her, high amusement coloring his own cheeks. "This is vermilion," he said, staring at her. Flummoxed. "Whore's paint."

Isolde glanced away, too embarrassed to admit she knew its common usage.

"You meant to use this to seduce me," he said, the odd catch back in his voice.

"Aye, I did," she allowed, beyond pretending false modesty after the bawdy talks they'd just indulged in. "But I lost it."

His dark eyes twinkled. "And here it is again."

"So?" Her heart began to pound.

Faith and mercy, he wanted her to use the nipple cream.

"I want you to put this on," he said, confirming what she already knew. He handed the little pot to her.

"If it will please you," she said, feeling somewhat disappointed. The surprise effect she'd hoped to achieve with the cream had been lost. "It won't be the same if you know it's there."

He shook his head. "Sweeting, surprising me is no longer the nipple paint's purpose."

Now he'd confused her. "Nay?"

He narrowed his eyes at her. "How bold can you be, lass?"

"As bold as your pleasure," the wanton in her replied.

"Then you shall please me indeed if you will let me watch you apply the paint to your nipples."

Isolde gasped, the idea first repulsing her, then arousing her.

Very much so.

She curled her fingers around the little earthen pot, her cheeks flaming.

Blush of rose.

An apt name indeed.

And she could scarce wait to sample its power.

Chapter Fifteen

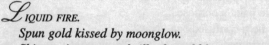

*L*IQUID FIRE.

Spun gold kissed by moonglow.

Shimmering, watered silk of untold luxuriance.

Donall's brows drew together at the sumptuous bounty presented by Isolde of Dunmuir's unbound hair. Blessed be, *she* whiled before the window, bathed by the night's silvery luminosity, whilst *he* lingered in the safe concealment of the shadows.

Hidden in the cool dimness outwith the reach of the revealing silver-blue light. A delicate glow spun of the night's magic, spilling into her bedchamber, and highlighting her charms so sweetly.

Bewitching him and laying bold claim to a heart no other maid had e'er heard *beat*, much less possess.

His scowl deepened.

He'd have to remove the hard-earned suffix from his name should she catch him making fawn eyes at her.

And, curse his bones, that was exactly what he was doing. Staring at her all agog, captivated as an untried youth scenting his first whiff of a bonnie wench's roused desire. And, saints stay him by, she had yet to completely loosen her braids.

She'd only unraveled half their glossy length.

The sheer temptation of what she'd displayed thus far bit so deep, the fetching sight had him composing lines more suited to an overperfumed French courtier than a red-blooded Islesman known as *the Bold*.

The only thing bold about him at the moment was the iron-hard press of his arousal against the snug confinement of his hose.

His mouth dry, his loins painfully tight, his heart . . . *lost*, he rested his shoulder against the wall, secretly borrowing from its solidity to help him to stand tall through the ongoing torture of watching her unravel her braids.

Her slender fingers released one sheened section at a time until the whole wealth of her bronze-gold tresses rippled free to spill in wild abandon around her hips.

The flowing length tested his knightly skills of restraint beyond even his well-practiced endurance and set loose a low moan of insistent need somewhere deep inside him.

A *lament*, torn from the very roots of his soul and born of the spell she'd cast over him.

A living thing, hot and fine.

An unrestrained fury whirling 'round the hard knot of nerves lodged in his gut, skipping past his slow-bounding heart, and then, with a boldness even he had to admire, plunging right through the tightness in his throat to burst from his lips with all the aplomb of a randy stag suffering a sore throat.

"Do I displease you?" Her voice, soft and sweet, dispelled his grousing demons with a greater ease than a well-wielded sword.

Her hesitancy, the way her fingers ceased arranging the

lustrous fall of her hair, tugged at Donall's heart. *Pulled* on the fool organ in ways far more troubling than the aching constriction in his throat, more disturbing than the fire licking at his loins.

Saints, the lass had his heart!

A comely maid, the finest he'd e'er seen, yet one who'd allow him tortured, lied whene'er she had the chance, would harvest his seed if allowed, and . . . and drank foul potions.

Sharp-smelling elixirs he knew had naught to do with banishing freckles and purging animals of fleas.

"Do I?" came her soft-as-cream voice again, teasing him, tempting him with its soothing melody, its warmth.

Donall blew out an aggravated breath, and glanced heavenward.

"I see I do."

"By the Rood!" He looked at her, stunned when she didn't bat an eye at how . . . how *exposed* he stood before her. And not simply his bared chest. Nay, 'twas his bared heart, the laid open secrets of his soul, he didn't want her to see.

But she simply peered at him, looking irresistibly vulnerable. "Do I?" she reverted to her original question.

Donall blinked, totally captivated. Saints, couldn't she *see* what she did to him? Was she truly unaware his heart, his very *soul*, rested at her feet?

"Do you what? *Displease me?*" The words came in a high-pitched tone.

Hellfire and botheration, but the fool squeak had caught him off guard. Turning away, he shoved his hair off his forehead, then covered his mouth with his hand and coughed.

Hopefully she'd think a coughing fit and naught else had caused him to speak with the voice of an eunuch.

"'Twas you who bid me to undo my hair, but you look displeased," she pressed, the note of pride underlying her words doing fine battle against the doubt swimming in her eyes.

"Shall I redo the plaits?" She lifted two handfuls of her bonnie tresses, offering him their bounty. Thick, satiny skeins of glossed bronze pouring through her fingers.

Donall's loins quickened, his pulse pounding hard through his veins. His great shoulders sagged in defeat. The effort of holding them straight and proud, a stalwart defense against his attraction to her, his *feelings* for her, crumbled as easily as a score of well-skilled sappers can topple a curtain wall.

"Nay, leave be with your tresses," he said, his voice thankfully low and deep again.

Low and deep, but oddly . . . *hoarse.*

Weary of riding vanguard in a battle he could not win.

Falling hard for Isolde MacInnes despite her potions and lies.

"It pleases me to see your hair thus," he said. *You ought tell her to shave it off and cover her bald head with a veil*, his last vestiges of good sense chided in swift rebuttal.

Looking curiously at him, she lowered her hands. The heavy, silken strands slipped from her fingers, falling to her hips, gleaming like fired silk in the moonlight. "As you wish," she said, and gave a light shrug.

"What I wish, my lady, is to love you." His hands clenched against the words his heart tossed so glibly at her feet.

Glibly and wholly unexpected.

And most disturbing of all, wholly true.

Something flared in her eyes, but then she gave a wistful little smile, and the something was gone. "Is that not why we are doing . . . t-this?"

"We are doing *this*"—he gestured to her and then at the little earthen pot of vermilion sitting innocently on the window ledge—"because you desired my affections, because it is—*will be*—pleasurable to us both, and because you are in sore need of enlightenment."

And because I have fallen in love with you, his heart added.

She smiled, surely unaware of the balled might of a MacLean man's love massing so near, and gathered her tresses into her hands, bunching its abundance into a glorious tumble she pushed above her head. "Enlightenment and knightly kisses." Her smile turned coy. "And do you enjoy enlightening me?"

His manhood stretched and preened, eager to show her exactly how much he enjoyed . . . *enlightening* her.

His heart swelled.

His soul melted.

"Saints, but you ask fool questions. Can you not see I do?"

"I see you look displeased," she said. "That is all I see."

Donall's brows snapped together. Could she not see the hard ridge of his arousal, fully charged with wanting her? Boldly displayed, if only she'd drop her gaze to *look*.

"Lady, your beauty steals my breath. As a seductress, you are most talented and adept." He glanced fleetingly at his groin, hoping she'd follow his gaze, but she didn't.

"Irresistible though your charms might be, you are quite blind." He pushed away from the wall, taking unwise leave of the dark corner. Stepping into the pooling light by the windows, he hoped she'd see his desire.

But she saw naught.

Her mere presence stirred his blood to a fever pitch and stiffened his tarse to such a painful degree he wouldn't be surprised if one false move caused the aching appendage to snap off.

Glancing away, he stared out at the silvered night beyond

the windows. He dragged a hand through his hair, drew a breath of the chill, tangy air.

Regrettably, it didn't cool him a whit.

He looked back at her, and promptly lost himself in her beautiful eyes, in the glorious mass of her rippling hair. Lost himself in his very fate, for her deftly working fingers had not simply undone her plaited hair.

Without him realizing she'd done it, the bold-hearted enchantress had undone his heart as well.

Smashed its casing first with her surprising refusal to accept his offers of ransom, then wrested it from his breast when she'd turned up her pretty nose at his gold brooch, and now laid further claim by turning those luminous eyes on him.

Eyes full of vulnerability, eager innocence, and entirely void of the glittering calculation he'd seen lurking in every other pair of female eyes that'd e'er peered at him.

Eyes that only saw his wealth and standing.

And mayhap his good looks . . . something he hadn't sought, but wouldn't deny.

All had wanted what he could *give*.

None had wanted simply *him*.

Until Isolde of Dunmuir.

Donall swallowed the bitter laugh rising in his throat. Reaching for the little jar of whore's paint, he held it tight, letting the earthen pot's coolness sink into his palm.

The saints knew, he was in sore need of a cooling.

Keeping his back to her, he watched a distant line of mist gather far out to sea. A soft, shifting line of gray-white, blurring the outlines of MacKinnons' Isle, changing the contours of the horizon itself until the drifting, billowy mass eventually blotted the wretched isle from sight.

He curled his fingers tighter around the little jar. Would that he could erase his cares so easily as a line of simple fog could swallow the view out a window, erase the truth that Isolde of Dunmuir didn't truly want him either.

But a shimmer of hope refused to be banished.

Enveloping sea mist or damning logic, be damned.

He would *make* her want him.

She didn't care a whit about how many baubles he could gift her with. Nor did his high standing amongst the gentle-born of the Isles impress her.

And, heaven help him, that knowledge made *him* want her.

In the worst possible way.

And not just to stave the itch in his tarse.

Nay, he wanted her to ease the ache in his heart.

An emptiness he hadn't known needed filling until he'd seen her eyes fire with indignation at his ransom offers, watched them spark with pride and hope when she'd confided the one thing she *did* want from him.

A child.

Not splendor and riches. Not fame. But a bairn to forge peace.

A fool notion, he'd thought at first, but one that had begun to please him. Feeling utterly defeated, Donall leaned against one of the window embrasures and breathed in the impassive scent of damp old stone.

The scent of capitulation.

Aye, even her ludicrous alliance scheme now struck him as appealing.

And she would ask if she *displeased* him?

Donall pinched the bridge of his nose. Truth to tell, the only thing displeasing him was not having met her earlier. In a less troubled time when he could have whisked her off to Baldoon and made her his bride.

As he'd sorely love to do.

Were such a feat possible.

Straightening, he drew back his shoulders once more, his knight's blood hot and ably reinforced.

Determined and prepared to lay siege to Isolde of Dunmuir's heart.

Isolde's heart tilted as she watched him at the window. She sensed the change the moment it happened, could almost see his resolve spinning away from him.

She needn't hear his gusty intake of breath to know he'd cast off the masterful control he'd displayed thus far and was steeling himself to . . . surrender.

She swallowed thickly and began undoing the fastenings of her bodice. Her hands shook, her fingers making slow, clumsy progress. Her heart, her body, her whole *being*, surrendering to him even as she sensed he was about to give himself to her.

A chill tripped down her spine, its cold footfalls admonishing her because her reasons for doing so had changed so dramatically.

The other reasons yet lingered, but the *true* reason she succumbed made her pulse pound as she freed the final laces on her bodice.

She wanted Donall MacLean regardless of who he was and what he represented.

Despite the doubts still gnawing at her.

Despite everything.

She was falling in love with him.

Had fallen in love with him.

Isolde swallowed, watched his shoulders tense as she slipped her arms from her sleeves and allowed the gown to fall and bunch around her waist. He tilted back his head and stared at the tops of the arched windows as if he sought to beseech the gods for strength.

Then he turned around.

Raw desire simmering in his eyes, he handed her the

little pot of blush of rose, his gaze boldly settling on the bodice of Evelina's borrowed camise.

The one crafted of see-through gauze silk with slits up the sides.

Something urgent and primal, a wholly male sound, came from deep in his throat. His nostrils flared and, though she wouldn't have believed it, his eyes went a shade darker.

He took her wrist and drew her into the pale circle of moonlight. "Stand here where I can see you better," he said, the huskiness of his voice stirring her as much as the warm, strong feel of his fingers moving on her wrist.

"You are more lovely than I'd imagined," he said, his words rousing her as thoroughly as the heavy-lidded gaze he let roam over every inch of her.

"By the saints, but you take my breath," he vowed, his breathing no longer deep and steady, but rapid, shallow. Releasing her wrist, he thrust his hands into her unbound hair. He reveled in the mass of it, smoothed his palms down its glistening length. Lifting, sifting, tangling his fingers where'er he could as if he sought to savor and touch each and every strand.

Isolde caught her lower lip between her teeth, so great were the delicious shivers his ministrations set loose in her, so pleasurable the tingles washing over her, *through* her at his touch.

So intense the longing. The sharply exquisite anticipation he seemed to prize so highly.

With a low moan, one that pleased her immensely, he buried his face in two great handfuls of her streaming tresses, the raven darkness of his own proud mane a stark contrast against the gold-bronze tones of her hair.

He groaned then, a strange man-sound. Half pain, half pleasure. A tremor rippled through his bowed shoulders.

Knowing his enjoyment of her hair rocked him thusly bestirred her in a most disturbing manner.

Faith, he *was* drinking of her hair. Slowly moving his head back and forth, nuzzling his face into her tresses. Seeing him pay homage to her thus did peculiar things to her.

And made her bold.

"And now you've indulged your need to see, feel, and drink of my unbound hair, Sir Knight," she said, her daring sending hot little jabs of pleasure to the secret place between her thighs, "what of your second wish? The vermilion cream? Shall I use the blush of rose now?"

The seductress in her warmed to the game. "Do you think I still require such . . . *enlightenment*?"

He nodded, but stayed her hands when she began to remove the little jar's stopper. "Oh, aye, you do," he said, a wicked gleam in his dark eyes, "but first, a kiss. To reward you for undoing your hair."

Isolde's heart leaped. "A knight's kiss?"

He nodded. Catching up a handful of her hair, he pressed his lips against the thick, glossy strands before he let its smoothness spill from his fingers.

His will to resist her spilling away as easily as the silken skein of hair glided from his hand, Donall gave in to the urge to take what she offered.

Everything she offered.

He smoothed his hands over her shoulders, down the bared softness of her arms, then around and up her back. Sliding his fingers into the smooth curtain of her hair, he caressed the silky warmth of her nape.

"A knight's kiss, then," he murmured, threading his fingers through the cool, satiny weight of her tresses, breathing deeply of her wildflower scent. "A thorough one."

He looked deep into her eyes as he eased his hands down her back. Searing need twisted inside him. Splaying his fingers around her hips, he caught her to him, drawing her as close as he could without taking full possession of her.

With trembling fingers, she traced the line of his shoulder. Her touch exhilarated him. Her grace and beauty near lamed him. She proffered her lips so sweetly, a raw primal urge tore through him, a need so fierce his heart thundered in his chest.

They locked gazes, each watching the play of light and shadow across the other's face. Then, patient no more, Donall touched a gentle kiss to the lone freckle he loved, and slanted his mouth over hers in a fierce kiss meant to brand her very soul.

Not lightly, not tender as before, but a powerfully possessive *taking*.

A thorough claiming of her warm, pliant lips.

But a *giving*, too.

For ne'er had he desired a woman more.

Ne'er had he wished to please one so greatly.

Ne'er had he loved.

Cradling the back of her head, he angled her face to accept a deeper kiss, used the gentle probing of his tongue to coax her lips apart, silently urging her to be the fine, bold lass he knew she was.

And she obliged, opening her mouth beneath his, accepting the glide of his tongue into her warm softness. Her lips, her passion, for once blessedly free of any traces of the noxious potion. He tasted her, drank of her breath, whisper-soft, sweet and fresh. A more potent elixir than anything her ancient crone could produce.

A thousand times more bewitching.

She clung to his shoulders, her need blossoming, her supple body pressing into his with ever greater urgency. His blood fired and he kissed her harder, thrust his tongue against hers in long bold sweeps.

She matched his sliding rhythm, her ardor pleasing him greatly as she tangled her tongue with his in a languid dance that mingled not just their mouths, but their breath, their hearts, their souls.

He crushed her against him, the intimacy of the kiss, its rough fierceness, softening his heart, rendering him wholly hers, while her eagerness to match his passion hardened him elsewhere.

And she finally noticed.

At last.

Drawing back, her eyes widened with a startled look of gold-cast perplexity. She stiffened, but only for a moment. Her soft, kiss-tender lips formed a sweet little "o," then curved into a hesitant, knowing smile.

She made a small breathy sound, and he caught it, enveloping her soft whimper with his own moan of pleasure, pulling her tight, capturing her sigh before it could fully form.

She melted against him. A haven of warm suppleness, her smooth-lined, pliant body molded to his. Again and again, he kissed her, consumed by a thunderous passion unlike any he'd ever known.

A shining and triumphant need only she could quench. A craving. He deepened each new kiss, plied her lips with a knight's mastery. Harder and increasingly demanding, until he recognized the fire raging inside him.

Until he recognized her.

Truly saw her at last.

Pulling her so close against him their hearts could surely beat as one, Donall lost himself in the glory of the one woman destined to set his strong-passioned MacLean heart aflame.

With ease, she ignited the famed love fires MacLean males were purported to harbor for their ladies. A supposed unquenchable inferno, the flames which Donall thought he'd been spared. Now he knew the folly of his doubt. He simply hadn't met his woman.

Until now.

And the knowledge almost brought him to his knees.

He gentled his kiss until it was naught but a light whisper of sweetness moving softly over her lips, a tender rain of achingly sweet kisses, delicate as down. Drawing back at last, he nuzzled her neck, lightly kissed the pulse beating at the base of her throat.

Only when she doubted she could remain standing did he finally lift his dark head. The heat simmering in his eyes undid the last tenuous threads of her modesty. "The blush of rose?" she asked, knowing instinctively what he needed.

Wanting it, too.

He captured her face between his hands, the compelling look in his dark eyes demanding the truth. "Are you aware of what will happen *after* you do this for me?"

Isolde nodded.

Aye, she knew.

And ached for him to take her in that final way.

Ached badly.

He leaned forward, dragged his mouth across hers, sealing her lips with the feel, the taste of him. Making her his, and his alone. "Then so be it," he said, his eyes turning dark as peat.

His gaze steady on hers, he skimmed his hands along her shoulders and down her arms. But this time, rather than reveling in her hair flowing wild and free over his hands, he smoothed her tresses off her shoulders, careful not to leave one strand shielding her near-bared breasts from view.

"You are more beautiful than I can describe," he told her, his voice cracking, so strong raged his desire.

She blushed prettily, and he would've sworn she thrust

her breasts forward a bit. As if she, too, ached for his touch, *burned* for the pleasure he was about to give her.

Teach her to give herself.

His manhood bucked and pulled at the thought.

"The paint," he breathed, the words heavy with his ardor. His enjoyment of their game.

A game more arousing if played with words.

"Open the jar of paint, Isolde," he said, and she did.

She watched him watch her, a hot, liquid-y feeling twirling deep within *that* part of her. "And now, Sir Knight?" she whispered, "will you tell me what to do?"

Donall drew a deep breath. "You are eager to continue our talking game?"

Her nod of acquiescence near undid him.

"Then let us begin." He rested his hands on her shoulders. "Your breasts are lush and perfect," he said, opening this new round, a more elevated version of the game than what he'd taught her earlier.

This time he meant to *do* what he spoke of, not simply regale her with *what* he wanted to do.

He peered at her. So closely his stare would soon burn a hole in Evelina's borrowed undergown. "Full and ripe, eager for my touch, they strain against the cloth of your camise," he said, massaging her shoulders as he spoke, his own blood thickening with every uttered syllable.

She hung on his words, watching him with a rapt expression, her eagerness so apparent he could all but taste it.

He smoothed his hands up the column of her throat, toyed with the lobes of her ears, the soft skin just beneath. "Their peaks, your *nipples*, are a beautiful dusky rose. They are tightened, hard little buds, thrusting toward me through the fine, sheer fabric of your camise. They've peaked because they ache to be caressed."

His wordy magic wove a wondrous enchantment 'round her, so titillating was it to hear him speak thus.

She burned for him.

"I ache for your touch," she breathed, the admittance shooting straight to his groin, lengthening him to a painful degree.

He trailed his fingertips across the top halves of her breasts—the bared flesh swelling above the edge of the low-cut camise. Unbridled longing spiraled through her. She sighed, aching to rip apart the camise front and fully expose herself to the heat of his gaze.

"And I ache for you, sweet Isolde," he said, gently kneading her upper arms, the magic he worked on her, pushing her past all maidenly decorum.

"Then take me," the wanton in her pleaded. "Take me now."

"And lose . . . this?" His slow smile returned, and its impact was devastating. "Nay, my love, to be a knight's steely maid, you must learn restraint, to endure. Even when you believe doing so will push you to the brink of madness."

Her tongue darted out to wet her lips, and he swiftly leaned forward, catching it with his teeth. He flicked his own tongue over the tip of hers, then suckled briefly on her full lower lip before releasing her.

"You see, Isolde, when the anticipation is keen and sharp, the later release is powerful enough to move the stars, and that is what I would give you. Nothing less." He looked at her. Deep and fully. "I want to move the stars for you."

His gaze dropped to the black linen of her half-discarded mourning gown. Still bunched around her hips, its abandoned state, gathered in wanton disarray, formed an irresistibly erotic frame for the lush bounty displayed so sweetly above.

It was time.

"Pull down your camise, Isolde."

A sharp stab of pleasure shot into her core.

Her hands began to tremble, almost in time to the aching throb between her thighs. Near swooning for want, she kept her gaze on his and eased her arms out of the camise's shoulder straps. The undergown's bodice dipped a bit when she dropped her arms to her sides, but the silky gauze still clung to the full mounds of her breasts, snagged there by her hardened nipples.

"Is this enough?" She played the game, the slow pulsing at her woman's center almost unbearable now. "Will this . . . suffice?"

He shook his head, his dark eyes a rich, liquid brown.

"Pull down the fabric, Isolde," he said, the words a command. "I would see you push down the camise until your breasts are fully exposed for my perusal."

Clenching her thighs together, for she could no longer stand the throbbing ache this word game unleashed in her, she curled her fingers around the top edge of Evelina's undergown, and tugged it down until nothing stood between her bared skin and the MacLean but the cool night air and the sheer pleasure of standing before him thus displayed.

Touch yourself.

The words came so soft, so low, she thought she'd imagined them.

"Touch yourself," he said again, more clearly this time. "Do this for me and then I shall do all manner of deliciously wicked things to you," he promised. "And not simply to your breasts."

He nodded to the little pot of vermilion she'd picked up. "Set that down for moment," he said. And she did, unable to resist whate'er he would have of her.

His eyes grew heavy with passion. "Lift up your breasts, Isolde. Lift them up, and toward me."

Very slowly, her entire body trembling, she placed her hands beneath her breasts and . . . didn't move them at all. She simply stood, holding them, feeling their weight against her palms, too embarrassed to do aught else.

"Show them to me, Isolde."

A ragged sigh tore from her throat as she did as he bade. He didn't moan or sigh, but his eyes were passion-drugged. Pure lust smoldered in their depths and sprang onto her, igniting similar fires in her own blood.

"Now touch your nipples," he instructed, and the hot pulsing at her core burst into wholly new dimensions. "Toy and play with them, Isolde."

She cried out the moment her fingers grasped the hardened peaks. Her knees buckled beneath her, but he caught her, pulling her tight against his warrior's chest as he leaned back against the table.

Holding her, he pressed a light kiss to her temple. "Can you go on, my love?" He trailed his fingers down her arm, carefully avoiding any contact with her aching breasts, with her nipples.

He sat back, cradling her securely in his strong arms. "Would you crave surcease now, or shall we prolong our pleasure a bit longer?"

She nodded. "More." The word came faint, pleasure-drowsed, but unmistakable.

Donall's smile flashed triumphant. "My fine bold lass," he said, his heart singing. "Then pull on your nipples, Isolde," came his voice, thick with need. "Let me see you *play* with them."

Her eyes drifted shut, so intense was the pleasure streaking through her. Her hips began to rock, her thighs instinctively inching apart, the pulsing ache between them begging for relief.

Infinitely gentle, he drew his hand, full-palmed over the

plump heat of her woman's flesh, warm through the folds of her gown. He caressed her need with a fleeting touch . . . a promise. "Soon, my sweet," he breathed, taking his hand away. "*After* I've had my fill of watching you toy with your breasts. After *I've* toyed with them. Now pull on the nipples, Isolde. *Please.*"

And she did. Hesitant at first, simple touches with the very tips of her fingers. Then light circles, scarcely touching the ruched peaks, until, urged on by his words and heated looks, she grew bolder, and began *really* playing with them.

Rousing herself with each tug, each pull. Watching him watch her do this stimulated her beyond anything she would have believed.

"The cream, Isolde," he said, his voice calling her from the haze of wanton delight. "You are ready, my love."

Still dazed, she felt him take one of her hands and smooth the cold, rose-scented unguent onto her fingers.

"The nipple cream. Use it, Isolde," he urged. "For me."

Another cry pushed up her throat, even as *that* part of her grew so heavy, she could scarce bear the exquisiteness. A heated, pulsing weight, driving her to the brink of all need.

"Rub the cream on your nipples."

Her right hand, the one he smeared the blush of rose onto, drifted toward her breasts. Almost of its own volition. Moving ever closer, then pausing just above the aching tip of her left breast.

"Do it, my lady." His words drowned her in lust, enslaved her to his mastery, his ardor.

His passion.

"Let me see you put the cream on your nipples, Isolde," he coaxed her, his voice a caress of warm silk sliding past her ears, bewitching her. "Slow, gentle circles, a pull or two, a good, sound *rubbing* to work in the color, and then . . ."

She looked at him. "And then?" she breathed, her voice so thick with need she scarce recognized it as her own.

"*Do it*, my sweeting." He tucked a strand of hair behind her ear, and the lust in his eyes sent her cream-coated fingers straight to her left nipple.

He flashed her a smile to rival the brilliance of the sun. "I am doing it, Sir Knight," she breathed, his smile giving her the boldness she needed to be wanton.

His wanton.

"And what shall you do, now that I am?" She rubbed and rubbed, her gaze holding his. "What is this 'and then . . .' of yours?"

"And then, sweet Isolde," he vowed, leaning forward to kiss her nose, "and then I shall call down the moon and the stars for you."

Chapter Sixteen

❖

"*Call down the moon and the stars?*"

"Every last one of them," Donall vowed, still leaning hard against the table, still cradling her in his arms. "I swear it to you."

"Every one?" She looked at him, shadows and candle-glow playing across her beautiful face.

"So I have said." Half-besotted with lust, he rubbed his thumb in slow, tender circles 'round one of her vermilion-tipped nipples. "And when the day breaks, mayhap I shall fetch you the sun as well."

She sighed, snuggling closer, her eyes limpid. "And you, my lord? What of your pleasure?"

His pleasure?

Could she truly not know simply holding her thus filled him with such pleasure, he'd soon burst from the sheer intensity of it?

"My pleasure is in the giving," he said, returning his attention to her rose-scented nipples. Hoping to lose himself in passion before his conscience smote him for what he was about to do: indulge his fierce craving for her, then leave.

And leave he would.

He'd take the key she'd so bravely relinquished, and escape at first opportunity, following not his pleasure, his *heart,* but his duty.

His pressing need to return to Baldoon before Iain's temper unleashed such chaos the tittle-tattlers would need centuries to tell the tale.

Her fingers—warm, smooth, and surprisingly strong—slipped over his hand, staying the sweet ministrations he dispensed so gladly. Banishing all thought of his hot-headed brother.

"The key is merely to afford you and your friend more comfort," she said, as if she'd read his mind, the words slicing through the thick shroud of his lust.

Donall glanced sharply at her.

Saints, but she was as great an all-seer as Gavin!

Something keen and hurtful hid behind the desire lighting her eyes, but before he could fathom the look, she spoke again. "Naught has changed."

He arched a brow. "Think you?"

She met his gaze full on, her courage bright and shining. "You and Gavin MacFie may while unhindered in your cell, but the door shall remained barred."

Hot fury sluiced through him, the cursed MacLean taint, and he struggled to tamp it down. Cool his brewing temper and not lose sight of *her* struggle.

And struggle she did.

Warring emotions flashed across her face, while the bitter edge in her voice heralded the weight of her cares.

He closed his eyes for a brief moment, silently cursing himself for a fool. Despite his own vexation, seeing her thus troubled bothered him greatly.

"You are blind, Isolde of Dunmuir," he said, his voice tight, rigidly controlled lest he bellow his frustration at her.

Remind her of the famed MacLean temper.

Toss tinder on her suspicions against Iain.

"Blind?" She tilted her head and the movement sent a sheaf of her hair sliding over his arm.

Cool, flowing silk, heating his blood, and firing his temper at his ineptitude in convincing her of his brother's innocence.

"Aye, blind." Willing the flare of ill humor to recede, he smoothed his free hand down her arm. He captured her hand and brought it to his lips. "A braw lass would look into her heart when seeking truths, and not out fool windows." He gentled the words with a soft kiss on the backs of her fingers.

Her eyes widened, but rather than dispute what he'd said, she pressed her lips together and simply stared at him.

Donall shrugged. "'Tis there, and there alone, your answer lies." He released her hand. "Not out yon windows or inside flagons of foul-reeking potions."

Her face colored at that, and she glanced away, despite his words, looking straight toward the row of unshuttered windows lining the far wall. Narrow, arch-topped eyes peering out on the silvered night.

Undaunted, Donall cupped her chin and turned her face back to his. "Fair lady, you are wondrous full of puzzles." He touched a fingertip to the lone freckle on her cheek. "How is it, you can dab whore's paint on your breasts without batting an eye, yet one mention of that sharp-smelling tincture and you blush furiously?"

The high color in her cheeks glowed near as red as the vermilion staining the tips of her breasts. Donall peered at her, curious beyond redemption. "What *is* the brew?" he prodded. "Have mercy and ease my wonderings, for I will not be gulled into believing it is what you've claimed."

His gaze raked her from the crown of her pretty head to where her gown and camise still bunched 'round her waist . . . and saw naught but unblemished creamy skin.

"You have but a single freckle," he said, his MacLean temper vanquished by the powerful swell of his lust.

He placed a light kiss atop the freckle. "And a most fetching freckle it is," he said, a genuine smile curving his lips.

"A bonnie freckle, indeed," he jested, extraordinarily pleased at the way her own lips lifted in a tiny half-smile at his teasing. Totally smitten, he kissed the freckle again. "I would sorely regret its demise."

"There were others," she began, fidgeting at the lie. "I b-banished them all wi—" she broke off when he shook his head.

Clearly defeated, the blush drained from her cheeks, quickly replaced by the soft vulnerability he found so difficult to resist.

A vulnerability alluring enough to melt the most jaded knight's heart, yet enough steel in her blood to make that same warrior's hardened soul swell with pride.

Despite his best efforts to remain impassive, a frustrated sigh welled in Donall's chest, and this time he didn't even try to hold it back.

"By all the prophets and apostles, lass, it cannot be that damning," he swore, his voice gruff, riding his aggravation. "What *is* the vile potion?"

She turned her head to the side and for one gut-wrenching moment, Donall feared she'd cry, but then a worse thought seized him. "Are you ill?" His fool MacLean heart twisted in anticipation of her answer.

To his astonishment, she smiled. Little more than slight

twitchings at the corners of her mouth at first, but blossoming into a beaming smile of such radiance, it rivaled the light of all of Baldoon's finest candelabra combined.

A smile to light the darkest night.

Or warm the emptiest heart.

"Aye, I am ill," she said. "Sorely stricken, and there is no cure. The potion was given to me as a p-preventative measure, but has proven itself worthless save in repelling all who catch its smell."

Something tightened in Donall's chest. Not because of her words, but because of the look on her face as she'd said them. Were he Gavin MacFie, he'd know what the look meant, but he wasn't, so he asked.

"And from what dire scourge is the wretched brew meant to protect you?"

She hesitated but a moment. "From you, milord," she said, looking right at him. "From you."

"From me?"

She nodded.

"A potion to protect you from me?" Hilarity began to overtake his astonishment. A bold conviviality, moving in fast and hard, ably crowding out his stunned surprise, and even his passion.

"Saints above, lass, 'tis not *I* who set out to seduce." He skimmed his fingers across the round swells of her breasts.

Her naked, exposed breasts.

Heated desire shot straight to his groin. "Why would you seek to protect yourself from that which you so openly sought?"

She blinked, had the good grace to appear chagrined.

"Sought and won," he added, heeding the urge to needle her when she didn't answer him.

Needle her and take the sharp edge off his growing need to possess her.

He grazed a fingernail over one hardened nipple. "So now you've worn down my resistance, you seek to safeguard yourself with rank-smelling potions?"

"Nay, such is not the way of it," she demurred. "I drank the potion to protect me from myself."

His brows shot upward, the pert nipple forgotten. *"From yourself?"*

"Devorgilla gave me the anti-attraction potion to render me immune to your charms," she said, bold as day, the steel he knew she possessed rising to the fore again. "Charms such as your bonnie chest and that slow, wicked smile you're e'er turning on me."

She stared at him, daring him to laugh. "Much is bandied about concerning your prowess and *airs* with the ladies," she declared. "I only wanted an alliance. Ne'er did I desire to fall prey to your legendary appeal. I was assured the potion would spare me such a fate."

His last trace of chivalry gone, Donall lowered his head and gave in to the urge to flick his tongue over one of her painted nipples. Unable to curb his lust once he'd touched her so intimately, he drew the nipple into his mouth, and swirled his tongue over its swollen, tender peak.

She arched her back, pressing herself against him, instinctively seeking more. It was the reaction he'd sought, all he needed to know.

"And have you been . . . spared?" he asked, lifting his mouth from her sweetness. "Do you still desire 'only a bairn'? Or would you have the whole man as well?"

Body, heart, and soul?

He touched a finger to her damp nipple. "Have you fallen for me, my lady?"

Silence answered him.

Silence and a most telltale stubborn set to her fine jaw.

Donall's heart soared. His fierce MacLean pride wanted

to shout with triumph. She'd said she wanted an alliance, naught else. But what she didn't say, and the look on her beautiful face, said more.

Whate'er fool notions had made her desire a child to seal her ludicrous pact, she wanted *him* now.

Donall was sure of it.

A maelstrom of fierce, joyous emotions surging through him, he gave her one of his guaranteed-to-melt-a-wench's-heart smiles. "And you vow the potion to be worthless?"

She surprised him by placing her hand on his chest and smoothing her fingers over the planes of his muscles. Donall melted, his jaunty smile tilting away. Banished by the darker urgings stirring inside him.

Easing her hand over his heart, she stilled her fingers, tensing them as if listening with their nerve endings for the manifest thudding.

The slow pounding of a heart conquered and besieged.

A tiny smile of recognition flittered across her face when her questing fingers heard what they'd sought.

"*This* is what I sought protection from," she breathed, her words balm to his soul. "Exactly this."

"The beating of my heart?" he could scarce speak, so thick was his throat.

"Nay, sirrah, what its slow, hard beat *means*." Showing the steel he loved, she captured his hand and placed it over her own pounding heart. "What *this* means," she said, and Donall was lost.

Totally, irrevocably lost.

A tremor, light and delicate, rippled through her. A sign as sure and true as the damnable thumping in his chest.

She cared.

Cared mightily.

As did he.

A floodtide of pure joy rose within him. Bold, fierce, and

shining. "And will you *tell* me what it means?" He slipped his hand from her grasp so he could caress her cheek. "I would hear the words."

She shook her head, and the refusal struck hard. Stinging and painful as a fired arrow striking its mark. But then she circled her arms around his back, and the pain diminished. "I cannot say the words, Donall of Baldoon, but I will show you."

Lifting her chin, she offered her lips for a kiss. Donall crushed her to him, slanting his mouth over hers in a rough, possessive claiming. A deep taking of her lips, her tongue, her very breath.

Her soul.

When he eased the kiss to an end, she gazed at him with luminous eyes. The pulse at the base of her neck pounded wildly. His pulse raced, too. Swift, hot, and urgent, an unrelenting stream of need pouring straight into his groin, filling him and demanding release.

But even as he held her, steel bands held him.

Invisible constraints forged of a steel harder than the most adept armorer could hope to achieve.

A forever bond crafted of his feelings, and hers, for there could be no doubt she harbored them. They shouted their existence, shone clear in her shining amber-flecked eyes.

Regardless of how many flagons of her fool anti-attraction potion she'd imbibed to dull them.

A wholly unexpected, giddy sensation swept over him. Wild and unrestrained. Exultant. He could call it naught else, and its fierceness threatened to bring him to his knees.

He pushed away from the table. Sweeping her up hard against his chest, he strode to her bed. With great gentleness, he lowered her to her feet beside the bedpost, *his bedpost*.

His dark eyes heavy-lidded with desire, he regarded her with a smoldering look so intense, sheer nerves made her slip out of her soft leather slippers and dig her toes into the floor rushes.

The stiff coolness of the rushes prickling her feet made a welcome contrast to the liquid heat of his gaze and the languid warmth weighing her belly.

"Your eagerness to disrobe pleases me greatly," he teased, his amused gaze lighting briefly on her bare feet before he swept back the bed curtains. He whipped down the coverlets, his swift movements revealing a sharp eagerness of his own.

Mayhap a greater eagerness, for of a sudden, hers was fraught with a slight twinge of trepidation.

He watched her, a slow smile curving his lips. "I am going to fondle your breasts now," he told her, placing his hands on them as he spoke. "And then we shall rid you fully of your clothes, and I shall love you until you cry out with your release."

"Will you kiss me?"

"I shall kiss you forever and a day," he vowed, lowering his head to her breast. He licked one nipple, caressing it with his lips while he palmed and rubbed the other.

Isolde dug her hands into the thick silk of his hair, gasped at her wonder. She clung to him, fearing she'd fall if she didn't, so overwhelming were the waves of pleasure swirling through her at his touch.

So exquisite.

Very gently, he grazed his teeth over her hardened nipples, then lapped at them, one at a time, until not a trace of the blush of rose remained.

"Would that I had a potion to save me from *your* charms," he murmured, so low she scarce heard him. But she felt his breath, warm and soft, against her flesh.

Reveled in it.

Straightening, he sent a pointed look at the garments still

tangled about her hips. "I would kiss all of you," he said. "Push down your gown and the camise so I can."

"You needn't have me naked to k-kiss me." The maid in her returned, not quite comprehending his intent. But the bawd in her knew, whispered to her exactly what kind of kiss he meant. "Oh!" she gasped, heat shooting onto her cheeks.

Delicious little flames of sharp pleasure stabbed her elsewhere.

There where her wanton side claimed he meant to put his mouth.

To *kiss* her, and the saints knew what else.

She took a backward step. "You cannot do that."

"Cannot . . . or will not?" His smile turned wicked. "Fair Isolde, I promise you I can and will, and shall do so most masterfully."

She gulped. Her heart knocked about wildly in her breast, the pulsing *there* cried out for what he meant to do to her.

"Push down the clothes, Isolde, or I shall do it for you."

Driven by the need he'd enflamed in her, she began struggling with the bunched folds of her garments until the last of her gown's laces finally gave. But just before she shoved it and the camise to her feet, she remembered Evelina's emerald bauble.

Mortification assailed her.

She'd forgotten the slim gold chain and large tear-shaped gemstone. A whore's trinket, bold, sassy, and resting brazenly against the abundant pelt of red-gold curls betwixt her thighs.

Her last bastion of hope had the MacLean shunned her efforts at seduction. Evelina had sworn, if all else failed, the sight of the bauble resting against her intimate curls would be rousing enough to stir any man.

Even one so braw and bold as Donall MacLean.

But she hadn't planned on him seducing her.

Her fingers dug into the fabric still bunched at her hips. "I-I cannot do this after all," she declared. "Can we not just . . . kiss?"

Donall placed his hands on hers, curled his fingers over hers. Over her fingers and the fabric she clutched so desperately. A wicked gleam danced in his dark eyes. "Kissing you is my intent," he said.

His gaze holding hers, he began easing down her gown, the camise with it. The tips of his fingers, dry and warm, brushed against her hips, the tops of her thighs, as he worked to release her grip on the fabric.

Each time the contact came, she grew more breathless, became more *eager.* Did the large emerald not adorn *that* part of her, she'd release her hold on the constricting garments, kick them aside, and part her thighs in wild abandon.

For him.

For his touch.

For the promised kisses.

Those kisses.

Sheer wanton need seized her, a liquid heat spilling the length of her, leaving her breathless, leaving her . . . *his.*

She began to sway, might have lost her footing did he not grasp her hips. "Do not fight what you're feeling, Isolde," he soothed, his fingers kneading the curve of her buttocks, this new touch sending waves of bliss swirling through her.

"Let the clothes fall," he murmured, his caresses working wondrous magic, making her fingers loosen their hold almost of their own volition.

He dropped to one knee. *"Let me give you this pleasure."*

Her fingers jerked reflexively against the linen and silk

clutched tight in her hands. "I do not want to be kissed *t-there*," she lied.

"You will," he said and yanked on the material.

Her fingers gave and the raiment dropped to the floor, pooling at her feet in a billowy heap of black linen and transparent gauze.

She wore naught beneath.

Naught but her desire and Evelina's bauble.

"Sweet Jesu!" The words tore from Donall's throat. A dark, feral cry rent from the very depths of his need.

By the holy sepulcher, her beauty *lamed* him.

The large gemstone winked at him from the wild tangle of her feminine curls. Heated blood rushed into his tarse, lengthening and swelling him to a degree that ripped away the last strands of his restraint.

His heart slammed rough against his ribs and his breath came fast and hard. He looked up at her, capturing her gaze as he pressed his lips against the warm, taut skin of her lower stomach in a fierce, openmouthed kiss.

"By the gods," he choked out against the soft curls of her woman's mound. "What siren's trick is this?"

He edged aside the bauble, nuzzled his face against her softness, drank in the light musk of her sweetness in great, greedy gulps. Its aroused tang fired his lust. He caressed his hands up the backs of her thighs, spread his fingers over the firm rounds of her bottom, drew her nearer.

Near enough to lose himself in her scent as he brushed his lips over the pleasingly lush vee of intimate curls.

He fingered the large gemstone, purposely holding back, not yet ready to touch the sweet flesh hidden beneath the wealth of red-gold curls . . . not yet wanting to *lick* at her lest he explode within his hose.

"So my lady does value baubles?" He rubbed his fingers over the stone's smoothness, its warmth.

Warmth gleaned from her heat.

She looked down at him, transfixed by the way his lips hovered so close to her femininity, incredibly aroused just watching him. Even the way his fingers moved over the emerald excited her.

A slow, languorous rubbing.

Touch me thus.

The throbbing at her core screamed the words, but he must have heard them, for he let loose the bauble and slipped one finger between her thighs, trailed its tip slowly along her very middle.

"The stone, Isolde?" He withdrew the finger and glanced up at her, the lust in his eyes stealing her breath. "Why did you wear it?"

She opened her mouth to explain, but a soft moan blocked the words. His eyes narrowing, he touched her again, using more fingers this time. He toyed with her, plucking at her damp nether hair, gently stroking and probing the sensitive flesh until she writhed with the sheer bliss of his touch.

"Why, Isolde?" he asked again.

"It was a friend's loan," she gasped, leaning against the bedpost, *needing* its support. "T-to push you past your limits should you shun my . . . advances."

His eyes widened. "What purveyor of nonsense suggested you have need of such ploys?" His hand closed over her, hard and rough. He palmed her, and the pressure increased the urgency pulsing so exquisitely at her center.

"I vow on my life, woman, a score of Infidel harlots wearing similar jewels would not sway my lust as much as one gold-cast glance from your beautiful eyes," he said, dragging his hand from her.

Catching her up in his arms, he eased her onto the bed's cool linen sheets. "We shall love now, Isolde," he said, his hands going to the waist of his hose, his fingers swiftly undoing the cord binding, then shoving down his braies, kicking them aside to stand proud and tall before her.

Standing *there,* next to the bedpost where he'd been chained for so many nights, her prisoner, yet now *she* lay sprawled before him, spread wantonly across her bedsheets.

His for the taking.

"You are beautiful," he said, his eyes heavy-lidded with passion, his manhood aroused and full, its swollen length riding hard against the darkness of his groin.

He touched one hand to his rigid shaft, let his fingers curl 'round its thickness. He stroked down, then up, his dark gaze trained on hers. "See well what you do to me," he said, his voice husky with need. "What you alone do to me."

To my MacLean heart.

Letting go of himself, he stepped to the edge of the bed and smoothed his hand down her side. "Look well and look your fill, for my honor would keep me from laying a further hand on you unless I honestly say you I shall leave here, leave *you,* at first opportunity."

Leave until I have gathered my wits, my sword, and my men. Then I shall harangue you the length and breadth of this fair isle until I've claimed your heart as well as your passion.

Until I've made you mine.

Isolde heard his words, recognized the threat behind the spoken ones, the promise in the unspoken ones.

The ones she heard with her heart.

"Is this still your wish, my lady?" His fingers skimmed over the thick curls of her woman's mound. "Speak now if it is not, for I can withhold myself but few moments more."

She watched him, too awed to speak. She gazed in wonder at the dark masculinity of his male parts, at the length and thickness of his manly flesh. Marveled at how well formed and beautiful that part of him was, how incredibly arousing.

How incredibly *aroused*.

Ne'er would she have guessed a man could wax so . . . *large*. Her heart leaped, her own passion soaring. Just looking upon him, long, thick, and visibly throbbing, sent purely wondrous thrills of pleasure streaking through her.

Something tore loose inside her. A careening *something*, and whatever it was, it made her hips rock. She arched upward off the bed, her body instinctively seeking relief from the wild urges twisting and spinning inside her.

An exquisitely painful knot, whirling ever tighter until she feared it would shatter into a million pieces if he did not soon spend her the surcease she craved.

"I see your desire, Isolde of Dunmuir," he said, the words proud, male, and triumphant. He touched his hand briefly to his swollen shaft. "As you can see mine. Tell me you still want this, and I shall come to you."

Lose myself fully inside you.

Give you my heart . . . my seed.

Know and love you in all your moods, find my own haven in the fair shelter of your embrace.

He waited, his MacLean heart thudding with a greater intensity than the hot throbbing of his charged shaft. And whilst he waited, he tried hard to block his ears to the foolery his heart and its annoying soft spot kept flustering at him.

Henpeckers both, the curse of every MacLean male e'er to be born: a full heart and a sore weakness for but one braw lass.

"Well?" he snapped, his temper and aching tarse winning the battle against his smitten heart.

Treat her gently, laddie, for she loves you.

Donall wheeled around, his sharply indrawn breath snagged fast in his throat, but no one stood behind him.

No old woman darted into the shadows, seeking a hiding place after chiding him to go easy with his lady.

His lady?

Aye, his, and with the acknowledgment came a queer sound, almost a cackle.

Gooseflesh rose on the back of his neck. He peered into each dark corner of the room but naught stirred save the embers glowing in the hearth and the tail end of the sea breeze that had just swept through the chamber.

Only the wind.

Not the hag he'd glimpsed spooking 'round Dunmuir once or twice.

Merely the wind.

As if to prove it, one of the shutters slammed back against the wall. Caught and tossed by the same sea wind whose high-pitched keening he'd mistaken for an old woman's un-asked-for advice.

He turned back to face her, a shade less irritated. "I would know if you still want this?"

"Aye, I do," she whispered and parted her thighs.

But 'tis you I want, not simply . . . this.

Donall started. He looked sharply at her, but her sweet lips were upturned in a soft smile, her luminous eyes unafraid. The wind had sought to bedevil again.

The wind or the sound of his own heated blood surging through his ears.

His patience flown, both with his overtaxed restraint and the damning voices e'er whispering at him, he joined her on the bed, settling himself on his knees between her parted thighs.

He raked his gaze over her, studied every curve. The sleek lines of her limbs, the round globes of her breasts, her sweet nipples peeking at him through the wild tumble of her bronze tresses. The nip of her slender waist, her smooth, flat belly, and the lush fleece of red-gold curls at the juncture of her spread thighs.

Especially the fleece of bronze curls.

Blood rushed to his shaft, swelling him even more. Slipping his hands beneath her knees, he gently bent her legs, urging them wider until she was fully open.

Totally exposed.

Lush red-gold curls, damp and fragrant. Pulsing, swollen flesh waiting for his touch . . . his kiss.

He nuzzled his face against her, pressed his mouth to her sweetness, licked and flicked his tongue over her. *Tasted* her. Drank fully of her essence, until the scent of her arousal rose up around him.

Her taste, her scent, her cries, sent pounding, urgent need thundering through him, stretched his shaft, and brought him to the very edge of his control.

She moved her hips, a gentle rocking at first, then more frantic, bold moves. Innocent attempts to bring her need closer to the pleasure he gave her.

And each time her limbs tensed, going so taut he knew her release neared, he upped the tender torment by lightening his kisses, reducing his slow wide-tongued lavings to soft, barely there little licks. Mere flickings of his tongue over her pouty, musk-scented sweetness.

Only when she strained so hard against his mouth, her hips raised off the bed, did he draw the swollen little bud of her sex into his mouth and suckle it, truly suckle it as if he meant to draw her release deep into himself, into his soul.

And when her passion verged, he pulled deeply on her, savoring her pleasure, holding her fast in its bliss by replacing his lips and tongue with his fingers.

Gently stroking, circling his middle finger over and over the tight bud of her desire. Keeping her need keen, as he stretched out atop her, and entered her with one swift stroke, plunging through her innocence in the same moment her sharp cry of release tore from her lips.

He stilled for but a moment, then glided into her snug, silken warmth again and again. Slow, languid thrusts, long and gentle, until he could hold back no more.

His own cry blending with hers, his seed poured from him in a blinding, rollicking deliverance powerful enough to blot out the moon and the stars.

Massive enough to extinguish not only the silver-hued cast of the night, but snatch the light from within the chamber as well.

Snatch the light, subdue the wind, and vanquish the very room itself, plunging him into a spinning vortex of the most intense bliss he'd e'er known.

As if from a great distance, he heard her soft moans, and knew a great joy, for they sounded of contentment rather than pain. But then those sounds faded, too, and the heavy aftermath of his release claimed him, pulling him down, down, down into a sea of dark drifting mists, a woman's sated sighs, and the exquisite peace of holding her close.

And as they slept, their ardor spent, their bodies and hearts entwined, an ever darker, thicker mist descended upon MacKinnons' Isle until not even a sliver of its stern-faced bulk could be seen.

The roiling sea mist—wet, gray, and drifting—blotted out its dunes and bays, its rugged cliffs. A dark shadow, blanketing the strewn wreckage of its once-feared fleet with an impenetrable shroud of dank, shifting fog.

Indeed, all that could be distinguished so far out to sea was a lone square-sailed galley bearing MacLean banners, and moving steadily through the curtain of mist, making its sad, slow journey home to Baldoon . . .

Chapter Seventeen

❧

$\mathcal{A}$ FULL SENNIGHT later, Iain MacLean paced the dais end of Baldoon's cavernous great hall and wondered at his folly in accepting the ailing MacKinnon laird's swiftly proffered offer of help.

Thus far, the only "help" proffered had been spent by the MacLeans' amply-stocked kitchens. Goods tendered, stores depleted, all to fill the bottomless bellies of the MacKinnon warriors who'd accompanied Iain and his men on the return journey from MacKinnons' Isle.

An isle not only littered with the broken remains of the MacKinnons' shattered fleet, but, did Iain care to believe their tales of woe, an isle plagued by all manner of ill fortune ever since a savage gale had blown its black breath o'er the MacKinnon holding a full year before.

And from what Iain and his men had seen, from the wreckage strewn along the isle's dune-lined shore to the shambles of its once formidable stronghold, and the sad physical state of its men, Iain believed them.

He'd even admit a grudging respect for the MacKinnon's

generous offer to send his best men-at-arms, those yet hale enough to swing a sword, to aid Iain in finding his lady wife's true murderers.

A two-edged offer, of a certainty. A down-on-its-luck clan reaching out to an old adversary, hoping to bridge past rivalries with a common goal, and mayhap desirous of a gentle grip under the arms until they'd recovered enough from their bout of misfortune to stand alone.

A two-edged offer, indeed, but one Iain had humbly accepted.

Doing otherwise would have been a gross breach of honor.

Even one as grief-stricken and quick-blooded as he could not refuse the outstretched hand of a foe on his knees.

Not if he meant to maintain his self-respect, hoped to walk proudly among his men. And since losing Lileas to the Lady Rock, naught much remained to cling to save his honor and his temper.

Sad bedmates, not always compatible, but all he had.

That, and his thirst for revenge.

A gentle but firm hand grabbed his arm. "Two more paces, brother, and you will set the hall a-fire," Amicia said, and snapped her fingers in front of his face.

She nodded to the tall iron candelabrum he'd almost walked into. "The floor rushes would've caught flame before yon guests can devour another joint of roasted boar."

Blinking, Iain fought the urge to topple the unwieldy taper-topped monstrosity anyway. Set loose the fires of hell to consume himself, his sorrow, and all else not wise enough to flee his wrath.

He heaved a great sigh, and raked a hand through his dark hair. "They do naught but eat and guzzle our stores of spirits."

Amicia folded her arms. "Had you but listened to reason,

they would not be sitting in our hall annoying you with their voracious presence."

"They offered help." Iain glanced at the MacKinnon men. They filled two of the hall's many trestle tables. In truth, they gorged themselves most generously. And appeared much at ease in the companionship of their old foes.

The MacKinnon warriors conversed easily with Iain's men, the lot of them jesting good-naturedly, exchanging boasts, and telling tall tales.

As if not a one amongst them carried a single care on his shoulders.

Iain's hands clenched at his sides. "I should have refused their laird's offer."

A soft look came into Amicia's dark eyes. A look appallingly akin to pity.

"Nay, Iain, 'tis good they are here, regardless of the reason," she said, an odd catch in her voice. "Father would have been proud of you. He and the old MacKinnon laird were once friends, as you know."

She touched his arm when he didn't respond. "*Donall* will be proud when he returns."

Iain rubbed the back of his neck.

A vain attempt to dislodge the growing lump of heat swelling in his throat.

"'Tis where that laddie's a-got hisself off to is what I want to know," Gerbert mumbled as he shuffled past with a platter of discarded gannet bones and other assorted table scraps. "Aye, 'tis mighty strange," he muttered, ambling off toward the dark shadows of the wooden screens passage and the kitchens beyond.

Iain sprinted after him. "*What* is strange?" He planted himself in front of the white-haired seneschal. "Have you heard word of Donall and Gavin?"

"Naught but what you should have heard with your own

ears, boy." Gerbert stared at him from watery blue eyes and, much to Iain's annoyance, the old bugger started clucking his tongue.

Just like he'd done when Iain and Donall were wee laddies and had been caught stirring up mischief.

"Mayhap I've wax in my ears, you clack-tongued old goat," Iain snapped. He braced his hands on his hips. "Now what is this about Donall?"

Gerbert drew back his scrawny shoulders, unimpressed by Iain's bluster. "'Tis a whole head o' wax you must have if you haven't paid heed to what the MacKinnons have been puzzling about ever since we departed from that blighted isle of theirs."

The tiny hairs on the back of Iain's neck lifted. He slapped at his nape. A reflex against the queer sensation that something, *someone*, had been standing behind him.

Someone who'd breathed down his neck.

A drawn breath, quickly expelled. As if whoe'er it'd been had meant to speak, then gave off, drifting away into the shadows instead.

He cast a wary glance over his shoulder but saw naught amiss. Only his supping men, the roaring fires in the three great hearths, and the equally healthy flames of the pitch-pine torches set in iron brackets along walls. A few hounds scrounging for bones amongst the rushes.

All appeared as it should.

All save the harried servitors bustling about, plying the MacKinnons' ravenous appetites with plenty of MacLean victuals and ale.

A bothersome state of being he could blame on none but himself.

He frowned and turned back to Gerbert. "What strangeness and puzzling are you talking about? Donall will still be in Glasgow."

Gerbert allowed himself one or two more clucks before he spoke. "Not if he ne'er set foot there, he won't be."

Iain's dark brows shot upward in a fine imitation of his older brother's favored look of astonishment. *"If he'd not set foot there?"* he mimicked. "What nonsense would you speak?"

The old seneschal shook his white-tufted head.

Iain glared back. "Donall set sail for Glasgow weeks ago, with the MacInnesses. You know when . . ." he began, then let the sentence trail off, not caring to voice the reason Donall and Gavin had set off for Dunmuir Castle.

Too painful was the memory of watching his brother and Gavin ride through Baldoon's gates, Lileas with them. Her shroud-draped body affixed atop a black-festooned cart, bell-ringers and candle-bearing children trudging respectfully in their wake.

"Set sail for Glasgow? With your dead lady wife's kinfolk?" Gerbert's reedy voice penetrated the fog of Iain's pain, the words catching Iain's attention with the swiftness of a stinging winter wind.

He looked sharply at the old man, only to find him casting a sideways glance at the MacKinnons.

"If we're to believe what *they* say," Gilbert mused, "no MacInnes galley has sailed past their isle in months."

The queer feeling stole onto the back of Iain's neck again, and this time it crept clear down his spine. "What are you saying?"

Gerbert shrugged. "Mayhap you'd best question them," he said with a nod toward their guests. "I only ken 'tis strange if, as they claim, they're e'er keeping a lookout on their waters yet didn't see the MacInnes galley a-sailing to Glasgow."

"Because . . ." Iain's mind reeled, grasping at snatches of conversation he'd had with the MacKinnon men. He dragged a hand over his face, struggled to clear the grief-inspired fog from his brain.

The thought finally formed.

". . . Because the MacInnesses would have to sail past MacKinnons' Isle to reach the mainland."

"Aye." Gerbert nodded in wizened satisfaction. "And *that* is what I find a mite strange," he offered, then shuffled off about his business, leaving Iain to gape after him.

Gape after him and rub at the odd tingling on the back of his neck.

About the same time, but far from Baldoon's vast and splendorous great hall, Isolde stood wrapped in the evening quiet of Devorgilla's thick-walled cottage, and gaped at the diminutive old woman. "A love potion?" she asked, promptly sinking onto a hard-backed chair.

Her heart sank as well. *"A love potion?"*

Apparently pretending to be deaf as well as half-blind, the *cailleach* ignored her questions and climbed onto a rough block of wood. She reached up to snap off a few sprigs of dried rosemary from one of the many clusters of dried herbs hanging from the ceiling rafters.

"Don't fret yourself, lassie," Devorgilla said, shooting her a cagey glance as she stepped down. "I ne'er said the potion was a love charm."

She hobbled back to her hanging cauldron and dropped the rosemary into what smelled like a most savory rabbit stew. "I said I may have accidentally added in a few of the wrong ingredients."

"Ingredients to incite passion and stir one's heart is what you said," Isolde reminded her, watching the old woman stir her bubbling stew pot.

Isolde's brow creased.

Stir mischief is what Devorgilla was doing.

Leaning against the chair's rough-hewn back, Isolde drew a deep breath of the cottage's homeyness. An atmosphere of warmth and welcome she'd always cherished.

Until just a few scant moments ago when Devorgilla had confirmed her suspicions about the foul-tasting tincture she'd let Isolde imbibe for weeks.

Not an anti-attraction potion at all, but a *love potion*!

And with the crone's upsetting admission, the cottage's homespun appeal had slipped right out the ceiling's chimney hole, its entire allure spiraling away along with the wispy ropes of smoke rising from the cook fire.

And neither the smoky-sweet smell of burning peat, the earthy tang of dried herbs, nor the tempting aroma of the simmering stew could fetch back the charm.

She'd had enough of charms.

Sitting bolt upright, driven to sheer madness by the firm grip *he* had on her heart, she blurted, "I have fallen in love with him!" She expelled a ragged breath of frustration. "I've wantoned myself, Devorgilla, and . . . a-and enjoyed it! *Craved* his touch, and 'tis all your doing."

Devorgilla lifted a straggly brow in mock astonishment, the simple gesture giving Isolde's heart a sharp jolt, so very much did it remind her of *him*.

Ignoring her distress, the crone hobbled to one of the unshuttered windows, the long-handled stirring ladle still clutched in her hand. "Did you see Lugh or Mab on your way here?" She stared out into the darkening night, her words as casual as if Isolde hadn't just bled her soul onto the stone-flagged floor. "The boy wanders ever farther of late, and Mab is getting too old to be about on wild and stormy nights," she fretted. "It will rain soon."

"I saw neither," Isolde answered, her voice flat, her irritation high. "Nor did I see a single cloud, but I ken better than to doubt you if you say a storm is brewing."

Nor did she fear the wrath of an approaching storm.

Nary a tempest could rise from the sea to rival the might of the tumult raging inside her.

But her resolve cracked when Devorgilla returned to the cook fire and dipped the wooden ladle into the cauldron, calmly stirring the stew as if Isolde's visit had been a purely social one and not a call paid in dire desperation.

"Oh, Devorgilla," she wailed, "how could you?"

"You should ken I'd ne'er do aught to vex you a-purpose." The crone slid her a guileless look. "'Tis possible I mistook an ingredient or two, but not with ill intent, my lady," she said, her thin voice steeped with contrition.

False contrition.

A tone as false as the contrived look of innocence on her face.

As mendacious as her use of "my lady." Devorgilla ne'er called her aught but lass or child.

Isolde frowned. The crone's expression, her tone, and her word choice, all boded ill.

All were but poorly disguised attempts to shield her treachery.

"'Tis my eyesight," Devorgilla droned on, warming to her deception. She set aside the ladle and rubbed at her eyes with knobby knuckles. "My vision worsens by—"

"Your vision was clear enough for you to spot teensy bog violets growing along the edges of the marsh pools the day I asked your assistance in getting my . . . m-my message to Balloch," Isolde protested, grateful when Bodo hopped onto her lap.

She wrapped an arm around him, pulling him close and reveling in the way he snuggled his soft weight against her. *He* would ne'er stoop to Devorgilla's deceptions, ne'er betray her trust. Ne'er . . .

Her thoughts petered to a most disturbing end when a

whole parade of images of Bodo and *him* rose up in her mind. The damning evidence of wee Bodo's betrayal marched heavily across her sensitivities.

Feeling as if she were drowning in one of the many bog pits dotting Doon's treacherous inlands, Isolde waited for the dog to settle himself before she railed on. "I think you tricked me a-purpose," she said, watching Devorgilla closely.

She didn't care for the way the crone pressed her lips together. "He's charmed you," she said.

"Charmed me?" Devorgilla shook her gray head, and Isolde thought she saw her fight back a smile.

"Aye, you," Isolde snapped, digging her fingers into Bodo's warm fur, seeking a hold on her world before it slanted from her grasp. "His bonnie looks have taken you in, and you've contrived to bring us together."

A strange twinkle glimmered in Devorgilla's foggy eyes and, of a sudden, the skin around them appeared more crinkled with mirth than wrinkled with age.

"It wasn't my idea to rid yourself of Balloch MacArthur by trying to get a bairn off the MacLean," the crone said, filling two wooden cups with her special heather ale. "'Twasn't I who wanted charmed yarrow sprigs to thrust beneath my pillow on Beltaine hoping to catch a glimpse of my true soul mate's bonnie face."

Isolde lifted her chin. "And is he the one you saw in your cauldron's steam that very same night?"

The crone's wrinkled face was wreathed in a smile. She tilted her head in a coy gesture better suited for a young maid of four-and-ten years. "Do you *want* him to be?"

Her ire rising, Isolde waved aside the froth-capped cup of ale the *cailleach* offered her. "I wanted an alliance, an end to strife and woe," she insisted. "Peace for this isle."

The crone set the cup of ale in front of her. Resting her

age-spotted hands on the tabletop's rough surface, she leaned forward. "A wise person know the gods oft give us not what we want or set out to achieve, but what we *need.*"

More perturbed than she cared to admit, Isolde glanced out the cottage's two square-cut windows at the gathering storm clouds.

Just as the *cailleach* had predicted.

Right as always.

A chill slid down Isolde's spine.

"And lo," Devorgilla barged on, straightening, "most times we surprise ourselves by discovering that what we need is also what we most wanted but were too blind to see."

That did it.

Isolde stood, causing Bodo to jump off her lap. He gave her a white-rimmed look of offended reproach.

"I am weary of having all and sundry tell me I am blind," she said, glancing down to dust off and smooth her skirts.

Mayhap not with your eyes, but what of your heart?

Isolde raised her head at once, but rather than peering at her with a wizened expression on her ancient face, proud of having spewed yet another noble-sounding gem of wisdom, the stoop-shouldered crone was already shuffling back to her steaming cauldron, Isolde and her troubles clearly forgotten.

Dismissed.

"Mayhap not with your eyes, but what of your heart?" Isolde muttered under her breath as she let herself and Bodo out the door. Closing it soundly behind her, she set off at a fast pace for Dunmuir and the night of passion awaiting her there.

"But what of your heart?" she mimicked in anger when she stumbled over a stone.

Clutching the soft, woolen folds of her *arisaid* more snugly around her shoulders, she hurried on. What she needed was to reach Dunmuir's sheltering walls before the storm broke.

What she *didn't* need, and a plague on Devorgilla, Evelina, and even Donall the Bold, his bonnie self, for telling her otherwise, was to go a-peeking into her heart.

She already knew what lurked there.

He stalked toward her the moment she let herself into her chamber, his whole demeanor rife with lordly bearing and self-contentment. His raven hair gleamed damp from his ablutions, and his dark eyes smoldered with hot need and something more fierce.

Something bold.

Something wild and furious. As untamed as the powerful storm just beginning to unfurl its might on the waiting night.

Someone, no doubt *he*, had not bothered to fasten the shutters, and a fast, keening wind swept into the room. The two cresset lamps swung on their chains, their flames dancing, while the more fragile tapers of the candelabrum guttered and extinguished, leaving tendrils of gray smoke hanging in the chill, damp air.

But they, too, were quickly vanquished.

The fragile smoke whisked away by the same swift-moving air licking coldly at her cheeks and every other inch of her exposed to the biting, wet wind.

Snuffed out and routed as easily as her well-laid plans.

And then he was upon her, his bold strapping self looming up before her. A pagan sea god risen from the storm-tossed sea, the wrath of the heavens blazing across his handsome face, in the tight set of his jaw and the proud, imposing spread of his shoulders.

And, merciful saints, he was shirtless again.

His discarded tunic rested on the foot end of her bed, slung impotently 'round her bedpost. A frightfully mundane bit of limp brown cloth, harmless and woefully unimpressive without *him* filling it out.

Filling it out so nobly.

So fine.

Isolde clutched at her damp *arisaid*. Something had changed. Though he was still her captive, the power between them had shifted. She'd seen the change coming, but it hadn't been truly apparent, not real, until this moment.

Even Bodo sensed the difference. The little brown and white dog stared up at him, tail wagging as always, but the tilt of his head and the quizzical look in his bright gold-brown eyes bespoke his puzzlement.

Isolde stared, too. She could do naught else. The sheer power of his presence left her breathless, stayed her limbs. She couldn't even lift her hands to remove her *arisaid*.

As if he'd read her thoughts, his hand shot out and snatched the plaid off her shoulders. "I do not want you catching an ague," he said, the husky tone of his voice a fine match for the dark fire in his eyes.

"I want . . ." His words trailed off as his gaze lighted on Bodo.

The dog stood with his forepaws braced on Donall the Bold's hose-clad knees. Peering up at him, Bodo looked every bit as awestruck as Isolde herself.

For a moment, the MacLean's imposing countenance softened, but then he glanced at her again, and the hard, resolute glint was back in his eyes. And stronger, more daunting than before. Without a further word, he spun away and strode to her bed.

Bodo, the wee furred traitor, trotted after him.

Her bold knight snatched his tunic off the bed, but rather than don it as she'd expected, he kept his broad back to her and appeared to fumble with the shirt, his wide-set shoulders rising and falling with whatever devilment he pursued.

His back and arm muscles tensed and bunched, and the sight made her breath catch in her throat. Hopeless longing welled inside her, an unquenchable ache she could no sooner deny than stop her heart from beating.

Bodo stared at him, too, the little dog's stubby brown tail wagging furiously.

As furiously as the mad rush of Isolde's pulse.

Her gaze clung to his powerful back, to the sheaf of raven hair just teasing his shoulders. Thick, silken tresses, high-glossed and gleamed by the cresset lamps' glow, caressed by the night wind pouring through the open windows.

Faith, but she ached to comb her fingers through the heavy silk of his hair, burned to gentle her hands over the smooth-muscled contours of his shoulders and back.

Touch him . . . *everywhere.*

Be touched by him.

But her feet, her arms, even her tongue wouldn't move. She stood transfixed, awed by his magnificence. The heated anticipation of his embrace, of his *loving*, swirled through her, unchecked and free.

A pleasing languid warmth to dispel the night's chill.

To warm her soul.

Even as her heart screamed the impossibility, the *shame*, of loving him.

Uncomfortable, she glanced away, then immediately wished she hadn't, for she glimpsed Lileas's anguished face, a fleeting image, briefly outlined against the wind-whipped clouds racing past the windows.

No shame, not hi— . . . the pale lips seemed to whisper, but a sudden burst of pelting rain and brilliant flash of lightning dissolved the illusion. Gusty wind and a deafening peal of thunder carried off the imagined words.

A brooding silence descended, thick and pulsing. A palpable quiet almost loud enough to block out the storm's fury.

An uncomfortable stillness to swallow the very roar of the sea.

Almost compelling enough to overpower the hard thudding of her heart. Silence the pounding of his as well, for she would have sworn she could hear its slow, steady beat.

Desire, wild and menacing as the storm, surged and tossed inside her. A hungry *wanting,* surely as dark and forthright as his own.

Demanding as the menaces of this strange night.

And then her feet carried her forward. To him, to her heart, and all she yearned for. She stopped an arm's length from him, trailed her fingers over the well-defined muscles of his shoulders.

"You want?" she murmured, urging him to finish the sentence he'd let hang between them.

He whirled around, his dark eyes heavy-lidded with desire, his jaw set with a new and formidable determination. "I want you," he said. "You, and naught else."

Isolde lowered her gaze, unable to bear the intensity banking in his. She saw the twisted shirt in his hands then, and her heart swelled at what he'd done. She watched him give Bodo the knotted tunic, her emotions wheeling out of control.

With a look of pure adulation, the little dog grasped the toy and bolted off with it before her heart could even comprehend the gift, the *pleasure,* this braw and strapping man's simple gesture had bestowed upon her wee champion.

How easily he'd won her dog's affection and trust.

How easily he'd won *hers.*

Her affection, if not quite her trust.

"Be you wise, my lady," his deep voice cut into her musings, "you shall make ready and give yourself to me of your own free consent, trusting and loving me as wholly as your four-legged companion."

He reached for her, taking her hands in his. "Be warned, for would you deny me, naught shall stop me from taking you." His dark eyes gleamed. "Not any dread consequences your misguided minions might attempt to visit upon me, not all the terrors of hell combined."

He squeezed her hands, a light but firm assurance he meant his every word. "Willing or otherwise, I shall have you."

"I have denied you naught." She looked up at him, knowing he meant more than the mere giving of her body, yet unable to break free of the one strand of resistance yet binding her heart.

The ghost of her sister yet rising between them, a barrier so impenetrable, physical need and not even the yearnings of her heart could breach it.

"You have had me in many ways and your touch pleases me greatly." She attempted a lightness, a teasing note, she didn't feel. Anything to ease the tension thrumming through him.

Through her.

Desperate to steer him away from that which could only pain them both, she pulled her hands from his. Hooking her fingers behind her neck, she twirled in a slow circle. "How shall I please you this night?" she sought to entice him. "Voice your will, and I shall indulge you."

Feeling quite the temptress, she said, "I have already heeded one of your desires. I wear naught beneath my skirts."

Donall's roguish smile reappeared. "Then dance for me," he said, scarce recognizing his own voice, so choked with lust were the words.

His desire surged, overmanning even his great discipline. Seizing her, he pulled her hips against the swollen length of his need, forcing her to accept his passion even if she wouldn't take his heart.

His love.

"Damn you, Isolde of Dunmuir," he swore, hating his weakness, thanking the saints for the loud clap of thunder that buried the terse words in the resonating rumble of its own ire.

"Dance for you?" she finally responded, her delicate brows lifting with interest.

He could see the spark of lust the idea put into her blood, and seeing her thus intrigued, fired his own passion.

Donall's loins tightened, his manhood swelling, while his heart hammered low and hard, fueled by the image of what he wanted her to do. By the vivid memory of the carnal dream he'd had of her so many weeks ago.

"Dance for you?" she asked again, her eyes limpid. She twined her arms 'round his shoulders, threading her fingers through his hair.

Mutual desire charged the air between them, while her arousal perfumed the damp night. Slipping her hands from his hair, she reached, trembling, for the ties of her bodice.

"For a kiss, I shall dance for you in any manner you desire, Sir Knight," she agreed, her fingers already plucking at her gown's bindings.

"You shall have all the kisses you desire," Donall promised, planting a light one on her freckle. "*After* you've danced for me."

"Knight's kisses?"

His heart melting, Donall flashed her a wicked grin. "Knight's kisses and many other kinds as well."

He lifted her hands from her bodice, gently urging them to her sides. Scarce able to draw air through the gathering thickness of his lust, he smoothed his palms over her back in slow, soothing circles. Massaging her, easing away her tension and coaxing her into a relaxed state lest she balk at what he wanted her to do.

"Have you a length of silk, my sweet?" he asked when she began to sway into his caresses. "Any length of silk?"

She shook her head, puzzlement clouding her eyes. "I told you, I have no taste for such luxuries."

She moistened her lips then, and Donall's control snapped. With a low moan, he caught her to him, pulling her flush against him as he took her lips in a searing kiss. His fingers dug roughly into the sweet rounds of her bottom, urging her closer still.

He drank of her, absorbed her taste, her essence, loving her with his mouth until all her doubts and hesitations loosened and fell from her.

Until she sagged against him, weak and besieged. Only then did he lighten the kiss. He eased back from her, but kept hold of her hips, his fingers gently stroking her.

"Do you truly not have a length of silk?" he asked, pressing his forehead lightly to hers.

She shook her head, brushed a soft kiss along his jawline. "Nay, I do not. I possess no frippery at all," she said, and blushed furiously. "Naught save Ev . . . my friend's bauble, and that was borrowed."

"And 'tis no need you have of such ornaments either. You shall dance for me without the silk, and I will be entranced," he promised, his lust straining hard against his braies and hose, his pulse keeping bold rhythm with the pulse of his need.

"I do not understand what you want of me," came his lady's soft voice, its magic wooing him back from the dark depths of want pounding through his veins.

"You will in a moment." He flashed her his most seductive smile. Holding her gaze, he lowered himself to the floor and stretched out on his back upon the recently strewn rushes.

Ignoring her surprise, he pushed up on his forearms and gazed up at her, the bold look on his face daring her to misunderstand.

And she didn't.

Evelina had told her of such things, had claimed indulging a man's basest craving in this manner would drive him wild. She swallowed thickly, and her breath grew rapid, shallow.

Excited.

He didn't say a word. Simply watched her, one brow cocked, a look of fierce want on his handsome face. Without breaking eye contact with her, he lay back and folded his arms behind his head.

"Step over me, Isolde of Dunmuir," he spoke at last. The request weighted her belly with warm, heavy pulsings of desire. "Come, my lady. Lift your skirts and stand o'er my face so I can truly see you."

Her whole body went liquid. She moved toward him, pausing but a heartbeat before she did as he'd bid, gave him what he desired.

A deep, feral groan came from his throat. He curled his hands 'round her ankles, held her fast in place, his grip pure iron, viselike.

Incredibly rousing.

"I cannot see you well enough," he said, his tone hot and smooth as the warmth pooling betwixt her thighs. " 'Tis too dark, my love. You must raise your skirts above your hips."

Waves of intense pleasure flooded Isolde, washing away all but her burning need.

"Hold your gown out and away from your body," he said, the words a command. "Lift and *air* your skirts o'er me, so I can gaze upon your sweetness."

Heat, fluid and languorous, twisted inside her.

Pulsed and throbbed, *there* where he desired to gaze on her.

Gaze on her while she moved her hips as Evelina had instructed her to do should he beg such a favor from her, should he desire to look on her whilst she circled her womanhood so lasciviously above him.

The sheer wantonness of such an act sent intensely pleasurable tingles whirling over and through her most sensitive parts. Seized by the rapturous sensations, Isolde dug her fingers into the folds of her skirts and began inching them higher.

So high as he desired.

Chill night air kissed her exposed skin as she met his demands, the bite of the cold, damp air soothed and tamed by the warmth of his hands moving up and down her legs.

"Higher. I would see more," he urged, letting his caresses roam higher as well. His stroking fingers stoked the flames of her own passion until any remaining shreds of embarrassment unraveled and spun away.

A moan slipped from her lips as sheer, visceral passion claimed her. Giving heed to the pleasure spun by his hands and the heat of his gaze, Isolde gave another little cry and yanked the bunched fabric over the tops of her thighs, gathering the whole of it up and around her hips.

"Sweet Christ . . ." Donall groaned, near spilling himself. The fire's glow slanted conveniently across her, gilding the lush bronzed vee to a gleaming gold, blessing him with a most tantalizing view of all she'd exposed.

"Circle, Isolde," he said, so drugged by lust he could scarce form the words. Too fired by his own need *not* to. "Move your hips slow and easy. 'Round and 'round, until I tell you to cease."

She did, and the sight of her lush intimate curls, her tender woman's flesh, circling so provocatively above him, yanked fiercely on his swollen shaft. A heated tug so urgent, his entire body shuddered with the force of his thirst for her.

The power of his *love* for her.

Smoothing his hands up her thighs, he slid his fingers into the tangle of damp curls, let his fingertips graze softly along her middle. Again and again, until her moans gave price to the pleasure she took in his touch, in having him look upon her so intimately.

"You are so beautiful," he murmured, his words glazed with need.

And then he stayed her, grasping hold of her thighs until she remained poised above him, unmoving and still. Biting back his own nearing edge, he played at her. Stroking her sweetness, caressing and *toying* with her curls and tender flesh until her own sharp cries of desire matched his.

Isolde screamed, a loud and unrestrained cry worthy of the night's wild magic. A raw and savage demand. A plea for release from the tight, coiling mass of exquisite throbbing centered at the very core of her femininity.

Wind, a loud and keening gale, raced into the chamber then, a surge of power so bold it knocked her legs from beneath her, its sheer force toppling her to her knees.

There, where he needed her to be.

The cry, so fierce, Donall could scarce believe it'd been ripped from his own throat, rivaled the scream of the wind. Beyond control, he pulled her down to him and slanted his mouth over her femininity.

Incredible need, blinding and ravenous, consumed him. He licked and laved at her, inhaled deeply of her, filling himself with her heady scent. He savored her as the prize she was, losing himself in the glory of her until she went limp beneath him.

Her legs began to tremble, unmistakably revealing the

approach of her release. Balancing on the edge of his own ease, Donall touched his tongue to the center of her passion.

"You are mine," he breathed against the tight little bud. He drank in the damp musk of her, the fingers of one hand tearing at the cords of his hose as he suckled her sweetness, teased and drew on her.

He fanned her desire, carrying her to the precipice of a fevered need so powerful she couldn't deny the possession he meant to take of her.

A claiming not only of her body, but of her very soul.

"You are mine," he swore, half-crazed from the softness of her nether curls, the musky tang of her arousal. "Do not e'er attempt to deny it."

"Aye, yours," he thought he heard her whisper, but the words lost shape, blended into a lusty, passion-tinged cry, when he grazed his teeth over the tiny bud of her arousal, drew even deeper on her.

Shaking with his own pressing ardor, Donall shoved down the hampering fabric of his own clothes, pushing the hose and braies just low enough on his legs for him to move over her.

For him to *take* her.

Rising up on his arms, he met her gaze, saw the same burning that consumed him mirrored in her beautiful amber eyes. He drew back his hips, holding her gaze as he reached between them to position himself, but her hand nudged his away.

She curled her fingers 'round him, easing him to her. The gesture, the *feel* of her hand on him, so soft, warm, and determined, near undid him. The last tenuous bands of his restraint tore free, and he plunged into her, claiming her with a bold and relentless force fitting of the night.

She reveled in the feel of him. Of his hard length, thick and full, gliding in and out of her, possessing her as only he could. His movements—masterful, slow, and knowing—

laid claim to her heart with the same skill he used to carry her body to the very edge of her desire.

And just when her need verged so tight she could scarce stand it, he guided her over the threshold, and she fell in on herself, imploding into a brilliant splintering of countless shards of pure, spinning bliss.

And still he moved in her. Slow moves. Long, gentle glidings, until he, too, collapsed atop her, his cry of release dark and full-bodied as the night around them.

Gradually, and oh-so-softly, she drifted back from the whirling abyss he'd plunged her into, barely noting he'd rolled onto his back and held her cradled securely in his arms. The solid comfort of his body cushioned her against the floor's prickliness, warmed her from the chill air.

With a sigh, she snuggled closer, gladly resting her head upon his shoulder. His nearness, the comforting shelter of his knightly arms, lulled her into the sweet oblivion of sleep.

She didn't awaken until just before the dawn, and only then because of the insistent rustlings of a mouse moving through the floor rushes.

Not wanting to lose the sweet languor still enveloping her, she tried to sink back into the mind-numbing bliss of deep slumber.

She rolled closer to him, the man she could no longer deny as her true soul mate, determined to ignore the pillaging mouse.

But the noise grew louder, the creature's foraging more frantic.

Angry now, she pressed her face deeper into the cushioning warmth of Donall's shoulder. His hair scratched and jabbed her, no longer silken and thick, but dry, coarse, and itchy.

Coming fully awake, she pushed herself upright on the bed of rushes.

Donall the Bold was gone.

Naught remained of the wild, lust-ridden night save the disarray of the flooring, the wrinkles on her gown, and the opened shutters. No longer admitting the whistling storm winds of the night, the glistening wet shutters granted entry to naught more daunting than a gloom-ridden drizzly rain.

A gray morning peopled only by herself, the still-slumbering Bodo, and the wretched mouse whose annoying scurryings had so rudely torn her from her sleep.

Only unlike the other unwelcome companions of the cold morn, the mouse was nowhere to be seen.

Vanished as soundly as the braw and handsome man she loved.

But, unlike Donall the Bold, whose low, seductive voice had disappeared with him, she could still *hear* the mouse's loathsome rustlings.

Scratchings now, ever louder and persistent.

Scratchings at her door.

Determined to bring vile spoliations on its source, Isolde pushed to her feet and straightened her rumpled gown as best she could. Squaring her shoulders, she crossed the empty chamber, a slow, cold dread building inside her.

No one would dare come knocking at her door this early lest grave ill had driven them there.

And the stealth of the scratchings boded an even worse ill.

Whoever had sought her out had news no one but *she* should hear.

With shaking hands, she opened her door, somehow not surprised to see Evelina standing there, her lovely dark eyes massed with concern, her beautiful face free of paint and pale.

Very pale.

"He comes, my lady," her friend whispered, grasping hold of Isolde's hand. "Balloch MacArthur's galley has been spotted. He should lay anchor within the hour."

Chapter Eighteen

❦

*Y*OU ARE CERTAIN?" Isolde stared hard at her friend.

The wall torch nearest Isolde's door had near burned itself out, but still spewed enough guttering flames to cast an eerie reddish glow over Evelina's beautiful face.

What Isolde saw there chilled her blood.

Evelina's full lips, usually curved in a quiet smile, were compressed into a tight, hard line. Long uncombed strands of her dark hair hung about her shoulders, the disheveled state of her tresses scarce concealed by the black cowl she wore.

Even if she'd stood before Isolde perfectly coifed and groomed as she was e'er wont to go about, the pale cast of her unadorned face bespoke the truth of her warning.

And the depth of her concern.

"You are certain?" Isolde asked again, a chill dancing up and down her spine.

"I would that I was wrong, but there can be no doubt." Evelina cast a furtive glance down the shadowy passage, empty and dark at this early hour.

With Donall returned to his cell, even Niels and Rory had hied themselves elsewhere, no doubt snoring peacefully on their pallets outside the entrance to the dungeons.

Isolde's stomach began to convulse. "There is no chance the ship has been falsely identified?"

"The approaching galley bears MacArthur banners." The answer dashed Isolde's last hope. "'Tis so near, my lady."

"Ne'er would I have believed he'd come." Isolde pressed a hand over her flat abdomen, tried to still the roiling dread churning there.

Wished something else tossed and turned inside her.

"It is too soon," she said, half to herself. Sharp talons of regret dug into her, squeezed so tight she could scarce breathe. "There hasn't been time . . ." She let the words die, her eyes filling.

"All may not be lost, but you must be wary. A journey worth taking is oft most difficult near its end." Evelina took her hand, gave it a brief squeeze. "The elders gather already," she added with another quick glance over her shoulder.

Isolde followed her gaze, her heart thumping. She could imagine the council's grim-cast faces, almost see their eyes grow cold with disdain, hear their wrath, their . . . shock, upon learning what she'd done.

"You must stand tall against their anger," Evelina urged, resting her hands lightly on Isolde's shoulders.

One of *his* favored gestures.

Isolde's heart twisted, her pulse racing ever faster. Hot panic clawed at her from within.

"Hold firm when Balloch confronts them," Evelina warned. "When he confronts *you*. He will be furious thinking you—"

"And how I wish I was!" Isolde cut in, then stopped at

the look of pity in Evelina's dark eyes. A tear trickled down her cheek. "I am not yet with child. All I am is . . ."

She paused to swipe a hand over her damp cheek. "I-I've fallen in lo—"

"I know you have." Evelina's own eyes gleamed bright. She stepped back, searched the shadows again. "I must go, my lady. I've an old debt to repay."

Isolde opened her mouth to speak, but no words came. Too thick was the hot lump swelling in her throat.

Her friend gave her a wan smile. "May God be with you," she said simply, and began taking backward steps, moving deeper into the shadows.

Before Isolde could question her further.

Or ask why she roamed Dunmuir's passages so early.

"Wait . . . *lady* . . ." Isolde called after her, lifting a hand, her legs too shaky to carry her after her friend's retreating form.

"Come back . . . *please* . . ."

But Evelina had already slipped away, her light footfalls hurried. And she was then gone, swallowed up by the corridor's gloom.

Isolde stared after her, dread cold and metallic on her tongue, her hands pressed hard against her middle, and trying desperately to find the steel Donall the Bold swore she possessed.

Donall came awake the moment one of his lady's buffoons began fumbling with the cell door's heavy drawbar. Despite his drowsiness and great desire to drift back into the bliss of his much-needed sleep, he couldn't help smiling at their repeated, *failed*, attempts to lift the fool bar.

The whoreson louts must've spent the night deep in their cups to have to struggle thus to unbar the door.

Not wanting to miss an opportunity to gloat at them, he

scooted up against the wall and folded his arms behind his head. Planting a broad grin on his face, he waited for the door to swing open.

Then he'd laugh.

But the mirth died in his throat when the cell door eased open but a margin, and an angel slipped inside.

An angel of death.

Garbed completely in black, a deep cowl concealing all but a shadowy glimpse of her night-black hair and beautiful face, the angel glided forward, her movements fluid, graceful, and full of stealth.

She stopped at the foot of his pallet. "Good sir, I can see why she loves you so," she said, smiling down at him, not a harbinger of death, but a desirable flesh and blood woman.

"Aye, 'tis most clear indeed," she said. "You are a fine braw man, Donall the Bold."

Her smile deepened, reached her sultry black-lashed eyes.

Donall smiled, too. The fool grin he'd plastered on his face in anticipation of *them* grew warm. Saints, but the woman's words filled him with joy.

Had she truly claimed Isolde "loved him so"?

Aye, she had.

"And I love her, my lady whoe'er-you-may-be," he said, springing to his feet, his heart swelling.

He made her a low bow. "Donall MacLean, laird of Baldoon, fair lady," he said as he straightened. "And you are?"

"Not a la—" she began but broke off when he snatched her hand to his lips and brushed a reverent kiss across her knuckles.

"Fair *lady*," he said, emphasizing his regard, "who are you, and to what honor do we owe your visit?"

"I am a friend of your lady's," she said simply, "but she does not know I am here." She glanced at Gavin, who still sprawled, snoring loudly, upon his pallet. Pale gray light falling through the window opening slanted across his boyish face. "I am come to repay a debt."

And make good a gross wrong I've done, Donall thought he heard her murmur beneath her breath.

"A debt?" he asked, choosing to leave go of the other faint words she'd uttered.

The ones he might have misunderstood.

Words his chivalry forbade him to consider.

He peered at her, mused at the wistful smile playing across her face as she watched Gavin. "I did not know he had a lady," he said, more than a little surprised.

Especially that the freckle-faced knave could win the heart of such an elegant, if somewhat older, beauty.

"Gavin MacFie and I are friends, naught else." She returned her attention to Donall, gave a little sigh. "His father and I were . . . more. Both men have done much for me, and I would repay their friendship this day," she said. "Laird MacLean, I mean to lead you from here, but we must hurry."

"What th—" Gavin finally stirred, a lopsided grin spreading across his face when he spied the dark-haired angel. "'Tis you, Evelina! Whate'er are you doing here?"

Donall reached down and grabbed his friend's arm, hauled him to his feet. "The most gracious lady Evelina is here to aid our escape," he announced, pleased at the surprise his words put on the all-knowing lout's face.

For once *he'd* been privy to something first.

"The lady Ev . . . ?" Gavin's words withered under Donall's sharp glance. But he caught himself as quickly, came forward, and embraced his old friend most heartily. "By the saints, my lady," he vowed, releasing her, "ne'er have I been more pleased to see you."

"We must make haste." She returned to the door. "I can only accompany you part of the way," she said, already stepping into the dimly lit corridor. "Then you shall be on your own, but hopefully not for long."

"Hopefully not for long?" Donall queried, but she'd already moved deeper into the dank passage.

Fully awake now, Gavin followed her, his broad grin bright enough to dispel the morn's murkiness, mayhap even chase the darkness from the low-ceilinged corridor.

Only Donall hesitated. May he be cursed for a hundred thousand fools, yet now, with his freedom looming so near, he dragged his cumbersome feet.

He was loath to leave *her.*

Suffer her the anguish he knew she'd feel upon discovering him gone.

Loath to suffer *himself* the anguish of missing her . . . if only for the short time it would take him to locate her sister's true murderer, clear Iain's name, then come back to Dunmuir and make her his bride.

"Do not tell me you've waxed fond of yon cell?" Gavin's voice called from a distance.

Donall blinked. He stared after Gavin and the black-clad angel, the lady Evelina. They'd already covered half the length of the passage. But when he didn't move, they turned and started back.

The lady Evelina spoke first. "You serve her better by leaving," she said, proving herself as full of all-seeing wisdom as Gavin. "She is strong. She will stand tall until you return for her."

Donall lifted a brow at her words. The look in her eyes filled his heart with bitter dread. "You speak as if she is in danger."

"I pray she is not." She grasped his hand, tried to pull him away from the cell. "But if she is, my lord, then the need for you to gather your men is all the more dire."

With ease, Donall pulled his hand from hers. He folded

his arms and braced his legs apart. Gavin muttered under his breath and rolled his eyes, but Donall ignored him. "I would know what intrigues you speak of, lady, or I swear to you I shall stand here until I grow roots."

The angel pushed back her cowl and ran a trembling hand through dark, unbound tresses. "Sir," she said, casting yet another furtive glance over her shoulder, "I shall tell you all I know, all I *suspect*, if you would but come with me."

She drew a long sigh and readjusted the cowl over her head when Donall didn't budge. "Pray do not ill wish me for my honesty, sir, but I know much of . . . men," she said, a sad, almost defeated note in her voice.

"I fear all is not as it would seem here," she went on, "and would hope you return with enough able-armed men to set things aright . . . if need be."

Ill ease sluiced hot and cold down Donall's back. "Lady Evelina," he vowed, suspecting her position but granting her honor for her bold heart, "you are a loyal friend, but your words make me more loath than before to leave. If my lady faces danger, I shall quell it here and now."

Turning, he set off in the opposite direction.

The direction of the hall.

Gavin loped after him. "Come, Donall, you are unarmed. What quelling would you evoke without your steel? If aught is amiss here, let us gather your men and return."

"Since when do we need arms to best a parcel of doddering graybeards?" Donall snapped, ill humor to rival Iain's rising inside him. "Saints, we could topple the lot of them with one hot breath!"

"And the red-haired giant and his sour-faced companion?" Gavin reminded him. "Both stout-armed and with steel a-plenty hanging from their belts?"

"I've dispatched men twice your size with naught but my

fists. As you have as well." He glowered at Gavin. "Since when has your nerve taken flight?"

"I vow about the same time your good sense abandoned you," Gavin said, his voice annoyingly smug.

Donall's temper broke, and he lunged at his friend. "It is my lady's safety I would secure, not yours or mine," he seethed, hauling Gavin up by the front of his tunic. "What is senseless in that?"

Rushing between them, Evelina placed a hand on each of their heaving chests. Donall swore, and released Gavin. That lout had the cheek to let one of his lopsided grins spread across his broad face.

He winked at the lady Evelina. "Love always brings out the best in a MacLean," he said. "Their temper."

Yanking down his tunic, Donall shot a murderous look at Gavin. "I say we stay and have done with whatever menace imperils my lady." To the angel, he said, "I would know what it is that troubles you."

A guarded expression came onto her face. "A ship will soon land here. I cannot reveal why, for to do so would break my lady's trust," she said. "Let it be enough to know I fear for her safety once those onboard make their tidings known."

Donall swore again, a darker stream of epithets than before. His ire thus vented, he tossed back his hair, drew a breath. "All the more reason we cannot leave."

Tamping down his vexation as best he could, he leveled his most lordly stare at her, warming it with just a hint of his most seductive smile. "Fair maid, I admire your heart and spirit, but I cannot protect the lady Isolde unless I know what foe she faces," he said. "You must tell me."

She hesitated, closed her eyes. When, at last, she looked at him again, Donall knew he'd won. "'Tis Balloch MacArthur," she said. "The man her clan council would see her wed."

"Sweet holy saints," Gavin burst out, earning him a dark look from Donall.

Ignoring Gavin, Donall narrowed his eyes at Evelina. "She is betrothed?" The words tasted like dirt on his tongue. "To MacArthur?"

The beauty swallowed, clearly uncomfortable. "Nay, my lord," she said, her ill ease evident in the slight tremor of her soft voice. "She is to *be* betrothed to him . . . or was."

Donall clenched his jaw. "Is or was?"

Evelina lowered her head.

Striding forward, Donall captured her chin, forced her to look at him. "Very fair lady, I've told you I admire your bold heart. Do not disappoint me now." His tone left her no quarter but to answer him. "What is with MacArthur? What tidings can he bring that could cause such grief?"

Evelina's brows drew together. "He is surely come to break the betrothal agreement because . . . because . . ."

"Because?" Donall urged when she faltered.

"Because my lady sent him word she carries another man's child," Evelina said in a rush. "Yours, milord. Or so she hopes."

Donall's jaw dropped. Shock, joy, wild elation began pumping through him. "And why did she send such tidings?"

He had a suspicion.

A wondrous one, but needed to hear the words.

He stared at her, lowered his brows in an attempt to look stern. "Answer me."

Evelina's face tinged pink. Casting a helpless sidelong glance at Gavin, she said, "She is not yet with child, sir. But she hoped by claiming so, she'd be able to rid herself of Balloch. I warned her otherwise, but she refused to listen. And now he is nigh upon us and will reveal what my lady has done. The elders' wrath will be great."

"Not so great as mine had they wed her to that fool swaggerer," Donall vowed, his mind reeling with Evelina's revelations. He released her chin, then shoved a hand through his hair.

A decision made, he turned to Gavin. "You go, fetch Iain and my men," he said, "I shall stay behind and speak with MacArthur."

Gavin glanced heavenward again. "And what, pray, would you bandy about with the whoreson? The man is not known for his fine conversing skills."

Donall smiled, amazed he could. But his decision, his *plan*, grew more appealing the longer he considered it. "I shall tell him and all who care to listen that the lady *does* carry my child and that her council erred in allowing him to believe a betrothal could take place," he said, his smile deepening. "Could not take place because she is already promised to me."

Gavin snorted. "You are a *prisoner* here," he argued. "If you do not come with me, those two guards will hie you back to the sea dungeon before you can spout one word of such utter nonsense."

He shook his head, a look of incredulity on his broad, honest face. "Saints, but you are a fool."

"*MacArthur* is the fool," Donall said, the control in his voice amazing him. "A blustering one. A braggart who'd run home with his tail betwixt his legs if faced with the bite of my steel."

"Steel you do not have." Gavin whirled away, threw up his hands in disgust. "You think to take on a shipload of armed and angry men? Without a sword to swing at them?"

He spun back to face Donall, his face flushed. "Nay, nay, nay, my friend, if aught so perilous is about to unfold here, I say we head to Baldoon and mass your men for a swift return."

"Swift?" Donall's brows shot upward. "We need *days*, two at best, to reach Baldoon by foot. Then add a few more to rally our men and ride back." He pinched the bridge of his nose in frustration. "Nay, we cannot afford the time."

"You may not have to, my lord. Your men should soon be here," Evelina said, surprising them.

They both looked at her, their haggling forgotten.

"My men . . . *here*?" Donall could scarce breathe, so great was his astonishment.

His hope.

The lady nodded, and Donall's heart swelled to bursting. "I sent Lugh to fetch them several days ago," she said. "God willing he made the journey safely."

"Lugh?" Gavin glanced between them.

Donall answered, his admiration for the lady mounting by the minute. "The dark-haired lad who spooks about the dungeon gathering cobwebs and the saints know what all," he said, pleased he knew yet something else Gavin didn't. "I heard the pock-faced lout call him Lugh," he added, glancing at Evelina for confirmation.

She nodded. "He is the *cailleach*'s grandson," she verified. "'Tis his poking about you owe your escape, for it was he who told me of the tunnel that opens off the sacred well's well shaft. He discovered the tunnel while fetching frogs from the stagnant water at the bottom of the well. He's explored its length and claims it leads to the open moorland."

Donall comprehended. "The moorland that stretches between here and Baldoon?"

"So Lugh claims," she said.

Another thought occurred to Donall, began to eat at his burgeoning hope. "I thought the lad couldn't speak?"

Evelina shrugged. "He speaks to me," she said, the trace of sadness in her voice again. "Men always do, even young ones like Lugh." She paused, gave another gentle sigh. "He will speak to your men when he reaches Baldoon, too. Because I've asked him to."

Donall's heart began to thud hard against his chest. "And you believe my men will be waiting on the other side of this tunnel?"

"Your men, and your steeds," Evelina promised, and smiled. "If young Lugh was able to lead the two horses there as he'd meant to do," she added. "And, of course, if he reached your holding."

"Come, Donall." Gavin seized his arm, his boyish grin back. "Of a sudden, I have a fearsome craving to see a swarm of ugly MacLean faces a-smiling at me."

And this time, when Evelina and Gavin hurried down the dark passage, Donall kept pace with them, a fool smile of his own spreading boldly across his handsome face.

Isolde stood in the shadows of the stair tower and stared across the hall at the erupting chaos, at the disaster unfolding before her eyes. The unraveling of her carefully wrought plans.

The unraveling of her life.

She drew a great breath and pulled back her shoulders. It was time to face her shame. The very air in the smoke-hazed hall rang with angry shouts. Accusations, taunts, and slurs. Both from her own kinsmen and Balloch MacArthur's men.

Her gaze sought and found Lorne. She locked eyes with him as she started forward. Of all those present, only he appeared unmoved. Not ranting, nor red-faced with rage as the others all appeared to be. The old knight stood off to the side, one hand resting lightly on the hilt of his sword. The look on his face revealed naught but wariness.

Niels and Rory stood in the midst of the storm, their faces dark with anger. But the loud clamor of voices raised all around them blocked out their shouts and she could only hope theirs were lifted in support of her.

Lorne.

Her cousin and Rory.

Bodo.

Her hopes rested on them. The few she trusted to stand beside her.

Naught else swayed in her favor save her last-minute decision to leave Bodo locked in the quiet safety of her bedchamber, well away from the vengeful wrath of Balloch MacArthur.

Would that she could sequester herself from him as well.

She scanned the throng as she elbowed her way through the jostling, furious crowd, but *he* was nowhere to be seen.

Only his man, and a party of hard-bitten angry-looking MacArthur warriors.

Despite her distress, the irony of his absence brought a wan smile to Isolde's lips as she pushed past the empty high table, making for the hearthside where they all stood, no doubt too riled to sit.

Both she *and* Evelina had been wrong.

Evelina, because Balloch had not come himself as she'd predicted.

Herself, because even though he hadn't come, his pride had not stayed his tongue.

Her secret tidings to him, her deceit, her shame, were on the tongues of all those present.

All save Lorne, and to her great dismay, even he had betrayed her. She cast one last frantic glance around the crowded hall before she squared her shoulders and pushed through the circle of men to stand in their middle and to face their wrath.

Lorne had vanished.

The old knight, her last hope in this sea of angry faces, had left the hall.

Chapter Nineteen

✦

CONSIGNING HERSELF TO their wrath, Isolde pushed through the circle of men. "Kinsmen, honored *guests*," she greeted them, her voice proud, her head high. "My humble regrets that I have kept you waiting."

"'Tis humble regrets for your treachery you should be a-tendering," someone yelled from the back of the assemblage of glaring men.

"A fornicator!" another voice rose above the swell of angry rumbles and slurs. "And with the cheek to give herself proud of such base depredations."

Her uncle nodded tersely at that, then stepped away from the knot of MacArthur warriors he'd been standing with. He strode toward her, his barrel chest thrust forward, his eyes aglow with a strange combination of zeal, anger, and . . . *triumph*?

"Well, lass," he said, coming up before her, "what have you to say for yourself?" He fixed her with a cold stare. "Since you seem disposed to wax so eloquent, mayhap you

can tell us what drove you to such flagrant and whorish behavior? And with *him*? Laird of the MacLeans?"

A chorus of riled men's voices roared approval of
Struan's aggression. Their faces blended in a blur of anger,
an impression made all the more intimidating by the glare
thrown out by the nearby hearth fire. It cast an eerie reddish
glow o'er their jeering countenances, giving them the look
of the devil's own.

Hell's minions come to wreak punishment on her for loving Donall MacLean.

Her sole solace was in noting the worst scowls graced
MacArthur faces. Her own kinsmen appeared vexed and
troubled, but not hate-charged as Balloch's men did.

Save her uncle, whose blood seemed to run hotter than
all those present combined.

"I'd mind you we await your answer," he said coldly,
glaring at her. "And have a care *how* you answer lest you
wish to pay most dearly for your sins."

"Sins?" A thin voice chimed from somewhere in the
crowd. "Be it a sin when a lass falls for a braw laddie?" The
voice rose a notch, grew a mite stronger. "Be that so, I shall
be in sore trouble when I meet my Maker, for many were the
lassies whose heads I turned in my younger day! And I par-
took o' way more than their bonnie smiles, I did!"

Ailbert.

Despite her distress, Isolde smiled inside.

"'Tis true! Our lady is not to be faulted," came another
MacInnes voice. "Had we not hauled the blackguard beneath our roof, this would ne'er have come about!"

"Aye!" a third joined in. "'Tis our own fool faults. The
MacLean is a known skirt-chaser."

"The MacLean is a known *murderer*!" Struan bellowed,
rage swelling his lungs until his outburst silenced all others.

"He is our sworn enemy, and tainted by his birthright to bear the weight of guilt for his clan's misdeeds."

Shouts of approval rose up again. Loud, boisterous, and blocking out the few amongst her clan who'd spoken in her defense.

"And *you*"—he pointed his finger at her—"you have broken all honor as chieftain. Honor to this house and honor sworn to the proud house of MacArthur."

A thunderous roar rent the hall. Furious foot stomping and the deafening clash of pewter tankards hammering on tables followed.

"A grievous state!" Her uncle raised his arms, shook his balled fists at the heavens. When he turned his heated gaze back on her, a fire to rival that of the hearth fire flared in his eyes. "Plead for yourself and beg forgiveness of Balloch's men, lest you force us to suffer most ungentle indignities on you."

Isolde clasped her hands tightly before her. As tightly as her heart clung to the unbending rod of steel shining deep inside her. Drawing on that strength, *his* strength, she willed herself to see laughing brown eyes and a slow-spreading smile.

A knight's smile.

Willed it until her eyes stung with the effort.

"I have done naught to plead mercy or beg forgiveness for," she said, fixing her gaze on the leaping flames of a wall torch across the hall.

Anything to blot out the jeering faces and taunts. "I only sought peace. An alliance to ensure an end to strife." She paused to blink away the burning in her eyes. "And I-I . . . followed my heart."

"An *alliance*?" Struan mocked her, his voice ringing. "The man was taken to serve justice for your sister's murder." His rust-colored brows snapped together. "And you would insult us by stating you *followed your heart*?"

"Nay, not her heart," a stranger's deep voice, one filled with lewd glee, boomed louder than the rest. "'Tis the heated flesh betwixt 'er thighs she's been a-heeding!"

"Whore!" This came so close to her, the vexer's hot breath nigh brushed her cheeks. Glancing to the side, Isolde found the man who'd slandered her thus and burned him with a look full of reproach.

Raising her voice above the din, she called out, "Aye, I followed my heart." She drew a deep breath, focused on the burning torch again. "And, my lords," she vowed, staring steadfastly into the flames, "where the heart takes one should be neither denied nor called to shame."

The rumbles around her spiked, then gradually stilled.

Low mutterings and the nervous shuffling of many pairs of feet on the floor rushes could still be heard, but for the moment, at least, the jeering receded.

But not for long.

"Our felicitations, then, fair lady of the heart," a sarcasm-ridden voice oozed behind her. She turned to see Balloch MacArthur's man push his way into the small space within the circle of angry onlookers.

He made her a mockingly low bow. "You speak noble words for a wench who cannot be trusted the width of her spread thighs."

The *zing* of drawn steel sounded as Niels and Rory shoved through the jostling ranks and placed themselves on either side of her. Swords in hand, but aimed at the floor, they swept angry gazes over the gathered men, MacInnesses and MacArthurs alike.

"Our lady did what she deemed best for her people, this isle, and, aye, for herself," Niels called out, his words sending a floodtide of relief coursing through Isolde.

Drawing himself to his full, formidable height, he looked pointedly at Balloch MacArthur's man. "She never wanted the betrothal to your liege. Nor does she owe loyalty to any isle but hers. 'Tis our folly we failed to heed her wishes. *She* cannot be blamed for refusing to honor a union she ne'er meant to acknowledge."

Balloch MacArthur's man's eyes bulged. Struan's face suffused a deeper red, and the remainder stood dumbfounded. Some muttered agreement, some staunch disapproval, while others appeared cowed into impotent silence.

Fingering the hilt of his blade, Niels seized the lull to look to those who still spewed malcontent. "Any who think otherwise may gladly test my sword arm." He glanced at Rory. "And his," he added, and Isolde was stunned to see Rory incline his head in curt agreement.

"Our lady's honor has naught to do with the MacLean whoreson's misdeeds," Rory spoke up, jutting his jaw. "*He* has a penance to pay, not our lady chieftain."

Scowls and more jeering greeted Rory's words. Isolde's heart sank, the burgeoning of hope that had been building in her chest swiftly deflated. Pierced and slashed by the furious, self-righteous calls for Donall's immediate execution.

Not on Summer Solstice, but with the rising sun.

On the morrow.

Less than a full night away.

"Nooooooo!!" She hurled her heart, her very soul into the cry. "I will not allow it!"

Struan's fingers curled 'round the tender flesh just above her elbow. He squeezed so tight, hot stinging tears jabbed into the backs of her eyes. "'Tis a blessing your sainted mother sleeps abovestairs. Witnessing the truth of your wantoning would push her further into the darkness she whiles in," he snarled for her ears alone.

Holding fast to her, he scanned the crowd, his glare

fierce. "Donall MacLean dies at cockcrow," he declared, his
voice commanding, the words plunging the hall into utter silence. "His death will avenge the loss of our own lady
Lileas, and purge the stain our lady chieftain has spilled onto
our honor by lying with him."

He turned to Balloch's man. "Send your liege our sorrow
for her behavior and tell him the man who dishonored her
has drawn his last."

"*You*"—he whirled to face Niels and Rory—"bear as
much shame as she for assisting her. You may purge your-
selves by accompanying me to the bastard's cell. I want him
to spend his last hours weeping and howling. If you can
make him entreat us for mercy, you may reclaim your
honor."

"No." The objection scarce passed Isolde's lips. A mere
rasp, not even strong enough to reach her own ears. "N . . ."
she tried again, but her voice had left her.

Died on her as surely as had her heart.

Withered and vanished.

Worthless and spent.

As useless as the cold lump of melted steel forming in
the very pit of her soul.

The sad remains of her shining backbone of steel.

Undoubtedly seeing her defeat, her uncle puffed out his
chest and spoke again, his words less heated now. Almost
jovial. "Kinsmen, men of the great house of MacArthur," he
rallied them, "victuals and drink are at the ready!"

He made a broad sweeping gesture with his free hand, indicated the far side of the hall where kitchen lads were
shouldering in large platters of roasted meats. Others carried
jugs of ale and leather-wrapped drinking jacks.

Preparations for a celebration.

A feast to mark the death of Donall the Bold.

"Excuse us while we tend a matter most grievously overdue, then see our lady chieftain to her bed, where she may dwell upon her transgressions." He paused, waited as if he thought some would defy him.

But no one spoke.

The MacArthur warriors eyed the feast goods streaming in from the kitchens, the hunger in their bellies winning out over their desire to serve their liege's vengeance.

Isolde's own kinsmen either looked at the floor or skulked off into the shadows.

"So be it then." Struan's voice rang loud. "Good men, have full pleasure of the feast goods until my return."

Without further demur or hesitation, he hustled Isolde through the throng, his fingers still digging painfully into her arm. Niels and Rory followed glumly in their wake.

They weren't there.

Donall washed down his disappointment with a deep, hearty draw of the cool rain-scented air. A damp chill lay over the high barren ground spread before him.

A damp chill and, sadly, not much else.

Gavin burst through the tunnel's narrow opening a scant moment after Donall's emergence, and he, too, breathed in an audible gulp of lung-filling air. Lugh's tunnel had led them to freedom, but the journey had been arduous.

They'd covered the last quarter of it on their knees.

And that in pitch-blackness with naught to sustain them but a foul, earthy-smelling cloyness.

"They are not here," Gavin said beside him, wheezing. Hands braced on his knees, he slid an astonished look at Donall. "Our horses are not here. There's naught to be seen but drizzle and mist."

Donall leaned back against the cold rocks that formed the mouth of the tunnel and scowled at his friend. "Think you I do not have eyes?"

Gavin stared up at the moon. It still rode the grayish sky, a near-full disk, pale and ghostly white, appearing to drift in and out the clouds, as elusive as the full panoply of MacLean men-at-arms they'd both hoped to discover waiting for them.

"I thought they'd be here," Gavin said, his voice still hoarse with the exertion the journey through the tunnel had cost him. "Saints, what are we to do now?"

Pushing away from the support of the rocks, Donall stretched his arms over his head and flexed his fingers. He stared across the wide expanse of moorland. A gray and black land at this young hour, awash with odd-shaped patches of shadow, the rolling hogbacks and bramble-covered ridges broken only by a few scattered copses of wind-stunted trees.

The whole of it stretching clear across the eerie silence all the way to Baldoon.

His mind set, Donall tossed back his hair and turned to face his friend. "We walk," he said. "If God has any mercy, we shall reach home in a day and a half rather than two."

"And then"—he balled his fists—"and then, we ride back and claim my bride."

"They are not there." Rory peered into the gloom-ridden interior of Donall and Gavin's cell. The leaping flames of the resin torch he held showed his high astonishment. "They're gone."

"They cannot be gone, the door was barred." Niels snatched the torch from Rory's hand and strode into the cell, Rory close on his heels.

"What . . . what foolery is this?" came Niels's stunned voice from the murkiness.

The two men stared out the window, an opening far too small for any man over eight years to wriggle through. They kicked at the empty pallets, dislodging naught but dust and dried bits of straw. Niels gave over first, spinning around to stare at Isolde and Struan.

Both still hovered outside the half-opened door.

Torchlight and shadows did frightful things to Niels's honest, open face, but the bewilderment in his eyes set Isolde's soul free.

It was true, then. Donall and his friend had escaped, were safe.

"Praise God!" the words burst from her lips even as hot tears spilled down her cheeks.

"Be silent!" Struan gave her arm a rough jerk. "They are gone?" he called into the cell, great waves of black fury rolling off him.

Shaking his head in disbelief, Niels started forward, a dark-faced Rory right behind him. "I know not how, but they've esc—"

The slamming of the door cut off Niels's astonishment. "An accomplishment you traitorous poltroons will not enjoy!" Struan sneered, and dropped the drawbar in place.

Isolde gasped, pure horror washing over her, her elation of a heartbeat before . . . dead.

Her flare of hope extinguished. Flat and brittle in her breast. "What have you done?" She stared at her uncle, stricken by the wild light in his eyes.

A crazed light that had naught to do with the flickering glow thrown by the wall torches.

He stared back at her, his hawkish features so familiar, but wholly strange. E'er stern and domineering, he'd never been her favorite, but she'd respected him.

Till of late.

Aye, she'd been losing her esteem for him, but ne'er had she feared him.

Until now.

"What are you doing?" The words sounded clumsy, slurred by the fear swelling her tongue.

"What am I doing?" He gave her an incredulous look as he dragged her away from the cell, pulled her along in the direction opposite from the hall and the safety of numbers. "Ridding myself of you, is what I am doing," he said, and increased the pressure on her arm.

Streaks of terror, black and cold, tore through Isolde, and she dragged her feet, hoping to slow his progress, hoping *someone* would come, would see them, but no one came, no one saw. She opened her mouth to scream, but fear had closed her throat so soundly, naught came forth but a rasped choke.

He gripped her arm in an iron grasp, his strength rendering her struggles useless, and swept her along with him toward a barred door half-hidden in shadow at the end of the passage.

The door to the sea dungeon and every bit of nastiness Dunmuir had e'er possessed. Or excreted, for the ancient stairs behind the door ended in a ruinous passage that served as a receptacle for Dunmuir's latrine chutes.

Alarm welled inside her when he kicked open the door and they began the slippery descent into the stinking morass at the base of the stairs. At the bottom, Struan's fierce hold on her was all that kept her from falling into the muck.

Stark fear seemed to have plucked the very bones from her limbs, wholly annihilating any last remnants of steel she might have drawn strength from.

Struan slogged through the foulness, dragging her behind him, his biting grip on her arm staying her feet but affording no comfort. At last, he paused before a narrow gap in the wall of the vaulted passageway, and Isolde found her voice at last, sheer terror retrieving it for her.

"T-the oubliette is in there," she gasped, her throat thick with fright. "Y-you cannot mean to plunge me into it?"

"Aye, I do," he said, snatching a torch from its wall bracket. "Into the chamber of little ease, or from your bedchamber's window," he admitted. "I've not yet decided. Either way, your passing will be accepted as having come from your own hand . . . the tragic result of your having given your affections so unwisely."

Isolde's heart stopped.

Slammed against her ribs and froze for horror.

Struan shoved her roughly through the narrow crevice in the wall. She slipped, fell to her knees, and quickly pressed the flats of her hands against the cold, damp floor, felt all around her before she dared push to her feet and inch toward the wall.

One false move would send her tumbling through the jagged gap yawning across the stone floor of the cavelike cell.

The opening into the oubliette, a cramped, bottle-shaped chamber cut deep into the bowls of the earth, a space so small that, once there, a soul could neither sit nor stand, simply wait, hunched over, until death gave its dubious release.

Struan stepped in then and thrust the torchlight into an iron holder on the wall. He positioned himself in front of the opening to the passage, soundly blocking her means of escape . . . did she possess the nerves to attempt one: as clan *ceann cath*, her uncle wore more metal than most mounted English knights.

His face twisted with a look of grim satisfaction. Mayhap because of the way she cowered against the far wall. "Be pleased you were able to know a man before you die," he said, the crudeness of his words foreign on his usually pious, self-righteous tongue. "Your sister knew love as well, or so it would seem from the hue and cry her husband let loose after he found her."

Isolde's blood ran cold. "W-what are you saying? Iain MacLean did not kill Lileas?" She pushed the words past the hot constriction in her throat, had to voice them even though a grim suspicion already assured her Donall the Bold had spoken true: his brother had not murdered his wife.

Iain MacLean had loved Lileas.

Struan was the murderer.

She saw it in the madness glittering in his eyes.

"W-why?"

Terror knifed through her, cold and laming. Numbing her mind, while pain and anguish squeezed the very breath from her lungs.

"Why?" Her uncle's lips curled. "To meet an end," he said. "Sacrificing her to the Lady Rock stirred up the old enmity and gave me the best means to lead Donall MacLean into a trap. I knew Lileas's besotted husband would ne'er stomach bringing his beloved wife home to Dunmuir, knew he'd let his brother perform the sad deed."

Iain MacLean's brother.

Donall the Bold.

Her love.

Her true soul mate . . . the truth of what her heart had refused to believe for so long pounded through her conscience, smote her for doubting him.

For doubting her heart.

Oh, love, please come for me. Come, and I shall plead forgiveness for not trusting you, will ne'er doubt your word again.

Tears burned her eyes, but she refused to let them fall. What she needed was time. Holding fast to the tiny flicker of hope that he *would* come, would find her, Isolde feigned a calm she did not feel.

"Why would you want to take the MacLean?" she asked, seeking to stall whatever fate he meant to submit her to.

She held his gaze. "After Da purveyed the marriage between Lileas and Iain, all thought the old feud o'er the Lady Rock had been assuaged, consigned to the distant past where the sad tale belongs," she said, purposely rambling. "We enjoyed a fair truce. Why would you seek to harm the alliance Da strove so hard to achieve?"

The odd light glinted in his eyes again. "Because *I* never wanted an alliance. I wanted, I *want*, Doon." He spread his hands. "All of it. But even I know I could ne'er seize it from one as able and stout-armed as Donall MacLean. With him gone, and his grieving brother stepping in as laird, it would only have been a matter of time before Iain MacLean's hot temper undid all of Baldoon."

Isolde frowned, a new thought raising its ugly countenance before her. "And left the gates wide for you to take it . . . with Balloch's aid. That is the true reason you sought to wed me to him."

"You have a wiser head on your shoulders than your sister and my sniveling peace-seeking brother had between them," he said grudgingly. "Neither one of them suspected aught."

"Neither one of . . ." Isolde couldn't finish the sentence.

A gloating sneer curled her uncle's lip again. "Aye, I eased your father's way to the heavens, too, though his death was not planned." He spat into the dark crevice of the oubliette, then shrugged. "When he became so ill with that last fever he'd caught, I couldn't resist taking a pillow and putting him out of his misery."

He spat into the gap again, a swifter, more angry spit this time. "'Twas a debt long overdue."

Isolde could feel the blood draining from her face, from

her heart. "How could you?" Her voice sounded hollow, distant. "'Tis mad you are, uncle. Full mad."

The strangest look yet crossed his hard-set features. "Aye, and so I am," he acceded, staring at her but seeing something, someone else. "I have been mad since the day our parents and your lady mother's decreed she should wed Archibald and not me. 'Tis *me* she loved, not your father."

His hands balled to fists and he began pacing the dark cell. "Me, me, me!" he railed, shooting her a glare that went straight through her.

Straight through her and into the past.

Of that, Isolde was certain.

"We were lovers!" He whirled to face her, his bearded jaw thrust forward. "She pleaded, cried, and came to me on her knees, *beseeching* me to intercede, to stop the marriage. But none would have any of it. She was to wed your father, the future laird, and naught else would do."

"You err." Isolde defended her parents' love. Something she couldn't, would not doubt. "Mother loved Da. All speak of their great passion. She waits for him still, every day, in her chair by the fire."

He rounded on her again, his face nigh purple. "Aye, she loved him, and loves him still!" he roared, the veins in his neck bulging. "My brother stole her heart, turned her against me. But she was mine first, and 'tis me she looks to for comfort now," he added, somewhat calmer. "Now she's lost her senses and remembers naught of the past."

Isolde pressed herself against the cold rock wall behind her. The odd light in his eyes had turned even more crazed. Each time he paused to glare at her, she feared he'd grab hold of her and send her hurtling through the crevice in the floor.

"But *I* remember." He thumped a fist against his breast.

"I remember, and I shall have her. Her, Dunmuir, this whole isle."

Pausing, he shoved back his wild mane of rust-colored hair. "Aye, I shall have it all. Everything Archibald stole from me and more."

He came to stand before her. So close she could see how glazed his eyes were, smell the ale on his breath, *taste* his madness.

"My plans would have worked, too, had you not ruined them with your meddlesome dalliances with *him*." He grabbed a fistful of her hair, yanked her head backward. "They still will, too. With you gone."

Her eyes watered with pain, but she forced herself to bear it, to shake her head in denial. "Nay, they will not. Donall will come for me," she said, a spark of anger beginning to reheat the cold clump of steel lying dormant in her belly. "He'll bring his men, the full might of Baldoon."

"The dead cannot be rescued." He let go of her hair and peered at her. Once again seeing *her* and not the past. "Your foolish twit of a sister wasn't rescued by a MacLean *husband*, what makes you think a MacLean *lover* can save you?"

"Because he will," she said, lifting her chin, finding her steel again. "Because he will."

My heart knows it.

Chapter Twenty

❦

$\mathcal{T}$HE NOISE WASN'T more than a vibration. A low tremor in the cool morning air, but enough to make Donall lay his hand on Gavin's arm, enough to make his breath hitch as he tilted his dark head to the side to better listen.

"By the Holy Mother, they come!" Gavin jerked away from Donall's grasp and pointed to their right.

Donall's gaze followed the direction of Gavin's outstretched arm. His heart slammed against his ribs, the breath he'd been holding bursting from his lungs in one great triumphant shout. And though he'd ne'er admit it, the whole of his body began to shake with joy.

A dark mass, denser than the gray-cast shadows and much faster-moving, swung around a distant hillock. An ever-increasing swell of pure, mounted might moving swiftly across the broad stretch of open moorland.

The very earth beneath Donall's feet trembled with the force of many pairs of pounding hooves, while the low rumble that had barely shaken the air moments before now erupted into the deafening, joyous drumming of powerful steeds tearing up the ground as they and the warriors atop them flew toward Donall and Gavin.

'Twas Iain.

Even at the great distance, Donall spotted his brother leading the van. Tall, furious, and broad-shouldered in his saddle as he thundered across the high moor, a small dark form clutched firmly before him.

Lugh.

He'd made it.

The strange lad had fetched Iain.

Iain and what appeared to be the entire MacLean army.

The MacLean garrison and . . . more.

A slight figure, far too scrawny to be mistaken for one of the powerfully built warriors, rode at the far edge of the left flank. The man's unhelmed white-tufted head a stark contrast against the gray sky.

Gerbert.

And the old goat led two horses!

"By the saints, Gavin, they've even fetched our steeds!" Donall whacked his friend on the shoulder.

A *hard* whack.

One he hoped was mighty enough to jar the hot moisture from his eyes and loosen the womanish lump burning in his throat.

"They come, Gavin!" he cried, his heart filling with such elation, he feared it'd soon burst. "'Tis over! They come, and ne'er have I been happier to see that hothead's scowling countenance!

"To see all of them, by God!" Donall threw back his head, stared up at the cloud-streaked sky. "Every last one of them, bless their souls."

"All of them?" Gavin's voice sounded strange. "That I doubt, my friend."

Astounded by the tone, Donall glanced sharply at Gavin

only to find him staring, slack-jawed, at the approaching riders. Donall looked, too, and immediately spotted the reason for Gavin's astonishment.

Amazed and dumbfounded, Donall stared at the tight phalanx of standard bearers riding close to Iain and the boy. The folds of the banners flying so proudly in the brisk wind bore not only the MacLean crest, but the MacKinnon insignia as well.

"What the devil?" Donall shot another quick glance at Gavin. "He has *MacKinnons* with him."

But before he could puzzle further, or Gavin could voice a reply, the riders were upon them, drawing rein all 'round them in a rowdy chaos of trampling hooves, horses' snorts, and jubilant men's voices raised in greeting.

Iain pulled up before Donall, his dark eyes alight with a rare twinkle. He held up his hand and the clamor ceased at once. "Do not ask," he said, jerking his head toward the MacKinnon warriors. For once, Iain's handsome face, so like Donall's own, wore a broad smile rather than a frown. "They come in peace and are friends."

Donall gaped at his brother.

Gaped at the MacKinnons.

They, too, wore smiles.

Smiles, and what looked suspiciously like MacLean armor. Not that Donall begrudged them the gleaming ware. He was too happy to see all of them. His men and the MacKinnons with them. He'd wonder later why Iain had outfitted them with MacLean steel.

Even the dark-haired Lugh sported a child-sized mail shirt of Baldoon origins. The lad grinned, too. The first smile Donall had seen on the quiet boy's face.

But the lad wasn't smiling at him. He'd twisted in Iain's strong arms and peered up at Donall's brother with a look of pure adulation shining in his eyes.

"Well, by the dark crack of the devil's arse," Donall muttered beneath his breath, a smile of his own curving his lips. "'Tis a time for miracles," he said, loud enough for all to hear.

Iain laughed, a wondrous feat in itself. He tousled Lugh's head. "Your young friend here tells me you've a lady in need of a few braw and ready sword arms?"

Donall opened his mouth to laugh as well, but snapped it shut as quickly and made do with a gruff nod.

Saints preserve him, but if he'd held his mouth open one second longer, the great wracking waves of relief and joy filling his breast would've flown out to shame him before the whole fool grinning assemblage!

And, of a mercy, they would have sounded embarrassingly like great, wracking *sobs*.

"Aye, he does have a lady awaiting our assistance," Gavin answered for him, his own voice suspiciously thick. "And a most fair maid she is," he added, catching the two sword belts old Gerbert tossed to him.

Looking quite pleased with himself, he also accepted the two fine MacLean swords the white-haired seneschal handed him. He gave one of the wide leather belts to Donall, and as he secured it low on his hips, Gavin clamped a rough hand on his friend's shoulder.

"It will soon be over, my friend," he said with a slight inclination of his head, an earnest look in his usually mirthfilled hazel eyes.

A private exchange.

A gesture of reassurance between friends, and meant for Donall alone. "The lass has a bold heart," Gavin said, his voice low, hoarse with his own emotion. "She will stand until you can pull her into your arms again."

Donall reached up and squeezed his friend's hand, his heart too full for him to speak. He didn't trust his tongue to form aught but foolish babble should he dare attempt to voice his appreciation.

To Gavin.

To them all.

Then Gavin handed him a sword, and he took it gladly. Not his own, stored somewhere at Dunmuir, but a blade near as fine. Equally deadly.

Comparably light and welcome in his hand.

Lifting it, Donall kissed the sword's cross-hilt, and at that instant, a great roar arose from the gathered men. "Onward to Dunmuir!" they cried. "Onward to Dunmuir and may God have mercy on any fool enough to try and hinder us!"

His chest still too tight for him to join his men's boisterous shouting, Donall held the borrowed blade high, thrust its gleaming steel upward at the cloud-cast sky.

"Onward to Dunmuir," he called out, but the shout proved too hoarse, too choked, for any but those standing nearest to hear. A squire led his steed forward then, and Donall sheathed the sword before he vaulted into the saddle, eager to be on.

He whirled his mount in the direction opposite Baldoon. Raising a hand, he found his voice at last. "Onward to Dunmuir!" he roared, the cry bursting from his lungs, from his heart. "On to save my lady!"

Then he kicked the beast in the sides and tore off across the moorland, leaving his men, his doughty seneschal, and his newfound companions-in-arms, the MacKinnons, no choice but to chase after him.

Not long after, the sprawling bulk of Dunmuir's half-ruinous walls rose up against the horizon. His jaw clenching, Donall drew rein and stared at the dark mass, black against the morning's gray, cloud-chased heavens. His heart began to pound in slow, hard thumps against his chest. His lady whiled behind those walls, and he prayed God she did so unharmed.

From his vantage point, still high on the open moors, MacArthur's war-galley could be seen riding anchor off Dunmuir's shingle-beached shore. High-prowed and low in the water, the single-masted warship banked what looked to be forty oars, and its mere presence made his stomach reel and put a taste like stale ash in his mouth.

Determined to see the galley's oarsmen straining at their long sweeps, its square sail flapping on a stiff *homeward*-bound wind, Donall spurred his horse and galloped the rest of the way to Dunmuir's gate.

The heavy, iron-spiked portcullis clanked upward at their approach, and without hesitation, he and all those riding hard behind him thundered beneath it. They clattered through the tunnel-like gatehouse, and straight into Dunmuir's silent and deserted bailey.

To his surprise, or mayhap not, two figures stepped from the shadows. Lorne, the old knight, and the dark beauty, his rescuing angel.

They hurried forward, Lorne's eyes mirroring a trace of reserve, his lady's glowing with relief. And Donall didn't doubt she was the valiant graybeard's woman.

Ne'er had a pair looked more at ease together.

Donall's heart lurched. Lorne and the black-garbed angel shared the air of trust and loving he hoped to share with *his* lady.

Share with her for all their days.

And nights.

Impatient to fetch her, he swung down from his saddle. "Lady Evelina, Lorne." He gave them terse nods.

She started to reply, but Lorne shot her a warning glance.

"My *lady* and I are relieved you've returned, Sir Donall," the old knight spoke for them both.

"He is a good man, as I've told you." Evelina slanted Lorne a pointed look. "As you have seen for yourself." To Donall, she said, "God be thanked, you came."

"Did you doubt it?" He angled a brow at her.

"Nay. I"—she glanced at Lorne again—"*we* knew you would return. Bless be, you made such haste."

Iain must've dismounted or lowered Lugh to the ground, for the boy dashed past Donall and threw his arms around Evelina's skirts. She rested a hand on his thin shoulder. "'Tis a braw lad you are," she soothed, tousling his dark hair. "I knew you'd get word to Laird MacLean's brother."

"And *he* would see his brother's fair lady," Iain said, stepping up to them. "Where is this lass who's done the impossible and claimed Donall's heart?"

Lorne cleared his throat. "Struan banished her to her bedchamber," he said with a sidelong glance at Donall. "Good sirs, you came swiftly, but we must make greater haste now. I do not trust Struan not to suffer a worse penalty upon her than merely locking her in her room."

"Then let us go fetch her down." Ill ease roiled in Donall's gut. "I shall deal with Struan afterward. First I would know her safe. I swear 'fore God the bastard shall regret being born if even a single breath that has passed my lady's sweet lips has suffered harm."

Not caring for the queer look moving over the old knight's face, Donall asked, "Where is Struan? Do not tell me he is yet with her?"

"I know not where he is," Lorne said with a glance over his shoulder at the hall's outer stairs. They loomed steep and rain-slick behind him. "No one has seen Struan since he hauled her abovestairs," he added, moving toward the steps.

"We must hurry." Already, he was bolting up the stairs.

"Niels and Rory have vanished as well. It is all full troublesome."

Donall ran after him, taking the stairs two at a time. His entire entourage followed suit, leaping from their steeds and drawing their blades from the sounds of it, their collective shouts and curses lost in the hiss, zing, and scraping of swords leaving their scabbards.

The instant he crested the landing, Donall shouldered past Lorne and wrested open the iron-shod door, yanking it wide so his men could pour into the hall.

An outcry rose up from those within. Shocked, angry rumblings that swelled to a great roar of outrage when *he* entered.

'Tis him!

Defiler of Isleswomen!

Skirt-chasing cur!

Impervious, Donall made straight for the dais end of the hall and the entrance to the stair tower yawning just beyond the raised area.

The curving turnpike stair that led to *her* chamber.

At the base of those stairs, he turned and scanned the throng. His men, and MacKinnons with them, formed a broad and menacing line around the entirety of the hall. Not that such a measure was needed to subdue the lolling mass of ale-headed feasters crowding Dunmuir's great hall.

All present appeared sorely spirit-fogged.

Regardless, his men and the surprisingly companionable MacKinnons would keep a watchful eye on them while he went to free his sweet Isolde from her chamber.

Well content to leave the glassy-eyed carousers to their cups and his men's competent charge, Donall turned and bounded up the winding stone steps, Gavin, Iain, Lorne, and Evelina hard on his heels.

As they'd expected, they found the door to the bed-chamber barred from the outside.

As they'd *not* expected, the room proved empty.

Wholly quiet.

Vacant save Bodo, who sat atop the great four-poster bed, staring at them with a troubled, crooked-toothed look of great consternation.

But not for long.

Before any of them could voice their surprise, the little brown and white dog leaped from the bed, shot out the opened door, and streaked down the darkened corridor as fast as his short legs could carry him.

He stopped once, glanced back over his shoulder, a pleading, eager look on his face, before he dashed off again, barking frantically as he ran.

Donall ran, too.

All of them did.

His sweet Isolde's wee champion was leading them to his mistress.

A familiar sound called Isolde out of the dazed state she'd drifted into to block out her uncle's mad ravings. For hours he'd paced the cell, at times stalking so near to the yawning crack in the floor, she'd held her breath, expecting . . . *hoping* . . . he'd step wrong and plunge into the crevice.

But he seemed more surefooted than a mere mortal man should be, not even blinking when, once or twice, he'd strode along the very lip of the opening.

And all the while he'd bemoaned his ill-fated lot in life, his hatred of her father, his love for her mother, his hatred of *her*.

His crazed plans to seize hold of all of Doon.

So she'd leaned against the cold stone wall, shut her eyes, closed her ears, and prayed.

Prayed for Donall to come for her.

Prayed for a miracle.

And now that miracle's barking sliced through the fog she'd let herself sink into, and filled her heart with renewed hope.

With joy.

Bodo, her sweet precious Bodo, was coming for her. And since she'd left him locked inside her bedchamber, his frantic, ever-nearing barks could only mean someone had let him out.

Someone who must've been searching for her.

Someone she hoped was Donall the Bold.

Struan heard him, too.

At last he ceased his pacing and whirled to face her. "It would seem your savior has four legs rather than the hoped-for two," he taunted, his mouth twisting into a sadistic smile. "I shall take as much pleasure in sending that yappy little beast into the oubliette as when it is *your* turn to follow him."

"Nooooo!!!!!" Isolde pushed away from the wall, blind panic chasing away her caution. "Don't you touch my dog!" she cried, lunging at him, her fear for Bodo making her bold.

Her steel, white-hot and glowing.

He laughed and danced away from her. "Have a care, lass, or you shall land in the pit without my help," he jeered, his eyes a-fire with a wild light.

"I cannot allow you to steal the recompense I shall enjoy by pushing you myself." His smile became a cruel sneer. "But before I do, I am desirous of watching your face when I drop your yelping cur down the crack."

"I'll kill you first," Isolde screamed, flinging herself at him again.

He laughed, easily sidestepping her. And rather than top-pling *him* into the crack, she stumbled herself. Her arms flailed, flying out for balance as she fell near the edge of the crevice. Pain slammed into her at the impact, the rough stone floor cracking her knees and abrading her flattened palms.

Struan leaned over her. "So eager to die, *chieftain*?" He nudged her with his foot. "Shall I ease you over the edge? I promise to send your wee beastie after you."

Her breath coming in ragged, painful gasps, Isolde crawled away from the opening, great shudders wracking her body. "Don't you dare touch Bodo," she panted, strug-gling to her feet. "Don't you da—*Bodo!*"

In that instant, amidst a frenzy of snarling barks worthy of a much larger, more ferocious-natured dog, Bodo shot through the cell's entrance gap and launched himself at Struan.

The little dog slammed into her uncle's legs, sinking his teeth deep into Struan's flesh. Howling with pain, Struan hovered on the very edge of the crevice, shaking his leg in a vain struggle to dislodge the animal.

For one agonizing long instant, Struan stared at her, his eyes wide with horror, his arms wheeling. And then he was gone. Over the edge in a blur of flailing arms, legs, and brown and white fur.

"*Bodo!!!!* Noooooo!!!!" Her own screams of terror blending with Struan's, Isolde dove forward, tried desper-ately to grab hold of her dog, but her arms closed on thin air.

Bodo had vanished into the oubliette.

Near blinded by tears, her heart crushed by the tight, searing pain in her chest, Isolde collapsed to her knees at the crevice's edge. "Bodo, no . . ."

Her cries came small now. Pathetic little gasps, wooden

and ragged, torn roughly past the hot swelling in her throat. "Oh, Bodo, no . . ."

And then she heard it.

A frantic *clacking* sound.

Claws on stone.

And a bark.

Bodo.

Opening her eyes, she saw him through the stinging veil of her tears. He clung to the lip of the crevice with his forepaws, desperately struggling to pull himself up over the edge.

Her heart bursting, hot tears spilling down her cheeks, she grabbed him, pulling him swiftly to safety.

Into her grateful arms.

Laughing and crying, she held him tight, stroking and soothing him while his panting subsided and his racing heart calmed. "Oh, sweet Bodo," she murmured against the warm fur of his shoulder, "You came for me, you came for me."

"And I, fair lady?"

Isolde's breath faltered. He'd come. "Donall?"

"I should hope you were not expecting another braw knight to save you?" he drawled, his smooth, deep voice spilling light over her.

Pouring love into her heart.

She blinked up at him, half-afraid she was imagining him, still too blinded by tears to see him properly. But it was he. That she knew. Ne'er could she mistake his tall, broad-shouldered form, his slow, disarming smile, his bold stance.

His magnificence.

His love.

It shone so bright in his rich brown eyes, its brilliance was almost more blinding than the salty wetness of her tears.

"You came," she said, the words choked. Thick.

"*We* came," he said, leaning down to gather her and

Bodo into the shelter of his strong, knightly arms. "We who love you."

"We who *love* me?" she asked, seizing the implication, her heart swelling with the joy of it. Then the others he'd meant gathered 'round, and another kind of happiness filled her heart as well.

The comforting happiness of home, family, and trusted friends.

Friends old and new, each with a bold and open heart.

Gavin with his lopsided, boyish smile. Lorne and Evelina, their own love shining bright in their eyes. Iain, her love's brother, her sister's widower, handsome and braw as his brother, concern and relief in his dark, *innocent* eyes.

And even young Lugh, smiling shyly from the cell's entrance, a look of wonder and a smattering of pride lighting his small face.

"'T-twas h-him, Uncle Struan. He's mad . . . he l-locked Niels and Rory in the cell," she stammered, needing to tell them, then block Struan's face, his last horror-filled scream, forever from her heart.

"He killed Lileas, even Da." Her gaze sought and found Lorne's. She saw his grim nod, saw he'd already guessed. "He would have killed me, had Bodo not . . ."

"Hush, you," Donall soothed her, smoothing back her hair, wiping the tears from her eyes, off her wet cheeks, as he carried her through the cell's narrow opening. "'Tis over now."

"And may God be praised!" someone said. She couldn't tell who, but the three words broke the tension and they all released their collectively held breaths.

Speaking all at once, they huddled close, clustered, smiling like fools, around Donall as he carried her and Bodo from the cell.

Murmuring love words against her hair, words for her

ears alone, he strode through the stinking muck of the latrine passage, up the sea tower's slime-coated stairs, and out of Dunmuir's dungeons.

An hour or so later, he carried her again.

A blissfully delightful state she could easily become most accustomed to.

A state she *intended* to become accustomed to.

Freshly bathed and so in love, she snuggled happily against Donall the Bold's bonnie chest as he strode into Dunmuir's great hall. She wrapped her arms soundly around his wide-set shoulders and twined her fingers in the heavy silk of his hair. With a sigh of pure contentment, she pressed herself to his braw and knightly form.

For once not feeling a single twinge of guilt or shame.

She looked up, caught his eye. *I love you*, she mouthed the words, still a bit shy about voicing them aloud.

"And I you, lass," he said boldly, without a trace of her own hesitation, his mouth curving into one of his seductive, heart-stealing smiles.

Lileas smiled, too.

For one fleeting and joyous moment, Isolde thought she caught a glimpse of her sister's face. The image wavered only briefly, well concealed in the wisps of peat smoke hanging in the air, but appearing long enough for Isolde to see the pleased expression she wore.

Long enough for her heart to catch Lileas's softly whispered assurance that now, at last, all had been set a-right.

And, truth tell, naught had e'er felt so . . . *right*.

Ne'er had her world, *their* beautiful Isle of Doon, been so close to perfect.

And if Donall kept his word, and she didn't doubt for a moment that he would, and if her clan members would but agree, as Lorne seemed to think they would, soon Doon would no longer be divided in twain, but jointly ruled.

Shared.

A common and loved home for MacLeans *and* MacInnesses.

The alliance her father had always sought, her sister had died trying to achieve. A desired alliance that had brought her so much more than just a truce.

A sharp, attention-demanding yap called her attention to Bodo. She glanced down, smiling at him through the moisture filming her eyes.

The little dog trotted along beside them, the extra spring in his step and the jaunty way he held his head a clear indication he knew the champion's role he'd played and was mighty proud.

Savoring the accolades.

Lorne and Evelina walked with them, too. As did Gavin and Iain. Each one of them freshly bathed. Even Bodo and Lugh. No traces remained of the slime and reek from the vaulted latrine passage, hardly a hint of the ordeal she'd been through.

Niels and Rory, newly released by their former captive, flanked them, both men looking a mite sheepish and subdued.

All smiled, though Iain appeared a shade less jovial than the others. Lorne's eyes, too, held a reflective note. But even the truth of Struan's treachery couldn't wholly dispel the joy in Isolde's heart.

Couldn't dim the triumph of the declaration about to be made.

Regrettably most of the hall's occupants, MacInnesses and MacArthurs alike, appeared too deep in their cups to comprehend what Donall was about to proclaim.

Shifting in the protective embrace of his strong arms,

Isolde smoothed a hand over the thick gloss of his hair, reveled in the feel of its silky coolness beneath her fingers. He carried her so well.

So fine.

Ne'er had she felt more secure.

More . . . *loved.*

Mayhap even cherished.

Full content, she rested a hand lightly on the solid warmth of his shoulder as they passed the massed ranks of hard-bitten MacLean and MacKinnon warriors. The men still stood grim watch around the circumference of the torch-lit hall.

Of her people, hardly a soul stirred. Those feasters yet awake turned glassy-eyed stares on them. Of *all* the revelers, MacInnesses and MacArthurs alike, some already sprawled on the rushes, mouths open and snoring loudly, while others slept with their ale-heads resting atop the trestle tables.

A hardy few still made merry, heartily exercising their tankard arms or entertaining themselves with ever bawdier songs and ludicrously boastful tales.

All appeared quite dull-witted, awake *or* slumbering.

And if their glazed eyes and limp forms weren't proof enough, the thick reek of stale ale hanging in the air betold their sorry state.

Not that Donall cared.

He had but one purpose.

To lay firm and irrevocable claim to his lady.

His mind set, he stepped onto the raised dais at the upper end of the hall. "MacInnesses!" He raised his voice to be heard above the carousing. Above the snores. "Men of Balloch MacArthur! Hear me well, all those with ears, for if you gainsay my words, I shall set loose upon you the balled might of the great houses of MacLean and MacKinnon!"

He swept his gaze along the ranks of his men. Not a one of them, nor the MacKinnons who'd come with them, had moved. They all stood proud and tall, a formidable circle of muscle, mail, and gleaming steel. Their blades drawn in silent warning, menacing to any malcontents even with the sword tips resting benignly against the floor.

Donall allowed himself a small stab of pride.

Well, mayhap a large stab of pride.

His men were at the ready, their faces steely and grim-set. One nod would have them pressing their blades against every unfriendly throat in the hall before the ale-headed louts realized they'd been set upon.

He eased his lady to her feet, then wrenched free his own sword, raised it over his head. "Word has come to me you mistreated my lady this day," he accused the feasters, letting his darkest, most piercing stare rake each man foolish enough to meet his glare.

Not surprisingly, an uneasy stirring rippled through the hall. Furtive whispers followed, accompanied by nervously exchanged and telling looks. A few muttered grumbles of displeasure.

Some had the gall to glare.

But no one challenged him.

Pleased, he took his lady's hand. Concentrating on his task rather than the smooth warmth of her hand in his, he threaded his fingers through hers and lifted their joined hands in an unmistakable show of unity.

"Dare sully my betrothed again, and I shall rescind my decision to seek peace with you, you of MacInnes blood," he shouted. "Let one MacArthur voice slander her again, and I shall fire your galley and force you to swim home." He tossed the challenge to all present. "Speak now and let us cross swords as worthy opponents, or accept our forthcoming marriage, this alliance, and forever hold your tongues."

"She cannot be your betrothed." One brave soul spoke up from the far back. "She is promised to our liege."

"Your liege believed thus in error," Donall shot back, his voice deep and calm though she could feel the tension thrumming through him. "She has e'er been pledged to me."

"You lie!" Another MacArthur voice rose in anger.

Donall released his lady's hand and eased her gently behind him. *Protectively* behind him. He heaved a sigh, then took a long step forward, sword in hand. "She is my betrothed. Say otherwise again and be harried all the way to hell."

Lorne looked sharply at him, his brows raised.

"A MacLean ne'er lies," a slight-figured, white-haired man standing next to Lorne called out. "Our laird in particular!"

A low, angry growling began in the far back of the crowd. It spread slowly forward, swelling and falling, as it crept the length of the hall, leaping from one crowded trestle table to the next, coming ever closer.

Until one thin voice rang out. "What he claims is true, I swear it," Ailbert lied, waving his walking stick in the air for emphasis. "'Twas her father's last wish, whispered to me on 'is death bed, it was."

Isolde swallowed, then moistened her lips. She fought back the heart pushing into her throat, blinked against the salty tears gathering in her eyes.

More of her kinsmen joined Ailbert in making similar proclamations, each one bolder than the last, until she could stay the quickening of her pulse, the swell of her emotions, no longer.

Tears began leaking from her eyes, and when Donall drew her close, she gladly melted into his embrace. Together, they listened to the tall tales her council fabricated for Balloch MacArthur's men.

Promised from birth, they were!

Aye, such was the way of it.

Handfasted for o'er a year, and with a wee bairn growing proud to seal our alliance.

'Tis soon they'll be wed.

Ne'er seen a pair love more . . .

"Ne'er seen a pair love more . . ." Isolde murmured the words to herself as, many hours later, she slipped from her sleeping love's arms. Climbing down from the great four-poster, she went to peer out the opened windows.

Naught but a peaceful morn stretched before her, reaching innocently from Doon's shingled shores to the distant MacKinnons' Isle.

The breaking of a calm dawn.

A calm peace reigned at Dunmuir, too.

Or had since Donall's bold declarations.

Since the last of her stubborn kinsmen had conceded to the wisdom of her alliance, then united in their efforts to convince the MacArthurs of its validity before stumbling off to seek their pallets.

Since Balloch's men had set hasty sail for home.

Since she'd learned to trust her heart.

Heaving a deep, satisfied sigh, a *sated* sigh, truth be told, she watched the pale gray-pink light tinge the eastern horizon. The new day's luminous light set MacKinnons' Isle aglow, too, and for once, she didn't shudder while gazing on it.

Its frowning cliffs and sandy bays had lost their menace now that they no longer stood between her and her true soul mate.

No longer presented a sad and damning symbol of his guilt.

Indeed, the sight now brought a smile to her lips.

Had Iain MacLean's temper not sent him there, the truth

might ne'er have been exposed. And now, she had not only her love, but the alliance she'd sought for Doon, and promising new allies in the MacKinnons.

Aye, looking at the isle made her smile.

But not as much as thinking about the things she and Donall had done after finally slipping away from the ruckus in the hall.

Thinking about the things he did to her *heart*.

Thinking about the babe she hoped would soon grow and thrive inside her. Smoothing her hand down her flat abdomen, she sighed.

And hoped.

Prayed that dream, too, would soon come true.

"Ne'er seen a pair love more," she said again, a mere whisper, caught and carried off by a gentle salt breeze as soon as the words had left her lips.

But no less true, no less powerful, no matter where the fickle wind carried them, for she held the knowledge in her heart, knew it to be true.

"And if you finally know the truth of my love for you, Isolde of Dunmuir," came a rich, deep voice behind her, "I would know once more if you shall truly have me?"

Her heart filled to brimming, she turned, half expecting him to be lounging against the bedpost, *his* bedpost, his arms crossed o'er his bonnie chest, one of his slow, sensual smiles spreading across his handsome face.

But he surprised her.

Donall the Bold, proud laird of the great Clan MacLean, knelt half-bent on one knee in the center of her bedchamber. He held his hands extended, palms out, in humble supplication.

Supplication to her.

"Well? Will you be my lady wife? Make an honest man of me after I pressed irrevocable claim on you before all and sundry?" His love for her shone true and bold in the depths of his deep brown eyes. "I warn you, I shall remain on bended knee until you answer me."

His lips curved into the wicked smile she so loved. "I swear to you I shall not move until you speak the answer I desire."

Her heart melting, the answer he wanted dancing on the tip of her tongue, she came forward and took his hands. Tilting her head to the side, she pretended to consider. "And if I have a condition?"

His dark eyes began to smolder. "Name it."

"I want kisses," she said. Her pulse quickening, she looked deep into his liquid brown eyes, dared him to laugh. *"Knight's kisses."*

His brow lifted. "You wish to be kissed as a knight kisses?"

She nodded, unable to stop the heat stealing onto her cheeks.

His smile deepened. "That, sweeting, can be easily arranged," he vowed, and stood.

He took her by the shoulders, turning the tables on her by peering deep into *her* eyes. "You shall have as many knight's kisses as you desire," he promised, leaning forward to place a light one on her freckle.

"I shall rain knightly kisses on you every night for the rest of our lives, my lady," he said, and winked at her. "Every conceivable kind of them."

Then he took her hand and led her back to the great four-poster bed, eager to prove the truth of his words.

Epilogue

❧

$\mathcal{O}$N A BRILLIANT sun-washed afternoon a little over two months later, several gaily festooned galleys rode anchor before the glistening black islet known as the Lady Rock. 'Twas a fine summer's day, blessed with a calm and sparkling sea, a warm and gentle wind, and a brilliantly blue sky marred by naught but a few fleecy white clouds.

Two of the galleys flew double banners: the MacLean banner and the MacInnes one. The third ship, a borrowed MacLean galley, bore the MacKinnon insignia.

And each vessel held members of all three clans.

Something Isolde had insisted upon in honor of the day.

In honor of an alliance long sought, almost lost, and so wondrously sealed this day.

And a glorious one it was.

A perfect day to celebrate a wedding.

The joyous union of clans MacLean and MacInnes.

The marriage of Donall the Bold, proud laird of the great MacLean clan, to his love, Isolde MacInnes.

And to celebrate the wee new life she suspected she carried so sweetly beneath her heart.

All fine reasons to bless the Lady Rock as well, to cleanse the tidal rock of its dark and dismal past by tossing votive offerings onto the deceptively well-mannered waves lapping benignly at its black and jagged edges.

Something the celebrants aboard the three galleys did with great enthusiasm.

Each clansmen or friend standing at the rails had been given a goodly share of small oatcakes and flowers to toss upon the waves. Not a single participant hadn't been presented with a flask of fine heather ale to pour upon the rock itself.

Potent measures to banish the Lady Rock's evil for once and all time.

Her own offerings tossed, and the wee pewter flask she held empty, Isolde leaned against the rail of the MacLean galley and stared across the short distance to where her husband stood talking with Niels and Rory at the rail of the somewhat smaller MacInnes ship.

Lorne and his own new wife, Evelina, stood near them, but the couple appeared more caught up in themselves than in the blessing ceremony. As she watched them, Isolde smiled in pleased approval.

Donall caught her gaze and flashed her one of his devastating smiles, lifted his hand. His dark eyes gleamed with wicked promise and just looking at him set her heart a-flutter, did unspeakably delicious things to the pit of her belly.

A sense of utter contentment washed through her, swelling her heart with enough love for him to last through this lifetime and well beyond. She could scarce wait until the galleys returned to shore, until the wedding feast planned for later had unfolded and spent its glory.

Until they could slip away, alone at last, and enjoy all the wicked things he'd vowed to do to her to make their wedding night unforgettable.

Holding fast to the rail, Isolde breathed in the brisk sea air, indulging her imagination . . . until a familiar bark and an equally familiar cackle disturbed her silent reverie.

She whirled around to see the *cailleach* making her shuffling way across the galley's gently rocking deck. Bodo frolicked in circles around her, undaunted by the slight tossing of the sea, much more interested in the rolled and twisted length of brown cloth clasped tight between his crooked teeth.

Her husband's shirt.

The tunic he'd made into a toy for Bodo.

One of the many things he'd done that should have alerted her to his good character, *would* have alerted her had her doubting heart not stood in the way.

"*He* is a wise one," Devorgilla said, watching the little dog run off in search of a more agreeable playmate than herself. "He knew well afore you," she added, stepping up to Isolde at the rail.

"Knew what?" Isolde glanced down at the tiny, black-clad woman. "What did Bodo know?"

Devorgilla cackled, her wizened features wreathing in a smile. "What I knew all along as well . . . that Donall MacLean was your true soul mate."

"The man you saw in the cauldron's steam?" Isolde asked, though she already knew the answer.

The crone nodded, her self-important glee barely contained. "Aye, that is the way of it."

Turning away from Isolde, she appeared to stare across the waves to where Donall watched them from the other galley. Or *would* have stared at him were her eyes not so clouded.

Swallowing her pique that Devorgilla had harbored that particular secret so long, Isolde asked the other question burning in her mind. "And if you knew he was the one, why did you give me an anti-attraction potion?" she prodded. "Or a *love* potion . . . *whatever* the foul brew was?"

Devorgilla cackled again. "I gave you neither," she said simply, her ancient gaze still on the other galley.

"Neither?" Isolde peered hard at her.

Devorgilla sighed. A low, sweet sigh that—for a moment—could have been made by a much younger woman.

A *lass*, even.

"Would such a braw man watch me with that kind of fire in his eyes, and were I a few years younger, I vow I'd climb o'er this rail and swim to his bonnie side."

Isolde started, gave the old woman a sharp look, the crone's cryptic words about the potion momentarily forgotten. "How can you tell if he's a-watching me or nay? Surely you cannot see that far?"

"Ah, lass, but I can," Devorgilla said, tearing her gaze away from Isolde's husband at last. She peered up at Isolde, and the new light in her once-clouded eyes, their surprising clarity, could not be denied. "I've been experimenting with a potion to cure blindness."

"To cure blindness?"

"Aye. 'Tis a wonder potion and works against all manner of blindness." The crone smiled. "'Tis the same potion I gave you."

Gooseflesh rose on Isolde's arms and a rapid chill streaked down her spine. *"The same potion you gave me?"* She was gaping now, totally flummoxed. "You admit you've been lying to me all this time?"

"Not lying, lass. *Helping.*" Devorgilla cast another quick glance at the other galley. "I once told you, we are oft given not what we ask for, but what we *need.*"

A smile began to curve Isolde's lips as she understood. "And what I did I need?"

"A cure." Devorgilla's newly clear eyes danced with mischief. "A cure against blindness of the heart."

More

Sue-Ellen Welfonder!

⊱⊰

Please turn this page

for an excerpt

from

BRIDE OF THE BEAST

available soon

from Warner Books.

Dunlaidir Castle

The eastern coast of Scotland, 1330

"What you need, my lady, is a champion."

Lady Caterine Keith stiffened her shoulders against her companion's well-meant counsel and continued to stare through the arch-topped windows of her tower bedchamber. Far below, the North Sea tossed and churned, its slate-gray swells capped with foamy white, its roiling surface a perfect reflection of her own inner turmoil.

A heavy curtain of silence fell between the two women until the crackle of the hearth fire and the hollow whistling of the brisk autumn wind reached almost deafening proportions.

Rain-laden gusts lashed at Dunlaidir's thick stone walls, rattling the window shutters with such fervor Caterine wouldn't have been surprised to see them ripped away and hurtled into the sea.

A niggling sense of foreboding crept up her spine, its portent unsettling. A cloying premonition as cold and relentless as the dark waves battering the cliffs upon which Dunlaidir Castle so proudly perched.

Still, she said naught.

Her companion's suggestion didn't merit comment.

Undaunted by Caterine's silence, Lady Rhona gushed on, "I can see him before me: a mighty warrior who swings a heavy sword, a belted knight of chivalric fame," she enthused, her young voice breathy with excitement.

Filled with flimsy fancies Caterine no longer believed in.

Mayhap had ne'er believed in.

Ne'er been *allowed* to believe in, much as her young heart had once sought to cling to such foolish dreams.

"My lady," Rhona implored, her tone striving to capture Caterine's ear. "Think of it! A battleworthy knight able to vanquish your foes with a mere glance. A braw man willing to hew them to bits should you but ask. A great champi—"

"I do not want a champion." Caterine swung around to face her friend. "I desire naught but to be left alone."

"And I vow it is desire you need," the ever-romantic Rhona blurted, then clapped a hand over her lips as a pink tinge crept onto her cheeks.

Slipping behind Caterine, she yanked the shutters into place, soundly closing out the rain and wind but plunging the chamber into semidarkness. "Of a mercy!" Rhona fretted, hurrying to light a brace of tallow candles. "I meant no disrespect. 'Tis only you've never kno—"

"I know fair well what you meant," Caterine stated before the younger woman could babble on and embarrass them both. Careful to keep her back straight, she sank onto the cushioned seat built into the window embrasure.

It mattered scarce little that the slanting rain had dampened the finely embroidered pillows. She had more serious issues to contend with than catching the ague.

"Your concern is appreciated but ill-placed." She leveled

a sidelong glance at Rhona. "I know much of men. Think you having outlived two husbands has left me an innocent?"

"Of a certainty, nay, my lady." Rhona busied herself lighting the remaining two candles. "No one is more aware of your plight than I. Did I have aught but your best interests at heart, I would not urge you to send for a champion."

Caterine made an impatient gesture. "You speak of desire. I need a solution to my problems, to *Dunlaidir's* problems, not a man to warm my bed."

Leaning down, she scooped her tiny golden-brown dog, Leo, onto her lap. "I will not seek another man's attentions regardless for what purpose. Leo is the only male welcome in this chamber . . . as you are full aware."

"Leo cannot protect you from a man as powerful as Sir Hugh. The man is a dastard craven capable of great and vile knavery. Your only recourse is to ask your sister to send help."

"Think you one Highland warrior will deter a Sassenach earl with a garrison of mounted knights at his disposal?" Caterine drew Leo closer, taking comfort in the soft warmth of his little body. "Even a mighty MacKenzie would be hard-pressed to deter de la Hogue from gaining hold of Dunlaidir through marriage to me."

Rhona tilted her dark head to the side. "Then you must render such a union impossible by wedding your champion."

Indignation flared in Caterine's breast. "I do not *have* a champion. Nor will I impose on Linnet's good graces by asking her to send one. And were I so inclined, which I am not, binding myself to such a man is no more palatable than marriage to Sir Hugh."

"How do you know if you haven't met the man your sister will send?"

Caterine gave her friend a hard look. "I will not suffer a third husband, champion or otherwise."

Rather than answer her, Rhona began pacing the chamber, tapping her chin with a forefinger as she went. Caterine braced herself for the absurd prattle soon to erupt from the younger woman's pursed lips.

After years of companionship, she knew her friend well. Fingertapping always preceded outbursts of foolishness. Nonsensical ramblings that made sense to none save Rhona herself.

"I have the answer!" Rhona cried then, clapping her hands together. A triumphant smile lit her pretty face. "Simply pretend to wed the man your sister sends."

Caterine's brows shot heavenward. *"Pretend?"*

"Aye." Her friend beamed at her, obviously waiting for Caterine to comprehend the brilliance of such a scheme.

But Caterine comprehended naught.

Naught save her growing aggravation with Rhona's persistent beseeching.

Pushing to her feet, she carried Leo across the rush-strewn floor and set him upon his sheepskin bed near the hearth. "I fear you do not understand. I will not plead Linnet's aid nor will I enter into marriage again. Not even a false one," she said, meeting Rhona's exuberance with what she hoped sounded like firm resistance.

Firm and unbending.

Above all, unbending.

"But doing so is your best chance to rid yourself of Sir Hugh," Rhona wheedled. "Have you forgotten he vowed to obtain an order from his king forcing you to acquiesce if you do not agree to the marriage by Michaelmas?" Rhona lifted her hands in supplication. "My lady, the feast of Michaelmas is long past."

"For truth?" Caterine plucked at an imagined speck of lint on her sleeve. "Since our stores have grown too meager to allow us to celebrate St. Michael's holy day, I hadn't noticed its passing. Nor do I care what Edward III declares I should do. Yet is this land held for young David of Scotland."

"Lady, please," Rhona entreated. "You have no other choice."

Stung to fury, Catherine clenched her hands to tight fists. Beyond the shuttered windows thunder sounded, the low rumblings echoing the churning bitterness deep inside her.

Rhona erred. She *did* have choices.

But, as so oft in her life, none appealed.

She'd e'er lived under a man's rule. Even now, newly widowed of an elderly but not unkind husband, a time when, at long last, she'd hoped to find some semblance of peace.

Peace and solitude.

Unbidden, Sir Hugh de la Hogue's thick-jowled face rose before her, his swinish eyes gleaming with satisfaction, the sound of his heavy breathing giving voice to his lecherous nature.

Caterine shuddered. The mere thought of the Sassenach's bejeweled fingers touching her made her skin crawl with distaste and sent bile rising thick in her throat.

"Lady, you've grown pale." Rhona's troubled voice shattered the loathsome image. "Shall I fetch the leech?"

"Nay, I am well," Catherine lied, flat-voiced.

Her dark eyes flooded with concern, Rhona rushed forward to grasp Caterine's hands. "Oh, lady, you must relent.

The MacKenzie men are able and valiant. Your sister's husband is a fair man, he will send you the most stalwart warrior in his garrison."

Rhona released Caterine's hands and resumed her pacing. "Do you recall when he and your sister came for a visit some years ago? My faith, but the castle women were all aflutter did he but glance—"

"There is more to a man than the width of his shoulders and the charm of his smile," Caterine broke into her friend's prattle. "I will not deny my sister's husband is pleasing to the eye *and* possessed of a goodly character, but I warn you, Duncan MacKenzie is nowise a man by which to measure others. One such as he is a rare find. My sister is much blessed to have him."

For a scant moment, Rhona appeared duly chastised, but soon babbled on, her face aglow with renewed wonderment. "On my oath, more than his bonnie looks impressed me. Ne'er will I forget how he unseated Dunlaidir's finest at the joust yet had the good grace to allow your late husband to best him."

Rhona aimed a keen-eyed stare at Caterine. "Aye, Laird MacKenzie is a just man. He will choose you a stout-armed warrior of great martial prowess, a man of honor to protect you."

A man of honor.

Caterine swallowed the sharp retort dancing dangerously near the tip of her tongue. She of all women had little reason to believe such a paragon existed. Though she'd seen many sides of the men who'd shared her life thus far, honor was one attribute most of them had sorely lacked.

Only her late husband had possessed a portion thereof.

A meager portion.

She folded her arms. "And you think this fabled and mighty Highlander, this man of honor, will lay aside his morals and agree to pose as my third husband?"

Rhona ceased her pacing and began tapping a finger against her lips. After a moment, the finger stilled and she smiled. "'Tis for honor's sake he will agree. What man of compassion, of worth, could refuse a gentlewoman in need?"

"Think you?"

"Of a surety." The tapping began again. "Especially if you inform the lady Linnet of the near ruination facing Dunlaidir. Once the severity of our situation is known, no man who abides by the code of chivalry would refuse you."

Saints cherish her, but Caterine didn't think so either.

Then so be it, she almost said but a loud clap of thunder silenced her before she could form the words, stealing them as surely as if a swift hand had snatched them from her lips.

The thunder cracked again, a tremendous and resounding series of booms powerful enough to shake the floorboards and jar the window shutters.

The storm's black fury was a portent, she knew.

A sign the saints disapproved of the sacrilege Rhona would see her commit.

Or worse, an indication they agreed and frowned on her refusal to heed her friend's suggestion.

Something she would not, could not, do.

Caterine waited for the storm's rage to abate, then smoothed the folds of her woolen kirtle. Before she lost her resolve, her nerve, she drew back her shoulders and forced herself to speak the words she must.

"Lady Rhona, I respect your counsel and ken you are ever heedful of my welfare," she said, her voice surprisingly calm, "but I forbid you to broach this matter again. I will *not* send for a champion."

A fortnight later, on the other side of Scotland, deep in the western Highlands, a lone warrior knight fought an invisible foe. Naught but the repeated swish of his great sword arcing through the chill predawn air marred the quietude.

Even Loch Duich, hidden from view over the list wall, was itself silent, its dark surface no doubt smooth as finely fired glass, for not so much as a ripple, not the gentlest lapping of waves on the pebbled shore, could be heard.

The hour was well before prime, the time of day Sir Marmaduke Strongbow favored for practicing his martial skills. Soon, Eilean Creag Castle would come alive, the empty bailey would fill with a bustle of activity and his overlord's squires would trickle into the lists to join him, each one eager for him to prod and teach them.

Help them hone their own sword arms.

But for the moment, he stood alone.

Free to challenge his secret enemies, daring enough to face down the most formidable of them all: his own self and the self-created demons he carried within.

He paused and drew a deep breath, then swiped the back of his arm over his damp forehead. The plague take his cares. The saints knew he had much to be grateful for. Soon his own castle would be completed. Indeed, were he not a man who enjoyed his comforts, he'd move into Balkenzie now, this very day.

But he'd waited long years to raise his banner over a stronghold of his own, a few more months would not cost him overmuch. Then all would be ready and he would take possession of his new home.

A castle he and his liege, Duncan MacKenzie, had designed with great care.

A strategically ideal fortalice to guard the southern reaches of MacKenzie land.

A home perfect in every way save one.

Unlike his liege and closest friend, Marmaduke lacked a fair lady wife to grace his side. His would be a castle filled with men.

Quelling the bitterness that oft mocked him when alone, Marmaduke adjusted his grip on the leather-wrapped hilt of his sword and lunged anew at his unseen foes. Faster and faster, his blade rent the morn as he spun and dipped, thrust and withdrew, skillfully slicing his doubts and regrets to ribbons, banishing them one by one.

Until the morrow when he'd challenge them anew.

"*Sir . . .*" The soft voice behind him was little more than a whisper to his ears but a great roar to his warrior's instincts. Instantly lowering his sword, Marmaduke wheeled around to face the lady who'd addressed him.

"Fair lady, I am always pleased to see you, but you should know better than to approach a man's back when he wields a sword," he said, sheathing his steel. "Nor do I believe it is good for you to be out in the chill morning air."

"I am fit enough," Linnet MacKenzie countered, drawing her woolen cloak more securely about her before resting one hand upon her swollen middle. "I would speak with you alone, now before the others stir."

Sir Marmaduke peered intently at his liege lord's lady wife. Her lovely face appeared more pale than it should and unless the vision in his good eye was failing him, she bore faint purple shadows beneath her eyes.

Nor did he care for the rapid rise and fall of her chest. That she'd overtaxed herself in seeking him out was painfully obvious.

"Lady, you should be abed," he admonished, trying to sound firm but unable to be duly stern with her. "Does your husband know you are about?"

The two bright spots of pink that bloomed on her cheeks gave him his answer.

"I must speak with you," she said again and placed a cold hand on his forearm.

"Then let us adjourn into the chapel." Closing his fingers over her hand, Marmaduke led her toward Eilean Creag's small stone oratory. "It is closer than the great hall, and private." He gave her hand a gentle squeeze. "I would know you warm before I hear what troubles you."

He'd scarce ushered her inside when the oratory's heavy wooden door burst open behind them. With a resounding crash, it slammed against the whitewashed wall.

"Saints, Maria, and Joseph!" Duncan MacKenzie fumed, ignoring the sanctity of the holy place. Ill-humor swirling round him like a dark cloak, he made straight for his wife. "Have you taken leave of your senses, woman? 'Tis in your bed you should be. The entire household is searching for you."

Bracing fisted hands on his hips, he tossed a dark glance at Marmaduke. "Why am I not surprised to find her with you?"

"Becalm yourself, my friend," Sir Marmaduke urged, his smooth baritone voice unruffled by the other man's bluster. "No harm has befallen her."

"Were she your lady, I vow you would want to know her safe, too, Strongbow." Duncan ran a hand through his disheveled hair.

"I care for her as if she were my lady, as you know." Marmaduke placed his own hands on his hips. "Her well-being is of equal import to me. There is naught I would not do for her."

"My lords, please." Linnet leaned back against the recumbent stone effigy of a former MacKenzie warrior, one hand still resting upon her midsection. "I have told you naught will go wrong this time. I know it. My gift has shown me."

Duncan MacKenzie peered hard at her, his handsome features as set-faced as his stone-carved ancestor. After casting another dark look in Marmaduke's direction, he swung about and strode across the oratory.

Dropping to one knee, he busied himself lighting a small brazier in the corner near the altar. "Have you told him?" he asked his wife when he stood.

"Told me what?" Marmaduke quirked a brow.

"My lady would ask a favor of you." Duncan slanted a glance at Linnet. "A great favor."

Sir Marmaduke did not care for the way his friend spoke the last three words, nor the ghost of a half smile suddenly twitching the corners of Duncan's mouth, but such reservations scarce mattered. He'd championed the lady Linnet since her arrival at Eilean Creag Castle five years ago, and she'd repaid his gallantry a thousandfold and then some.

With kindness, and the goodness of heart few gentlewomen possessed. In her presence, he could almost imagine himself rid of the scar that marred his once-handsome face and believe that, once more, his *looks* and not his well-practiced charm could turn female heads.

Indeed, he revered her greatly.

"A very great favor," came his liege's voice again, this time laced with unmistakable amusement.

"No request Lady Linnet may ask of me is too great," Marmaduke vowed. Turning to her, he made her a slight bow. "How may I serve you, my lady?"

Rather than answer him, Linnet cast her gaze downward and began scuffing her toe against the stone flagging of the chapel floor.

Ignoring his friend's ill-concealed amusement, Marmaduke lifted her chin, forcing her to look at him. "Name your desire and it is yours," he sought to encourage her.

She met his gaze but kept her silence. After a moment, she moistened her lips and said, "Now that I stand before you, I fear it is too much to ask."

Marmaduke shot a glance at Duncan, then immediately wished he hadn't. His handsome friend now wore a bold smile.

A too bold smile.

Somewhere in Marmaduke's gut, a tiny shard of unease broke loose, a jagged-edged shard that jabbed his innards and grew more unpleasant by the moment.

The smile on Duncan MacKenzie's face grew as well.

Worse, an amused gleam danced in the ofttimes dark-tempered Highlander's eyes and there could be no doubt the smile and the gleam boded ill for Marmaduke.

Of a sudden, the neck opening of Marmaduke's tunic seemed extraordinarily tight, but he forced himself to ignore the sensation, and his friend's gloating, and turned back to Linnet. "I cannot help you if you will not tell me what it is you wish me to do."

"I cannot," she whispered, shaking her head.

"And *you*?" He glanced at Duncan, alarmed to see that his friend's smile had now turned into a silly grin. "Will you divulge this great secret?"

"With pleasure," Duncan said, the mirth in his voice undeniable. "My lady wife's sister is in need of a champion."

Marmaduke lifted a brow. "I see naught amusing about a lady in need."

"Then you will go to her aid?" Linnet asked, the tremor of hope in her voice going straight to Marmaduke's heart.

Iron control hid the mounting tension swirling in Marmaduke's breast, the dull thudding of a heart filled with other plans than riding off to slay some unknown gentlewoman's dragons.

"Think you I am the man to champion her?" his valor asked before his heart could stay his tongue.

"We know of no one better suited," Duncan answered for his wife. "The lady Caterine is newly widowed and plagued by a persistent Sassenach earl who would press her to marry him. Her holding, Dunlaidir Castle in the east, is sorely failing. Without help she will lose both the peace she craves and the home she holds dear."

He laid his arm around Linnet's shoulders and drew her close. "Nor is it in our best interest in these troubled times to see as strategic a stronghold as Dunlaidir fall into English hands."

Marmaduke rubbed the back of his neck. "Why not send a contingent of able men to assist her? Many are the warriors you could choose from."

"Name one whose sword arm is mightier than yours."

Duncan's fingers kneaded the woolen folds of his wife's cloak. "Who better than you, a Sassenach of noble blood, to challenge an English earl? You, with your martial skills and smooth tongue, are more suited to the task than a score of fighting Gaels."

Unconvinced, Marmaduke shook his head. "A full retinue would serve her better than a single man."

"Dunlaidir is possessed of a stout garrison. They only need direction. A firm hand and a clearheaded man to lead them. Nor can I spare more than a few men with Balkenzie nearing completion. Nay, Strongbow, the task falls to you." His smile gone, Duncan aimed a penetrating stare at Marmaduke. "Or would you deny my lady's sister your skill?"

"You know I cannot. It is only—" Marmaduke broke off, near stumbling over his unusually thick tongue. He ran a finger under the neckline of his tunic. The chapel's somewhat stale, incense-laden air closed in on him with such pressure he almost gagged. "I'd planned to take occupancy of Balkenzie soon."

A lame excuse, to be sure, but he'd so hoped to hoist his own banner before Samhain.

"I'd hoped to see the castle well garrisoned and secure, secure for *you*, before the onset of winter," Marmaduke said, his words casting down the gauntlet of his hesitation.

"And so you shall." Duncan's flashing smile reappeared. "Upon your return."

Marmaduke opened his mouth to rebuke the notion but Duncan silenced him with a raised hand. "You shall be snugly ensconced within your own keep's walls by Yuletide at latest," his liege declared. "Then we shall all gather at Balkenzie's hearth and drink to my lady's health."

"And to our bairn's," Linnet added, the conviction in her

voice and the look in her eyes doing more to dismantle Marmaduke's resistance than all her husband's bold words combined.

As if he sensed his friend's crumbling will, Duncan clamped a firm hand on Marmaduke's shoulder. "It will not take long for a strong-armed warrior such as yourself to have done with one odious Englishman?"

Taking his hand off Marmaduke's shoulder, Duncan gave him a playful jab in the ribs. "A fat and ill-fit one, if we choose to believe the tongue-waggers."

Marmaduke swallowed hard.

Something was amiss.

And whatever it was, it slithered up his back, cool and smooth as a snake, to curl deftly around his neck and squeeze ever tighter the longer he watched the merry twinkle dancing in his friend's eyes.

Marmaduke frowned. "There is something you are not telling me."

Linnet glanced away and Duncan stretched his arms over his head, loudly cracking his knuckles. His fool grin widened. "As ever, I can hide naught from you," he said, his deep voice almost jovial. "I've long suspected you're as blessed with the sight as my fair lady wife."

Lounging against the cold stone form of his long-dead forebear, Duncan finally tossed down his own gauntlet. "Lady Caterine wishes you to pose as her husband. Only if word spreads she has wed a third time, does she believe she can rid herself of her current woes."

Marmaduke stared at his friends, too stunned to speak. None would deny he revered them well. Saints, he would gladly give his life for either of them. But what they proposed went beyond all lunacy.

Impossible, he should *pose* as any lady's husband no matter how great her plight.

No matter who her sister.

Never had he heard anything more preposterous.

"You ask too much," he found his voice at last. "I will offer the lady full use of my sword arm, and I shall guard her with my life so long as she requires my aid, but I will not enter into a blasphemous relationship with any woman."

He bit back a harsher refusal on seeing the hope fade from Linnet's eyes. "By the Rood, Duncan," he swore as softly as he could, "you should know I am not a man who would pretend to speak holy vows."

"Then don't," Duncan said, triumph riding heavy on his words. "Make the lady your bride in truth."

Make the lady your bride in truth.

His friend's parting comment lingered long after Duncan and his lady took their leave. Like the repetitive chants of a monk's litany, the taunt echoed, increasing in intensity until the words seemed to fill not just his mind but the close confines of the oratory as well.

Make the lady your bride . . .

By the saints, did his liege mean to mock him? Duncan MacKenzie knew better than most of the loneliness that plagued Marmaduke in the darkest hours of the night, was well aware of Marmaduke's most secret desire: to have a fine and goodly consort of his own once more.

And a sister of the lady Linnet could be naught but a pure and kindly gentlewoman.

Was there indeed more behind his friends' insistence that only he could champion the ill-plighted young widow?

A tiny smile tugged at the corner of Marmaduke's mouth

and a pleasant warmth the likes of which he hadn't felt in many years began to curl round his heart.

Make her your bride . . .

The words came as a song now.

A joyous one.

Hope beginning to burgeon deep within his soul, Sir Marmaduke went to the altar, sank to his knees, and bowed his head.

Sometime later, he knew not how long, a shaft of multi-colored light fell through the chapel's one stained-glass window to cast a rosy-gold glow upon his folded hands. The beam of light illuminated his signet ring, turning it to molten gold and making the large ruby gleam as if set afire.

Then, no sooner than had the colored light appeared, did it vanish, extinguished as if a cloud had passed before the rising sun.

But Marmaduke had seen it rest upon his ring.

A portent from above.

Once more, Marmaduke murmured a prayer. One of thanksgiving and hope. When at last he rose, his decision was made.

As soon as he could muster what few men Duncan could spare him, he would journey across Scotland to aid a damsel in need, a lady he would offer not only his warring skills and protection, but marriage.

A true one.

If by God's good graces, she would have him.